PRAISE FO
JAI

The Second Letter

Gold Medal winner of the Independent Book Publishers Association's 2015 Benjamin Franklin Awards, Best New Voice: Fiction

"**L**ane has created a winning hero in Jake Travis, someone who is super-skilled, super-fit, glib, oddly bookish, funny as a stiletto . . ." —*Florida Weekly*

"**A** captivating book with lies and deceit as well as love and loss." —*Readers' Favorite*

"**F**ans of Michael Connelly, Ace Atkins, and Dennis Lehane will likely find Lane's book satisfying on how it hits all the right notes of a truly suspenseful story."

—*SceneSarasota*

Cooler Than Blood

"**L**ane delivers a confident, engaging Florida tale with a cast of intriguing characters. A solid, entertaining mystery." —*Kirkus Reviews*

"**G**ripping and highly enjoyable." —*Foreword Clarion Reviews*

"**E**ntertaining and enjoyable." —*SceneSarasota*

The Cardinal's Sin

Finalist for the 2015 Foreword Reviews INDIES Book of the Year Award

"**A** cinematic tale . . . the prose is confident and clear, and the pacing smooth and compelling . . . readers will care about its characters. Another entertaining mystery from Lane—possibly his best yet." —*Kirkus Reviews*

"It starts with a bang and never lets up . . . a sophisticated exploration of the relationship . . . in which the killing power of words vies with the powerful finality of the assassin's rifle. [An] exciting reading experience. Florida noir at its best."
—*Florida Weekly*

"**T**his brilliantly calibrated thriller bests the leading sellers in its genre. Lane's writing is sharp, evocative, and engaging . . . a novel that not only entertains but enriches its readership."
—*Foreword Clarion Reviews*, Five Stars

"**E**ngaging thriller . . . a compelling, quick-read novel."
—*BlueInk Reviews*

The Gail Force

Finalist for the 2016 Foreword Reviews INDIES Book of the Year Award

"**T**he plot crackles with energy and suspense. The pace is breakneck, the writing is crisp . . . clever. A consistently entertaining and self-assured crime thriller."

—*Kirkus Reviews*

"Written with a razor-sharp wit and a keen sense of impending doom. *The Gail Force* is a page turner to the end."
—*Midwest Book Review*

"A powerful rush of suspense. Jake Travis is one of the best leading men to take the thriller-fiction stage in recent years."
—*Florida Weekly*

"Charm and humor permeate the pages of this surprising thriller. There's little chance anyone will turn the last page before developing a craving for the next installment."

—*Foreword Clarion Reviews*, Five Stars

"Full of action, great characters, and tips on living the good life. This is one you don't want to miss." —*BookLoons*

Naked We Came

Finalist for the 2017 Foreword Reviews INDIES Book of the Year Award

"*Naked We Came* is an emotionally austere and endlessly surprising thriller that brings new depth to the Jake Travis series. Replete with the wit and charm that characterizes Lane's singular style, this is a thrill with heart."—*Foreword Clarion Reviews*

"A psychologically engrossing thriller. Lane artfully constructs an intricate mystery around the equally complex psychology of the protagonist."—*Kirkus Reviews*

"Jake is sharp and humorous. A perfectly imperfect hero. A taunt, tense psychological thriller with an exciting plot."— *Readers' Favorite*

"This heart-racing thriller is dripping with style."—*Florida Weekly*

"The story line is engaging and fast paced. Lane's excellent writing will keep readers intrigued."—*Readers Views*

A BEAUTIFUL VOICE

ALSO BY ROBERT LANE

The Second Letter

Cooler Than Blood

The Cardinal's Sin

The Gail Force

Naked We Came

The Elizabeth Walker Affair

A Different Way to Die

The Easy Way Out

A BEAUTIFUL VOICE

A JAKE TRAVIS NOVEL

ROBERT LANE

Copyright © 2018 Robert Lane

All rights reserved.

Mason Alley Publishing, Saint Pete Beach, Florida.

All rights reserved. No part of this book may be reproduced, scanned, or distributed in any print or electronic form without the author's permission.

This is a work of fiction. While some incidents of this story may appear to be true and factual, their relation to each other, and implications derived from their occurrences, is strictly the product of the author's imagination. Names, characters, places, and incidents either are the product of the author's imagination or are used fictitiously. Any resemblance to actual persons (living or dead), localities, companies, organizations, and events is entirely coincidental.

Cover design by James T. Egin, Bookfly Design.

"Without a family, man, alone in the world, trembles with the cold."

Andre Maurois

"There is a land of the living and a land of the dead and the bridge is love, the only survival, the only meaning."

Thornton Wilder
    The Bridge of San Luis Rey

A BEAUTIFUL VOICE

PART I
THE BOOKKEEPER'S DAUGHTER

1

STEPHEN COLE

A chill shivered Stephen Cole. He stood in the sky and gazed down at the earth twenty-six floors beneath him. Summer echoed everywhere. It bathed the ground and the stratosphere and all places in between. It had been heartbreaking for Stephen to leave his sleeping girls on such a glorious and promising day. He had checked on April last. She rested peacefully in the shutter-slatted dimness of her bedroom, recently decorated with Pooh and his friends from the Hundred Acre Wood. A thin shaft of sun had streaked her face as if God was reaching in and lightly touching her with the tip of Her finger. Stephen Cole had stared with awe at his youngest daughter. He could not understand why the sun didn't wake her. Stephen Cole could not understand that at all.

While not daydreaming, Stephen pondered the will of the late Ms. Eleanor Greenberg—"Ace" to her friends. Crystal, Stephen's redheaded secretary who was prone to smacking gum, a trait he found more endearing than annoying, poked her head into his office.

"There's a couple of men in the lobby who would like to" —smack—"see you," she said.

There's a couple of men in the lobby who would like to—smack—*see you.*

Later, after Stephen had relocated, those words, and that smack, would drop out of the pastel-blue Florida sky with no warning, like rain without clouds. How could life pivot on such a simple sentence? From his gum-smacking secretary, for Pete's sake?

He could not understand that, either.

Although he shared Crystal with another attorney, Norbert "Nobby" Larrison, she allocated the majority of her time to Stephen. Nobby, the dark and brooding type, constantly mined Crystal for information on other attorneys' clients. He was of that class of men who, like schoolgirls, habitually needed to know what everybody else was doing. His insecurities, masked by his gruff manner, required constant pandering.

"Do they have an appointment?" Stephen asked Crystal, squinting his left eye.

"Would have told you."

"Who are they?"

"Wouldn't say."

"What do they want?"

"Ditto. But one's a cop."

"A cop?"

"Either that or one of the Village People. Didn't one of those guys dress like a cop?"

She spun away without waiting for an answer. Stephen checked the watch his wife, Julie, had given him for Christmas. 11:43.

Julie was due at noon with their two girls: April, age five; and Corrie, age seven. She frequently brought them downtown to have lunch with him in the summer when the trees were hung full with their summer clothing and everything was painted green. They would grab sandwiches and then locate to a shaded patch of grass in the park that bordered the Scioto

A Beautiful Voice

River, careful not to camp out too close to goose droppings. Julie would bring coloring books for the girls. While they scrawled colored wax upon white pages, he would make up a story, and when he paused, searching for words, April would say, "Keep it rolling, like a drummer." Some silly phrase she'd overheard and fallen in love with. Impatient, that one was. He would hoist both of them on his shoulders so they could reach into a tree to pluck a leaf. The leaves ended up in a jar at home. He couldn't make himself throw them away. Silly. But that's who Stephen Cole was.

Relaxing along the banks of the river with his family—like in one of those impressionist paintings he saw in the Chicago Museum of Art when he and Julie visited her hometown—Stephen's world would slow to a crawl. And then it would stop.

Interpreting law, once such a noble aspiration, would seem so petty. Trivial. He inwardly acknowledged that he was happiest when singing in the church choir. *Good God, how gay is that?* He didn't necessarily believe any of the stuff—the end product, so to speak—as much as he liked the *act* of believing. The rituals. The songs. The purple robes and fresh cut flowers on the altar.

Julie would dress up April and Corrie every Sunday as if Easter came fifty-two times a year, doting on them like childhood dolls. April singing. Corrie laughing. What sweetness the day brings when garnished with little girls in bright dresses. They never escaped the house without snapping a dozen pictures. The pageantry would continue after they piled into the SUV. Corrie belted behind her mother and April in her booster seat behind Stephen where, true to her name, she would chirp away like a bird on a crisp spring morning. Stephen considered the birds of April to be the archangels of nature, announcing Earth's resurrection after a long Ohio winter of unrelieved cloudiness. He had lobbied hard for her name—Julie, at the time, had been enchanted by Sophia—

and April honored his winning efforts, for she saw no reason to talk when she could sing. That one can certainly carry a tune, everyone told Stephen. Just wait; she'll be a singer like you one day. You'll see.

Oh, what a lucky man he was.

An obnoxious phone ring jolted him back to a world that he suspected was as empty as his place in the sky. It had recently begun bothering Stephen Cole that he didn't spend his days with his feet planted on Mother Earth. No reason. It just didn't feel right.

Keep your head in the game, he lectured himself. *Got a mortgage. Need to slip a little cash into those college funds. Julie's Christmas bank. Birthdays. The weekly happy gifts that Julie springs on the girls.* (The Cole household did not require a calendar to dictate when to shower each other with gifts.) The world was full of fatherly obligations, and Stephen Cole, age 34, took his seriously.

I am the family soldier.

Watch the lucky man march.

"Airhead, you with me?" Crystal said as she stuck her head in the door.

"Show them in."

"They'd like you to come to the lobby."

"Why?"

"Wouldn't say."

Stephen Rolodexed his mind through his client base. Probably the pizza man.

His firm represented a policeman, Sean Wright, who—while off-duty and in a particularly nasty mood—shot an eighteen-year-old pizza employee. According to Wright, the kid had given him some lip when he whined about the temperature of the pizza. Wright blasted the senior trombone player point-blank with no further provocation. "I didn't like his attitude," the buzzed-head cop had calmly informed his lawyers. He chewed his tongue, humped his right shoulder, and added, "So I shot the little fucker."

"You mean he threatened you in some manner?" his attorney had asked, desperately fishing for something to base a defense on, and praying the cop didn't see the fear clouding his eyes.

"Zit face?" He snorted. "Hell no. Kid was a dweeb. But you boys tell me what to say. You got my back, right? So, yeah. Now that you mention it, he had a knife in his hand."

"What type of knife?"

"Hell if I know. You figure it out."

The law firm planted someone in the pizza joint to discern what type of knives were used.

Rumor was, the cop was protecting drug dealers on the near east side. Speculation was that the drugs were being laundered through the pizza store. But Stephen's law firm knew not to probe rumors and speculations. His firm was on retainer by the police union. It kept the lights on. The hell with bliss—ignorance was continued employment. Who knows? Maybe the wasted kid was involved in the drug trade. Some leggy federal drug agent had even come sniffing around a week after the kid's head got pulverized, making everyone nervous. Acted like she'd known him. Had an attitude herself.

But why him? He was only involved in the periphery of the case.

The police likely wanted him to take a more active role in defending the pizza-killer. Good ole goody-two shoes Cole. At age ten, he had looked like an altar boy on a Christmas card, and there wasn't much development after that. As a founding partner had observed, Stephen Cole had the perfect face for a defense attorney. No doubt the partners wanted that choirboy face in the courtroom. Lose the police union account, and heads would roll. It was all a game.

But Stephen had his own game plan.

Exit, stage left.

He was defecting to the prosecutor's office at four in the afternoon. No one at his firm knew except for Nobby. Stephen hadn't wanted to tell Nobby, but Crystal was leaving with him, and he thought it the gentlemanly thing to do. He was done with the scum. Time to put them behind bars instead of pretending they were goddamn rock stars. While he couldn't use any of the information he was privy to in the cop-killer case, he knew it would rattle his former colleagues to see him grinning from the opposing bench. And if he dipped his toe over the client-attorney line, what? A killer goes to jail? A bad cop off the streets?

Stephen Cole needed to believe in what he did. Because little girls perched on his hip and gazing at him with round, innocent eyes will do that to a man.

He stood up and said to Crystal, "Ace has property in Florida. The Ocean Reef Club in Key Largo. We'll need to probate it."

"Awesome," Crystal said, stepping into his office. "How about I fly down there and check it out?"

"How about you find what the parcel number is so we can enter it in the estate."

"Roger that." She hesitated. "All set? Four today, right?"

"Remember, take no files."

She winked, double-smacked her gum, and twirled away.

He hesitated at the door where his jacket hung. It was a blue sports coat, with a light checkered pattern that Julie had sprung on him one day after shopping at Von Maur. He wore sports coats and beige dress pants in the summer. No tie. The omission of the tie helped to differentiate the seasons, and in some indiscernible manner, made him believe he was doing more with his life than just falling into place. It helped convince him that his inebriated college aspirations had not become totally compromised, they'd just got smacked—you know, rearranged a little—by reality. Happens to us all, right?

"Living the dream," he said, stuffing his arms down the sleeves. "Living the big, fat, corporate dream."

The air goosed him again. Must have the AC on high.

A Beautiful Voice

Halfway down the hall to the reception room, he spun and quickened his pace back to his office. From his top desk drawer, he took out two mints he'd pocketed from his business lunch yesterday. He didn't want to take the chance of forgetting to go back and get the candy if his family happened to arrive when he was in the lobby. He hesitated, then pocketed a third. He also snatched a pamphlet on Hilton Head from his briefcase. They were driving there in a week for their annual trip, and it was fun to flip through the pictures. The girls were already pumped about road food—there are no written words, no composed notes, no brushed strokes that have ever described the smug joy of French fries and a milkshake in the car. When they arrived after eight happy hours in the car, the girls would scurry to the beach before Stephen even unlocked the door to their condo.

They planned to break the news to the girls while on vacation. They'd always wanted three, and three it would be.

Oh, what a lucky man he was.

Stephen Cole, graduate of The Ohio State University Moritz School of Law, past managing editor of the Ohio State Journal of Dispute Resolution, the youngest partner at Friedman, Leonard, Puleo, Larrison and Enslen—loving husband, doting father, proud son, lighthearted brother to two sisters, (geez almighty, could he make them laugh) and first tenor in the Worthington United Methodist Church choir, for Stephen Cole had a beautiful voice—walked out of his office for the final time.

2

Church bells reverberated the December air. Kathleen and I were at the boat show in downtown St. Petersburg, Florida. It was Sunday afternoon and crazy good weather. The leading edge of winter had barreled through and washed the air clean, and you could even see through it better. Winter is never stubborn in Florida. It has a two-day visa and scampers out of the state, knowing it is an unwelcome guest and has strayed far from its place of birth.

I had a beer in one hand and Kathleen's hand in the other. There was no need for a third hand. We stood on a dock facing the aft deck of a forty-foot Downeast blue trawler. Its beam spread wider than Tennessee, and it boasted mahogany deck planks that an Amish carpenter would swoon over.

"K?" I said to my future wife.

"Yes?"

"I've found another woman."

"As have I."

"You gave no indication."

"This is how you learn. Shall we?"

We kicked off our shoes and stepped aboard. The boat was used, but in terrific shape. The dash had enough electronics to power the Atlanta airport flight tower. I thought I heard someone whistle, but it was a bird.

Kathleen planted herself in the middle of the aft deck and surveyed her surroundings as if taking inventory.

"Gorgeous," she said. She managed to draw the word out, starting on one note, peaking in the middle, and ending as if she were delicately placing it on a cloud.

"Don't," I warned her.

"I *really* like it," she effervesced, ignoring my command. She strode, with both hesitancy and confidence—don't ask me how—into the cockpit, trailing her fingers on the teak side rails. "The wood is sensuous. The outside area is incredible. It's so large."

"As is the price tag," I pointed out.

"It's used," she countered in a firm voice as money nearly leapt out of her purse. "We can negotiate. Besides, I can—"

"I'm going to grab a hotdog."

"Let's go through this first. It just feels so . . . us."

She rubbed her hand over a soft vinyl seat that not a drop of sunscreen had ever touched. It was impossible not to like the boat and what it represented, or at least what we believed it represented, for boats are the dream that is always a day away.

A retractable awning was attached to the hardtop. I instinctively reached up and touched its aluminum case. I seek the sun, just not on my skin.

"A real beauty, isn't she?" A salesman approached us. His bushy eyebrows were like a fireplace garland, and his tennis shoes had neon-green laces. The features in between weren't as impressionable as the bookends.

Kathleen intercepted him and introduced herself. They shook hands, and her face brightened with a genuine smile that was her special grace. I marveled at the vastness of that smile when meeting strangers. The beaming sincerity. I could never muster such enthusiasm for someone I didn't know, especially one who may profit off our relationship.

"Does this cover the entire back?" Kathleen jutted her head toward the awning. Already plying my weak spot. A sly woman, that future wife of mine.

"It does. Would you like to see it?"

"Please."

Another bird screeched. Or did it? My ears aren't the leading component of my body. No. That wasn't a bird. That was someone attempting a tune.

A man in a straw hat with a black band around it walked by. He whistled Dixie, although he was not a man gifted at whistling. He navigated the crowded dock, holding a hot dog in his hand, his eyes straight.

"Back in a flash," I said.

"She's got low hours," the salesman said to me as the awning inched shade over the deck. "Generator's hardly been touched."

"Trust me, pal," I said to him. "I'm not the bread."

I didn't need to see any more of the boat. I'd spotted it from two docks over. It was a keeper. Renowned manufacturer. One owner. Tip-top shape, and priced at a fraction of a new one. New boats lose their value faster than last year's Miss America. None of that enticed me as much as it made it something to avoid. A boat that size would need constant upkeep. Despite Kathleen's lunar sway over me, I didn't need the commitment to a large boat in my life.

I slipped my Sebagos back on, fighting a bad feeling about the boat. Kathleen had been hinting at doing some prolonged cruising. "Shed ourselves of the days and weeks," she had lobbied. "I'm tired of classroom walls." She taught English lit at a local college and no longer planned to teach during the summer semester. When we lay in bed after making love, she'd recently started chatting about breaking free in the summer. Exploring points south. Recapturing one's youthful days—that magnificent moment when the school doors flew open in early June and the empty highway of summer beckoned. "We need to lay our heads down and listen to the grass grow," she had said.

Well, good luck doing that on a boat.

I, on the other hand, was maniacally devoted to a strict morning workout that would be impossible to duplicate at sea. Besides, Thoreau said our lives are frittered away on detail and that a man is rich in proportion to the number of things he can let alone. I'd reminded Kathleen of that. She claimed she'd never heard of this Thoreau fellow.

The straw hat took a right onto another dock. I brushed past two men gawking at a center console with four engines across her stern. I came up behind the straw hat and started whistling "When Johnny Comes Marching." He kept his head level and headed into the open-air concession tent.

A spacious, octangular bar was set up under a white circus tent. Women in T-shirts a size too small darted behind the bar dishing out draft beers, their foaming heads trailing down the sides of plastic cups. White tables were strewn around the wood deck, every one choked to occupancy. A guitar player pitched the sailing life from atop a stool in the corner. Next to him was a table with his CDs and tip jar. It was the last day of the show. The place was Florida high, with everybody nursing a beer and a boating dream.

I squeezed next to the man in the straw hat and plopped my beer on the counter.

"Where've you been?" he demanded. "I've been whistling all day."

"That ain't whistling."

"I can carry a coal shaft better than I carry a melody."

"You'd be quite a sight dragging a coal shaft around a boat show."

Janssen and I rarely engaged in banter. Oddly, I didn't mind. Was a white picket fence in my future?

He wore khaki slacks and a blue long sleeve shirt. The man never wasted time in his closet. His polished, reddish-brown dress shoes didn't belong within a nautical mile of a boat show.

"You know why I'm here?" he said.

I nodded.

"You need to rethink precaution," he said. "Mexican drug lords will blow the devil out of hell."

"What do you got?"

He placed his hotdog on the counter, where it rested in a white paper cradle. He picked up the hotdog and took a bite, leaving it in his hand while he chewed.

I glanced down at the hot dog cradle.

"Mustard?" I said.

"Umm?" he uttered while chewing.

"You got mustard on it."

He swallowed. "You going to"—he suppressed a belch—"write it down?"

"No."

There was a four-digit number on the paper, with a yellow blob over one digit, either a five or a six. Next to it were longitude and latitude coordinates as well a military time. On the side of the paper cradle was an address in Pass-a-Grille. Maybe a mile from my house.

"Is there anything else I need to know?"

"Uh-umm." He rolled his tongue. "That was a nice boat you and your girl were on."

He spotted me before I spotted him.

He worked his tongue in the same place, like when you get food trapped in your teeth and it bugs the hell out of you.

"You up to speed?" he said.

"I am."

"Mission?"

"Slay bad guys. Sail away with the dame."

"Your mouth." He shook his head.

"Beats smearing a number with mustard."

"History has turned on less."

"How many am I picking up?"

"A man and a woman," Janssen said. The man's method of speech was more rhythm than notes, as if he had never ventured from the percussion section of an orchestra. His thin mouth anchored a face scarred by a decade of desert battlefields followed by a decade of bureaucratic entanglement. It was impossible to tell which decade had exacted the greatest toll.

"Sergio 'Donald' Flores—"

"The Mexican cartel leader?" I said.

Janssen knifed me a look. "Flores operates a drug cartel that kills thousands of Americans with tainted drugs, drains our system of productivity, and costs us hundreds of millions each year to fight. That doesn't boil me. This does: He's taken out two DEA agents—that we know of—and killed over a hundred of his own countrymen. He doesn't discriminate against women and children.

"A man named Richard Bannon runs a sliver of books for his U.S. operation. We found a snitch in Mexico who we think can squeeze Bannon. Says he runs numbers for Flores and Bannon. We want to bring that man in and stick him in front of Bannon. We'll make it clear: Bannon skates if he helps us pin Flores."

"Bannon's toast whichever direction he goes."

"Should've thought of that before he applied for the job."

"Who's the snitch?"

"Alejandro Vizcarro. He's an accountant. A bookkeeper. Without his testimony, we can't turn Bannon. Without Bannon, Flores slips through our hands . . . again." He leaned in toward me. His face was blotched with sunspots. "Bring Vizcarro and his wife ashore. Get him set up. Protect them. This is the best shot we've had in years."

"Any help?"

"No."

"You're kidding."

"We surround him with a battalion, and we tip our hand. That's what they'll be looking for. We want to keep a low profile." He settled his empty eyes on mine. "You're as low as we go," he said with a smirk. He got a kick out of that line.

"Alejandro's wife's name?"

"Martina."

"Does Bannon know you're after him?"

"They always know. He may be watching us now. Has a condo downtown. Laid out over three million for it."

"Why here?" I asked. "Those boys favor Miami."

"He married a woman from this area."

"For how long?"

"Why the hell would I how long he's been married?"

"How long do I need to babysit?"

He popped open his fingers. "Three, four days. Week on the outside. We need to arrange transportation, and there's jurisdiction infighting. Vizcarro wasn't initially scheduled to come ashore until next week. We had to bump him up."

"The longer it takes—"

"You do your job," he interrupted me, "we do ours. Engage in nothing to gain attention. A single boat. A dark rendezvous. A quiet cottage. No heavily armed guards that some drone will spot in a nanosecond. Keep them inside. No walks on the beach. I don't want his goddamn head out of the house, got it? I'll give you twenty-four before we pick him up. You're done after the handoff."

"Any backup on the water?"

"An eye in the sky. If there's a problem, we can be there within fifteen minutes."

"If there's a problem," I said, "I, and your cargo, will be at the bottom of the gulf in half that time."

He leveled his eyes on mine. "Then you will have failed. When you approach the boat? Four short lights. They will respond with two shorts and a long. Anything other than that, and you better have more horsepower on your ass than the other guy. If you clear that, when you get within earshot, say, 'I used to live in New York City.'"

"What do I want to hear in reply?"

"Everything there was dark and dirty."

I'd heard it before, but it took a second to register. "The Mamas and the Papas?"

"Vizcarro collects vinyl from the sixties."

"Boat size?"

"I don't know."

"Picture? Description?"

"None."

"You're joking."

"I don't joke," he said. "Or kid."

"You should."

"He helps run the books for a cartel. You think he's got a Facebook page?"

"You're asking me to do a rendezvous with a man whom I cannot identify?"

"Ordering you."

"You know his music but not his looks?"

"We're done."

He stood. I did likewise. I wasn't pleased about the lack of physical description, but had nothing to gain by prolonging the point.

"Keep them under a blanket," he said.

He strolled away and tossed the paper cradle into a trash bin. A man far too buff and confident to be a trash collector gathered the bag, tied it, and tossed in into the back of a trash cart. He took off, ignoring all other trash containers he passed.

I went back to the boat, whistling "When Johnny Comes Marching Home," *sotto voce* and half-time, like a funeral dirge.

"Jake, dear?" Kathleen said as I stepped aboard.

I don't believe I'd ever heard her say those two words in

that particular tone—a tone which, like her indecipherable walk, contained both hesitancy and confidence. Yet I knew what it represented. It was the universal sound of your will being sucked away by the one person in the world you bow to. Paperwork was spread out on the teak table. Kathleen had substantial funds due to the estate of her deceased husband. She was not frivolous with money, and the boat was easily affordable for her.

"How bad?" I said, but I was already envisioning myself docking in Key West, the Jolly Roger flapping in the breeze. Might pierce my ear. Move happy hour up to 9:00 a.m. And why not? It's hard not drinking before noon. Think I'm flip-flopping here? I said I didn't *need* the commitment in my life. That is not to be confused with not wanting it.

"Your wife got me at the last hour of the show," the salesman said with a collegial smile that I didn't fall for. "You can probably wax her and flip her in a year. But I don't think it's a boat you'll ever give up."

"She's not my wife," I corrected him. "I never saw her before today."

"It is okay, isn't it?' Kathleen said. Buyer's remorse must have settled in, for her eyes searched mine for approval. "I know we've been supporting the refugee house, but this won't impede that, and it's a dream we've always discussed. I gave him a stupid price. He took it."

I didn't want her to feel bad about her decision or keep her from *our* dreams. After all, we were engaged. I'd buried my knee in the sand at the southern tip of Pass-a-Grille beach. The lava red sunset had witnessed the act as my mother's stone, mounted on a new ring, reflected the low rays of the dying sun. The tender moment was confiscated by a woman blubbering out of a two-piece bathing suit and playing football with a pair of pudgy boys in the shallow water. They were a hard act to ignore.

"No problem," I said, although I had no recollection of

discussing or listening to such a dream. I said Kathleen chatted away after we made love. I fell asleep.

She wrapped her arms around me and kicked up a leg in a playful manner, like they did in the old black and whites.

"Where *shall* we go?" she gushed theatrically, strengthening her wizardry over me and nearly buckling my knees with the sheer volume of the question.

3

"Not to sound trite," Morgan said, "but they don't make them like this anymore."

"They do," I said. "The new ones just have more zeros after a comma."

"Strange that the number signifying nothing imparts greater value."

We had cruised *Lauren Rowe* through Pass-a-Grille channel and to my vacant inside lot where Morgan docked his sailboat *Moonchild*. *Moonchild*, a classic in her own category, moored motionless on the other side of the dock. They floated like a pair of good-looking cousins. Morgan and I jostled with the husky blue dock lines, allowing for five feet of tidal surge. We tied on a twenty-foot spring line.

"I'll run home and get cleaning supplies," Morgan said.

"No need. Kathleen hired her house cleaner to do the boat every two weeks."

"A cleaning lady for a boat?" Morgan squeaked out, as if his life had just been torn asunder by a new and unimaginable paradigm.

"It's a brave new world."

"For you as well. You now have three places to bunk."

"Don't remind me."

At my bungalow on Boca Ciega Bay, the sun rose like a trumpet fanfare over the water. We could walk to the Gulf of Mexico, and Morgan lived next to me—no knocking required. Kathleen's downtown condo was within an enjoyable stroll to the bay, numerous shops, museums, a concert hall and twenty-eight restaurants/bars—we'd counted. We had no intention of selling either place. Another man might wonder if such an arrangement was masking a lack of commitment, or a tarnished glitter of doubt. I am not another man.

And now a forty-foot boat.

Yikes. Thoreau was laughing his New England ass off at me.

Morgan faced me. "When's the first big cruise?"

"Something came up." I wiped the sweat from my forehead with the end of my T-shirt. "I've got to hang around here for a while."

"A while?"

"A week, tops."

"Insurance work?"

"Other."

A boat idled out of the canal, its fumes lingering behind. I dig the smell of gasoline on the water. I gave a final tug of the spring line around a pitted cleat, and then cheesed the excess line on the dock into a tight coil. Morgan picked up the extension cord—it was thick enough to supply juice to the whole island—and plugged it into the shore outlet. A faint tone emitted from the *Lauren Rowe* as her circuits hummed to life.

The name had been put on at the boatyard where I had her surveyed before Kathleen wired the money. That was after I'd explained to my giddy fiancée what a boat survey was, and that, no, you don't just putter out of the marina with the salesman waving adios at the end of the dock. The insurance company needed the survey before they would pick up coverage, I'd informed her.

"Bon voyage," Kathleen had said, upon the completion of my lecture.

"Pardon?"

"He would be waving bon voyage, not adios."

I wasn't sure she'd gotten the point.

Lauren was her middle name and Rowe—Dr. Rowe to her students—was her new last name after she went into a quasi witness protection program. I liked the boat's name. It represented the before and after of her life. Mine as well.

"I could use a little help on the other job," I said to Morgan. Even with GPS, finding another small boat in the pit of night on open water was tricky business.

He eyed me curiously. "How so?"

"A rendezvous at 2:30 a.m. About seven miles off shore."

"When?"

"Tonight. A man and a woman. I'm stowing them for a few days in a cottage in Pass-a-Grille."

I jumped on the boat and opened the rear refrigerator. It was well stocked. That had been my modest request from the selling agent. I opened a beer, tossed the cap in a bottle holder, and reached up and hit the button for the awning. The overmatched engine groaned as it labored to extend the cover. Two-thirds of the way out, it stopped, started again, and surrendered. I took a long draw from the bottle. It was cold and the best thing in the world.

Rule number one of boating: Everything breaks.

"Track likely needs to be greased. I got a tube at home," Morgan said. He climbed onto the boat. "What time do we head out?"

I gave him the time and told him who we were bringing into the States and why. Janssen would have a conniption if he knew I confided in my neighbor, who at that moment was inspecting a loose screw in the teak rail, his ponytail flopped over the side of his face. His moon talisman necklace dangled over the water, reflecting the sun. His T-shirt was bleached beyond recognition and his boat shoes, fermented by the sun and salt, were speckled with drops of suntan oil and fish guts.

When I'd finished, Morgan said, "Alejandro and Martina Vizcarro?"

"Correct."

"Where's the cottage?"

I drained the bottle, lifting the end high into the fierce blue sky. "Third Avenue. I need to get provisions."

"It is a shame to leave this boat," he said appraising her like a lost dream.

"Not to worry," I said. "In time, the *Lauren Rowe* will know open waters."

I expected Morgan to reply, but he did not, leaving a niggling silence that took on a life of its own.

4

Alejandro and Martina Vizcarro's new home was yellow with Caribbean-blue and white trim. The front door canopy appeared to be freshly painted, although the weather was starting to leave its mark. The canopy looked like the sun, with blue rays that fanned out to a dolphin bargeboard. A worn doormat read, "If you're not barefoot, you're overdressed."

The cottage nuzzled between the bay and the gulf with an untrimmed wall of green foliage isolating it from its neighbors. A few dozen paces in one direction provided box seats to the sunrise. Similar paces in the opposite direction unveiled the idyllic sunset beaches of the west coast of Florida. A smattering of restaurants, retail stores and art studios were within a few blocks. Retirees, hippies, people on the lam, and those chasing the elusive tropical dream coveted the location, creating a hodgepodge fruit basket of people with a tenuous common thread: they'd all decided on the same few grains of Florida sand to call home. Their dreams, their escapes, their beginnings, and their ends had gathered them at the southern end of a barrier island, a toe of sand that struggled for survival only a few feet above sea level.

"No go," Morgan said after entering a combination into a lockbox. He jiggled the doorknob. "And we might want to get a better lock. One good shove and the door's gone."

"If they need a lock, we're in trouble. Try it with a five," I said.

"Bingo."

He opened a lockbox, extracted two keys, and unlocked the front door. I followed him in, my fingers webbed with a dozen plastic bags of groceries.

It was closed-up stuffy. Morgan turned on a raspy wall AC unit and opened the windows to circulate air. The kitchen was a picnic-blanket-sized room in the rear that had been remodeled the last time green and gold linoleum rocked the world. The single bathroom was the same era as the kitchen, but clean and tidy. Fresh towels hung on pitted towel racks. Salt kills everything.

A high fence protected the back yard. No garage. The cottages on either side were of similar size, and it would be difficult for anyone to see in the yard. Alejandro and Martina should at least be able to get some fresh air. The heck with what Janssen said. There was no way someone could stay inside day after day.

"Could you stay inside for a week?" I said, soliciting support for my decision, and then disappointed that I had. Self-doubt is like salt—it kills everything.

"I'd agree to it," Morgan said as he inspected a window lock. "And then I'd go out. It's difficult to imagine anyone finding them here. My father tells me, though, that difficult is not a synonym for impossible."

Morgan's father drank himself to death years ago, but Morgan welcomes the presence the deceased exert on our lives.

I left him fussing with the lock and hiked the quiet streets. Cars rested tight against the curb, some snuggled under fitted covers. I waved at a woman washing the outside of her windows. She waved back, like you do when you think you're supposed to know someone, although you don't. She adjusted her hat and returned to her task, confident she'd done the neighborly thing. Alleys veined between and behind the homes. The developers must have hijacked the zoning committee, grabbed a shovel with one hand, a bottle of moonshine in the other, and set off to work. Not that it mattered. Only one road led onto Pass-a-Grille. Water, however, was a threat. It surrounded the thin peninsula. I'd have to do my Paul Revere act and keep a watchful eye on sea as well as land.

When I arrived back at the cottage, a man stood in the front yard of the house across the street. He had a stringy beard and baggy shorts. Although it wasn't cold, he wore a loose-fitting Ohio State sweatshirt. He ignored me, picked up a rake that was leaning against a tabebuia tree, and went to work. The sun filtered through the clattering palms, and his face appeared to be much younger than his deliberate and measured movements indicated. He raked as if each stroke was a conscious act, each leaf a prized possession. After a half dozen passes, he stopped, although a great many leaves still smothered the ground awaiting his attention. He stared at his creation and then placed the rake where it had previously rested. He glanced in my direction, but if he saw me, he gave no indication. He turned and went into his house. Behind him, the pile of debris stood as a testament to his day's effort.

Another over-ripe piece of fruit in the jumbled Florida basket.

5

RAFAEL

Rafael Cherez pinched his chin with his thumb and forefinger and peered out of his first-class seat as the British Air 747, direct from Heathrow, made its final approach to Tampa International Airport. Such a swampy place, he thought. All flat and dimpled with lakes, as if this part of Earth couldn't decide whether it was solid or liquid. Farm or sea. Cow or fish.

He'd been to Florida on one other occasion. That was years ago, when Sergio Flores had summoned him for a job in Miami. A Columbian drug lord's wife had been on a shopping spree with her girlfriends, celebrating her fortieth birthday. Her body was never found, but the drug lord did receive a single Jimmy Choo ankle strap gold sandal in a box. Her blood-crusted foot was still strapped in. After that, the drug lord agreed to pull out of the Texas delivery routes. Not that it mattered, for a bullet found his head within a month. Aspiring young South American and banana republic venture capitalists got the message: You will die, but your loved ones will go first.

The Frenchman had stayed a month in Southeast Florida. He found it advantageous in his profession not to move immediately before or after he completed an assignment. That was for amateurs. There was no better way to draw attention to yourself than to pretend you could slip in and out within days of a job—just what every intelligence agency on the planet was looking for. Be inconspicuous. That was what mattered. Arrive early. Stay late. Blend in.

Obscurity is your friend.

As for Miami, he'd found the city soulless. A sexed-up city of heat and skin that shunned the day and worshipped the night. There was no *reason* for the place. No purpose. He'd longed for the hills of Bordeaux. The grapes hanging patiently in the sun so man could drink the ancient ground and all the sweetness it brought forth. The city itself. How the muddy Garonne River curved along the waterfront like a voluptuous woman lying on her side, pressed against her lover. He had longed for her statues, her history, her open markets with cheese and bread. The young prancing by, scarfed up in wool and cashmere and hats with dark hair tumbling out. He did not understand women who did not realize that clothing was sexy, and that parading around in as little cloth as possible was not only cheap and vulgar, but left nothing to the imagination. And what is life without imagination?

No, you could keep Miami. Let the rising sea sweep it away. It had been a challenge to pass time, although he found the golf attractive. Unfortunately, such a leisurely schedule was not an option for this job. He'd only been contacted a week ago, and the summons had come on the heels of another job he'd orchestrated in North Carolina. My, my. Such a rush to kill people these days. But this one was different; murder and kidnapping. He'd also been told that an accomplice would assist him, supposedly to aid him in the kidnapping. Can't have someone out there who could pull him from a lineup, let alone bear witness to a murder, can we? He would need to settle that on his own. Did Flores know he was sending the accomplice down a one-way street?

There's a thought.

Mon. Mon. The rush to *meurtre* these days.

Murder.

Rafael shunned the word. Staging "accidents" was more . . . diplomatic. Tasteful. While far more elaborate, the lack of intent thwarted investigations. The second Ohio job, over a year before—*has it been that long?*—had been his test. He'd been forced to come up with a new trademark, since Jimmy Choo and the Ohio eight had only been two years prior to that. They had brought too much attention, although the Ohio eight had gone well.

You call that "well?" Eight dead and not a clue? That, my friend, is a standing ovation. The crowd. The curtain. The lights. Ladies and gentlemen, I give you **Monsieur Rafael Cherez!**

But Rafael was not one to press luck. The North Carolina and the second Ohio job had been masterpieces of deception. He'd been sipping Pomerol, six time zones away, when North Carolina occurred. The Pomerol—he tried to remember—was the balance a little off? Too much tannins for the acidity? He'd decided to let it age a few more years. Good wine is like good murder—it takes time to do it right.

"You need to put your tray away, sir," a stewardess informed him. Her skin was flawless, and her red hair rested on her freckled shoulders like a frozen waterfall. He'd wanted to smother his face in it since they took off eight hours ago.

"*Je ne comprends pas.*"

She gave him a knowing grin. He'd spoken perfectly good English to her when he settled into his seat as the plane loaded at terminal four at Heathrow. She reached over and retired his tray. As she did, her hair tumbled over her left shoulder. He scooted forward, opened his mouth, and took in a deep breath. A few lose strands tickled his tongue.

"*Merci bien, mademoiselle.* Your hair is strawberries on a June morning."

She faked him another grin and continued down the aisle.

Enough, he thought. It is time for business.

He reached into the pocket of his sports coat and took out a picture.

Such a beautiful woman. So young to be a mother.

C'est la vie.

No, he chuckled to himself. That is death.

6

It was three o'clock in the morning. Morgan and I were dressed in black, and black ensconced us. On the water at night, black is not a color; it is the world—the left, the right, the high and the low. You breathe it in and hope it doesn't stain your lungs.

Impulse, my thirty-foot Grady White, rose and fell like a child's fishing bobber in the dark swells of the gulf. The red spinnaker bag in the cockpit under the dash contained passports, currencies, satellite phones, a locator beacon, a Surefire tactical light, and new Steiner eOptics night goggles. The goggles had cost the GDP of Uruguay, but they let me see at night without the other guy seeing me. That's assuming the opposing player didn't have a pair himself.

A gun mount inside the cuddy held a Remington sniper rifle and a Mossberg Maverick double barrel shotgun. A Yukon Titanium Night Vision Rifle Scope was in the radio box. Whether or not I would need any of those toys didn't matter. You're better off having it and not needing it, than needing it and not having it.

If forced to run, I was cooked. *Impulse* was an open bow, dual console cruising and fishing vessel. In a race, despite her twin Yamaha 300s, she'd lose to a gimpy turtle with a favorable tide. Her unattractiveness in that regard is what made her perfect for my type of work. Go out in the gulf in a narrow-beamed boat with five engines crowding its stern, and you can bet your wet fanny someone's watching you. You might as well fly a smuggler's flag. Lumber out in a Grady White, and whoever's at the controls that night will go back to phone porn. There is no benefit in trying to be the fastest boat on the water—you will lose that battle. There is, however, an incalculable benefit to being the least conspicuous boat on the water.

Obscurity is your friend.

"Two o'clock," Morgan said. He had the Steiners tight on his face.

"One?"

"Affirmative."

"Size?"

"Like us."

I swung *Impulse* to the starboard and dropped her into neutral. I reached over and picked up the Surefire light.

"Now?" I said.

"Noon."

I gave four short bursts of light.

Nothing.

I repeated it. Two short and a long came back.

"We're on," I said.

We switched positions. Morgan went behind the wheel, and I maneuvered to the bow. I put the goggles up to my face.

"Eleven-thirty," I said over my shoulder.

Morgan adjusted a few degrees port.

I stuck the goggles under the front seat. We came upon the other boat as if we were mating with a demonic apparition.

"I used to live in New York City," I called out.

"Everything there was dark and dirty," a voice sliced through the dark. It carried no accent, and I assumed it was the captain.

"We'll pull aside you," I said. "Do not climb aboard until I give you the order. Understand?"

"Understood."

We drifted closer. The other boat was a cuddy cabin. I didn't like that. I had no idea what they had below deck. I unlatched my Sig Sauer from its holster.

Morgan threw the engines in reverse for a second to facilitate a complete stop, and then scampered over to the port side and tossed a line to the other vessel. The captain caught it and secured it to a side cleat. A wave raised both boats at once, and it was all we could do to just hang on. When we settled, we tied two large blue fenders around the cleats to keep the boats from knocking each other. We secured both forward and aft cleats.

The captain and I eyed each other with hawkish intensity. He looked ex-military. Square shoulders. Buzzed hair. Arms loose at his side. He wore a black jacket, and I assume a gun or two was on him. He was likely a DEA agent, but I wasn't drifting offshore in the middle of the night looking for camaraderie. A smaller man cowered behind him.

"Alejandro Vizcarro?" I said.

"That is I," the smaller man said. His frail shoulders made his head seem large.

"Welcome to Florida. Get in."

He hesitated.

I raised my gun.

"Get in now or we leave. *Comprende?*"

The captain said, "There's no need—"

"Yes. Yes," Alejandro spurted out. "I come. Of course. I need to get my . . . wife."

He headed for the closed cuddy cabin door.

"Step away from the cuddy," I said.

"But my . . . Martina. She is down below. And I have a small suitcase." He had only a trace of accent. His eyes darted to the captain and back to me.

"Everything's fine," the captain said. "Keep your gun in your hand, if it makes you feel better."

It did make me feel better—it kept me at the top of the food chain. I didn't like my situation. Morgan was exposed, and I had no idea who, or what, was in the cruiser's cabin.

"You go in slowly, you come out slowly," I instructed Alejandro. "Push the suitcase out first. Then you, then your wife. You both come out, hands on head."

He gave a staccato nod. He opened the cuddy door and disappeared. A moment later, he pushed out a bulging, ragged suitcase. Then he emerged, his open palms raised.

"I said on your head."

He placed them on his head and tottered as another swell raised the boats.

A woman with dark hair bundled high on her head and shouldering a backpack emerged. The bundle of hair was nearly the size of her head. Although difficult to see in the dark, she appeared to be younger than Alejandro. Her hands rested on her hair like it was a cushion. Her eyes canvassed me, but then flashed to her husband. She took two steps and stopped. She glanced nervously at the cuddy door. She lowered her hands.

I raised my gun.

A young girl escaped the cuddy. She ran straight to Alejandro and hugged his legs. He placed his protective arms around her. She also had a backpack.

Then another girl snuck out—taller than the first. She was clutching a small boy. She trotted to Martina, who took the boy in her arms. Then she, too, scampered over to Alejandro.

"The hell is this?" I demanded to the captain. The cuddy door was still open.

"His family. He wishes to—"

"Shut the door."

The captain shut the cuddy door.

"This is my family," Alejandro announced proudly. He

stood tall for such a diminutive man and had wiry Albert Einstein hair.

"My instructions are to transport you and your wife."

"This is my family," he said, as if no further explanation was warranted.

The boats heaved together as another roller caught us broadside. I reached down to the stainless steel rail to steady myself. Alejandro stumbled to his right, catching the rail with one arm.

"They were to have other arrangements," the captain said. He gave a dismissive shrug. "But that didn't work out so well. We had no choice. Nor do you."

Martina and their son stood a few feet away from Alejandro and their two daughters. The girls, both in dresses, eyed me with hope and defiance, as if they were not sure what I represented and equally unsure, therefore, how to view me.

Alejandro glanced down at his older daughter. "This is Ana Maria. And this," he nodded to the shorter girl, "is Gabriela."

"And this is Little Joe," Gabriela rushed out, as if eager to get the introductions in. "Aunt Rosa always wanted a girl named Josephina. But," she fanned her hands, "guess what? Joe turned out to be a boy."

Like her parents, her voice carried only a thread of accent.

"Hush, Gabriela," Martina said.

"But that's what you said—"

"Enough," her father admonished her.

"Lock the door," I told the captain.

"Papa said Little Joe was on a TV show once," Gabriela said, immune to her parents' admonishments. "But he really wasn't little."

"*Gabriela,*" Alejandro said.

"The door." I kept my eyes on the captain.

He bobbed his head in approval of my move. He fumbled

with the ignition key and locked the cuddy door. He placed the keys back on the console.

"I understand your caution," he said. "But he will not board you without them. I can assure you of that."

"You got a dog too?" I said to Alejandro.

"We don't have one," Gabriela said. "But Papa said we—"

"Shh," her father said.

"We're going to name him Epcot," Gabriela said. "Know why? Papa's always—"

"*Gabriela Louisa!*" Alejandro scolded her and wrapped his arms around Gabriela, pulling her into his legs.

"Board them," I said to Morgan. I didn't have a choice.

Morgan came forward and extended his hand to Ana Maria. She glanced up at her father. He nodded. She stepped aboard and quickly moved away from me as if I carried the Black Plague. Alejandro boarded next, and Martina passed Little Joe to him. He handed the boy—I would guess he was between three and four, but I'm not good with kids—to Ana Maria. Morgan took Gabriela's hand, but she was an independent little firecracker and jumped onto *Impulse* by herself. She landed next to me, steadied herself, and then spread her arms, like a gymnast who had just vaulted off a pommel horse. The moon broke free of a cloud and bathed the boats in a soft light. With her arms still raised, Gabriela looked up at me and said, "Look at me, I'm a moonbeam. Have you been to Disney World?"

"Gabriela," her father said, his voice soaked with weariness for what I sensed was an ongoing battle.

Alejandro hesitated, and then helped his wife board. They avoided eye contact. I couldn't imagine bearing the responsibility of sneaking three children out of Mexico and into the States. My plan had been to stash Alejandro and Martina in the Grady's cuddy. Unlike a cruiser, though, my cuddy was a single side door on the port side. It held the commode and a bunk only a couple into contortionist sex could appreciate.

Still, it would have to do. No way did I want some bird in the sky to notice that I had two warm bodies going out into the gulf and seven on the return trip.

Morgan untied us. I instructed the other captain to leave first. He gave me a brotherly salute, spun his boat, and roared off to God-knows-where.

"Inside," I said. I motioned with my gun toward the cuddy door.

"Please," Alejandro said. "Is the gun necessary?"

I holstered my gun and opened the door. I unlatched the Remington and Mossberg, and passed them to Morgan. There was no need to shut them in a cuddy with guns.

"You stay in until I open it. If we get stopped, do not even breathe. We clear on that?"

"I get the bed," Gabriela squealed as she jumped down into the cuddy.

I pointed my finger at Alejandro. "Put a lid on that one. Understand?"

"Yes, sir."

"I'll take care of her, Papa," Ana Maria said and tumbled in after her sister.

Martina, clenching Little Joe, went in next. After Alejandro, I shut the door, perhaps a bit more firmly than was necessary.

I laid the guns across the back so they wouldn't slide when the bow rose. Morgan thrust the twin throttle forward, and *Impulse* reared up like an angry thoroughbred before her bow settled down. Her twin three hundreds skimmed the hull over the water's surface as if we had the wings of Pegasus. I think she was out to prove wrong my quip about losing to a turtle.

We split the night back to the west coast of Florida with Alejandro Vizcarro, his wife Martina, their oldest daughter Ana Maria, a spitfire named Gabriela, and Little Joe.

How I would keep them bottled up in that little cottage was anyone's guess.

7

Morgan guided *Impulse* through a narrow channel shrouded with tangled mangrove roots. It could have passed as the mythological river Styx. I wondered what Greek tragedy awaited us and tried to shake the thought, but that just gave it tenure.

I jumped out onto a dilapidated dock and secured the bow while Morgan tied off the aft cleat. We were at an isolated piece of property that had recently been gifted to Pinellas County through the estate of a man named Walter 'Mac" MacDonald. It was a refugee house that, per Mac's will, was administered by Morgan and me.

We herded the Vizcarros into my truck and set out toward the cottage. It was only a ten-minute drive, but by the time we got there, I was ready to throw Gabriela back into the Gulf of Mexico. Or jump in myself. Or fall upon my sword. Motor mouth could not shut up. She was annoyingly happy. Chipper. She had the lung capacity of a baby whale and stuffed every silent second with a chorus of words, delivered with exhausting exuberance. Maybe family life was great. How would I know? My older sister and only sibling vanished out of my life when I was seven, nearly eight. My parents died within a few years of that. *Family* was a dictionary entry to me.

When we entered the cottage, Gabriela tore through it like a child opening a Christmas package.

But again, what do I know?

Martina and I stood in the kitchen, our bodies a few feet apart. Her stance was wide, as if she were wary of being dislodged from her ground. She had a sinewy figure of boyish hips and thin shoulders. She reached over her shoulder and untied her hair. It sprang free and cascaded down around her. Its volume was disproportionate to her frame. Her midnight eyes were both dark and inviting and her breasts small and pointy, although I tried not to notice. I put her around fifteen years younger than Alejandro.

"How old is Gabriela?" I asked her.

"Nine."

"The others?"

"Ana Maria is thirteen. Joe is three. He is Alejandro's nephew."

"Why do you have his nephew?"

"What is your name?"

"That's not an answer to—"

"Your name?" she demanded.

I was beginning to see where Martina's youngest daughter got her spunk.

"Jake."

"That is not a name," she said. "That is a syllable."

"Best I can do."

"I'll tell you, *Jake*, why we have Little Joe. They killed Alejandro's brother, wife, and their three other children. Joe was left as a reminder. An *advertencia*. They also left a note instructing us to think of death every time we look at him. To remember our family, and to do what is best for them."

"You can ignore—"

"They had a guard to protect them. But he was more

professional than you. He did not have long hair. He did not stare at my breasts."

"You'll be safe here."

"We are in danger you cannot dream of," she said, as if the future were unalterable.

"I have a vivid imagination."

"You are no match for them," she scoffed at me.

"Fine, lady. You'd rather all die in Mexico?"

It wasn't my kindest comment, but if I was going to protect the family, I required at least a measurable amount of gratitude.

"We will die wherever we are. And, yes. I would rather die in my home country."

"You might get your wish, but not on my watch."

"I have met men like you before. Macho. Cocky. You are all the same. You will not even mourn us when we are gone."

"What do you want from me?"

"There is nothing you can do for us. We are dead."

"How about a consolation prize: I'll kill whoever kills you."

She shook her head as to rid herself of me. "Treat me like a fool. It is you who is a clown."

"Keep your children inside. Do you understand that?"

"You think thin walls will protect us?"

"I said, do you understand?"

"Yes," she said.

"Empty your suitcase."

"Why?"

"Syllables don't repeat questions."

Her jaw tightened and she spun around. We went to the bedroom. She heaved up the bloated leather suitcase and dropped it on the dresser. Her arms were stringed with muscle and bone. She opened it, took items of clothing out, and started to place the clothing in a drawer.

"Let me feel them first," I said.

A Beautiful Voice

She hesitated and then passed me an undershirt. One by one, she handed the contents of the suitcase into my probing hands. I passed the clothing back to her and, in a stark contrast with her previous behavior, she placed them considerately into a drawer. She patted each garment, as if to touch a world gone by and assure herself that all was not without hope. When the suitcase was empty, I took out a pocketknife.

"I'll buy you another one," I said. I ripped the suitcase open.

Nothing was sewn into the stitching. No bugs. It would find a new home in a dumpster, far from the safe house. I did the same with the two backpacks, and then flipped through the books they had brought.

"You think they are that simple?" Martina said in a resigned tone.

"If they're good, they are even simpler than this."

"You are no match for them."

"I wrestle dolphins for exercise."

"You make me cry, not laugh."

She went back to fondling the clothes in the drawer, dismissing me as if I weren't worth the effort. Maybe I wasn't.

I punched out my breath and left the room. Perhaps Martina was upset with her husband for his profession—running numbers for the cartel—or his decision to squeal on Bannon. Or maybe they had a squabble over who was going to read to the kids at bedtime. I didn't know or care.

Morgan instructed Alejandro to keep the blinds down and showed him how one window lock needed an extra twist. Alejandro listened with intense interest and patience, as if by obeying, he would incrementally increase his and his family's chance for survival. I felt a rush of pity for the man. If he provided enough information to force Bannon to testify against Flores, what waited for both men? A life on the run? New identities? Anyone who snitches on a drug cartel invites fear and paranoia into their lives. He had to know this—as did his wife. Yet they were together. A family. I vowed to perform my task so that he could be a proud father and rise to the expectations of his family.

Ana Maria attended to Joe with the proficiency of a hired nanny. Joe, a pudgy little fellow with a mop of black hair and cheeks stuffed with grapes, was always moving, although there was no harmony to his motions. He was a different build than his sisters. They were thin with longer faces, like their father and mother. He was thick with a round, stick-figure head. He jabbered between Spanish and English as if he were speaking in tongues.

"You are to keep your family inside until I come for you," I said to Alejandro when Morgan was finished with him. "Do you understand this?"

"It will be very hard with the children. I noticed the backyard is fenced. Can they at least go out there?"

"Officially? No."

"But, in your opinion?"

I didn't want to answer that.

"Keep them inside," I told him.

He hesitated, and then said, "Will it be you who comes for us?"

"Yes. Allow no one in besides myself and Morgan."

"When will you come?"

"Tomorrow."

"No. I mean to take us away."

"I don't know."

"It will be you?" he repeated.

"It will be me," I assured him, although I wished I had something more to offer him. "Others may transport you, but I will be the one to open the door."

He gave that a solitary nod and his face sagged, as if a great worry had manifested itself to him.

"It is only to be you and your friend who protect us?" he asked.

"You are in hiding. We're not planting a flag announcing your presence."

"No guards at the door, or on the street? How can you call that protection?"

"That invites curiosity. You're a rabbit in a hole. Put a guard on the hole, and a fox knows the rabbit is home."

"A fox will not approach the hole if he knows a lion is guarding it," he said.

"I don't make the plans. I just execute them. I'll be by in the morning. You have no cell phones, correct?"

"We have no phones."

"Any pocket electronics?"

"None," he said. "They told us to bring only clothing."

"Did anybody approach you before you got on the boat and ask you to carry anything, or give you a farewell present?"

"There is no farewell when you sneak out of your country at night."

"Answer the question."

"No."

"Did the man on the boat give you anything?"

"No."

"Enjoy your stay." I turned toward the door.

"My girls," he said.

I expected him to say something, but he froze, as if he'd momentarily forgotten his train of thought or was embarrassed that he had spoken.

"What about them?"

He folded his hands in front of himself and massaged his fingers. "When they come for us, save the children. Only Martina knows of our danger, of evil in the world. The others—"

"No one's coming for you."

"Sometimes boys are more desirable in my country, but girls—"

"You'll be—"

43

"On your mother's grave, promise me that you'll give them the opportunity for a good life."

"Have a good evening, Alejandro."

"You make this promise to me now," he nearly shouted. His eyes widened as if startled by his own outcry. "As one man to another."

"Nothing—"

"*Promise me.*" He took a step toward me.

The cottage roared in silence, and in that silence I heard him scream.

"Sure. I promise."

8

A super moon hung low over the water an hour before sunrise like a faltering party balloon from the previous night. A partial lunar eclipse marred it, creating a rare red and blue moon combination. It brightened a wide swath of the gulf. The beam got narrower as it approached the shore, tracking me as I ran. Bulbs flashed as I sprinted past cameras set on tripods. I thought of packing in the run and taking a seat on a bench, as others had done, and enjoying the phenomenon—but my circuit board isn't wired for that. My pool rules don't allow it.

Haunted by Alejandro's outcry, I'd spent half the night slumped in my truck parked at the end of their street. Alejandro and Martina believed their deaths were a foregone conclusion. A preordained scene that I could in no manner alter or affect. Hopefully, after an uneventful night they would both relax and breathe a little easier. After all, Florida is not Mexico.

I climbed the footbridge—the lower steps were lost in the sand—over the protected dunes with sea oats, and then strolled down the sleeping southern streets of Pass-a-Grille. I traversed First and Second Avenue and broke back into a run down Third Avenue before again hitting the beach for the return trip to the bridge that rose over the slim channel and onto my island.

At eight-fifteen, after hitting the grocery story, I stood at the front door of Mr. and Mrs. Alejandro Vizcarro.

I knocked once, paused, knocked three more times, another pause, and then once. That was the agreed upon signal. I repeated it, which was also understood. The curtain covering the window on the door peeled back. Alejandro opened the door. I stepped in, a box of doughnuts in one hand, flowers in the other, and a winning smile on my face.

"The toilet is clogged," Alejandro said.

I'm sure he meant to say good morning and thanks for the pastries, but oftentimes things get lost in translation.

"No plunger?" I said.

"*Nah-dah.*"

"I'll get one."

I texted Morgan.

Martina ignored the flowers and shot dagger eyes at the doughnuts. "We do not eat those," she said with contempt. "They are bad for the children."

"Is that their vote?" I said, trying to inject cheer into a deteriorating situation.

She snatched the doughnuts from my hand and spun away from me. She just as quickly spun back around and thrust them into my chest. "We have no place to dispose of them. Take them. What are we to do with our trash?"

"I can—"

"We need a bigger trash can. You see the . . . the *minuscule* one under the sink? *Estupido.* We are a family of five."

Alejandro ran off a salvo of Spanish words that was met with an equally sharp barrage from his wife. She capitulated with a harrumph, grabbed my doughnuts, took three steps to the kitchen, and dropped them on the counter, on top of a copy of

Giraffes Can't Dance. It rested cockeyed on one of the Harry Potter tomes. I fumbled around the cabinets searching for a vase, but found nothing that would hold my bouquet. I propped the flowers up in the sink, and several yellow tulips slumped in the corner like embarrassed houseguests who knew they were unwelcome.

Martina shook her head, opened a cabinet, and took out two water glasses. She hacked groups of two or three at a time with a knife, using enough force to fell an oak tree, and bunched them together in the glasses.

A bedroom door flung open and Gabriela, giggling, came dashing out. Ana Maria was hot on her tail.

It was a cottage. They had no place to run. Gabriela smacked into me like a northerly January wind that fights me on the beach during a morning run. Her momentum dissipated as she slid around my thigh. Ana Maria pulled up just short of colliding with me. She regained her composure and smoothed her lavender blue dress.

"Doughnuts?" I said holding up the box.

"Father?" Ana Maria asked tentatively. He must be more lenient than her mother.

"Of course," Alejandro said nodding. Gabriela attacked the box, while Ana Maria held back and allowed her little sister to select first.

"I'll get you a larger trash can," I said to Martina.

"Thank you," she said in a polite voice that was in sharp contrast to her previous contentious comments.

"And fresh fruit tomorrow," I said, sensing that progress would be measured one grocery trip at a time.

"Why not today?" Martina prodded me.

"I don't want to be seen coming and going from the house too often. Activity arouses suspicion."

"My girls like strawberries," Alejandro said. Martina narrowed her eyes. Maybe strawberries weren't on their diet.

"And Joe?" I asked.

"He'll eat anything," Gabriela interjected. "You never answered my question."

Her eyes, three feet below mine, searched my face. They were like tiny round portholes of life. She held the same stuffy in her hand she had clutched the night in the boat. It was a small, tattered brown monkey, worn bare by years of coddling.

"What question was that, Peanut?" I said.

She giggled. "Hey, I'm not a peanut."

"You look like one to me."

"You look like a giraffe with a lion's head." Her hands kneaded her stuffed monkey, perhaps sensing that she had gone too far.

"Gabriela," her father said.

"What's your question, Peanut?" I said.

"Have you been to Disney World? I asked you on the boat. But you didn't answer me."

Kid had a good memory.

"Yes, you did ask, and no, I didn't answer."

"Have you?"

"I have."

"What's it like?"

Ana Maria took a step away from her father and closer to me, as if to get in on the great secret.

I kneeled so that my face was level with Gabriela's. I jutted my chin toward her stuffed monkey. "What's your buddy's name?"

"Bongo."

"You'll need to hold on tight to Bongo. Disney World is full of trolls with warts on their faces. They eat little children, and then dance in the street playing with the children's toys, which they rename. Bongo will become Rummy the Monkey."

Gabriela gave a nervous giggle. "No they don't," she said and twisted one of the monkey's arms with her finger. It had a loose thread.

"Oh? You tell me, then, what it's like."

"I think there *are* trolls with warts on their faces," she bleated, calling my bluff. "But they eat giraffes that have lion heads," she said with gusto. "And take *their* toys."

"Stop it, Gabriela," Ana Maria said. She eyed me studiously. "What is it *rea*lly like?"

"You know they call part of it the Magic Kingdom?" I said.

She nodded and leaned her head in.

A knock on the door interrupted us. The signal came again, and Alejandro let Morgan in. He carried a plunger.

"Let's hit that toilet," I said.

THE NEXT DAY I BROUGHT FRUIT AND A VASE. MARTINA struggled mightily not to show her appreciation. A few flowers were already in a small, cut-glass piece on the table. She'd done an admirable job with the other flowers, placing them in drinking glasses and partitioning them around the cottage. Each one was centered neatly on a red square cloth so as not to stain the furniture or windowsill. I also surprised the girls with coloring books and crayons.

Morgan and I each canvassed the neighborhood three times that day. I staggered our times, jogging the streets at five a.m., and walking them or riding my bike at different hours of the day and evening. Apart from the house across the street—the beard with the rake—all was quiet. The beard was a restless soul and had lights on at odd hours. At night, he was visible through the thin curtains, slinking around his house in a sweatshirt, a cold ghost trapped by walls.

ON THE THIRD MORNING, I RAPPED THE SIGNAL ON the door while armed with a handful of children's books that Kathleen had selected for me. I remembered I'd never told Ana Maria about Disney World. Why hadn't she asked me again? I knocked again. Janssen hadn't contacted me, but I assumed their time in the cottage was drawing to an end.

A plane droned above. The growl of outboard engines carried down the street from the bay. Two birds got in a bitter argument. An army of teensy-weensy red ants frantically marched single file cutting a corner over the doormat. Heigh-ho, heigh-ho. It's off to work we go. If you're not barefoot, you're overdressed.

After my third series of knocks, I dropped the books, drew my gun from my behind my back, and kicked the front door. It flew open, and I realized it had not been locked. Morgan had observed when we first entered the cottage that the door was weak.

Martina Vizcarro slumped in the corner of the cramped kitchen. She stared at me. Her hair cobwebbed the sides of her face, and a small hole centered her forehead. Alejandro was face down on the floor a few feet from her. I turned him over with my left hand, my right hand still holding my worthless gun. A similar mark dotted his forehead and blood puddled on the floor. The flowers I had brought them ringed the room like a funeral parlor.

The children were gone.

9

"You're out to pasture," Janssen said.

"I can't help if I'm not on the case," I said.

"Help? Alejandro Vizcarro is dead. You do recall that is a permanent state."

We were at the hotel beach bar a mile from my house. The hot tub on the ground to my right served as the steamy, liquid home of a solitary woman with a pink visor and dangling gold earrings. Her elbow rested on the paver bricks and propped up a book. A man thrashing laps had the north pool to himself. The speakers played to empty lounge chairs. Green umbrellas, with the breeze billowing their fringes like women's skirts, shaded deserted tables. Not many people take a vacation in Florida in early December. They should.

My world was a world away from a vacation.

I'd notified Janssen. Three hours later, he was next to me sipping iced tea. I didn't think he'd fly in from D.C. and assumed he'd been at MacDill, where CENTCOM is headquartered. I didn't care enough to ask.

He glanced around at the resort, granting it the aloof disdain he reserved for his surroundings no matter where he was.

"What do your pictures show?" I asked.

"We don't have any," he said, finding something more interesting to look at other than me.

"You told me you had an eye in the sky."

"Not at night." He looked at me. "The idea was to generate as little activity as possible in order to minimize suspicion."

"How did that work out?"

"You failed."

"My job was to stash them away," I said, scrambling to salvage a pitiful piece of self-esteem. "No one knew of their location due to action or carelessness on my part. It had to be on your end. Any clues?"

Janssen already had a team at the cottage.

He grunted. "No. But it stinks of professionals. No brass. So either a revolver or they picked up their casings. We'll dust the place and cut out. It resembles the Ohio eight, but on a smaller scale. Nothing solid. Just conjecture."

"The Ohio eight?"

He explained that in rural southern Ohio, eight family members who were excessively fond of cultivating Cannabis plants had been executed in their homes. Children had been spared—some who had been sleeping in the same bed as an executed family member. The crimes remain unsolved. Janssen had become involved on the theory that Mexican cartel hit squads were now operating on U.S. soil.

As he spoke, my memory kicked in. "Ohio was a group effort, correct?"

"We think they needed at least three men to pull it off."

"Why take Alejandro's children and Little Joe?"

I'd previously informed Janssen that the Vizcarros came with their children. He claimed to have no knowledge of the children.

"Little who?"

Apparently he hadn't been paying attention.

"Joe, Alejandro's nephew," I explained for the second time. "Martina said the cartel killed Alejandro's brother, wife and three of four children. One survived. They smuggled him in with their two girls."

"You think the assassin snatched them?" Janssen said. "Get your head out of the sun. They split. They'll show up on a beach. It's not our concern."

"You should gift your heart to science so they can discover how a stone pumped blood all those years."

He shifted his scornful gaze toward one of the TV screens where men and women on mute were discussing the calamity of interest rates rising faster than the sea level. Ticker news scrolled along the bottom on the screen like child's train set. The Euro crashed through a support level. Trade wars were erupting. Emerging markets under severe pressure. Lions and tigers and bears.

If Ana Maria ran with her younger sister and Little Joe, they shouldn't be hard to find. I owed that to the Vizcarros. Before I left the cottage, I'd taken inventory. Some of the children's clothing and both backpacks—I'd bought them new ones—were gone. So were the books they had brought with them, although one of the coloring books I'd given them was left behind.

I took a sip of beer and glanced out at the gulf. It used to tantalize me like a hungry lover beckoning for me to join her so she could suffocate me with her warm and salty waves. But recently it struck me as nothing more than curling swells of indifference relentlessly pounding the beach. I miss the lover. It was a more pleasurable, if inaccurate, take on the world. But why shy from romanticism? It's the perfect antidote for cruel reality.

I said, "What do we know about Alejandro before he got on the boat?"

"Meaning?"

"Who handled him in Mexico?"

"We don't know. But he wasn't followed into the gulf, nor were you. We checked the tape again. Nothing. There was no one close to you on your return trip."

"But they knew."

He nodded in agreement. "It's likely that the Vizcarros were carrying a tracking device. You searched their suitcase?"

"I did."

"Take the seams apart."

"I did."

"They carry anything for a friend?"

"Said they didn't."

"Maybe he saw a dentist last week and a bug was in his mouth. We may never know." He stood. "I won't waste my breath telling you not to look for the children. If you find them, see what they know. Every bit of intelligence helps."

He strolled away without a glance at the gulf or the pools. He rounded the corner past the display board that listed the events for the day along with the time of sunrise, sunset, and temperature of the gulf. He disappeared into the garden where the outdoor weddings were conducted and where they had recently dug up the grass and put in artificial turf to accommodate more seating. I doubted he knew or cared for any of that. For a man who shunned defeat more than he coveted victory, he seemed languid, considering the person who could have jailed a notorious drug dealer had just been eliminated under his supervision. Maybe he was getting soft as he aged. Or perhaps after so many defeats, he no longer fought them but accepted them as part of the package.

I took a swallow of beer. A guest who enjoyed his food sat up in a beach lounge and surveyed the resort, like a prairie dog coming out of its hole. His belly and chest were apple red, and his sides and back banana white. He hesitated and then lay back down, sacrificing his body again to the cunning sun. You can always spot a rookie. On the other side of the pool, Jaffe, one of the pool attendants, prepped four lounge chairs for a group of women. A girls' trip. He carefully tucked in the towels under the cushions. Nothing loose. Not even a thread.

"Bongo," I said.

"Come again?" Eddie, the bartender said. I wasn't aware that he was across from me.

"Bongo had a loose thread."

"Don't we all?"

"So simple," I said in admiration.

It hadn't occurred to me to sacrifice Gabriela's stuffed monkey to make certain a tracking device wasn't inside. What kind of man would rip open a child's stuffy?

A smart man.

I'd tartly prophesized to Martina that if her adversaries were really good, they would be simpler than we imagined. That I was right—as was she when she declared me no match for them—were issues I was in no mood to contend with. But I felt them gathering and mushrooming inside like a dark thunderhead.

I slid off my stool, marched through the garden level of the hotel, climbed in my truck, and gunned it down the street to the cottage. Janssen's team had cleared out.

Bongo, the stuffed monkey, was gone.

If a tracking device was in Gabriela's stuffed monkey, someone had known every move. I couldn't know for sure, and I already doubted my theory, but it was all I had. They killed Vizcarro and his wife, created three runaway orphans—or kidnapped them—and destroyed our chance to turn Richard Bannon against his boss, Sergio Flores.

The box of doughnuts sat on the counter in the kitchen next to the vertical paper towel dispenser. A doughnut with a child's bite mark rested under the cellophane cover. I thought

I should do something with it, but nothing came to me. No thoughts. No emotions. The wall unit air conditioner grew louder and louder, like a jet tearing down a runway. I flipped it off.

The silence nearly broke me, and I wish it had.

10

Morgan and I bruised our knuckles for hours. We pounded every house within three blocks of the cottage. A third of them were vacant. Someone in the neighborhood had to see something. If the children ran, they couldn't have gotten far. Wandering children draw attention. With each negative reply we absorbed, the likelihood that they were kidnapped increased along with our foreboding sense of futility.

The first door I had knocked on was the door directly across the street, where the nut had been raking the thin leaves from a tabebuia tree a few days before. No one had answered. It was late afternoon when I approached the house for the second time. The bells of the community church tolled in the clear air. The sound was incongruous with a beach town. Church bells belong up north, in a Norman Rockwell town. A town that's the picture for October on the calendar Kathleen keeps in her office at the college. Where the bells echo through rolling autumn hills of brilliant trees dripping with yellow and red and gold. Where the residual summer wind smells like dry leaves and carries a whisper of cold on its tail. That sounds like a nice town, but it's not my town.

The front porch held a pair of rusted metal chairs and a plastic side table. The planked gray floors appeared to be recently painted, except for one corner. Someone had run out of paint, energy, or both. I lifted the brass dolphin knocker and flipped it hard into the corroded plate. Nothing. I roamed around the property and peeked in the back windows. Posters of impressionist paintings decorated the walls. Books were strewn around the room and fishing poles curved into the far corner.

"May I help you?"

I turned and faced the bearded man I'd seen before with the rake. He was a cub scout with a beard, for his beard failed to hide a porcelain and youthful face. He had on cargo shorts and a washed-out T-shirt with the longitude and latitude of Pass-a-Grille on the front. I have the same shirt. It struck me —unlikely as it seemed—that as this man and I had both chosen the same hidden peninsula to live on, and had the same shirt, we held other things in common. Perhaps things internal in nature, and not so easily identifiable.

I introduced myself, explained that there had been a break-in across the street, and asked if he had heard or seen anything. He listened as if the words were wind, and either went around him or through him but did not stay on him. I was standing between him and his house. He peered around me as if he longed to be back inside, where he had sanctuary from a world he didn't understand, or that was, in some manner, suddenly threatening to him.

"I didn't see anything," he replied flatly to my questioning. He rubbed his arms, like when you're trying to warm up.

It was the gazillionth time that day I'd heard "I didn't see anything."

"It happened right across from you," I said.

He shrugged. "Suit yourself." He circumvented me and entered his house. He left the door open.

I followed him inside.

It was a charmer; dark wood floors and a white tongue-and-groove ceiling. A desk faced a paned window, and on either side of it, stacked bookcases climbed to the ceiling. Sections of them were arranged like a shrine with pictures of smiling faces at different angles, as if each one had a specific place upon the shelf so that it could be properly viewed in the intimate room. A plate rack ran under the ceiling. A hodge-podge of books and glass vases were evenly spaced on it, although one space was open.

"You live here long?" I said.

"About a year."

He picked up a baggy gold sweatshirt off the back of a chair and slipped it on. He pulled it down evenly around his waist.

"What do you do?" I asked.

"What do I do?" He spoke as if he were upholstered in gravitas.

"How do you make a living?"

He considered the question as if it were one he'd never heard, or ever given serious thought to.

"I'm a fishing guide," he said as if it just popped into his mind.

"Every day?"

"Slow this time of the year, but good money during the season. On my own, I go out every day at seven, back by ten."

I waited for more, but my fisherman went under an arched entry to the kitchen. I considered cutting my losses and heading home.

But he was my last stop. If I left, I would be defeated. I would stalk out of his door with nothing to show for my efforts that day. Like Janssen, I'm motivated more by the bitter taste of failure than by the pleasing accolades of success.

I wandered over to the bookcases. My fisherman cast far and wide, although he held a peculiar affection for the devastating wars that trembled the world from 1939 to 1945. A turntable with a smoked plastic lid rested on a nearby table. Underneath it were two shelves stuffed with vinyl. A pair of floor speakers anchored each side, large enough to blow the roof off the house. On top of one was a snow globe holding a palm tree on an island. I picked it up and shook it. Glittery white flakes fell on the tree and fake sand. I put it down next to a jar with dry leaves in it, but they appeared to be nothing from around here. The shit people collect. On a shelf above the turntable were pictures of a happy family. They looked fake, like when you buy a frame and it already has a picture in it.

"Nice family," I said over my shoulder. "Yours?"

He came up beside me with a beer in each hand.

"My brother's," he said although his gaze slipped sideways.

I squinted at a Christmas picture of four people sitting in front of a brick fireplace. A mother, father, and two girls who were clutching stockings to their chests as if they were afraid someone might rip them out of their hands. Candy canes poked out of the top of the stockings. The girls beamed high voltage smiles of inestimable joy.

"He looks like you," I said.

"Always did. But I got the brains."

"What's he say to that?"

Another shrug, dismissing everything as pointless. He seemed a man incapable of smiling, as if like a feral child, he had never learned the act.

"I didn't catch your name," I said.

"Cole."

"That first or last?"

"Last."

"Got a first name?"

"Stephen, but I don't go by it."

"You drinking both of those, Cole?"

He hesitated—*was he really holding two for himself?*—and then handed me a beer. I took a cold swig. His house was warm, yet he'd put a sweatshirt on.

"What happened across the street?" Cole asked.

He had a disturbing way of gazing at me, as if he were constantly reevaluating me, rebooting his opinion of me as we went along. I wondered if he viewed the world in a similar manner or reserved his tepid analytical judgment just for me.

Before I could answer, he added, "Was anything stolen?"

"You could say that. A pair of lives. A woman and a man were executed."

His face was hard and blank. He seemed to be buying time, as if to formulate his response.

"Did you hear me?" I said.

"I didn't see any cops."

"You fish today?"

"I did."

"They were in and out," I lied. It would have been a sealed military investigation.

"That's too bad," he said.

"You're a geyser of emotion."

"What can I say?"

"More than that."

"Was it a random act?" he said. "A domestic dispute?"

"Don't know. Three children were in the house as well. They're missing."

"Who are you?" he asked with more bravado than I would have expected.

"I'm their guardian."

"You should probably check the neighbors behind the house."

"Why?"

"Because I didn't see anything, so maybe someone in the back did."

"I've knocked on every door in Pass-a-Grille."

"Lot of doors," he said.

"I got a lot of time."

"Sorry I can't help you."

"There was a double murder across from you," I said. "You're hardly swimming in grief."

He humped his left shoulder. "Nothing I can do."

I took a patient sip of beer, not letting my eyes drip from his. "I run at odd hours. I've seen you early in the morning when it's still dark. Think. *Any*thing strike you as unusual the last few days?"

"You," he said.

"Come again?"

"You," he repeated with defiance, which seemed out of character for him. "You circle by in the morning, afternoon and middle of the night. You take grocery bags into the house, but never open the door very wide. Another man—with a ponytail—has been riding his bike on the street the last few days."

I took a few steps over to his record collection. A Fred Waring and the Pennsylvanians Christmas album were sitting out. I picked it up.

"I collect vinyl myself. You play these much?"

"Some."

I put the album on a table. "I'm tired, Cole. It's been a long day, and I think you're holding back. What did you see, hear, or smell last night from the house across the street?"

"Sorry I can't help you. I've got some things I need to do. It was nice meeting you."

"You're done fishing for the day."

"House chores."

"Small house."

"Sorry," he repeated.

"If I find out that you're holding back on me, I'll—"

He snorted. "Save it."

"You understand?"

"Wish I could help."

We did the two-second stare. I couldn't get the pulse of the man. We categorize people when we first meet them. Place them in a labeled slot unconsciously constructed by years of experience. But Cole didn't fit anywhere. He seemed to have a burdensome sadness inside. A tumor implanted by some vile god, which would neither grow and snuff out his indifference, nor shrink and free his soul.

"Thanks for the beer," I said and slammed the door behind me.

11

"I'd like a whiskey, woman," I said over my shoulder to Kathleen as she strode down the dock.

"Is that hyphenated?"

"Either way."

She pivoted and went into the house. She emerged a few minutes later carrying a blanket and a glass tumbler. The insulated ones keep the ice longer, but I like my drink in a glass, and my whiskey woman knows that.

I'd been staring at the water from the end of my dock, hoping it held restorative powers but knowing it didn't. It echoed Alejandro's charge back to me. *On your mother's grave* . . .

Why was he so confident of his demise? If I was the bookkeeper for a Mexican cartel and I'd decided to sing on my boss, the head moneyman, wouldn't I have—

"How old was the oldest girl?" Kathleen handed me my drink and sat next to me. My previous thought melted like snowflakes drifting above a bonfire. I tried to bring it back, but it had lost all form.

"Thirteen."

"And the other two?"

64

"Gabriela is nine. Little Joe is three."

The sunset sailboat *Magic* slithered past us on her way out to the mouth of the channel as if she were trying to pass unnoticed. Her flags battled a dying wind although her main sail was stretched full with the setting sun. Under our feet, a school of box jellyfish drifted by. Their white, ghost-like tentacles trailed them in the water. The bay had been full of them for days. They are not something to mess with.

Kathleen wrapped the blanket around her shoulders and fluffed it high behind her neck as a shaft of cool air banked off the chilly water. Her hair was down and she wore loafers with socks. She unhesitatingly ditched style in favor of comfort. Sheepshead nibbled on the crusted pilings while on the sandbar, birds gathered like a Kentucky family reunion.

"My turn," she said.

I passed her a cigar. She took a long draw on it, curved her head back, and exhaled a cloud of smoke. I tracked the smoke into the sky where a gull took wing higher into the air. As it did, it caught the sun's rays and its underbelly became white like snow. The bird dipped back in the shadows, darkening itself, and then rose once again like a dove of peace into the gentle light of the setting sun.

"I'm good," she said, handing the cigar back to me.

I took a drag, flicked ashes into the bay, and placed the cigar on the edge of the dock. The red glow of the smoldering end hung suspended over the feasting sheepshead. A dolphin blew off to our left, and we both instinctively looked in that direction. A pair surfaced no more than twenty feet off the stern of *Impulse* that hung high in its lift.

"I still don't see how three children could vanish," she said, her head still turned in the direction of the dolphins.

"Morgan and I knocked on every house."

She looked at me. "Every?"

Cole had questioned my statement as well.

"Within half a dozen blocks."

"No clues?"

"Nothing."

The breeze freshened and she tightened the blanket around her. "Either they were kidnapped that night, or someone is sheltering them."

"Kidnapping is out," I said. "The man who killed their parents would have no interest in them."

"How do you know that?"

"They are professional killers. Their interest was in Alejandro."

"How do you *know* that?" she repeated.

"I was told," I admitted, and the first hairline crack appeared. "But what motive could possibly exist to kidnap three orphan children?"

"One was a double."

"Come again?"

"Little Joe. You said he was Alejandro's nephew. He's been orphaned twice, now."

"So I was told."

"And so you believed," she said with a note of piety.

I picked up my cigar and started to bring it to my lips. Instead, I tossed it into the bay. It met its fate with a protesting hiss, although the fish paid it no attention.

"You know something I don't?" I said.

"You went out to the gulf to gather two and came back with five, and within a week, two are dead and three are missing—they are *not* your responsibility—and Janssen was understandably ticked, but not as much as one would think, and now it's over, and I don't care about any of that. I just don't want you to shoulder the blame."

"That was a lot."

"Did you get the last part?" she asked.

"Sure. Do you think they'd sell Ana Maria and dump the other two?"

"Don't. You know——"

"Toss Little Joe into an outgoing tide—Gabriela as well, but Ana Maria was more than an enterprising assassin could resist. Cash in hand, baby."

Kathleen was quiet, but her thoughts were loud. She'd had a long day of classes, and now I was dumping my imagined problems on her. She didn't need that.

"I'll find them," I said.

"Thank you," she said, and we both knew what she was thanking me for.

I was glad I'd opted to keep my theory about Bongo to myself. It was, after all, just speculation. Maybe the Vizcarros had been tracked by some means other than a planted bug in a stuffed monkey. Maybe I wasn't responsible for the death of two people and the whereabouts of three children. I like keeping things inside, and I questioned whether that didn't make me a less than ideal candidate for marriage. But who wants a lover who dumps on them all day?

THAT NIGHT I DREAMED THAT I WORKED IN A flower shop, but I had no vases in which to place the flowers. A woman sneered at me and asked me how I ever hoped to find a vase if I couldn't even find the children. I told her if I found the vase, I would find the children. Then I was in bed. Martina came to me. She laid her tawny, nude body on top of mine, her pointy breasts pressing against me. I stroked her smooth and flawless back. She spoke to someone off-camera, and I wished I knew who it was. I didn't mind her not speaking to me, as our unspoken bond was stronger than any words could forge. I awoke. Kathleen was pressing up against my side. I got out of bed and cracked the blinds. I slid open the window and stared at the dark bay and the red marker, blinking like Rudolph's nose. I thought of the dolphins, and the box jellyfish, the bird rising to catch the sun, and all the life in the night and in the water that we cannot see.

The damp, cool air streamed through the window. I laid another blanket on top of Kathleen and tried to re-enter sleep, but that gate was closed.

12

"Since when did punctuality become paramount to you?" Kathleen asked. She stared into her tabletop vanity mirror and delicately touched up her eyebrows. The mirror had belonged to her mother, and Kathleen had told me once that her mother commented that she'd watched herself grow old in that mirror. I always expected Kathleen to add to that, or toss the mirror, but she did neither.

"Since it rhymed with Champagne," I said.

"You'd fail as a poet."

"Me and Faulkner."

"That's right." She put her eye brush down and rested her eyes on mine in the mirror. "He considered himself a failed poet. We touched on that the first time I went to your house."

"We did?"

"We did. But we missed Conroy. I recently learned that he, too, sought refuge in the novel after butchering poems."

I remembered her first visit—how she had picked up objects and books from my shelves as if trying to get to know the man through his artifacts, and how I had pined to touch her hair—but had no recollection of discussing William Faulkner.

"You don't remember, do you?" Kathleen could read my mind as easy as picking out E on an eye chart.

"I do."

"Liar," she said.

"I don't?"

"That's better. When is Morgan meeting us?"

"Ten minutes."

"I won't make it," she said.

"You know how much this means to—"

"Skip it," she said. "Pour yourself another drink—and show a little more respect for poets. They're a dying breed."

We were attending a gala at the Museum of Fine Arts in downtown St. Petersburg. Richard Bannon was chairing a capital improvement drive, and tonight's bash was the kickoff. I looked forward to bumping into him. I had no plan other than to stir the waters and hope for a reaction. Float around like a box jellyfish and hope to sting him.

The dream from the previous night had never released me. I'd not understood a word Martina had said to whomever was out of sight. Yet I'd never felt so emotionally attached to someone as when she had lain upon me. My dreams are often a second person accompanying me throughout the day. I suspect I'm not alone in that regard—at least I'd like to believe that to be the case.

On the steps of the museum, Morgan greeted Kathleen with a kiss on the cheek. His hair was tied back, and he wore long linen pants and a coral sports coat over a white shirt. I had on slacks and a blue blazer, an outfit that had taken zero thought. Kathleen wore a short-but-not-too-short black dress and a checkered, chestnut cashmere shawl that she draped over her bare shoulders. She held a rose-gold quilted purse in her hand. I knew it was rose-gold because I called it pink and received a lecture in return. I'd also mistakenly referred to the shawl as tan. After that, I threw in the white towel on color commentary.

We hadn't purchased tickets in advance, so I paid the jacked-up admission/donation to a woman behind the counter. She had cinnamon hair and the eyes of a nun. Her cheeks were freckled and she looked as if she'd just come in from picking apples at a Wisconsin orchard. She also smiled when she talked. Kathleen had that same gene. I've often wondered if women were aware of the incalculable power of their smiles, of the irrepressible image they create in such a casual and offhand manner. If they had any clue that such a fleeting and innocuous moment chipped away a little souvenir of my heart.

Her nametag read Charlotte. I thanked Charlotte, and she told me to enjoy my evening. I think she meant it.

We'd been to the museum numerous times, as every Thursday they lowered the price of admission and served drinks and hors d'oeuvres. Despite those tantalizing incentives, it was not my favorite time to browse. Museums are best frequented midweek, when the galleries are hushed in solitude and the pictures themselves are your living companions. When the only stimulus is what you bring to them and what they bring to you. In such seclusion, your relaxed mind is free to contemplate the oil-painted expressions of those you will never know and whose time you did not share. They reach out and touch you with a depth that is lost and forgotten in the digital world.

As George Bernard Shaw said, "You use a glass mirror to see your face; you use works of art to see your soul."

The museum was jammed, with more people gazing than picture gazing. Crowds and I don't mesh, nor do I possess the muscle for small talk. I abandoned Kathleen and Morgan, both chattering with acquaintances, and weaved my way toward the Stuart Sculpture Garden. The massive, nineteenth-century oil painting *Gathering at the Church Entrance* hung next to the door to the garden. It depicts a scene outside a church in Saint-Germain-des-Prés in Paris. Well-dressed Parisians are gathered on the steps while, amongst them, a pauper mother holds her child wrapped in a brown blanket. I gave a conciliatory nod at the peasant mother, with whom I'd bonded with years before, and went outside to the welcoming, fresh December air.

Richard Bannon stood straight as a stalk of celery in the center of the courtyard. A throng of worshippers circled him.

He was appropriately attired in a dark, tailored business suit and a red tie dotted with green palm trees. A powder-blue presidential pocket square protruded out of his suit. His fashionably trimmed, peppered hair projected the image of civil stability and leadership. Disciples surrounded him, drinks in their hands, superficial smiles on their faces, eyes darting and feet shuffling.

His back was to Paul Jennewein's sculpture *The First Step*. It was of a woman kneeling behind her little boy as he tried to walk. The boy had one leg extended and his hand was symbolically reaching out in front of him, fingers parted, as if he were trying to touch Bannon's robe. Behind the sculpture, fronds from an Alexander palm bowed in royal incarnation.

An aristocratic couple who had been planted in front of Bannon backed away. I seized the opening. I extended my hand, introduced myself, and tacked on, "I just wanted to thank you for your good work."

He took my hand with as much thought as a dog grabbing a bone. "My pleasure." His pocket square was a tad crooked —I wanted to straighten it.

"I understand you have a successful wine importing business—West Coast Distributors. Family origins, or did you start it?"

"All mine." He twisted up the corner of his mouth as he freed my hand. "I'm totally self-made."

"That lets God off the hook. What brought you to the west coast of Florida?"

He hesitated, not sure what to make of my riposte. "Business initially," he said. "Then I fell in love with the sun and a woman." His voice was higher on the scale than I expected it to be.

"In what order?"

"The sun by day, the woman at night."

"That makes for pleasant evenings."

"It does indeed," he said.

"How is business?"

"Another record year."

"Even in today's competitive environment?"

"All business is competitive," he said dryly. His eyes flicked, indicating the first hint of boredom. Several people shifted their weight around me, waiting for an opening.

"Here's to money and wine." I raised my glass in a mock toast. "Two liquids that need to be moved. Do you have any particular challenges in that area?"

"What area is that?"

"Moving money. Laundering it through the system, so to speak."

His eyebrows furrowed. "I don't know what you referring to. Now, if you'll—"

"You're not missing three children are you?" I blurted out in an attempt to rattle him.

"What on earth are you talking about?"

"I misplaced some children. Alejandro Vizcarro told me you might be of assistance."

His eyes rested on me with dullness bordering on contempt. "I'm afraid I don't know who or what you're referring to. If you'll excuse me, I have other guests to attend to." He turned to a man with a handlebar mustache who had entered our circle. They greeted each other by name.

I circulated through the galleries, refilling as I moved. I wasn't the only loner. In the Mackey Gallery, an effeminate man posed with his glass of Champagne as he studied Richard Miller's painting of a woman sitting at a table, titled

Woman Sitting at a Table. Great artists understate. Our eyes connected briefly before he moved on, leaving me alone with a woman sitting at a table.

I reverently view the picture on every sojourn to the museum. I could only fantasize what Miller saw in the young lady from turn-of-the-century Paris, who appeared to be flirting with a less-than-respectable lifestyle. Her dress draped off her left shoulder and revealed enough of her breast to draw one's eye. Her face failed to mask her disillusionment, for her eyes were cast down, never to be seen by those who would view her for eternity. Her finely drawn hands surrounded a teacup, but they didn't touch it. They would never touch it. I wanted her to step out so that together we might unveil the masked ball of life.

I moved on.

Bannon's wife, according to a picture I'd seen of them at a fundraiser at the Mahaffey Theater, was a blonde with shoulder length hair who packed a nightclub figure. I caught a glimpse of her standing in front of Monet's *House of Parliament, 1904 Effect of Fog.* The museum had placed the blue painting by itself on a deep blue wall. But she wasn't blonde. Her hair was black and cut short. She wore a flapper's silver headband, and a pair of heels added six inches to her stature. She looked as if she could have walked out of a Jay Gatsby party. Several women were gathered around her. One was tall and austere with bony and wide bare shoulders.

What the heck. I had already made a fool of myself. There was no point in breaking character.

"I love your hair," I said, stepping rudely in front of Emma Bannon.

"Pardon me?" She did not draw back from my physical intrusion, but held her ground. Her eyes searched mine for recognition. Despite her inquisitive stare, her eyes held nothing and gave nothing.

"Your hair. At the Mahaffey...oh what was it . . . I know,

the Pinellas pre-school fundraiser. *You*, my cupcake, were a blonde."

"And the verdict?" she said in tone both questioning and challenging.

"It depends upon the mood."

"And what mood are you in, Mr . . . ?"

"Travis, Jake Travis."

I extended my hand. She dropped her cool hand into mine, and I brought it to my lips and kissed the back of it. I believe that is appropriate museum behavior.

"The verdict is that you look dashing in Spanish black," I said.

"Really? What would you think of me as a ravishing redhead?" she said in a tease, warming up to our game.

"So unnecessary. You don't require fanfare."

"What makes you so certain?"

"Sometimes you just go with your gut."

"How's that work for you?" Emma said, her voice husky and laden with unexpected sincerity.

"Let's find out."

"My you're fast. Do you come with a flight attendant?"

"I fly solo."

The tall lady—her legs ran up to her shoulders—took a half a step toward me, keeping her eyes level on me. I stretched myself a little taller.

"Who's your friend, Emma?" she said. Her lips were an advertisement for Botox.

"Evidently a gentleman named Travis. Jake Travis. That is correct, isn't it?"

"It is." I offered my hand. She squeezed it more than she shook it. "Pleased to meet you, Ms . . . "

"Tina Welch," she said. "And you weren't at the Mahaffey."

"No?"

"No."

She had penetrating, steel-blue eyes and a Roman nose. Her brunette hair was pulled tight behind her head, creating a noble forehead. A black hair clip had some sort of spider design on it. While slender, she seemed to be a mass of trapped energy, like a cheetah waiting to pounce. I didn't like her—despite her height.

"Why are you so sure?" I said.

She tilted her head in a dismissive move. "You don't fly solo—you arrived tonight with the woman with the tan shawl. You're familiar with her—it's not the first time you two have hit the town. You're comfortable enough in your relationship to wander by yourself and leave her with your male companion, who greeted you both warmly when you arrived. I remember faces, Mr. Travis, and neither she nor you were at the Mahaffey."

"It's chestnut," I said.

"Pardon?"

"The shawl. I bought it for her. She claims that it's chestnut. But now, with your vote, we can overrule her. How fortunate that we met."

Emma giggled. I double-like any woman who giggles at me.

Welch—I went with her last name, as she wasn't warm and cozy enough for a first name basis—shifted her weight like an antsy boxer waiting to charge from the corner.

"And what do you claim to be?" she asked. "A pick-up artist who cheats on his date?"

"Tina," Emma said. "I believe our Mr. Travis was just having a little sport. Isn't that right?"

"Just trying to keep the evening poppin'," I said, keeping a steady gaze on Welch.

"Tina has been working recently with my husband, Richard," Emma explained.

"What it is you do for Mr. Bannon, Ms. Welch?"

"I'm his executive assistant."

"And an observant one at that. Are you normally so keenly aware of the guests, or does your passion truly lie with chestnut shawls?"

"I treat all guests equally."

"Certainly a woman of your stature does more than memorize faces. Perhaps you count his nickels, or you pick up his shirts. Mr. Bannon must require a lot of laundering."

She rocked on her heels. She smiled, although it was not a smile I would ever want to wake up to. Tina Welch impressed me as the type of woman whose favorite part of cooking was slicing the meat.

"Yes," she said. "I retrieve his shirts."

I shifted my stance so as to square off before her. "And if a few children went missing, would you retrieve them as well?"

She hesitated. "What are your intentions this evening?"

"Just making conversation."

"Are you missing children?"

"If so, do you know where to find them?"

"You're speaking nonsense," she said. "Tell me about yourself."

"You did so well. Remember? A petty pick-up artist who cheats on his date."

Welch took a patient sip of white wine. She sucked in her cheeks. "Perhaps we'll have the pleasure of meeting again."

"I would enjoy that."

"I'll catch up with you later," Welch said to Emma, touching her lightly on the shoulder. She spun around and marched her attitude into the adjoining gallery.

"Is it true?" Emma asked from behind me.

I turned to face her. "What is that?"

"You didn't attend the Mahaffey?"

"Not the same night you did."

"You *are* a naughty boy."

"One must try."

She gave me a playful smile that indicated she and I were fine. A smile would start any day off right.

"I need to make boring, meaningless chitchat with the guests," she said. "It's an obligation, seeing as how Richard and I are hosting the event."

"And I have obligation to the bartenders, seeing as how I keep them employed."

"That's an old line, Mr. Travis."

"As was your flight attendant one."

"Tell me, do they still work?" she asked with a tilt of her pretty head.

"They do for me."

She let her eyes linger on mine for a second. She landed a parting smile and only got in a few steps before the crowd engulfed her. I had the feeling I would run into her again, but I have that feeling every time I fall victim to the white gunnery smile of a woman.

I wanted to follow Welch and see who she talked to, but Ms. Observant might be wary if I were on her trail. Instead, I corralled Morgan in the Parrish Gallery. He was in front of crude Mexican carvings of a man and a woman holding their hands up. They looked like something that, with a little coaching, even I could produce. Morgan gave me a lecture on their importance. I faked listening. We went searching for Kathleen and found her deep in conversation—she could talk to anyone about anything—and voted not to interfere. Morgan wanted to view the glass in the Brown Gallery. I craved night air and mapped my way to an outdoor patio I had not yet been to. It was sparsely populated.

I parked myself at the iron gate that fronted Bayshore Drive and took a sip of Champagne. Kathleen had asked earlier in the evening if we could take the *Lauren Rowe* out for a four-day cruise. I'd demurred, saying that Morgan and I needed to conduct sea-trials before any serious cruising. It was an itty-bitty lie, totally acceptable under *Jake's Guide To*

Lying to Your Lover, Vol. II. Page one clearly states that a partner can lie when the truth to the speaker is more painful than a lie to the listener. Here's the truth: I had no business cruising anywhere. My silent moment with the doughnut box in Vizcarro's death cottage had created my own iron gate, forbidding me entrance into a world of leisure and pleasure.

Cole entered the courtyard with Charlotte—my apple-picking woman who had checked us in. I was surprised he was there. He didn't strike me as someone who had the dough to support civic causes. They didn't notice me and took an immediate right into a corner by wrought-iron chairs, where they huddled, deep in conversation. I was maneuvering over to them when Welch burst through the side door and intercepted me.

"Mr. Travis," she said.

"You do like me, don't you?"

"Mr. Bannon is having a party on his boat next Saturday. He'd be most pleased if you could attend."

"A shame. It's my night to bake cookies."

"Suit yourself." She sashayed off. My smart mouth. She didn't get more than a few feet before I countered with, "But that can wait."

She turned triumphantly back to me. "I thought so. Seven. The Vinoy Marina. And Mr. Travis?"

"Jake."

"Mr. Travis?"

"If you must."

"Feel free to bring your friend in the *chest*nut shawl. And your affable friend in the ponytail as well. He is quite the life of the party."

She turned, took no more than three strides, and abruptly marched back to me for the second time. She took one step beyond protocol, invading my personal space. Our faces were inches apart. Her perfume carried a hint of honeysuckle.

"Who are the cookies for?" she asked. "Your missing children?" She bolted before I could reply.

I glanced across the courtyard, but Cole and Charlotte were gone. I started to take another sip of Champagne, but it hadn't tasted right all night. I left it on a table next to a dirty plate with a half-eaten crab cake on it.

WE BUNKED AT THE CONDO. WHEN MY HEAD INDENTED the pillow, my dream from the previous night flashed back to life like a hologram. As if Martina had passed the day lying in bed, waiting for me to return.

"We can talk, now," she said. But then she, and the dream, were gone.

The next morning before sunrise, I ran along the water at Straub Park and then up Central Avenue. My morning run often serves as the final rinse of the previous day, as stubborn thoughts and images are prone to survive the night. Life is a twenty-four cycle of flushing and reloading.

I fretted that all I'd done was announce my presence to Bannon. That put me at a disadvantage—down a couple of chess pieces right off the bat. But I saw little choice. The search for the children was teetering on despair. Worse, the only logical conclusion was that whoever killed their parents had taken them as well. If the assassin wanted them dead, he would have finished the job in the cottage. If he wanted Ana Maria, he would have likely taken all three and killed Gabriela and Little Joe later. Whether or not I'd learn anything by another encounter with Bannon was doubtful, but it wouldn't be due to lack of effort, however haphazard that effort might be.

I went back to the condo and showered in the guest room so as not to wake Kathleen. I put on jeans and a long-sleeve white shirt, grabbed my laptop, a banana, and took an elevator back down to Beach Drive. A man was hosing down the sidewalk while whistling "I Saw Mommy Kissing Santa Claus." I stepped out of his path and ducked into a Kahwa coffee shop after opening the door for two women. One smiled and said "thank you." The other, clutching a purse that looked like an AM radio, passed without comment. I ordered a coffee and a pastry with some sort of cherry goo in the middle and won the lottery when a man stood and vacated a table by the window.

Google Flores: A gazillion hits in a blink. Bannon, not so many. Tina Welch was a whiff, assuming she wasn't a redheaded porn star in a different life. I was searching for the proverbial needle in a haystack.

I dialed Mary Evelyn, Garrett's secretary. Not only was she aware of the work Garrett and I did for Janssen, but her research skills took backseat to no one's.

"Mr. Travis," she said in a perky voice after the third ring. Mary Evelyn: Ex-nun. Resides east of Cleveland. Worships the Browns more than she does God, but I don't think she puts much faith in either of them anymore. She insists on formally addressing me. It's a little game we perpetually play—and I am doomed to lose.

"Not too early, is it, M.E.?" I asked.

"Not even close. I'm on my way out to the church. Pancakes for the volunteers who will be delivering presents to those who work so hard, yet have so little."

"Why do I always feel insignificant when I talk to you?"

"I understand you and Morgan are doing wonderful things with the new refugee house."

"It's Morgan. I'm just stuffing my resume in the unlikely event St. Peter takes a peek. Maybe good works do count."

"I'd take one good deed over a basket of prayers every day. What can I do for you?"

I gave her Sergio Flores and Mexican drug cartels, asking her to dig for something beyond the obvious. She said she'd have time later in the morning, and we disconnected. I dribbled coffee on my chin, snatched a napkin from the counter, and got to work.

Richard Bannon's background was drier than toast, other than an abrupt plunge years ago into wine distributing. I switched to his wife. Emma Bannon had attended a private school in St. Petersburg, where her father, Edward Stratford was a real estate developer. She'd graduated cum laude from Rollins College in Winter Park, Florida. She and Bannon had wed six years ago. At the time, Emma was employed in the family business, Stratford Management and Development, but their website currently made no mention of her. I wanted to believe she knew nothing of her husband's association with a drug lord and clicked open a picture of her and her husband at a fundraiser—as if that would help vindicate her name. She flashed the same winning smile she had for me.

And I'd thought I was special.

I slapped the laptop shut. Enough screen staring. No way would I find the children sitting on my butt and sipping coffee. It was time to hunt down Cole—he had to be holding back.

As I strode out of the café, a man wearing a baseball hat backwards growled by on a Harley. On the gas tank were the words Last Laugh. My eyes tracked him until he took a corner and was gone, although the rumble of the engine resounded down the street.

13

Cole wasn't home. I trekked a few blocks and took a counter stool at Seabreeze.

A new sign on the pine walls read, "I'm in favor of gun control. I have both hands on my gun." Why do people who have never served in the armed forces seem far more eager to embrace guns than those who have? On army bases, we kept assault rifles under lock and key—they are designed to kill as many humans as possible in the shortest period of time. In Florida, they're tossed into the back seat of a pickup truck next to the child's car seat. What's the purpose of defending your country only to return and—

"Why the long face?" Carol interrupted my rambling mind as she poured me a black stream of coffee.

"I'm a horse today."

"That's old. You need new material."

"So I've been told."

"The usual? Lots of onion, right? And bacon that cracks?"

"You got it."

I picked up the *Tampa Bay Times* and forced myself to read in a vain attempt to forget, as least for a moment, my failures and the topsy-turvy world. I scanned a follow-up story about a semi-truck driver who crashed into an SUV in North Carolina, killing the SUV's driver and wife. The truck driver and witnesses stated that another car had cut the SUV off, forcing it to break hard. The semi, while not tailgating, had no choice but to slam into the rear of the SUV. Authorities never found a red four-door that had fled the scene. No charges had been filed against the semi driver, who was reportedly distraught and unable to continue driving his rig. He lived in Tampa, which was why, I presumed, the paper picked it up. I folded the paper and left it for someone else to figure out.

I checked the time, as I'd told Morgan that I would drop by the thrift store he operated for the church to see how Life, a Jamaican man he'd recently hired, was getting along. Morgan was spending more time at the refugee house. He'd instituted an English as a second language class, using volunteers from local colleges. The weekly foot-count was picking up dramatically. Between the thrift shop and the refugee house, he was putting in 80-hour weeks. He'd also confessed that he was rising at 5 a.m. and writing a book on his days as a charter sailboat captain. *Your Password is About to Expire* held Morgan's observations on his passengers who tried to squeeze lost decades on land into seven days on the water.

If man's ultimate quest is to find usefulness in the world—somebody said that—then Morgan was well on his way. I increasingly found myself riding his coattails, but what's wrong with that?

"Coffee to go?" Carol asked, stopping in front of me.

I checked the time. "Make it two."

COLE WAS ON HIS ON FRONT PORCH WHEN I PULLED IN to his drive. He glanced up from a fishing reel he was oiling, showed no interest in me, and recommitted himself to his task. I took a seat next to him. He kept his focus on his reel.

"Coffee?" I placed a Styrofoam cup next to him.

"You didn't come here to give me that," he said.

"Take it easy, slim. I'm not here to take your cattle."

"But you're here."

He used a red, square cloth to clean the reel. On a table next to him was a small packet of more cloths.

"You never talked to them, right?" I said, staring at the red squares in the package.

He put the reel down and leaned back in the chair. "You're persistent."

"Not even the tip of the iceberg. Where are the children?"

"Told you I don't know."

"You're lying."

"Suit yourself," he said. "Maybe you took them and you're trying to deflect suspicion. I told you that I noticed you at odd hours dropping by the house. Do the police know they're missing children?"

"No."

"Why not?"

"I can't say."

"You're lying." Cole threw my words back at me. He landed a defiant stare, stood, and went inside his house, leaving the door open.

I rapped on his doorframe.

"It's open," he called from inside.

He had left the rear door open during our previous encounter. Cole seemed conflicted; he wanted to shut me out yet invite me in at the same time.

I stepped in and glanced at the plate rack where a space was still unoccupied. Whether a book or a vase had been there, I wasn't sure. But I had a good idea.

"You're not worried, are you?" I said. "About whether it was me who took the children or not. Whether I'm good or evil. You're not worried because they told you about me."

"I don't—"

"You're missing a vase." I poked my chin toward the empty spot on the shelf.

He didn't bother to follow my lead, but kept his focus on me.

"What about it?" he said.

"I took them flowers. Martina—the mother—said there was no vase in the house. Next trip, there was."

"The mother?"

"Martina. That was the mother's name."

He gave that a second as if he was considering his reply.

"She must have found one," he said in a dismissive tone.

"She placed the red squares you use to oil your rods under water glasses."

"I don't—"

"He knocked on the door, didn't he?"

Silence.

"Alejandro—that was the father's name. He came to your house. Did you invite him, or did he come on his own accord?"

Cole flipped open his hands. "He wanted to know if he could borrow a plunger, but I didn't have one."

"Everyone has a plunger."

"Been meaning to get one."

I swung my head in disbelief. Had I not made it clear? *Do not leave this house.* But Cole's admission also sparked a glimmer of hope. Maybe it wasn't a tracking device in Bongo after all. Maybe I wasn't to blame.

"You gave him a vase instead of a plunger?" I said.

"No. He came back later and asked for a vase. He'd seen the collection earlier."

"He was over here twice?"

"Red cloths were later."

"Three times?" I couldn't control the rise in my voice.

Cole nodded. "He wanted to place them under water

glasses. His daughter didn't want to get condensation on the wood windowsills."

"You mean his wife?"

"Said his daughter, but I never met any...one except him."

I wondered if Vizcarro had misspoken or if Ana Maria had been put in charge of placing the flowers.

"What'd you two do, chat it up?"

"He liked my books," Cole said. "He's a bookkeeper—an antiquarian."

"*Was* a bookkeeper. I told you there was a double homicide outside your front porch—people it now appears you were chummy with, yet no tears for the dead. Did you ever call the police?"

"Never much trusted them myself. Besides, two black SUV's pulled up the day after. These guys weren't Five-O. They smelled like government. I figured you knew that, even though you don't look like Hoover material. What are you? Some sort of Dick Tracy?"

"He was a cartoon character."

"My question stands."

It was a senseless round. I let him have it.

Cole acted unfazed by the double homicide, missing children, and my presence. When I had first told him about the murder across the street from him, I'd thought his reaction was measured. Now, he seemed inured to the world and all it dumped on him. Fisherman, my ass. The man had dirt on his shoes. I just didn't know what.

"My job was to protect them," I admitted, searching for a foundation stone to build a relationship with Cole.

"And now what? They want you to find the children?"

"I'm off the case."

"And a better world for it," he said.

"If you got a chip against me, let's hear it."

He twisted up the left side of his face. "Withdrawn. A shame about the children. No one's looking for them?"

"They were smuggled into the country. No one even knows there're here."

"Government's not looking for them?"

"Could care less," I said.

"Any other family?"

"Why so curious?"

"You can't fault me for not being concerned," Cole said, "and then fault me when I am."

"I can do whatever I want."

Cole nodded. I gave him a scrutinizing stare, as if my concentrated effort might unlock his secrets.

"What did you and Alejandro discuss?" I asked in an even tone, hoping to keep the conversation from deteriorating any further.

"Nothing solid. When he came the first time, for the plunger, he didn't stay. But later that day he came back. We talked about books. Albums. Why would the government have interest in a peasant bookkeeper from Mexico? Why would someone murder him?"

"Depends whose books he was running," I pointed out.

"He was a bookkeeper. An antiquarian."

"You keep insisting on that. He had a side job."

"Was he in witness protection?"

"I can't tell you."

He dropped eye contact and went back to the front porch. I followed him. A couple strode down the street walking their dog. It held its leash in its mouth and pranced joyfully. We took seats on the porch, looking directly across at my failure. A thin chill blew in from the water, as if someone had opened a refrigerator door. The water had lost its summer heat, and was cooler than the air. But when the cold fronts assaulted us from the north, the water would be warmer than the air. It would wrap us in her arms and keep us warm. You don't live on the water without the water being part of you.

"Those are tough cases," Cole said, but I wasn't sure what

A Beautiful Voice

he was referring to. "You can groom a witness for years, then you lose him and . . ." He cocked his head and took a drink of his coffee.

"You have experience?" I said. I realized I had inadvertently confirmed that Alejandro Vizcarro was headed toward witness protection.

"I read books."

I didn't believe that was the source of his comment. Nor did I pursue it. Instead I asked him what he knew about Alejandro Vizcarro.

"He preferred the word bookkeeper," Cole said, "as in one who keeps books, instead of antiquarian. He liked the word—the three letters in a row that are repeated—double o's, double k's, double e's. We played word games trying to come up with other such words, like sweettoothed."

"If you forgive a hyphen. That also allows hooffooted in the club."

"We missed that one. We talked about first editions. I have a few, nothing of value, just what I picked up in used bookstores. He has . . . had a rare-book business on eBay."

I made a mental note to verify Cole's comment.

"What else?" I said.

"He loves vinyl records as well—sixties stuff. We tossed around older music. Sunshine pop. Mamas and Papas. Spanky and Our Gang. Stuff like that."

"Seems an odd flavor for a Mexican bookkeeper."

"That was just where our interests coincided. He also had a deep interest in classical guitar, but I know nothing of that."

"How long was he here?"

He squinted his left eye. "Which time?"

"Did he stay longer one time versus another?"

"The middle visit."

"And?"

"Maybe an hour? Don't think he meant to, but time flew."

"Incredible."

"That a problem?" he said.
I puffed out my breath. "I told him not leave the cottage."
"Where do you think the children are?"
"I don't know, Cole. You tell me."
"Kidnapped."
"Why do you say that?"
"It's the only plausible explanation remaining," he said.
"Assassins kill, not steal."
"Is their stuff gone?"
"Some."
"There you go."
"Not necessarily," I said. "That might have been just to throw someone off the trail."

I tried to reconcile the gentle Alejandro Vizcarro I'd met and who Cole described, with a man who ran numbers for a Mexican cartel. A man who packed enough knowledge to send a bean counter, Richard Bannon, to prison unless he ratted on his boss. It was easier to see Vizcarro as a mild-mannered bookkeeper, but I'm not always the best judge of people. I form opinions too quickly and am reluctant to modify them, as that is an admission of error.

"Did he mention his children at all?" I asked.
"Just that he had three girls."
"His three girls were two daughters and his wife. Did he divulge any names?"
"No," he said, staring at me as if I were a puzzle.
"Mention a little boy?"
"No."
"Don't knock yourself out."
"We talked books, not kids."
"His business on eBay was a front," I said.
He furrowed his eyes. "How so?"
"He ran numbers for a Mexican drug cartel."
"Really?"
"Really."

"Alejandro?" Cole said in disbelief.

"The one and only."

Cole gave that a moment and then declared, "I don't think so."

"Trust me," I said, although my mind was picking up a strong scent. "His gift was numbers, not books."

"Well, you never know, do you?" Cole said with an easiness that bordered on callous indifference. He rose and went into his house. He was fond of doing that, moving without comment. He returned a minute later with a book.

"Careful," he said as he handed it to me. "It's quite valuable. My great-grandfather was in Paris in the 20s. This is a family heirloom—it's not something you pick up in a used bookstore."

It was a copy of the book *Fiesta* by Hemingway.

Cole said, "Only a few runs were done with that title. Most in Europe, by a publishing house in London. Soon after, the title was changed to *The Sun Also Rises*. Hemingway thought it good marketing to bestow a Biblical theme to his friends' drunken romp in Pamplona. Alejandro knew of this book."

"That doesn't mean—"

"He—Alejandro—knew of the type of letterpress, where it was published, other books that came off that same press. He collected and sold books from that letterpress. It's like people buying vinyl today because of the purity of the sound. The authenticity of it. The *zeitgeist*. Alejandro felt that way about books."

"Words are words," I pointed out.

"Not to him. What's your next move in finding the children?"

I had no answer to that, so I returned to something that had bothered me. "You said he mentioned having three girls and that his daughter didn't want to get condensation on the windowsills."

"What about it?"

"Did he ever mention his wife?"

"No. Said he had three girls."

"That was just his way of describing his family. He had a wife and two daughters."

"You're not married, are you?" Cole said.

"No."

"Ever have children?"

"No."

"Then you don't know what you're talking about," Cole said flatly.

"And you do?" I said.

Cole slumped, as if he'd been shot in the heart with an arrow.

14

Kathleen's class was having a reading that evening at seven in the college theater. Students would select a favorite passage from a book, offer a brief explanation of why they found it particularly attractive or moving, and then recite the passage.

"It will only be about an hour," Kathleen said in response to my whimpering. We were enjoying cocktails on my porch before the ten-minute drive to the college.

"Is there a reception in the student center afterwards?" I asked.

"There is."

"Open bar, courtesy of their hot English lit professor?"

"Hmm. Do I sense growing enthusiasm?"

"I'll always be there for you."

"Nice shirt, by the way," she said, as if just noticing it. "Did I buy it?"

"I found it at the thrift store today when I checked on Life."

"You? Browsing the racks?"

I had no comeback.

I'd called Mary Evelyn again and given her the additional

task of seeing if she could find Alejandro's business on eBay. My cursory run at it came up empty. It was possible that he discontinued it before boarding the boat. Maybe his book-keeping business was integral in helping Bannon launder money. Janssen had claimed he didn't even have a picture of Vizcarro, but I began to suspect that Janssen had not put his best effort into the cause. If that were the case, then a tsunami of questions flooded me.

I SLOUCHED IN THE BACK OF THE AUDITORIUM, LEAFING through the program. I'd snuck my drink in and wished I'd put it in a plastic tumbler. The tinkle of the ice invited envious glances.

Kathleen's intent was more than to just give her students practice speaking behind a podium. She passionately believed that one's ability to stand erect and to speak confidently in front of a group, regardless of the topic, was an invaluable asset, no matter what one's academic major or eventual line of work. She often kidded—although she was serious—that the college should offer a course on etiquette. On walking. Eating. Meeting people. Talking with intelligence, confidence, and clarity because you *are* intelligent, confident, and of clear thought. On the wall in her classroom, she had a poster with a Ben Johnson quote on it: "Language most shows a man, speak that I may see thee."

My phone buzzed in my pocket. I squirmed in my seat and glanced at it. Mary Evelyn had sent information on Flores and Alejandro. I'd look at it later. I wiggled the phone back as a student read a passage from Ralph Ellison's *Invisible Man*. Kathleen would be proud of her. Shoulders back. Face straight ahead. Her diction was slow and clear, and her voice exuded authority. She described an unnamed narrator telling of a world in which he was not noticed. How all people, regardless of race, could at some point in their lives relate to the narrator.

At the reception afterwards, I congratulated the student on her reading, while attempting to feel hip and younger than I was. That was getting harder, for the low drumbeat of advancing age trembled the ground. Strangers propped behind counters called me "sir." My last name was prefaced with "mister" and delivered with an undeserved tone of respect. I'd known more people who fell short of forty than who had celebrated sixty, and the years were galloping by at a dizzying pace, the days nothing more than a flurry. A page had turned, yet I'd had no hand in the deed. No desire in the advancement.

"You're Dr. Rowe's man, aren't you?" the student said. "I've seen you around."

Dr. Rowe's man.

"I'm on her payroll." I introduced myself.

"Danielle," she said and thrust out her hand. "It's a pleasure meeting you. I like your shirt."

"Likewise," I said, reveling in my thrift-store GQ moment.

About Danielle's shirt. It was white and puffy-large with four unemployed top buttons that granted a clear view of her black bra and the upper edge of a tattoo on the beginning slope of her left breast. I thought I had noticed the tattoo during her reading and was glad to confirm that my eyesight was still spot-on. The placement of her tattoo had nothing to do with why I was impressed with her stature, or my attentive demeanor while she had spoken.

"Danielle," Kathleen said, sneaking up beside us. "You did exceptionally well this evening."

"Thank you."

"Now learn how to use buttons and find someone your own age."

"See you around, Jake Travis," she said. Her eyes fell to my glass. "I wasn't aware that we have glasses like that here."

She gave a courteous nod to Kathleen. "*Dr.* Rowe." She pirouetted and waltzed away.

"That one has spunk," I said and then shifted my eyes to Kathleen. "That is what you teach, isn't it?"

"You're not looking at her spunk."

"School's out. Toga party?"

"I've got essays to grade first."

"We'll invite Danielle and—"

"Danielle." She rolled her eyes. "I don't know how many more young women I can handle who have just discovered the power of their sexuality and can't wait for the sun to rise so they can hit the reset button."

"If you ever need a sub."

"The killer is she's great at her work, plus she volunteers to be a teacher's aide at a local elementary school. She's one of those people who checks off every box."

"I think you like this woman."

"She has her moments."

"My place later?" I said, trying to rid my mind of Danielle's tattoo on the bunny slope of her breast.

"I'm going downtown tonight. I want to get up early and get a jump on my work."

"That hardly sounds like a Roman splash."

"Debauchery," Kathleen said, "will await us another day."

She mixed with her students, and I bought a new Trident coffee cup. My previous one had taken a spill and cracked.

When I entered my house, Hadley III meowed and rubbed up against me. I'd not seen her since the previous morning.

"Miss me?"

She didn't answer, which was fine. I didn't want to get into the habit of talking to a cat. Who knows where that leads? She was increasingly more affectionate. Probably because I'd taken to feeding her fresh fish several times a week. I rummaged through the refrigerator and came out with pan-

A Beautiful Voice

fried flounder from a few days back. I cut it in pieces and placed them in a bowl. Hadley III hunched her paws underneath her and delicately consumed her dinner in a civil and dignified manner. Cats are the Audrey Hepburns of the animal world.

I flipped through my record collection, which was housed in the new wall piece I'd built while remodeling my bungalow, and pulled out a default original Sinatra album. I read Stan Cornyn's classic liner notes on the back for the umpteenth time, brought it up to my face, and inhaled. It smelled like a nightclub the morning after.

The smell of music.

I thought of Cole's little speech on books while I bathed ice cubes with whiskey. I settled into a cushioned chair on the screened porch and opened Mary Evelyn's attachment on my tablet. Frank moaned about getting older. Tell me about it.

Little was known of Sergio Flores until his calling card became bodies leaking blood on pavement. It was believed that his empire was waning due to the appearance—and dominance—of synthetic drugs. He was suspected to have made inroads into the opioid trade in Ohio, one of the leading states for the disbursement of painkillers. He was believed to have funded a south side Columbus clinic where two doctors each wrote 100 prescriptions a day for pain pills. Six days a week. The doctors charged a hundred dollars cash up front per appointment, raking in half a million a month. The local paper reported that before the authorities shuttered it, patients could be seen lined up for hours before the clinic opened. One of the pill mill doctors had struck a plea bargain, but had been executed in his affluent suburban home. There were no arrests.

There was nothing about Flores being responsible, or wanted, for the deaths of DEA agents, as Janssen had reported to me. That wasn't surprising. The agency kept its agents secret, even in the grave. M.E. noted that she had visited over four dozen websites, but could not find any evidence that Flores had children.

Alejandro did have a business on eBay, although it had been closed for months. He, as Cole had said, was particularly fond of letterpress books from the 1920s to 1950s. I couldn't bridge the connection to Richard Bannon. I doubted that a book dealer would garner enough traffic to help launder millions of dollars—but that would create a perfect cover for laundering money. Maybe Alejandro's business was strictly a sidecar.

There was no evidence corroborating Martina's claim that Alejandro had a brother and sister-in-law who were murdered by the cartel. A footnote in her research indicated how *meaningless* (emphasis Mary Evelyn's) this lack of information was. Over 70,000 people had been murdered in the past ten years in Mexico as a result of "organized crime incidents," although various sites quoted dramatically higher figures. Pick a number. Any number. Many murders weren't investigated, or even officially reported. Estimates of unsolved homicides in Mexico ran as high as 98 percent.

She included several pictures of Alejandro, confirming my belief that Janssen hadn't done basic research. Disturbing. Most were at book fairs—the California International Antiquarian Book Fair as well as the Guadalajara International Book Fair. In both pictures, he was standing behind a table where, presumably, he had his books on display or for sale. He certainly made enough money to travel, which defused Cole's theory that he was a peasant bookkeeper. Perhaps he used his trips to conduct business for Bannon.

A fish jumped in the water and I glanced up. A great blue heron screeched. It took flight, its stately wings beating without apparent effort until it was lost in the dark. The raised drawbridge across the bay sounded its horn five times and the giant arms patiently folded down.

The last picture was of Alejandro standing in front of a

book display. He looked happy, nothing like the anxious face he'd worn the short time I'd known him. The picture wasn't dated, but it was at the Frankfurt Book Fair—the *Frankfurter Buchmesse*—a year ago in October. Next to Alejandro stood a heavyset woman with short hair. I put her around his age. They smiled into the camera, their arms comfortably around each other. I read the cutline. I read it again.

Alejandro Vizcarro and his wife, Nicole.

15

"Grease," Morgan proclaimed, "is a gift from the gods to combat salt."

He hit the switch to the awning on the *Lauren Rowe*. It glided out silently from its coiled position and extended over the aft deck.

"You think Alejandro was married to two woman?" he said.

"It's possible."

"So we brought five people in from the gulf. Two are dead and three are missing. And the woman we thought to be Alejandro's wife may be his second wife, or they may not be married at all."

"Cole thinks he had three daughters."

Morgan gave that a moment and then said, "I can see that. We never knew Martina's age, and appearance is deceptive. If Alejandro and Nicole had Martina when they were very young, and then paused fifteen years—then they had three daughters."

"Or not."

"Or not," he concurred.

A Beautiful Voice

Between Cole's assertion that Alejandro was truly just a bookkeeper, Janssen's faux outrage over my failure to protect him, and a picture that claimed Martina was not Alejandro's wife, it was time to rethink the universe. In order to find the truth, you must first dismantle what you know. Jake the Great said that.

I sat on the side of the boat and pulled my baseball cap down, as if shielding out the world would help me concentrate. A manatee surfaced a few feet from the sea wall. It was unusual to see it that late in the year. The unexpected always stands out more than that which we expect to see.

Janssen said Alejandro was a bookkeeper for a Mexican cartel. I believed it. Why would he lie, unless—

"Ready," Morgan said. We were planning to take the *Lauren Rowe* downtown for an early lunch with Kathleen, followed by a day cruise.

"You got the wheel," I said.

I untied the lines, and Morgan piloted the *Lauren Rowe* through the narrow channels and into Boca Ciega Bay. He let the engines loose, and they thundered through the open water, shaking all thoughts from my mind. Spray from the bow fanned out on both sides as the heavy boat displaced the stagnant and unsuspecting water. A man who has never yearned to be at sea on a large cruiser is a man intimidated by the world.

We switched halfway to downtown St. Pete, and I was at the helm when we motored into the public marina. We tied up, after I banged her around a little getting her in. We met Kathleen at an outdoor table at Mangroves.

I explained to her the picture I'd seen of Alejandro with Nicole. She listened as she sipped iced tea through a straw. Kathleen had recently fallen in love with straws. Only coffee and wine entered her mouth without the benefit, and fun, of a straw. I'd encouraged her to enjoy them while they were legal, as plastic ones were being banned in many places due to legitimate environmental concerns. Apparently, she would have to start slurping her drinks through an assault rifle.

"Did they—Martina and Alejandro—act like husband and wife?" she asked.

"Hard to tell," I admitted. "They were under duress."

"Answer the question," Kathleen said tartly. Must have been a tough morning grading exams. It wasn't like her to snap.

"No."

"Why?"

"He was older than her. That was my first impression. But he ran books for the cartel and was likely well compensated."

"Really—you assume young, attractive woman are easily lassoed by money?"

"I didn't—"

"Skip it. What else did you notice?"

"The girls," I said as it came back to me. "They seemed to gather around their father, and Martina was focused on Little Joe."

"The nephew?"

"Correct. Also, Cole said Alejandro called them 'my girls.'"

"A figure of speech," she said. "He felt responsible for all three."

"Perhaps."

"Morgan?" Kathleen tilted her head toward him.

"When we picked them up in the boat," Morgan said, "Gabriela told us that it was their Aunt Rosa who always wanted a girl named Josephina. Martina scolded her for talking, but Gabriela said 'That's what you said' and then was cut off by Martina. I thought it odd, as if the children had been coached on what to say."

We batted around more discrepancies, but nothing solid. How do people you don't know act under trying circumstances? Morgan countered that people are more similar than we think and to put ourselves in their situation. It wasn't a total waste of time. The red snapper sandwich flaked off the bun.

The three of us boarded the *Lauren Rowe*. Morgan took her out of the harbor while I fixed afternoon imbibements. We headed into the Gulf of Mexico, the *Lauren Rowe* flattening the swells under her solid hull. She rode smooth and clean, a vessel confident of her heritage. We chased the sun south to Egmont Key and down to Longboat. Her twin diesels hummed with a steady and reassuring confidence.

Kathleen took the wheel for an extended period. She was determined to be a capable pilot. She'd never shown much interest in boating before, other than being a willing and thankful passenger. She listened intently as Morgan explained the controls. In Robert's Bay, Morgan had her practice reversing and spinning the boat on a dime. While newer boats had joysticks, the *Lauren Rowe* had twin throttles and gears. After an hour of practice, Kathleen mastered the relationship between the four levers and was able to successfully dock the boat in calm water.

"Can I take her back?" she asked Morgan when class was over.

"You're the captain."

"I don't know about that. Isn't there some course I should take?"

"You can, but nothing beats TOW."

"Tow?"

"Time On Water," Morgan said. "Beats time behind the desk."

Kathleen confidently put her hand on the wheel.

She puttered out of the bay and swung wide off Longboat Key. I took a back seat and let the salt air have at me. Kathleen turned the wheel over to Morgan and disappeared into the cabin. She emerged a moment later wearing a large white sweatshirt. She started to take the wheel again, when I whistled and patted the seat next to me. She smiled and joined me, sitting as much on me as she did beside me. The sun was setting on our port side, warming that side of our faces. I put my arm around her and felt her through the thickness of the sweatshirt.

"Penny for your thoughts," she said.

Four dollars later, she said, "They would do that?"

"They would do anything."

"How will you find out?"

"I'm going to Washington in the morning."

"Janssen know you're coming?"

"There's no fun in that."

"Why the ruse?" she asked.

"Don't know."

"But you'll find out, won't you?"

I didn't answer but snuggled her even closer. The sun dipped into the water, and high above us clouds exploded into an oceanic display of fall colors. One streak of angelic yellow was the color of her hair as the wind whipped it in my face.

16

Janssen lived in McLean, Virginia, on a street where stately white houses stood well back from the fumes of traffic. Trails of paver-brick walks bisected their manicured front yards. The houses served as proud sentries, guarding the power and intrigue that resided behind their glass-paned windows.

The last of the autumn leaves drifted down on the windshield of my rental car. It started to drizzle and the wipers came on, smearing the windshield. A red leaf got stuck in the blade, and it rode it back and forth like the sole occupant on an amusement park ride. Back and forth. Up and down. Back and forth.

For all I knew, Janssen was out of town. But I wanted to surprise him. I'd caught a direct flight from Tampa with a return ticket the following day. Richard Bannon's boat party was tomorrow night. I didn't want to miss it.

I cranked up the heat and turned on the radio. Drive time. Nothing but ads. I turned it off. Darkness pushed in. I lowered the heat. Twenty past seven, a car pulled into his driveway. Janssen got out of the rear seat. The car backed out. I gave him a minute in his house before I rang the doorbell.

A Latino woman answered the door. She wore an apron and held a flowered dishtowel in her hand.

"May I help you?" she asked. She looked puzzled, as if she feared that she'd forgotten that someone was coming for dinner

"Jake Travis to see—"

"The hell you doing here?" Janssen charged out of a study on my left. His belligerent attitude was not unexpected. I'd been at his house one other time, also uninvited, and he had ordered me not to make that mistake again.

"What's for dinner?" I asked his cook.

"I'm preparing a—"

"He's not staying, Isabelle. I've got it from here."

"Perhaps dessert?" I said to Isabelle.

"Cut the shit," Janssen said. "What do you want?"

He stomped back into his study. I trailed him inside the dimly lit, wood-paneled room. An open laptop cast a faint glow on a cut-glass tumbler. It held an olive and ice cubes suspended in amber liquid. He flipped the laptop shut, darkening the drink.

I said, "You weren't ticked enough when I supposedly failed."

"You got two more dead bodies on your resume. I was being considerate."

More stung a little, but I shook it off.

"You're never considerate," I said.

He grunted.

I sauntered over to his bookcase and picked up a small award statue of a man shooting a basketball. League runner-up, two years ago. Janssen played B-ball. Never would have guessed that. I put it down. I turned to him and crossed my arms over my chest.

"Who were they?" I said.

He didn't immediately answer, choosing to register his contempt for my presence with the weapon of silence. "Does it matter?" he finally said. "If you feel bad two people died on your watch, then—"

"They were red herrings, weren't they?" I took a step toward him, letting my arms fall loose at my side.

"I don't have a—"

"Now they're dead herrings. The killer took your bait. That means whoever you're really protecting is safe. How many red herrings did you put out there? How many died?"

His eyes rested on mine, but I doubt he saw me. "It is important that we get Sergio Flores. Bannon's not his only laundry man."

"How many did you bring in?"

"Decoys?"

I nodded.

"Not your concern," he said.

"Hell it is."

"Hell it isn't."

"The assassin would have known he plugged the wrong person," I pointed out.

"If he knew what he looked like. If not, he would have snapped a shot and found out later. Either way, your failure bought us valuable time."

"And at such an inconsequential cost. A couple of stiffs and three children AWOL."

"If you can't take the heat."

"The missing children," I said.

"What about them?"

"I assume they were kidnapped. That doesn't fit anything you've said."

His chest rose and fell. He walked to his window. The rain pelted and pinged the glass, angry that something so transparent and thin could be such an effective deterrent.

He faced me and said, "We can't make sense of it. They were just . . . kids. They have no tie to anything."

"Then you're missing something."

"I won't deny that." He hesitated. "You find out, let me know."

"Anybody else on it?"

"No."

"Why Alejandro Vizcarro and his family?" I asked. "And don't tell me you picked him out of a lineup, or Isabelle will be preparing the guest room."

"He was more than a decoy," Janssen admitted. "We have someone on the inside. DEA. We were given information. A lead. While not the head numbers man—that man is tucked safely away—Vizcarro is connected. We were led to believe Vizcarro had incriminating evidence. Every bit helps. We brought him in. I don't think your bookkeeper is as clean as others think. We'll never know, though, will we?"

Janssen wasn't beneath delivering cheap shots.

"What did you promise Alejandro to get him on the boat?" I asked.

"America."

"There's got to be more."

"You think? Whole goddamn country would immigrate if we let them. We told him we'd pick him up. Explained the risks. He was a willing participant."

"Any more red herrings find a bullet?"

"Does it matter?" he asked.

"Everything matters."

"We lost one a while back in a car accident, North Carolina. Maybe legitimate, maybe not. The cartel has gotten creative in how they kill. A bullet to the head indicates the victim knew something and sparks an investigation. Someone falls off a curb, cracks their head, no one pays attention. Your executed couple is the only one we can confirm."

"Perhaps I had the only people the assassin had interest in."

"Deal with it however you want. You can find your way

out." He flipped open his laptop, finding its flat screen more engaging than he found me.

"What if they didn't make a mistake? What if they really wanted Vizcarro?" I said.

"If that makes you feel better," he said without looking up.

I pulled out a picture of Vizcarro and his unknown wife—Nicole—at the book fair. I dropped it on his keyboard.

He picked it up and clenched his jaw. "What's this?" he demanded.

I told him.

He gave it a few seconds, more out of obligation than of genuine interest, and handed it to me.

"I don't know what this means, if anything," he said and again focused on his computer screen.

I slammed the lid shut.

Hs sucked in his cheeks and kept his head down. His nostrils flared. He bobbed his head a few times. I'd likely just blown my Christmas bonus.

"You were used, Colonel," I said. "What if *you're* the willing participant? What if Flores led you to Vizcarro by leaking to an undercover DEA agent?"

He glanced up at me. "I know what you're getting at." He leaned back in his chair. "Flores was the source. Did he play us? I don't know, nor do I have the luxury of entertaining every idea or chase every half-ass lead. Vizcarro indicated he could help. His story checked out. He was known to have been at parties at Flores's house in Mexico. They knew each other. We're firm on that."

"I think Martina was his oldest daughter. You know anything about that?"

"No."

"Nothing?"

"I've answered your question," Janssen said coolly.

"There's nothing worse, Colonel than when you think you're running the scam, but it's really on you."

"You're giving me advice?"

"You need it."

"Have a safe trip home." He flipped open his laptop again. I knew not to slam it shut a second time.

I was halfway to the door, and getting a good whiff of Isabelle's talent, when Janssen called out, "Travis."

I turned to face him. He looked up from his desk.

"Those kids. You find anything, you let me know."

He didn't wait for a response but sank his head into the shadows of the desk lamp, his hand reaching blindly for his drink.

17

"You're wearing shorts?" Kathleen said when she came out of her bedroom. Morgan and I were in her condo having cocktails before the Bannons' boat party. Apparently, I wasn't up to snuff.

"It's a warm evening," I said. "We'll be on a boat."

"It's likely business casual."

"Anyone who does business casually is out a job."

"You look nice in slacks."

"I'm a shorts guy."

"Saddle up," she said.

"You could have just ordered me to in the first place."

"I thought I'd give you a chance."

I changed into white linen pants while I considered what other chances she was giving me. I snatched a black blazer from the closet. I put it back and grabbed a tan—some would say chestnut—blazer instead. Loafers and no socks completed my ensemble.

"Much better," she said when I emerged from the bedroom in proper boating couture.

"I couldn't find my ascot."

"Don't push it."

The three of us dodged families with children as we strolled through Straub Park to the Vinoy Marina. White lights dripped down trees, and children ice-skated on the small rink that was set up every December. We paused to drink in the scene. A mother and a young girl held hands as they teetered and tottered around the rink, fighting to keep their balance. Their hair coiled out of matching red knit hats with green pom poms that the weather did not warrant. Bing crooned his song. Kathleen stared.

"Jake?" she said.

"Yes?"

Pause.

"Never mind."

Great.

Never mind is the cellar door of the English language. You have no idea what's behind it; the junk, the mess, the cobwebs, the hoarding, the indecision, the Tolstoian meaning of those two words.

I took the traditional, gutless, and manly way out. I did not probe.

At the gangplank, a woman asked us our names and checked them off her tablet. Once on the boat, I deserted Kathleen and Morgan and went hunting for Bannon. He was drowning in people, laughter and drinks. Although that hadn't deterred me from barging in during our first meeting, I didn't think that act would work twice. I slipped through the crowd and discovered that the aft starboard side was sparsely populated. A lone guitar player strummed softly. His lowered head swayed with the beat as if no one else existed in his world. Behind him, the lit condos of downtown stretched into the sky, twinkling like concrete Christmas trees, with smaller, miniature white trees, visible through some of the windows.

"Mr. Travis." Tina Welch had maneuvered behind me. "May I get you something to drink?" She wore a black dress that was slit up to her thigh and had a high neck. Her lips were seasonal red.

"You're the bartender as well?"

"I perform a myriad of trivial tasks," she said as we made our way to a makeshift bar.

"Still working for Mr. Bannon?" I asked.

"Why do you wish to know?"

"Idle chat."

"You hardly strike me as a man who idles, let alone chats."

"Nor you a woman who squanders her time in trivia, let alone a myriad of it."

"Jameson on the rocks," she said to the bartender and then turned to me. "That is correct, is it not?"

I gave her a solitary nod. "And why would the personal assistant of a wine importer know my bad habits?"

She gave me the smile I'd seen at the museum. The one that made me want to get my safari gun out for protection.

"It's my job," she said.

"How so?"

"You seemed rather . . . suggestive in your questioning the other night. Mr. Bannon does not like any threats to his business."

"I hardly think my comments could be construed as a threat."

"What if I disagree?"

"You just don't know me."

"Don't I?" She leaned against the railing, a naked leg jutting out. "Jacob Francis Travis. You recover stolen boats for insurance companies. But that's down time for you. You served five years in the army, received the Purple Heart, the Distinguished Service Medal—although both incidents are sealed—and attended courses run by the Defense Intelligence Agency's Military Attaché School as well as the Joint Military Intelligence Training Center. You were questioned years ago for multiple murders at Fort De Soto. You disappear for weeks on end with no explanation of where you've been."

"You've been talking to my neighbors. Did they tell you I also bring their empty trash containers in?"

"When you were seven, your sister and only sibling was abducted from a—"

"That's enough," I said and stepped into her. She held her ground, unrattled by my physical presence. Her knowledge of my intelligence courses was impressive. She'd done some digging.

"Why have you suddenly dropped into our world, Mr. Travis?" Her breath was mint-fresh and it flicked out of her mouth like an invisible lizard's tongue.

"I heard a rumor that three children were abducted from Pass-a-Grille."

"Ah, back to the missing munchkins. And in what unimaginable scenario do I or Mr. Bannon factor into this?"

"The children belonged to a man, Alejandro Vizcarro, who helped Bannon launder money for Sergio Flores."

It might have been a stupid thing to say, but sometimes you throw your high card on the table. Mine wasn't an ace, but it was a face card.

Welch opened her mouth and rolled her tongue over her lower teeth that remarkably had no trace of her lipstick. A thin smile morphed her sumptuous lips. I feared I had just awakened a sleeping—and hungry—lioness.

"Mr. Bannon mentioned that you dropped this Vizcarro fellow's name at the museum," she said. "He is clueless as to whom you are referring to. And Sergio Flores—he is what, a bullfighter? Or perhaps a Spanish painter like Dali?"

"He's a ruthless drug lord who kills for a nickel, tortures for a dime, and sells young girls into sex slavery."

She let out a low whistle that under different circumstances would buckle my knees and split my heart.

"My, my," she said as if she were enjoying the moment.

"The jobs people have these days. You may wish to stay clear of such an animal."

"Perhaps if the children were returned, my interest in Mr. Bannon would correspondingly diminish."

"That has not been my experience."

"Why would an executive assistant for a wine merchant have experience in such vile matters?"

She took a patient sip of wine. A sea breeze swept off the harbor. It had no effect on her plastered hair, which again was pulled tight behind her head. She leveled her eyes on mine. "Have a pleasant evening." She strolled away. I reached for my phone.

"Ms. Welch." She turned. "Something to remember our moment by." I snapped a picture.

"You should not have done that," she said as if in some manner I had let her down, or disappointed her. Her face was expressionless as she spun away from me.

I dawdled around and located Kathleen and Morgan laughing with a circle of strangers. Morgan was a spring breeze—welcomed where he went and missed when he left. I passed them by in favor of another drink. I never got close to Bannon. It didn't matter—I'd spoken to his lieutenant. My comment to Welch concerning Flores was brazen and revealing. With luck, my desperate act would force Bannon to commit an unforced error. That my plan depended on luck proved how desperate and rudderless my efforts were.

I wandered over to the port side facing downtown, where only a sliver of water separated the boat from the park. The woman and young girl who we saw skating walked by on the sidewalk, each holding a cup. They laughed. The woman's hat was off, and I wondered where she'd stashed it. They were so close, yet a world away. I thought I should say something to Kathleen about her earlier comments, her hesitation, but I never did.

18

RAFAEL

Rafael considered time to be the most valuable asset in the world. Objects that measured that rarest of commodities, broke it into measureable units, were a great source of personal pleasure and artistic expression. Today's artifact was a Swiss Venus from the mid nineteen-fifties. Its simplicity, clean lines, and soft leather band blended well with his thin bone structure. It wasn't easy finding a man's watch that looked exquisite on his delicate wrist.

He rode the elevator down to the lobby of the Vinoy Hotel. Ignoring the air cologned with coffee and croissants, he strode to Beach Drive, where he'd enjoyed coffee and pastry the day before. He liked routines, and when traveling, quickly developed them as a method of integrating himself into new surroundings. He took a seat outside and observed the people hustling by. St. Petersburg is not a business city, but a residential one. Rafael admired that, although he did not allow that admiration to taint his overall view of the lawless state of Florida, or, for that matter, the bullying country it was a part of. He brought up his phone and checked the weather in Bordeaux. Cloudy and 48. He took a sip of steaming coffee and begrudgingly admitted that Florida was not such a bad place in the winter. He would not be sitting outside at home. He would be bundled in his wool sweater observing the dank world through lead-beveled glass that was no match for the piercing cold.

Richard Bannon marched up to the table, pulled out a chair, and took a seat. "Will you be leaving soon?" Bannon blurted out.

Rafael took a sip of coffee. He detested men who did not practice the art of conversation. Who did not realize that words were brushstrokes in the air. "Good morning," he said. "That is not for me to say."

"But your job here is finished." Bannon said.

"I may be given another assignment."

Bannon squirmed in his chair. "Travis?"

"Why are you so interested in him?"

"Who said I am?"

"You wear insecurity like a peasant's coat," Rafael said.

"Whatever. He's a threat," Bannon shot back. "I told you what he dropped on me at the museum. He's like a fire hose that no one's holding onto."

"He is trying to goad you into revealing something because he has nothing. He is an amateur."

"He insinuated that I move money," Bannon said.

"What business man doesn't?"

"Not in that manner."

"Lucky guess," Rafael said.

"The comment about missing children, and Vizcarro-somebody. What was that about?"

"How would I know?" Rafael said.

"He didn't pull it out of his ass."

"What did I just say?"

Bannon studied the man across from him. He'd been notified by Flores's lieutenant, a surly man who went only by

Davido, that a man was entering the United States. He was a threat, and Flores had dispatched a solution. He'd been told to cooperate with Rafael, although concerning what was never made clear to him. "He'll be in and out in a few days," Bannon had been assured. Those few days had stretched on, and Bannon didn't like the uncertainty. It reeked of failure. That Rafael's appearance coincided with Welch's unannounced audit made Bannon even more nervous.

"This man, Vizcarro," Bannon said, "did he have kids? Is this what it's about?"

He instantly regretted his questions. If Vizcarro did have children, and Rafael took care of them in the same manner he probably took care of Vizcarro, then Bannon didn't want to know.

When Rafael didn't immediately answer, Bannon moved on quickly. "What should I do about Travis?" he asked.

"Nothing."

"No?"

"That is not your job. Tell me about Tina Welch."

"She's a rug muncher," Bannon said. "I can tell you that."

Rafael winced as if stricken in the face. "Her sexual preference is no concern to anyone but herself."

Bannon shrugged. "She was dispatched a week or so ago to audit my books. I get a different person every time. Unannounced. It doesn't bother me. I'm clean and happy to prove it." He eyeballed Rafael. "Why do you want to know about her?"

"She accompanied me the other night."

"When you visited this Vizcarro guy?" Bannon asked.

"Keep your voice down."

Bannon leaned in. "It's not a coincidence that you and her are both here at the same time, is it?"

When Rafael didn't reply, Bannon pressed him. "I was told there was a threat—that was this Vizcarro, right? And what? He brought his family? What was Welch's role—shield their little faces? You don't give a spider's tit about that."

"Do you trust her?" Rafael asked.

"Me?" Bannon spit out. "She works for the big man. Ask him."

"I'm asking you."

"She's an auditor. You telling me she's more than a bean counter?" He nodded. "I'd buy that."

"Why?"

"She's got an attitude."

"So do you," Rafael said.

"You know what—"

"Your judgment is compromised because she does not want to have sex with you," Rafael said. "She finds you repulsive."

"Listen, I don't—"

"You belong in the corner of the world where they stick people with little minds."

"Whatever, pal," Bannon said.

"Did she engage in any suspicious activity while around you?"

"No."

"We went to where Vizcarro was hiding," Rafael said. "There were supposed to be children there. She did not know this, nor did I tell her. The children were gone. If you learn otherwise, let me know. Understand?"

"Why the interest in the children?"

"Do you understand?"

"Yeah. I come to you. Why the interest?"

"That is not for me to say."

"Was Vizcarro ever a threat?" Bannon asked.

"That is not for—"

"Yeah, yeah. I got it," Bannon said. He crossed and then uncrossed his legs. "Where does Travis fit into this?"

"I do not know."

"Sounds like the cards are crumbling."

"That is not your concern."

Bannon grunted. "Not much seems to be."

"Perhaps there is a reason for that," Rafael said. "After all, I never know who my next job might be."

"I'll keep that in mind," Bannon said, but he was embarrassed by the shake in his voice. He should have just shut up.

Maybe it's time for my exit plan, he thought. *Time to punch my one-way ticket out of here.*

Bannon had been the mastermind behind a box stuffed with greenbacks that had the same weight and appearance as a case of wine. When the boxes were delivered to his kingdom of wine stores throughout the state, that cash was filtered into the banking system. The deposits were always under $10,000. Eight million last year. All profit. He'd taken a chunk of that and bought some of the strip centers the stores were in. He'd gotten them cheap—strip centers were on the ropes. But they don't make land anymore, and Bannon was picky about what centers he bought. He understood the three rules of real estate: location, location, location. The country was exploding with apartments, condos, nursing homes and retirement centers, and they needed dirt to stand on. While most of the properties were in shell corporations for Flores—those guys were always trying to legitimize—he'd taken his cut and bought some in his name. He could skate anytime.

"If you talk with Travis, let me know," Rafael said.

A young woman sauntered by. Her untucked flannel shirt failed to conceal her figure. Bannon tracked her down the sidewalk.

"Did you hear me?" Rafael said.

"Pardon?"

"You slobber over women."

"What do you—"

"Leave," Rafael ordered him. "Our meeting is over."

Bannon hesitated, stood, and scuttled away.

Rafael observed that Bannon struggled with his gait, as if he was uncertain at what pace to walk. If Flores sought his opinion, Rafael would not hesitate. The world would not miss Richard Bannon.

19

Cole sat on his front porch picking "Seminole Wind." He didn't stop when I took a seat next to him, crossed my legs, and settled back in the chair. After several bars, and a final angry, out-of-tune strum, he leaned the guitar against the side of his house. I asked him how long he'd been playing.

"Six months." He shrugged.

"Sounds good."

"Don't patronize me."

"Don't give up fishing," I said, although I hoped it didn't cut too deep. I'd been enjoying his performance.

"Did you check out Alejandro?" he asked with an edge to his voice.

"I did."

"And?"

"A bookkeeper—at least on the surface."

"A bookkeeper to the core."

"And you know this because what—you're intimate with drug dealers?"

Cole paused a beat. "Why do you keep bugging me?"

"I think you're holding something back."

"I am. I'm a non-practicing attorney, not a fisherman."

Before I could toss out a retort, the screen door swung open. Charlotte, the woman who had been at the ticket counter of the museum, and who had huddled with Cole in the courtyard, stepped out of the house. She held a stack of papers.

"This is what you wanted printed," she said as she came through the door. "It looks a lot like what hap—" She saw me and stopped.

I popped up, extended my hand, and introduced myself. "I was at the museum the other night, although we never formally met. You wished me a pleasant evening. I think you meant it."

She fumbled her holdings and shook my hand. "Charlotte Ross."

"I didn't mean to take your seat."

"No, no. That's okay."

"I'll look at them later," Cole told her in an instructional tone.

"I'll look at them now." I meant it as a lighthearted comment, but it struck a fuse.

Charlotte clutched the stack of papers to her chest and her eyes darted to Cole. She wore shorts and a long-sleeve T-shirt. No shoes. Little makeup. She was comfortable around Cole, and I assumed it was more than a casual relationship. Cole stood and took a step as if to protect her, or the contents of her hand.

"If it's between you two," I said, "then I apologize for intruding. But if it has anything to do with dead bodies and missing kids, then I'm not leaving."

Charlotte kept her eyes on Cole. She was going to let him make the call, and Cole was thinking.

"Let's have a drink at Hurricanes," Cole said.

Cole locked up and the three of us legged over to Hurricanes, a restaurant with a rooftop bar a few blocks away. We climbed the winding, outdoor metal steps to the top floor where the infinite waters of the Gulf of Mexico took my eyes and emptied my mind. The feeble December sun hid behind a cloud, creating a propane-blue sky with streams of copper. It was an hour before sunset, and I assumed the Ding Dong man would be on the beach that night. He kept a log of who rang the bell at sunset and had viewed over 7,000 sunsets from the same spot since retiring and moving to Florida over twenty years ago.

We opted for corner seating at the bar. I was at one end next to Cole, and then Charlotte so that we faced each other. I ordered a beer and an iced tea. Cole asked for an IPA, and Charlotte said she was fine. Then she changed her mind and asked for a "diet whatever." Emerson, Lake, and Palmer came over the speakers.

Oh, what a lucky man he was.

Before we left Cole's place, Cole had gone inside with Charlotte while she got her shoes. Who knew what they had discussed. In addition to her shoes, she had emerged wearing a zip-up sweatshirt.

I took a sip of cold beer that didn't hit the mark and decided to let them start at their own pace. It didn't take long.

"Charlotte's been spending some nights with me," Cole said. "I couldn't say anything, and neither will you. Her divorce isn't final."

"I have no interest in that."

If she had seen something, that may have contributed to his reluctance to call the police. But Cole seemed to have a deeper mistrust of the men in blue than mucking up a divorce settlement.

"I need your word—however good that may be. Charlotte and I are out of this. Nothing comes back to us."

Was Cole running from another life? The IRS?

"You have it."

He gave a shake of his head as if he'd grown weary of the game and it was hardly worth the effort. "One night—"

"Charlotte, I'd like to hear it in your words."

She positioned herself higher and took a sip of her diet whatever. She didn't look at Cole for approval, and I liked that. Instead she looked at me as she had at the art museum, her deliciously brown eyes wide as if excited to take in the world and equally eager to share what she knew. Her hair was tied back and a trace of eye shadow, which I hadn't noticed previously, matched her brown eyes. She was attractive, but in a careful manner, as if she was wary of drawing too much attention to herself. As if she knew that she could turn every head in a room, but what's the purpose of that? I didn't really know Charlotte, and I certainly couldn't finger Cole, but they'd be fools to let each other slip away.

This from someone who had already admitted that he is somewhat flawed in judging people.

"It wasn't the night that it . . . happened," she said, and my hopes rattled around the rim and hit the floor. There would be no easy points in this game. "It was the night before. I couldn't sleep. I was thinking about"—she waved her hand —"it doesn't matter. I got up and went to sit on the front porch. I like the night. The quiet."

"What time was this?" I said.

"About 3:17." She gave me a bashful smile. "You've got to love the digital age. I went to the bathroom first, so let's call it 3:18."

"You were asleep?" I said to Cole.

"Sawing lumber."

"I've seen you roaming inside at night."

"At that moment, I was out cold."

"I'm sorry," I said to Charlotte. "Go ahead."

"No, that's fine. I started to go out to the front porch when a car crawled down the street. For some reason, I held back until it passed. But it didn't."

"It stopped?"

"Not for long. Maybe a few seconds? There's a lamppost

in Harriet's yard—she's across the street, catty-corner toward the gulf, with the blue shutters. It cast a glow on the car. Their heads were turned toward the house where those two people died."

"Heads?"

"I'm sorry?"

"How many people where in the car?"

"Two."

"Both in the front?"

"Yes."

"What direction was the car traveling, east or west?"

"I'm not sure—"

"Was it coming from Gulf Boulevard or from Pass-a-Grille Way?"

"From Pass-a-Grille."

"Go on."

"I'm afraid there's not much more."

"There's always more. The people: Tall? Short?"

"I think one might have been a woman. The passenger was . . . thin, but still tall. You know, narrow shoulders, and I thought I saw hair pulled back."

"The driver?"

"Not real large either. But not the narrow shoulders of the passenger."

"You said they came to a complete stop."

"Yes. Then they drove off."

"What did you think, Charlotte, when you saw this?"

"I don't know. I—"

"I apologize. What did you *feel* when you saw this?"

She brought her hands together and cast her eyes down at the bar. "Fear. Creepy." She glanced over at me. "All those silly emotions that you have no rational basis for, but they don't seek rationality, do they? I mean, there is no reason for anyone to be driving on that street at that time of the night."

I leaned back and started to reach for my drink, but rested

my hand on the counter instead. Two people. That wasn't a surprise. A double murder followed by a triple kidnapping would be a tough, if not impossible, solo assignment.

"The car?" I asked Charlotte.

"A four-door. Black, but maybe dark gray, it was hard to tell."

"Plates?"

"I didn't look."

"Okay. So they paused, and then what?"

"It kept going. I took a seat on the porch. A few minutes later, it returned, from Gulf Boulevard." She shot me a look. "The west. But this time it only slowed down in front of the house."

"You were on the porch?"

"No. I went inside when I saw the headlights."

"Did Harriet's lamp afford you a better look the second time?"

"Not really. But I was pretty sure that the passenger was definitely a woman."

"Pretty sure and definitely don't hang together."

She blushed. "It's my best guess."

I pushed my beer away, buying time. "So we got two people, twenty-four hours before Alejandro and his oldest daughter got killed."

"You've come over?" Cole said. "You now believe that Martina was his daughter and not his wife?"

"I do."

"It wasn't my weak powers of persuasion."

"I found a picture of Vizcarro at a book fair standing with a woman identified as his wife. Not even close to Martina. With what you told me—how he referred to his three girls—and how I witnessed them interact, I think she might have been his daughter." I gave Charlotte a conciliatory nod. "It's my best guess."

"The girls' age difference?" Cole said.

"Not improbable. Alejandro and his wife would have had Martina when they were young, and then waited before adding to their family."

"Why would someone kill one daughter and kidnap three children?" Cole asked.

"How many possibilities can we conjure?"

"Based on our pitiful knowledge? Endless."

"Is that it?" I said to whoever wanted to field the question.

Cole reached into his pocket and brought out his phone. He punched it a few times and gave it to me. "This is what Charlotte was printing when you arrived."

I took his phone and read an article about an accident in Wildwood, Florida. A semi truck had slammed into a car, killing the driver and its sole occupant, Sean Wright. The truck driver was not charged, and the police were still looking for the driver of the car that had caused the accident by cutting sharply in front of the victim's car. A woman driving in the opposite direction witnessed the crash. I'd read an article while at Seabreeze regarding a similar accident in North Carolina. Janssen mentioned losing a red herring in North Carolina. I didn't think anything of it at the time and wasn't sure I should now. I had no clue, out of the 35,000 road deaths in the country every year, how many were caused by a truck rear-ending a car.

Or if any of those might have been staged.

"What about it?" I said.

"The victim, Sean Wright, was a crooked ex-cop. We helped him beat a charge. I think his death was a drug hit."

I leaned back in my stool and welded my eyes to Cole.

"What happened to I'm just a lonely fisherman?"

"I never said lonely."

"Go on," I said, eager to get to the point.

"My old firm represented Wright. Brokered the deal that got him off on a slam-dunk murder charge."

"Your firm?"

"I was a lawyer up north."

"You knew Wright?" I said.

"Met him."

"Is that why the Cat Stevens act?"

Cole ignored my gambit. "Wildwood was a hit job. They, the cartel, feared he knew too much. It was designed to look like an accident. I think . . . they've gotten proficient at that." Charlotte reached over and touched his arm, but Cole didn't know she was there. "I have other examples as well, but Wildwood is our—your best chance of proving it."

He snatched his phone from me and tickled his fingers over its face. He gave it back. I read a follow-up article that had been published a few days after the first article. It identified Robin Bashinsky as the witness who had given a description of the driver to the police.

"She might have seen one of the two people Charlotte saw," he said as I handed his phone back to him.

"You have no basis for that."

"No, I don't. But two drug killings not far apart in time or distance certainly piques one's curiosity."

I took a sip of iced tea and let an ice cube slide in my mouth. I cracked the ice. Wildwood was less than two hours north. It was rural Florida that was in the process of being engulfed by The Villages, a retirement community that boasted over 100,000 residents, 65,000 golf carts, and was splitting at the seams as the collective population of 55-year-olds blew out of the northeast, Midwest, and other parts of Florida that had become cost prohibitive.

Was it worth a day to check out Cole's unsubstantiated theory?

"Give it a whack," Cole said, as if I had broadcasted my dubiety and indecision. "Nothing ventured crap. Your hit was a cartel job, and I'm telling you—" He nodded at his phone on the bar. "Pepperoni was too."

"Pepperoni?"

"That was the code name we—my old firm—gave Sean Wright."

"Why pepperoni?"

"Look into it." Cole stared at me, but his eyes were a few inches off, as if he was looking past me, not at me.

I was about to tell him that I'd enjoyed his guitar playing earlier when Charlotte sniffled. Tears dotted her smooth cheeks, like summer raindrops on a waxy apple. She was so pretty to be so sad, and it had happened so quickly that I was afraid to say anything else. I looked away toward the gulf so as not to embarrass her, but the water held no place to anchor my unsettled eyes.

20

Robin Bashinsky, the woman who had witnessed the fatal accident, lived on a side street off County Road 466A outside Wildwood Florida. I took a right off 301 past a business called Sharky's. A sign boasted that they repaired vacuum cleaners and also did sewing—because you always think of taking your vacuum cleaner to your tailor.

I parked on a street carpeted with brown leaves. An oak tree in Bashinsky's front yard, hung with limp Spanish moss, dwarfed the house. Its massive protective branches stretched over the roof. I stabbed the doorbell, knocked, and stabbed it again. There was no car in the driveway and no garage. I ambled around to the rear of the house.

There's a chunk of Florida, less manufactured than the costal extremities, that is overlooked by the tourist bureau. Texas-sized pastures with cows and horses instead of sand and water. Circling vultures with wingspans that block the sun like an Old Testament omen. Suffocating summer heat and winter arctic fronts that blast in from the Yukon Territory. The cold panics the snowbirds, and they'll scramble to arrange a flight to the eastern Caribbean—but then it's gone.

There was nothing manufactured about Robin Bashinsky's back yard. A pair of Washington palms had never been trimmed. Their dead fronds draped toward the ground like soiled debutante dresses. A shed might have served a purpose at one time, but its rusted tin roof was gashed open and the front door hung by a gimpy single hinge, creating a wide gap at the top. The gravel drive surrendered to a packed dirt yard with tufts of grass and weeds struggling for a sparse existence amongst mounds of Spanish moss.

From behind me: "Can I help you?"

A young-to-middle-aged woman stood on the back porch. She wore a T-shirt that read, "The Titanic. The Irishmen built it and an Englishman sunk it." Oatmeal-colored hair fell on the left side of her face and then disappeared behind her.

"No offense, ma'am. I knocked and rang the bell, but there was no answer."

"You think that gives you the right to hike around my property."

"No."

"Then why you doin' it?"

"Bad manners and I apologize. I—"

"What's your name?" she said.

I told her. "Yours?"

"Robin Bashinsky. Never heard of you."

"I'm just here to ask you some questions about the car accident you witnessed. If you want me to leave, say the words and I'll waltz right off your property."

"Never met a man who could waltz. You're not the police?"

"No. Private investigator."

"You read the papers?"

"About as well as I waltz."

She cracked a smile. "Well if you did, you'd know I didn't see much."

"I won't take much of your time."

"Are you helping the family of that man—Sean Wright—who got squashed like an accordion when the Peterbilt rear-ended him?"

"I am."

In for a dime, in for a dollar.

"I can give you ten minutes. My daughter, Lee Ann, is due home any moment."

"I'd appreciate that," I said to her back as she turned and started walking inside. I took that as a sign to follow her and stepped onto her porch.

She said over her shoulder, "Take a seat out there."

I plopped into a metal rocker that hit the house when I leaned back. A minute later, Robin came back out with two glasses. One was etched with Looney Tunes characters, and the other was a Pepsi-Cola glass. The smell of slow-cooked beef wafted from inside the house. It mixed with the cooling air and stirred something deep within me that I'd long forgotten and cannot talk about.

"Have some lemonade." She handed me Daffy Duck. "It got hotter today than they said it would. Always does. That weatherman needs to plant his heinie in my backyard sometimes."

"Thank you. You make it yourself?"

"Mixed the powder with my own spoon."

Her face still held vestiges of youth. I'm drawn to faces like hers—faces that straddle youth and wisdom and can jump fifteen years in either direction. Lines that tell stories, foreheads that are novels. She was thin, the type of thin you get from an active life, not a gym routine. She wore white frayed shorts along with her green Titanic T-shirt.

I took a sip of lemonade. It was painfully sweet.

"Are you Irish?" I said.

"Why would—no, I got this at the thrift store the church runs. Bargains and Blessing. Just liked it, that's all. Picked it up on the way home from work one day."

"Where do you work?"

"Why?"

"Small talk."

She sighed. "Most men do that about as well as they waltz. I'm a receptionist at a Urologist office. Five days a week, I sit behind a desk facing a wall with a poster that says 'Urine leakage doesn't need to be a sign of aging.'" She took a drink of lemonade. She swallowed hard, as if she'd been looking forward to that drink for the past few hours. "Can't say that was ever in my dreams." She took another drink. "That's as small as we get, and right now your clock's ticking faster than our patients drip."

"How do you get to work to stare at your pee poster?"

"I can make fun of my job, you can't."

"I'm—"

"I catch a ride with another woman who works with me. On days I need the car, Lee Ann's friend, Gloria, takes her."

"And you had the car that day?"

"'Course I did."

"You were driving east when you witnessed the accident?"

"No, west."

"That's right."

She eyed me as if trying to ascertain whether I'd made the error on purpose, which I had.

"It was on route 44 by the Chevy dealer," she said. "A car pulled out of the dealership right in front of Sean Wright's car. The truck was following too tight behind Wright—riding his ass. The car didn't seem in no hurry or anything, and the truck just slammed hard into the rear of Wright's car. End of Wright. End of story."

"Where were you when the actual impact occurred?"

"Sorta just past it. But I was going in the opposite direction, remember? It happened real fast."

"What did the driver of the other car look like?"

She scrunched up her face. "White. Male. Not too old. Like I told Sam, I didn't get a good look at him."

"Sam?"

"He's the sheriff."

I asked her questions about the make and color of the car that pulled out in front of Wright. I also drilled her on anything else she could extract from her memory that would help identify the driver. She stuck by her earlier version that she remembered little.

"The accident happened *after* I passed the car. How many random people do you remember from your drive today?"

"Very few," I admitted. "It was about this time of day, wasn't it?"

She eyed me curiously. "It was."

"Did anyone at the sheriff's office ever question the dealership for a description of the car?"

"That's a question for them."

"The car that pulled out in front of Wright, it must have been at just the right speed so as not to get hit by Wright."

She took a sip of her lemonade and stood. "Good luck, Jake. I gotta get dinner on the table. It's been in a crockpot all day."

I gave her my card and the line about calling me. As I talked, the gravel crunched on the side of her house and a red Honda came to a stop. A young woman bounded out and hopped onto the porch.

"Hey Mamma." She gave Robin a peck on the cheek. "You better have that brisket ready." She turned to me. "Hi, I'm Lee Ann, but everyone just calls me Lee except my mom." She thrust her hand out and we did a business shake. She stood with the confidence of a runway model. She wore workout shorts and a loose, short-sleeve, green and gold T-shirt with "Buffalos" printed on it. Her hair was iron straight and the color of smooth, wet sand.

"Pleasure to meet you," I said. "Are you just getting in from school?"

"She's a member of the Golden Girls, that's the school's competitive dance and cheer squad," her mother rushed in, flag flying. "Top five at nationals last year. Lee Ann's co-captain of the squad. She tumbles like a five-year-old. She doesn't get that from me. I can't even clap my hands." She turned to her daughter and touched Lee Ann lightly on her shoulder. "Coach Quay hard on you today?"

"The usual."

"Quay's a task master," Robin said to me. "They win competitions, but they earn every trophy three times over."

"Anyways," Lee Ann said with a slight roll of her eyes. "I'm famished. I got tons of homework to do, and I haven't practiced my flute in days. There's not enough time in three days to do what's expected of me in one day."

"The glory days of high school," I said, attempting to sound like a family man.

"Yuck, you can have them. I'm up at 6:00 every morning, drive myself to school, back ten to twelve hours later, and rarely get to bed before 11. If I get five free minutes in between, I'm thrilled. Weekends aren't much better. Saturdays, I work the afternoon shift at the Panera in Sumter Landing. I'm trying to save money for a car."

"Lee Ann's got a scholarship to UF next fall." Her mother beamed. "She got in on early admission."

"How long does your cheer season go?" I asked Lee Ann. Robin shifted her weight.

"I'm the biggest fool in central Florida. I do both football and basketball—do *not* ask me why. So we got the same schedule every day for nearly two-thirds of the year. But I like it. My friends tell me college will be easier. I'm looking forward to that." She turned to her mother. "I'm going to take a shower." Back to me. "Nice meeting you, Mr. Travis." Another boardroom handshake.

Lee Ann breezed into the house and said over her shoulder. "Gloria's car is in the shop *again*. You okay if I keep it the rest of the week?"

She didn't wait for an answer, but got one anyway as Robin called out, "That's fine."

Robin turned to me and said, "I worry about them girls drivin' that road to school. Everyone thinks a straight road is a safe road, but there ain't no such thing. I can show you the exact place where a young girl riding her bike got hit by some day-time drunk checking his phone. I can pinpoint the spot where Frog Gebhart rolled his rod three times. They found his girlfriend—I can never recall her name—fifty feet away in a ditch. They say she launched through the moon roof like a rocket. Now with Wright, we got us another one."

"Frog?"

"On account of him bein' such a good jumper on the track team. I think of Lee Ann on that road every day, passin' all the death spots."

"Every road has its stories."

"Yeah? Well I don't care about every road." Robin fluttered my card in the air. "If I think of something, I'll let you know. Have a safe trip." She spun around and went in the house, shutting the door behind her.

I moped around the side of the house, carrying my dejection like a suitcase. I hadn't learned anything, nor was I certain that I'd given it my best effort. The red Honda Accord was clean—a little road dirt behind the front tires, but that was to be expected.

Mother and daughter shared the car.

One car.

I stomped back up on the porch and rapped on the door. Robin Bashinsky opened it. She centered herself in the middle of the doorframe. I knew why.

"You and Lee Ann share the car?"

"What about it?"

"On the day of the accident, you had the car?"

"Like I said. On days I need the car, like that day, Lee Ann's friend, Gloria takes her."

"And Gloria's car wasn't in the garage that day."

"No. It was not," she said with too much bluster.

"And you drive that straight stretch of road to get to work."

She paused. "It's time for you to leave."

She started to shut the door, but I stuck my foot in. Robin eyed me with fear, and I felt bad for intruding in her world.

"I need that road's story. There's a possibility that what she saw was not an accident. It may be related to another crime. A double homicide. I'll keep your daughter out of it."

"I've told you everything. You leave or—"

"I'm not a threat to you, Robin. I'm a man seeking answers and I need your help. Two people were murdered. Three young children are missing."

Her face crinkled with indecision. "I saw an accident. Nothing more. Sorry I can't help you."

"You didn't see a thing, but your daughter might have seen someone get murdered."

She clenched her jaw and narrowed her eyes.

"I'm from a long line of basket cases," she said. "And all I ever did was honor that heritage. I was pregnant before I got my diploma." She punched her words out, taking a free swing at the world. "That ain't no excuse, but it guarantees a crooked road, and I just told you how dangerous even a straight one is. I wouldn't trade Lee Ann for all the gold in China, but there is no escaping having a baby and no high school diploma. That's not going to happen to my girl. She's going to UF and getting out of here. I can't afford—"

"It's okay Mama," Lee Ann said stepping behind her mother. I hadn't noticed her arrive. "I told you, it's going to get out someday." Lee Ann looked at me with wisdom that belied her physical years. "Are you looking for the children?"

"I am."

"This might help?"

"It might."

"Then why don't you join us for dinner, Mr. Travis?" She turned to her mother. "Go ahead and call Daddy. You know it's the right thing to do. It'll make you feel better having him here."

21

Robin presented the brisket on a fresh onion bun smothered with coleslaw. It melted in my mouth like hot cotton candy. She had not offered me anything alcoholic to drink, nor had I seen any devil's brew in the house. We ate at a small table next to a refrigerator plastered with magnets. Disney World. Key West. Rock City. Weeki Wachee Springs. A smiling realtor with a football schedule under her picture. And Lee Ann. A Louvre gallery of Lee Ann radiating excitement with her friends and her mother. I felt bad for my naked refrigerator. It was capable of so much more.

I couldn't see how my efforts would circle back to finding the children. But if Wright's death was related to the Vizcarros' demise, then that doubled the leads I could follow. Sometimes you've got to put the effort out there and have faith it will come back. After all, half the trajectory of a boomerang is moving away from you. It's the second half that makes the flight a thing of beauty.

"I get the coleslaw at Fresh Market," Robin said to a question I'd asked. "But I make up the sauce and mix it in. It's too dry when it comes out of the bag."

"Give my mom a one-step meal, and she's queen of the kitchen," Lee Ann said.

"That is true," Robin said. "I heard once that when cake in a box first came out—you know, just add water and bake—no one bought it because women didn't feel like that was real cooking. So the company that made it changed the recipe to read add one egg along with water, even though the egg wasn't needed. Sales took off after that. That's my idea of cookin', add an ingredient to make *me* feel special."

"Best homemade coleslaw I ever had," I said.

"You catch on fast," Robin said. She bit into her sandwich and added between chews, "Maybe you do know how to waltz."

I expected her to smile, but she did not.

We didn't talk about the accident over dinner; Lee Ann had a French quiz the next day, and she and I batted her required vocabulary around. She asked if I'd ever been to the country and I replied that I'd made several trips. UF had a study abroad program, and Lee Ann said she kept the brochure by her nightstand and leafed through it at night. When we were finished, I helped Robin with the dishes. Lee Ann excused herself to take that long-anticipated shower.

"Sam should be here in a few minutes," Robin said, placing a plastic container into her refrigerator. "He was just finishin' up some paperwork."

"Sam the sheriff?"

She nodded.

"I thought 'daddy' was coming."

"Same difference," she said.

"Are you married?"

"We got married twice and never had an anniversary. But he was a good sperm donor."

"Third time's a—"

"Don't you even go there."

Robin and I relocated to the back porch. The day was pulling out. The clean night air arrived with the purple dusk, as if they were holding hands. Crickets chirped and trees become silhouettes in a colorless world. An unmarked car pulled into the driveway. It swung confidently around the Honda and came to a stop in the dirt, as if that was its assigned parking place.

A uniformed man climbed out of the car. His thick forearms bulged out of his short-sleeve shirt. He moseyed up to the back porch, a can of beer in his hand.

"Robin."

"Sam. You know I don't allow that in my house."

"And I knew you'd be sitting out here, using my beer as an excuse to keep me out of the house that I built."

"You built it for me."

"The point was to share."

"Well, la-di-da. I changed my mind," Robin said. "When you going to fix the door on the shed? It looks junky like that."

"Get to it this weekend. Put a new roof on too. Who's your friend? Not a new bunkmate, is he?"

"I told you, he—"

"Jake Travis," I said, standing and extending my hand.

He shook it out of obligation and then said, "I need to see some identification." His row of lower teeth—Hollywood straight and neat—was visible when he spoke. Thick hair was clipped department regulation short around his ears, but it looked as if he tested the limit in the back.

I surrendered my driver's license. He went to his car and sat in the front seat. He came back, handed me my license, and said, "How long did you serve?"

He didn't get that off my license.

"Five years with the Rangers," I said.

He took a sip of beer. "Why are you here?"

I explained that I was looking into a homicide and there was a remote chance it was related to the fatal accident on Route 44 last month.

"Hey, Daddy." Lee Ann bounded down the back steps and pecked him on the cheek. "Didn't see you at Howard's house last Sunday."

"Doin' a little fishing. I'll be there this week, though. How was your day, Minnow?"

"Super. I got about three hours of homework and one hour of energy left."

"I told you, you need to call in sick every once in a while. Do you a world of good. You need a day to just catch up."

Robin said, "Don't you be tell—"

"Robin and I are desperately in love. She just doesn't know it," Sam said to me, cutting off his ex-wife—or current wife, for all I knew. He shot Robin a boyish grin that likely had done the trick nearly eighteen years ago, and the memory alone might be good for another eighteen.

"You love your badge," Robin said. "Three's a crowd."

"I'd drop it anytime."

"And blame me every day."

"You two need to get a new act," Lee Ann said. "Let's start. I really do got a *ton* of homework."

Sam grabbed a folding chair that was leaning against the wall. Robin and Lee Ann sat at a round table, and I situated the metal rocker to face them all. Sam drilled me with some questions about what led me to his family's back porch. I kept it simple, telling him I was a friend of Cole's and was investigating whether there was a connection between Sean Wright and the deaths across from Cole. As a way of tying them together, I noted that Cole's ex-firm had represented the police union that Wright had belonged to. I held back that Wright had been accused of murder, deciding only to play that card if necessary.

"I don't think we can help you," Sam said. "But before we kickoff, you need to know the ground rules. My daughter's name is not to be dragged into this. Robin was driving that day. You hint to anyone that that's not the case, and not only will we deny it, but—you listening to me?"

He'd got me glancing at the granite orange sky ribbed with streaks of blue.

"I am."

He said, "You squeal, and I'll have you thrown in jail for accosting an officer of the law."

"I've done no such thing."

"Don't matter. Deal?"

"Deal."

"Go ahead, Lee Ann. Keep it simple. Your homework is more important."

Lee Ann squirmed in her seat. "I'm afraid, Mr. Travis, it was pretty much like my mom said, except I was driving that day. I approached the car just as the other car swung out in front of it. I saw the accident in my rearview mirror. I stopped and called 911."

"We logged that as Robin calling," Sam said.

"You can do that?"

Sam took a leisurely draw from his can.

I asked Lee Ann if she could describe the driver of the car that pulled out in front of Sean Wright's car.

"Not really. A young man with a cherry-red baseball cap on. No beard. Fat lips. Thin chin."

"Fat lips?" I said.

"Like Botox."

"That's pretty good for a drive by."

"I remember thinking he had smooth skin. That he was a man, but his skin was so pretty. I think that's why maybe he stuck with me."

"Was he a woman dressed to look like a man?"

Her eyebrows knitted together. "I never really thought about it, but it's possible. But I can't say for sure, other than that he/she had smooth skin. And tall. You know, his head high in the car. I'm sorry, but the moment came and went."

"Can you describe the driver of the truck?"

Lee Ann glanced nervously at her father. "Lee Ann," he said, "didn't get a good look at the driver."

"You certainly questioned the truck driver," I said to Sam. "I'm just curious as to whether Lee Ann got a look."

"My daughter did not see the driver of the truck," Sam said, ending that vein of conversation.

"But you spoke with him?" I said, keeping my attention on Sam.

"He's innocent. Nothing more than failure to maintain a safe distance."

"Not even vehicular homicide?"

"We don't need that publicity."

Sheriff Sam was not interested in an investigation. His sole interest in the death of Sean Wright was to shield his daughter. I changed course and looked at Lee Ann. "Was Gloria with you that day?"

"Yes, but her head was buried in her phone. She never looked up until we heard the crash behind us."

My phone rang. I pulled it out of my pocket. It was Kathleen. I clicked it on mute and was wedging it back into my pocket when Lee Ann piped up. "Is that the ten?"

"The eight."

"Does it have Live Photos?"

"It does."

"Those are so cool. Can I show my mom?"

"She's been trying to explain it to me," Robin said in a pleasant voice, eager to switch the conversation to something other than the accident. "She can get a new phone next month, but I keep telling her that doesn't mean she *has* to get a new phone."

Lee Ann rose and patted her mother on the top of her head. "And *you*, Little One, can get a new one any day. You don't know what you're missing." She glanced at me. "May I?"

"Be my guest." I brought up some fishing pictures and handed it to Lee Ann.

"See," she said showing it to her mother.

"Oh, my gosh," Robin said. "It's like a little movie before it settles into a picture. I don't know if I like that. It's almost creepy, like something Stephen King would come up with."

Lee Ann took the phone over to her father. "See, Daddy?"

"What is that, a trout?" he said, staring at the phone.

Morgan and I had gone fishing a few weeks ago.

"It is. That was a good day for us."

Lee Ann swiped the screen with her hand, flipping through more pictures. "It is *so* —" She stopped and stared at the screen. She put her thumb and forefinger on it to work the picture in and out. She looked up at me and then at her father.

"Who is she?" she said staring back at the screen of my phone.

She must have been looking at a picture of Kathleen, but I couldn't recall the last one I'd taken.

"Let me see."

Lee Ann flipped the phone around. It was the picture of Tina Welch that I'd taken on Bannon's boat.

Botoxed lips.

I didn't want to give Lee Ann a leading comment.

"A woman I casually met," I said.

Lee Ann turned the phone back around and stared at the picture.

"What do you see, Minnow?" Sam asked as he scooted forward in his chair.

"Those lips," she said. "What I *real*ly remember was getting a flash glance, my eyes locking on his lips, and thinking I'd never seen a boy with such pretty lips."

"Was she driving the car?" I said.

"I don't know."

"Put a cherry-red baseball cap on her," I said, nudging her just a bit.

She handed me back my phone, like it was too hot for her hands. She nodded her head in an affirmative manner. "I remember thinking that was a girlish color for a man to wear —too pinkish, not enough red. But I don't know why I didn't tell you that just now."

"Where was that picture taken?" Sam asked me.

"On a boat. In Saint Pete."

"Let's go." He stood up.

"Pardon?"

"You and me. To my office. Now. We need to talk."

I couldn't blame Sheriff Sam for not being too keen on me having a picture of the driver, and wanting to move the conversation away from his daughter. He told me to follow him. I thanked Robin, again, for dinner, and wished Lee Ann good luck on her French quiz. She said she was done studying and was going to practice the flute, as she had skipped it for too many days.

When I got in the truck, the heart-tugging and maudlin melody of "The Theme from *Love Story*" floated out of the glow of an open window in the front of the house. The vibrato of the flute was clear and strong. Lee Ann played it with great patience, as if she had all the time in the world. The oak tree loomed over the house, a somber and reverent giant in the presence of the kingdom's princess. As I drove away, the sorrowful angst of love faded, washed away by the noise and confusion of crickets and the cool night air whooshing through the moon roof.

22

Sam parked me in a room with a picture of a high school football team on the wall and a flickering light bulb in the ceiling. The picture was from two seasons ago. A Florida Gators coffee cup was on the laminate table in front of me. It rested on a crumpled napkin and contained the residual of an oil spill in the Gulf of Mexico. He said he'd be "back in a second" and walked out.

Ten minutes later, Kathleen called. I'd forgotten to ring her back.

"Where are you?" she asked.

"Sheriff's office, couple hours north."

Pause.

"What did you do?"

"Robbed a bank."

"You did not," she said.

"Stole the sheriff's horse?"

"Stop it."

"We're just doing a little Q and A," I said. "But it will be late when we're done."

"Everything okay?"

"Smooth as smoke. See you tomorrow."

We disconnected. I tried not to focus on the football poster, but there was nothing else on the walls, so I stared at a bunch of rosy-cheeked guys with faux menacing faces and flexed muscles posed in the backs of jacked-up black pickup trucks. What did the theater group do for a picture? Everyone dress like Puck?

Before Sam planted me in the room, he had voiced that he didn't buy my explanation—that I was listening to his daughter play flute—as to why I initially fell so far behind him when he left Robin's house. He thought I might ditch him. To get us on common ground, I'd given him the cell number of Detective McGlashan of the Lee County Sheriff's office. I'd worked with McGlashan on a couple of cases, and he would vouch for me. I hoped. Sam had left me with the toxic coffee while, I assumed, he made the call.

He came back in the room and yanked out a chair across from me.

"What's your next step?" he asked.

"Did you get hold of McGlashan?"

"I did. You're not stomping around my county any longer than you need to."

"What do you have on the truck driver?"

"You remember my comment I made earlier about if any of this comes back to my daughter?"

"Who was driving the truck?" I asked.

"You answer one question before launching another."

"I never met your daughter. You have my word."

We did an eye shake and then he started in.

"Truck driver's name is Kenny Strawser. Kenny's got a frequent customer card. His rails don't run together. Been that way since grade school. Last visit here was 'cause he got so drunk he ordered a cheeseburger from an ATM machine and refused to move until he got served. Now he's suddenly found resources that have eluded him his entire life. He's driving a new Mustang and got himself a new fishing rig. Pretty impressive for a man who can't keep a job."

"Were his priors serious?" I asked.

He nudged the toxic coffee cup away. "He's about as harmless as a drunk gerbil. Got busted last year for masturbating in a Belk's dressing room with a naked black mannequin—claimed he got her permission. Like a lot of guys, he's just a drain on the system."

"Anything more indicative of what he might have gotten involved in?"

"He's got a drug problem. We're a rural area here. It's pretty common. But in the Wright case, like I told you, we kept it at failure to maintain a safe distance. He was genuinely distraught. Strawser's not a man who plans things—he's not that bright. He's not a killer, either. I recognize that streak in a man, and he doesn't have it."

"Was anyone at the dealership of any assistance?"

"That car that pulled out in front of Wright's? It was a Tesla. Lee Ann wouldn't know a Tesla from a Toyota Tundra, but the boys at the dealership noticed it parked in the lot for about ten minutes before Sean Wright came barreling down the road. It's quicker than a jackrabbit to sixty. The perfect car for the deed."

"They get a look at the driver?"

"No."

I thought of pursuing that, but let it slide. "Wright was an ex-cop," I said, hoping to get some brownie points before I asked Sheriff Sam for a favor.

"I know that."

"Might have been involved in a drug gang," I said, laying down the card I'd held back at Robin's house.

He chewed his cheeks and bounced his head a few times. "Now that, I didn't know. But I sensed you think it was premeditated, and I didn't want my girls to hear any more."

"I don't have motivation."

A Beautiful Voice

"But where there's smoke," he said. "Why do you have that woman's picture on your phone?"

"She works for a man suspected of laundering money for a drug cartel."

"In my county?"

"No."

He leaned in on the table, shoving the coffee cup, and its napkin, even farther away as if in his mind he wasn't satisfied with his first attempt. "But you aim on getting' to the bottom of it."

"I do."

"But not in my county."

"If it leads me here."

He paused and then said, "Do I need to explain the lay of the land to you?"

"I think you've—"

"Keep it out of my yard. My wife and daughter are not to be approached by you or anybody ever again. You got that? You come through me and me only. Until you cross the county line, I want to know where you are. Understand?"

"You've made your point, Sheriff."

"And you've got a problem with direct answers."

"I understand," I said. "What's Strawser's story?"

Sam leaned back in his chair and rubbed his jaw. He dug his finger into his lower left cheek. I wasn't sure we'd settled the previous point, but he moved on. "We planted a guy at a bar Strawser hangs out at. Strawser muttered something about it wasn't supposed to happen that way, but we can't make a case on that. Sober, he clams up. We're no longer investigating the case."

"Don't need the publicity, right?"

"About as much as I need you."

I didn't challenge him on his lack of incentive in pursuing the case. It was time to ask my favor.

"You can save me the trouble and give me Strawser's address."

"I can't have any shenanigans on my watch."

"You'll never know I was here."

"I doubt that. I'm only doing this 'cause you'd find him anyways. My helping you just hustles your ass out of my county a little sooner." He took out a pen from his pocket, reached over to the displaced Gators cup, and took the napkin from underneath it. He jotted something down.

"Make sure you drop by before leaving," he said.

"I'll do that."

We both stood.

"Who's Howard?" I asked.

"Who?"

"Howard. Your daughter said she missed you at Howard's house last Sunday. Is he anyone I should be talking to?"

He coughed out a laugh. "I won't give you advice on that. When Lee Ann was little, we took her to church all the time—well, at least some of the time. You know the Lord's Prayer, 'hallowed be thy name?' Lee Ann told us later that for years she thought it was 'Howard be thy name.'" He shrugged and allowed himself a fatherly grin. "She thought Jesus' daddy was a guy named Howard. We've called church Howard's house ever since."

"You've got a nice family."

The smile vanished as it were never there. "Don't screw up. We clear?"

"Yes, sir."

He walked out the door. I picked up the soiled napkin. It had an address on it.

IT WAS LATE WHEN I CHECKED INTO A HOTEL THAT fronted a small lake in the town of Lake Sumter Landing. It was a Disney lake with fake warehouse signs and moorings, but the water was real, although it was so still that it, too, could have been fake.

"What are you whistling?" the older lady behind the desk asked. I'd inquired about a room on the water. Her glasses were too small for her flabby face, and she wore a necklace of seashells.

"Not sure," I lied.

"Sounds like that song from *Love Story*."

"It's stuck in my head. You want it?"

"No. But I know what you mean. Only thing we got left is the Pelican Suite. We've got high school reunions going on, so we're pretty packed."

"Reunions this time of year?"

"Hurricane last fall postponed it."

"I'll take the suite."

"I hated that movie. Just too mushy for me."

"Bet it made you cry."

"Oh, you know it did."

The room was the size of a small gym and appointed about as elegantly, but it had water on both sides and a balcony. After dropping off my bag, I went down to the lounge. I cut a path to the bar, although mapping the virgin Amazon would have been easier. I ordered a whiskey. The room was a splitting headache of people competing to be heard.

I escaped down a hall. Signs taped outside of doors indicated what class was in what room. A few people buzzed around in each room cleaning up plundered buffets. The various class years met in separate rooms, and then everybody nuked the bar. At the end of the hall, I came across the sign for the class of 1942. It was written on a different paper than the other class dates.

It was empty. There were no remnants of a buffet, or any other type of activity.

I walked in, took a seat, and relished the quiet. I nursed

my whiskey in solitude, figuring that whoever was representing the class of '42 must be off visiting some other ancient classmates. 1942: the war was snuffing out the depression the way Johnny Carson once quipped that California mudslides were putting out the wildfires.

I thought of Robin and Sam. Married twice without an anniversary. Would they try it a third time, or do people give up on their lives? Grow weary of the constant faltering, only to surrender their burdens to their children, like passing down busted dreams and wasted hope. But the empty room held no answers, and the whiskey honored its tradition of great promise and hollow results.

The next morning, the sun rose over the lake and clouds floated on the water. A rowboat appeared as if it was moored on a mirror. After forty minutes of laps in the pool, I strolled into town for a cup of real coffee and a newspaper that covered events more than half-a-county over. Music played through concealed speakers. It was like pumping oxygen into a casino. People in golf carts glided through the early morning streets, and the rising sun channeled brilliant knifes of light into the awakening town square. The town sounded happy. Looked happy. Felt happy. It was a Brigadoon world crafted and created for the enjoyment of its inhabitants. They did not seek, nor need, approval from the outside world.

I feasted on a ten-dollar breakfast buffet, which I consumed on the patio overlooking the water. Scullers gleamed their boats over the placid surface of the small lake. The coxswain called out the rhythm, and the oars dipped into the water in harmony, leaving a timid and finely patterned wake behind them. I walked along the waterfront and then entered the hotel through a side door. A janitor in a crisp white shirt was cleaning the rooms where the different classes had met. He took down the sign for 1942.

"I didn't see anyone in that room last night," I said, stopping in front of him. He held a purple plastic bucket in his hand. It looked like a child's sand toy.

"They're done making their mess. Had one guy there five years ago. Jus' sat all by his-self. Tried to get him to go to other rooms, but he jus' sat."

"Did he RSVP?"

"Who?"

"The man who was here five years ago."

"Oh, no sir. They all gone. That's what I heard anyways. This here is somethun' I do for every reunion. I always fix up a room for the most recent class to have no known survivors."

"Why do you that?"

He slung the rag over his shoulder. "We all in that room soon enough. Be there before you know it. I'm just lettin' them —rest of the folks round here—know what the final reunion looks like. They don't mind. They expect it from me."

"Does that make them happy or sad?"

"It's up to each person. I expect it make some folks party all that much harder. Others? Maybe makes them a little quieter."

"Which is the right way?" I asked the man with the purple bucket.

"What's that?"

"Do we party or reflect?"

He chuckled. "You be better off tryin' to catch the wind than answer that. Some questions are born with no answers. That's why it's such a mystery."

"But we keep asking."

"We do. Not that that be very long. We are born in a second and we die in the nex' one. In-between is nothin' but a hyphen on piece of granite when they bury you—my daddy always told me that. But that hyphen is all we need. Yes sir—it makes us imperishable."

He dropped 1942 into a trashcan.

"Seventy-five years," he said. "I was hopin' that old codger would hang on. You have a good day."

He shuffled down the hall and out the side door, where his form gathered in the bright glare of the sun.

"Excuse me, sir?"

A woman with a laptop bag slung over her shoulder and holding a box had come up behind me.

"Yes?"

"Do you know if this is the Panther room? We're having a pesticide meeting here and I need to set up. Bugs are gettin' more terrible every year. We just don't get the cold snaps like we used to."

23

Strawser lived in a brick ranch off a two-lane county road with a faded yellow line down the middle. The only other structure within a half-mile was a windowless white block building. A sign on the roof proclaimed "Discount Porn." A busted-down Greek food truck, with a picture of Zeus holding a gyro, had the gravel parking lot to itself.

Needle palms crowded Strawser's house, and earthquake sheets of concrete passed as the driveway. A bright yellow Mustang parked tight up against the closed garage door sat next to a sparkling red Lund fishing boat. A pair of earmuffs with a hose running from them clamped onto a Mercury 150 outboard engine.

I opened an aluminum storm door and gave the weathered wood door a couple of hard knocks. Nothing. I pounded on the door. Muffled footsteps came from inside. A beefy man in a splotchy brown T-shirt and jeans opened the door. He had a three-day beard and a sweating can of beer in his hand. The thickness of his neck made everything above his shoulders look like a thumb. His eyes were buried deep in his forehead. A stale odor skulked out of the house as if seeking freedom.

"Kenny Strawser?"

"Who's axin'?"

I gave him my name.

"Whatdaya want?"

"I'd like to ask you a few questions about the accident."

"Why? You insurance? I can tell you ain't law."

"Sure, Kenny. I'll be the insurance guy. Where can we talk?"

He eyed me from his withdrawn sockets. "Get lost," he said and started to close the door.

Pushing the door open, I stepped into the house. Then I saw the dog. Whoever heard of a dog that doesn't bark when a stranger pounds on the front door?

It was a crooked old pit bull mix with shoulders you could break a two-by-four over. It lunged at me just as I stepped back outside and slammed the storm door. An old dog was not going to spoil my new day.

Strawser wrapped his arms around the dog and shouted, "Dontcha hurt her."

"Tie her up," I yelled at him.

"She won't hurt you."

"Tie her up."

"Okay. Okay." Strawser took her by the collar. "Her stake is out back."

I opened the door. "Go."

I followed him into the house. It would have been easier to follow a deer trail through a thicket. Strawser was a serious hoarder, and junk layered every surface. We made our way to the kitchen where a five-foot tall cage sat in the corner. Inside it, a green parrot perched on a swing jerked its head sideways when we entered.

"I'm a pretty girl," the parrot squawked.

"Hush now, Peggy," Strawser said.

"I'm a pretty girl."

"I taught her that," Strawser explained. "Now I can't get her to shut up."

"Out back," I said.

"I'm goin'."

"I'm a pretty girl."

Strawser led his dog—it emitted a guttural *boof*—through the back kitchen door, carrying his beer in the other hand. He clipped her collar to a line that was tied to a picnic table. Seedlings sprouted between the cracks in the boards, and bird droppings crusted the surface.

"She's a good dog." He plopped down on the bench as if the walk had exhausted him. "Lost her hearing years ago when some damn fool let off a few rounds too close to her ears. I don't think she would have hurt you."

"Tell me why you were following Sean Wright too close the day you rammed him."

His head fell. A rooster crowed and blue jays bickered in a nearby oak tree. He brought his face up to me, and I was surprised to see tears cleaning tracks on his cheek. The man was 250 pounds of sadness.

"Why you want to know?" he said.

"Not your business."

"I told Sam. It was an accident."

"Sam the sheriff?"

"Is there another one?"

"Someone paid you to cause an accident," I said.

"Ain't no such thing happen. I didn't cause nothin'."

"Where'd you get the money for the Lund and the yellow banana in your front yard?"

"Workin' my whole life. Car cost me an ass and a half."

"And your uncle died, right?"

"Oh yeah. That, too."

"Come on Kenny, you're going to do have to better with me. I'm not the law."

"I don't much give a duck's butt who you are."

I got down on my knees so my face was level with his. "You're going to tell the truth, Kenny. The only question is: How much damage do I do before you tell me the truth?"

"I'm not axin' for trouble."

"And I'm not delivering it, as long as you cooperate."

"I just need a little shot. I got a needle in my bedroom."

"Kenny—hey, look at me, big man."

His eyes had started to stray, as if he were searching for a way out. He was a drug addict, a beer addict, and a man who knew he was slipping away. What glued such men together? The thought of someone they once knew and who had believed in them? One who'd uttered kind words? A ghost from their past they didn't want to let down? I didn't want to find out.

"No one will know I was here," I said. "There will be no repercussions from our conversation."

"We both know you're lyin'."

"Who put you up to it?"

"No one you'd know. I gotta take a TUMS, my stomach's been actin' up." He squirmed into his pocket, took out a sleeve of something and popped one in his mouth. He stuck the rest back in his pocket. "You got me up early—all that poundin'. I just need to— 'Cause every morning 'bout this—"

"You talk to me first."

"You said you'd hurt Elizabeth."

"The dog?"

He nodded like schoolboy who'd gotten in trouble and was now eager to please.

"I'm not going to hurt your—"

He lurched at me, and we both tumbled to the ground. He took a clumsy swing at my head. I rolled him face down on the ground and put him in a full nelson.

"Are you going to try that again? Kenny?"

"No?"

"Kenny?"

"Yeah?"

"No more freebies. Understand?"

"Yeah."

I released him and sat on the end of the picnic table bench where the supports where. Kenny slumped to the ground and rested his forearms on his raised knees. He took in a deep breath.

"Pass me my beer?" he said. I handed it to him. He took a swig. "I could use some money. I spent everything payin' people off and then I bought that boat. Always wanted one. Then I bought that car. That was stupid. Now I got no gas money for neither."

I reached into my wallet and tossed a pair of fifties that floated next to him. It was open betting on how long it would be before they found their way into his bloodstream.

"Talk."

He scooped up the bills.

"I drive a dirt truck—pretty good driver, really. Some guys, you know, they say they drive a truck jus' to get a little Saturday money, but I'm pretty good at it, have been my whole life. I've been dri—"

"Tell me about that day."

"All right . . . sure. I was tol' to follow that car. Wright's. I got nothing against the man, didn't even know him. But they said to bump him, you know, nudge him a little when I got to that Chevy dealership."

"Why there?"

"Shit if I know."

"Did you ask how they knew Wright would be there at that time of day?"

"I did," he said with a note of pride. "They jus' said they'd arrange for that."

"You had to suspect something."

"No." He looked at me with fear. "Not a-tall. Nothing like

what happened. Like I said, I'm a pretty good driver. Nudge him a bit. That's all. Never meant for no accident."

"Tell me about the accident."

"I told it to the sheriff straight. I was followin' too close, and that car pulled out in front of Wright. He slammed his brakes. I pushed my foot through the floor. I never hurt nobody in my whole life. That damned car that pulled out caused this whole mess."

"Who are they, Kenny? Who put you up to it?"

"No one you would know."

"Never heard of that name."

He chuckled. "Told you you wouldn't know 'em."

"Someone at the trucking company?"

"Naw. Couple of guys that supply me. They called me over one night—we was at the booth at Pig Floyd's Barbecue listenin' to the Allman Brothers, 'Melissa,' I think. They had some woman with them. Rangy thing with fat lips. She wore a baseball cap—she was cute in that thing. I axed her what her name was. She said 'Stan.' Stan, my ass. I knew then she was stuffed with shit like a Thanksgiving turkey.

"I owed them some money, and I thought they was goin' to throw me on the fire pit. Instead, Zipper—he's my main source, skinny as a palm so everyone calls him Zipper—anyhow, he axed me how I'd like it if my debt was to be forgiven and how'd I like to make some real spendin' money. I said sure. Then the woman took over. Said all's I had to do was tailgate that car. 'Teach him a lesson,' she said when I axed the purpose of the whole thing."

"Tell me about the woman."

"Shee-it—like no one I'd ever seen. Tall, I can tell you that. When she stood up, she just kept standin'. Thought that pretty head was gonna poke right through the ceiling. Know what I mean?"

"What else?" I asked.

"She looked at me like I was lower than a snake's belly."

A Beautiful Voice

"Details, Kenny."

"Her face was like a magazine picture."

"Hair color?"

"Brunette, but hell, I don't really even know what color that is. Brown, ain't it? She had it stuffed up under that John Deere hat. Don't see many women like that, least 'round here. Not that I would know. I haven't left my area code in ten years, 'cept for the time we went over to Daytona for the race, when Junior won for the second time."

"You're a truck driver."

"That ain't goin' nowhere. Just means you sit on your ass without ever leavin' the cab." He gave me the sad stare of an empty life. "Oh, I've been plenty of places, all right. Warehouses and piss-stops. That's my America."

"Dirt trucks aren't long-haulers."

"I've done it all."

"How did they know you'd be driving that day?"

"Tol' you, they asked me when I was scheduled to drive."

"You never told me that," I said.

"Didn't I? Hmm. Thought I did."

My eyes got lost over an uncut field of grass where a soft breeze curved the tall blades, and I thought of Cole's fishing poles leaning into the corner of his house. Sean Wright was murdered, likely the victim of a fractured drug deal, and there was no investigation. Murder is less risky if it can be passed off as an accident. It also helps when the local sheriff has a vested interest in not investigating. Whoever was responsible would also have needed a backup plan in the event that Wright had only been seriously injured.

I took out my phone and showed him the picture of Tina Welch.

"Oh no, no, no." His voice quivered with fear. "That ain't her."

"It's not what you think, Kenny. I'm no friend of hers."

Kenny might have thought I was working with Welch and had come to clean up after her.

"Who is she?" he asked.

"A nasty person. Is she the woman in the John Deere hat?"

"I don't know, there's jus' no way—"

"Is she?"

"Yeah." He nodded. "You know she is. Why you even axin' me? You gonna kill me now?"

"No."

"You jus' sayin' that?"

"I'm not going to lay a hand on you." I stood to leave. "Thank you for your time."

"You don't have another fifty do ya? You pulled them other two out pretty fast."

"You think of anything else, you give me a call." I tossed my card on the ground, but he didn't scoop it up like he had the bills. I made my way through the kitchen and toward the front door.

"I'm a pretty girl."

TINA WELCH WAS LIKELY A CONTRACTOR WORKING for Flores. But what Sean Wright had to do with my problems was anyone's guess. Perhaps nothing. He might be unrelated to the Vizcarros, but Welch was in the neighborhood so she got the call. Based on Charlotte's description, her phone might have rung for the Vizcarro job as well. One thing was certain: I had to tread lightly around her.

I swung back to Sheriff Sam's office as requested and briefed him on my meeting with Strawser. He'd played it straight with me, and I owed him the same respect. He thanked me and said he never wanted to see me again.

On the way down I-75 to St. Pete, I gave up on music and rode the highway in silence. I also gave up on Wright, Flores, Welch and the whole gang. I recalled the crooked man with the purple bucket. I tried to make sense of his comments, but my thoughts wallowed in the mire.

Seeking firmer ground, I switched to Sam and Robin and their daughter Lee Ann. I contemplated whether there was any room in my life for something, or someone, like that and if the three of them were going to Howard's house on Sunday. The thought flittered away, leaving my mind as empty as a conch shell—but not for long. Janssen's and Martina's voices filled the dark void with unforeshadowed quickness.

Janssen: "You're as low as we go."

Martina: "It is you who is a clown."

I didn't know whether my vainglorious attempt to find the children was as much an attempt to save them as a despairing act to save myself. A flailing venture to keep me from becoming the low rung on the ladder. I tried to rinse my mind, but there was nothing to rinse. It was empty as if everything had been subtracted from me.

24

Later that day I picked up Garrett from the airport after being repeatedly whistled at for loitering in the passenger pickup zone. The man in a yellow vest was out to save the world. His piercing instrument never left his lips as he conducted his task with Teutonic efficiency.

We fought rush-hour traffic to Bannon's office, arriving a tick before four-thirty. I opened the pebbled glass door, etched with West Coast Distributors, and asked for Tina Welch.

"She's no longer with us," the saucy receptionist with a streak of red in her hair said. Judging by her tone, Ms. Welch was not missed. A plaque on the desk read Lindsay.

"Know where she flew off to, Lindsay?" I said.

"Timbuktu for all I care."

"Miss her madly?"

"I know she was here to audit books, but it's a busy time of year. I hoped she'd stay on to pick up some of the workload. Evidently, that's beneath her calling. Now we're on the street soliciting part-time help. Is there anything else I can help you gentlemen with?"

"Is Richard in?"

"No."

"Tell him Jake Travis dropped by."

"And your friend?" She glanced up appreciatively at Garrett.

"DEA," Garrett said.

She crinkled her nose. "DE—what?"

"Just give Ricky the message," I said.

THAT EVENING AS A SNOWY EGRET PACED THE GRASS BY my seawall, I placed three filets on a 600-degree grill and uncorked a 1995 Chateau Kirwan Margaux. I'd been holding onto the bottle of Bordeaux for years and don't know why I popped it that night. Some days the clock ticks louder than others. Some days it's a pipe bomb waiting to blow. Morgan couldn't join us, as he was working late—again—at the refugee house.

"You think that Tina Welch is a hit man?" Kathleen said.

"Hit woman," I said.

"Nooo," she drew out. "How's this: She is a transgender, asexual, bisexual, pansexual, have-I-forgotten-any-sexual, person of a legally identifiable racial, ethnic, and culture orientation, and who, pending a trademark on said combination, actively seeks to prohibit anyone from representing any element of her—who kills other people."

"Academia getting to you?"

"I don't understand why we need to wear nametags. It seems to me that . . ."

"What?"

"I don't know. But don't call me jaded."

"I didn't."

"And I'm telling you not to."

"More wine?"

"Please." She handed me her glass, and I gave her a generous pour.

Magic drifted past the end of my dock. Only a few people

braved her deck, bundled in jackets and huddled together in a picture that would never grace a Florida postcard. A spineless northwest breeze ruffled the five country flags on her mast. A pod of dolphins surfaced farther out by the channel marker. My kingdom was like a Live Photo. Despite the leading motion, it settled into a predictable photograph.

Garrett and I had stopped by the Museum of Fine Arts after our visit to West Coast Distributors. We caught Charlotte on the way out. I showed her the picture of Tina Welch. She remembered her from the fundraiser, but couldn't say for certain if she was the passenger in the car that prowled outside Cole's house. She admitted Welch had the height, and then apologized that she couldn't be of more help.

"Do you really think I'm getting jaded?" Kathleen asked. I'd thought we'd finished that scene.

"No," I said, hoping to throw a bucket of water on a fire before it spread.

"I don't want to become *jaded*."

"You're not."

"You said I am."

"No—you made that up, remember?"

"But you thought it."

"I was thinking more like cranky."

"Cranky?" She shook her head in disgust. "That's just the masculine form of jaded. Where do you think the children are?"

"Self-pity time over?"

"I just had to blow. The children?"

"In the wind. I put a notice up at Seabreeze, Riptides, and Dockside. Maybe a tourist saw something."

I flipped the steaks and twisted the knobs to turn the burners to low.

Garrett brought a salad he'd prepared out to the porch. It's not the best news when he volunteers for KP. He's wacko about health, and his salads possess the consistency and taste of freshly mowed grass, with a collection of squirrels' nuts tossed in.

"Time to turn up the heat," he said. "We need to force Bannon's hand."

"And how do you propose to do that?" Kathleen asked him.

"He launders money," Garrett said. "We catch him on that, we own him."

"You two are hardly the first to think like that," she said.

"We might be the first to deploy less than normally accepted procedures," I said.

"You mean break the law?" she said.

"Skirt the law."

"You mean break the law."

"Now you're being jaded," I said.

"I *knew* you'd say it. Don't overcook my filet."

"That's entrapment."

"The filet."

I took a steak off and left the other two on. I thought of Kathleen longing after the mother and daughter at the skating rink the other night. *Never mind*, she'd said when I questioned her stare. I didn't know why that popped into my head at that moment. My mind is often at its best when in a relaxed and unknotted state. When it is free of life's petty demands. During such moments of mental solitude, events and conversations float to the surface, bathed in new light and understanding, although I fail gloriously at acting upon insights gleaned from such serendipitous moments. I instinctively took a sip of wine for the wisdom and enlightenment it might impart upon me. That's never worked, but lack of effort will never be cited for its failure.

Over dinner we decided that the straightest road to Welch, and ultimately the fate of the children, ran through Bannon. And the surest means of securing Bannon's cooperation was to catch him laundering drug money and propose a quid pro quo. We might even get Bannon to sing on Flores, which was the original goal. Whether or not our methods would produce anything admissible in court was another matter.

The waxing crescent moon ascended over the bay, silvering the water with ripples of light. It was a silent observer to our quiet discussion. It cast a black shadow of *Impulse* on the water, and the shadow looked just as real as the boat. Then the shadow looked more real than the object it was reflecting, and everything jumped a hundred years.

My winged emotions that carry me through the day were gunned down. Everything lay in Ozymandias ruins.

What do we have left—maybe fifty years if we're lucky? Then death knocks us off one by one, like a zit-faced kid throwing darts at balloons in a carnival booth. I wrestle such dark moods myself. To involve others in the embittering battle within is only to burden those whom I love. There is no church service. No support group. No anthem to lift the spirit. Kathleen and Garrett droned on, but I was done for the night.

In the morning, I would run, flush it all out, and once again rule the world. But what if one day that pill stopped working?

THAT NIGHT I DREAMED I WAS AT WALT DISNEY World, but Walt Disney World was in Iowa. A troll popped out from underneath a bridge. It held a stuffed giraffe with a lion's head. The troll, a grotesque figure with warts for a face, giggled like Gabriela and then disappeared. Poof. Gone. A man wearing a plaid kilt, T-shirt and construction hard-hat approached me. Banded to the top of his hat was a rubber duck, facing forward. He peered over the side of the bridge and then at me.

The man said, "Who's the woman sitting at the table?"

25

"You want her to do what?" Cole asked. I had solicited his approval for a job I had in mind for Charlotte. I felt I had a better chance of success if the request was channeled through Cole.

"Apply for a part-time job at a wine distributor and then give me access to who they distribute to."

I rubbed my right calf muscle. I'd sprinted at the end of my run that morning and must have stretched it too far. The run had done its magic. My despondency from the previous evening had washed out, leaving me ashamed that such petty thoughts had commandeered my mind.

"You mean steal from her employer," Cole said.

"I can see how one might construe—"

"What do you plan to do with the information?"

"Blackmail Bannon into telling us who killed your neighbors. Maybe pick up a lead as to what happened to the children."

"You think Bannon launders money for a drug cartel?"

"I do."

"And you want to jump into that pond?"

"If necessary."

"You got a flashlight battery for a brain," Cole informed me.

"One of those big searchlights?"

He studied me for a moment and then took a sip of coffee. A rainless blast of frigid air had gusted through during the night. It white-capped the gulf, fought me every step on the beach when I ran north, and shoved me from behind as I ran south as if trying to scoot me clean off the planet. The air was crisp and clear, and everything was bright and focused, even the house across the street. My apocalypse stood prim and proper, eagerly awaiting its next guest.

"And over here—never mind that slight discolor on the floor—that's where the previous tenants took one to the head. Now, pardon me, if I could have your attention—"

"What makes you think she would go along?" Cole said.

"Excuse me?"

"Why would Charlotte do this?"

"She'll do it for you," I said.

"And why would I want to get involved?"

"You haven't told me yet."

Cole copped a look at the street. "I'll ask her," he said, as his eyes followed a woman jogging. Her ponytail bounced from shoulder to shoulder with the reliability of a metronome.

"Would it help if I talked to her?" I asked.

"No." He shot me a look.

"I'll need to explain—"

"Let's take it one step at a time."

"Call her today," I said. "The position could fill at any time."

"I'll let you know."

"Either way?"

"Either way."

26

In Florida, the old people water the flowers in the middle of the day. It is the simplest of jobs, yet one that carries its head high, for flowers are the melody of nature and they need water to sing.

Sean Wright's mother, Elaine, hunched over white gardenias in her backyard. She waved a red watering can over the flowers like a magic wand. She tilted the handle high in the air to empty the last drops as the petals vibrated in the breeze. A burnished-brown, creosote split rail fence separated her lot from a field where a turtle ventured out of his mound and into the high, dry grass.

While waiting for Cole to get back to me, I'd decided on a day trip to The Villages to see if I could learn more about Wright. Maybe there was a connection between him and Alejandro and Martina Vizcarro.

Cole had informed me that Wright did twenty-four years as a cop in Columbus, Ohio and abruptly retired short of the twenty-five-year mark. He had one public incident on his record. During his last year, he was the subject of an internal investigation for killing a pizza restaurant employee. Wright had shot the young man point-blank. The investigation concluded that an argument over a pizza had escalated. The off-duty policeman felt threatened when the pizza man—an 18-year-old—pulled a knife. Wright, who had provided a detailed description of the knife, was cleared of all charges. The deceased employee had a troubled juvenile past. There had been suspicion, but no proof, that drug money was being laundered through the restaurant and that Wright was on the take. Wright then moved to Florida, where Kenny Strawser's truck killed him.

Not wanting to startle Elaine Wright, I called her name from fifteen feet back, and then at ten feet. At five feet, she turned and said, "I don't need my trees trimmed, thank you. Although my robellini is looking pretty sad, but I can still reach that." She recommitted herself to her task.

"I'm not here to trim your trees."

She turned around to me. "My roof is fine. I just had a new one put on a little over a year ago."

"Not a roofer, either. I'd like to ask a few questions about your son."

"Which one? Michael?"

"Sean."

Her arm holding the red sprinkling can fell just a tad. I'd managed to trim the joy out of watering the flowers. "He's deceased."

"Yes, ma'am. I'm sorry about your loss."

"What's your interest?"

She appeared to be in her young eighties. She wore bright blue shorts and a gold embroidered white shirt.

"I have reason to believe that your son's death was not an accident."

"You didn't tell me your name."

I gave her my name.

"I need to finish watering the flowers."

"Let me fill that for you."

I walked over to her and she handed me the sprinkling

can. I took it to a hose reel at the rear of the house and filled it halfway. I feared it might be too heavy if filled to the top. While the water ran, I scooped out a handful of small brown oak leaves that cluttered the opening of a downspout. The leaves were brittle and felt like plastic. I gave her the can.

"You could have put a little more water in it."

I tossed the leaves over the fence.

She showered a thicket of orange marmalade that surrounded a birdbath filled with pristine water. I sought refuge from the sun in the shade of an umbrella that was over a round table. When she finished, she sat down next to me. I would have expected her to sit across from me.

"Would you like something to drink?" she asked.

"I'm fine, thank you."

"I told the sheriff that Sean feared for his life, but he wasn't too interested in my story."

"Why did he fear for his life?"

"What?"

"You said your son feared for his life. Why was that, Mrs. Wright?"

"I don't know."

"He must have said something?" I swatted a gnat off my arm.

"Your name again?"

I repeated my name and added that I was investigating an accident similar to the one that had resulted in her son's death and any information she had would be beneficial. I added that I knew her son had been a policeman.

Strangely satisfied, she said, "Sean told me he put a lot of bad men behind bars and some might be out by now, but not to worry."

"That's not the same as fearing for your life."

"Sounds like it to me. He never really talked much about his work."

"Did he tell you anything more specific?"

"I don't believe so."

"Did Sheriff Bashinsky ask you many questions about your son?"

"That's his last name. I was lying in bed the other night and couldn't remember it. What nationality do you think that is?"

"I don't know. Did he ask you many questions?"

"No. He mostly offered me his condolences. He was a very polite man. I told him I voted for him, but I don't recall whether I did or not. But you always want them to think so. He needs to trim his hair, though. It was pretty long in the back."

I pivoted in my seat and gazed out over her backyard. The turtle lumbered away from a pile of dirt and settled in thick grass, its shell forming a small dome above the blades. My luck with my phone and Lee Ann popped into my mind.

"Did your son leave any pictures? Memorabilia? Any letters or correspondence?"

"He wasn't that type. There was this one picture, though, he kept staring at. I was over at his house one night and he had it out. But it was a picture of a party, not just one person."

"You wouldn't have it, would you?"

"I think I might." She got up and slid open the rear door. She used both her hands and leaned her weight into the door. "Sean was going to grease this for me. I got some grease in the garage, but he never got around to it." She went inside, and Barry Manilow's voice drifted outside. She came back out holding a color four-by-six photograph.

"He left it here a few nights before the accident. I'm not even sure why he brought it over—he lived down toward Brownwood. Said it was in his legal files. He'd been charged with something up north when he was on the force. He killed a drug dealer and had to defend himself. Terrible thing to protect citizens from crooks and then have to defend yourself, don't you think?"

I decided not to contest her point that her son had killed a drug dealer. There had been no evidence of that, and I wasn't there to tarnish her deceased son's name.

"Not fair at all," I said. "Are you referring to the pizza store killing?"

Her eyes widened. "You know about it?"

"No real details. What did he tell you about it?"

"Only that some people didn't believe the man he killed was a drug dealer. There was a law firm that worked for the police. They're good people. They got him cleared of the charges."

I waited for her to say more or to hand me the photo. When neither occurred, I asked, "Where did he get the picture from?"

"One night after dinner at his house—I was watching Jeopardy and he was going through kitchen drawers looking for . . . I forget what he was looking for. But he must have come across this, and he just stared at it."

"Do you know how he originally came into possession of it?"

"Oh, that's what you're asking. I'm afraid I don't."

"Why did he leave it with you? He must have said something."

"Said it was a souvenir from his police days."

She started to hand me hand the photograph and then pulled back.

"I'm giving it to you because I think it must be more than just a souvenir, but I can't figure it out."

She handed the picture to me. Sergio Flores stood off to the left side of an affluent backyard swimming pool that was rimmed with topless women. Mouths were open as if they were talking, and at least one appeared to be in the middle of a dance move. Pictures have no soundtracks, but if this one did, it would have been deafening. Flores held a cigar in his mouth. A cloud of smoke shrouded part of his face, like a morning fog. He seemed to be gazing out of the picture, as if none of his immediate surroundings, as enticing as they were, held his interest. Few photographs of the man existed. Perhaps Wright *had* kept it as a souvenir. The picture was in poor shape, as it had been folded numerous times and humidity had dulled the images.

"May I keep it?" I said, expecting a hard no in return.

"I don't want it—it just makes me sad. You think maybe he kept it to look at those women?"

"No. You don't have any idea how your son came into possession of this?"

"No more than I already said. I asked him what the picture was of. He said 'a party in Mexico, someplace.'"

"You said he pulled it out of a drawer, but earlier you mentioned it was in his legal files."

She shook her head. "Maybe he had misplaced it. Why is it important how he got the picture?"

"Just curious, ma'am."

Wright likely knew he'd stumbled across a picture of Sergio Flores and might have kept it for no other reason. If nothing else, I could pass it up the chain as another picture of the notorious drug czar. It occurred to me that perhaps Tina Welch had arranged Wright's death because of his ability to identify Sergio Flores—confirming she was on the drug lord's payroll.

I tossed out a few questions about whether she'd ever seen, or her son had ever mentioned, Tina Welch or someone matching her description. I also delicately revisited the charges in Ohio that he'd killed an innocent man. She was adamant that the courts, and internal investigations, had cleared him of all charges.

"Do you think your son ever took money, or cooperated in any manner with drug dealers?" I said.

It's strange what your voice says when your mind takes a moment off. I had nothing to gain by the question other than hurting her.

Her eyes tightened and her mouth sagged. "No. Why do you say that? You don't think so, do you?"

"No ma'am. I apologize for the question. Where's that grease?"

"The what?"

"Grease for the door. Allow me do that for you."

When I left, she could slide the door with one hand. I also trimmed her robellini palm after she admitted that a few of the fronds were too high for her reach.

A BOLD MOON BROKE THE HORIZON LIKE A GIANT Cyclops eye taking a peek at a dark world. It chased away all the stars around it. The moon is not fond of sharing its part of the sky. Kathleen, Morgan and I sat in the screened porch. Garrett, who does not believe in conditioning his body to exercise at the same time every day, was on a night run. Better doing that than being in the kitchen.

We'd been passing the picture of Sergio Flores back and forth, trying to extract meaning. I left them to change records. I flipped through a dozen covers, but couldn't decide. I put *Dusty in Memphis* on and turned the volume down. On the way back out to the patio, I plucked a sweater draped over a couch and tossed it on Kathleen's lap. Hadley III, as if she'd been lying in wait, jumped on the sweater, and, in a move the yoga class on the beach would envy, folded her front legs under her. She purred as Kathleen stroked the back of her neck.

Morgan said, "May I see it again?" He extended his hand toward Kathleen.

"The cigar smoke makes the picture surreal," she said, handing the picture to Morgan. "It's more brushstrokes than pixels. More Degas than digital."

Kathleen, like myself, saw it as a random picture of a pool party. Nor did she discount the possibility that Wright had saved it for its porn value. It had a raw sexual edge to it. The date of the photograph, four years ago, was stamped on the back. No clues as to the location.

"Perhaps he had no reason to save it," Morgan said. "But he was equally not inclined to throw it away."

"That's my thinking." I took a sip of watered-down whiskey and placed the tumbler on the glass table.

Morgan squirmed up in his cushioned chair and took out his phone. He turned on the flashlight app and held it over the picture. "He's looking at something, or someone. Maybe not in the picture, but it's hard to see with the smoke and the creases." He placed the picture down and turned to me. "Do you have a magnifying glass?"

"No."

"Back in a sec."

He bolted out of his chair. Hadley III tracked him intently as he tramped across the back of the yard to his house. A moment later, he returned with a wood-handled mariner's magnifying glass. He settled in over the picture.

"This is my father's," he said while keeping his head buried. "He would spread maps over the dash of our sailboat and study them. He never made the switch to screens. That's not how he saw the world." He brought the magnifying glass up and down. "Why do these voluptuous woman bore you so?"

"Must be dreaming of true love," I said.

"Maybe he found it," Morgan said. He looked at me. "How old is Little Joe?"

"Three. But whether he's closer to two or four, I don't know. Why?"

He handed me the picture and the magnifying glass. The finish on the wood handle was gone, but the wood was oiled and smooth from decades of handling.

"Follow his gaze," Morgan said. "It takes you right out of the photo. But see the room?" He reached over and hovered his index finger above the corner of the picture. "Right there? There's a mirror. It's hard to see as the picture's been folded so many times. Tell me who you see."

I brought the picture up and down like a yo-yo, trying to get the best distance for my eyes. A hall mirror in the far right corner of the picture caught the reflection of someone off the picture. She was only visible from the waist up. It appeared she was part of the staff, as she wore a simple white shirt and her hair was pulled back. Acres and acres of hair.

I knew that hair.

The noise. The near-naked women. None of that mattered to Sergio Flores. He was staring at a pregnant Martina Vizcarro.

"The bookkeeper's daughter," I said. "It was never about Alejandro Vizcarro or Richard Bannon, or money laundering. It was about smuggling Sergio Flores's only son into the country."

PART II
TINA WELCH

27

Sergio Flores, from the information Mary Evelyn had provided me, had no children. If he and Martina had a tryst, and she bore him a son, then Flores might have orchestrated the whole plot himself. He would have leaked false information that Alejandro ran numbers so that he could employ the U.S. government to smuggle his son into the country for him. The prize in the package wasn't Alejandro's knowledge of Flores's drug operation, for he had little to none. It was Little Joe. I went with that version, as the children had genuinely baffled Janssen himself.

I decided not to inform Janssen of our discovery. There was no deep thought behind my decision other than he had not been truthful with me, so I'd return the favor. I believe that is some version of the Golden Rule.

Why did Vizcarro try to pass Little Joe off as his nephew? Vizcarro might have sensed that Flores was behind it all and opted to shield Little Joe's true identity. Maybe he thought it would insulate the little guy in some manner. We had a hundred questions, and they each spawned a thousand maybes.

As for the whereabouts of the missing children, they were

likely victims of a drug war. We've got your son. We'll trade him for your empire. That wouldn't bode well for the girls. No wonder Vizcarro begged me to take care of them.

He knew.

MY PHONE RANG. COLE.

"She's in," he said.

"Got hired?"

"Yes. Part-time."

"When does she start?"

"Tomorrow morning."

"I need to talk to her."

"It's her day at the museum and she's got a lot going on. She applied for the other job over lunch. Come by the house about six this evening."

At 6:15, I explained to Charlotte, West Coast Distributor's new part-time employee, that I wanted a list of the wine stores throughout the state that Bannon distributed to. She kept glancing at Cole. When I was finished, he urged her to do nothing illegal.

"How do I steal from an employer without crossing the line?" Charlotte asked. She had the kindest eyes I'd ever seen. I'd noticed them when I first saw her at the museum, and they flooded with guilt for what I was asking her to do.

"Make it a mistake," Cole said.

"A mistake?"

"Copy something that you didn't mean to copy. Pick something off a desk only to discover later that you also erroneously picked up papers you didn't intend to. But above all, don't get caught."

She gave that a second, shrugged, and said, "Okey-dokey."

. . .

A Beautiful Voice

"PIECE OF CAKE," CHARLOTTE ANNOUNCED triumphantly the following evening as she handed me pages stapled together. Cole had called me over to his house, saying she would be there.

"How so?" I took the pages.

"I worked for the French resistance in another life," she teased, clasping her hands, and I sensed that teasing was not an act that came naturally to her. As if remembering the gravity of the situation, she added, "This stuff is normally under lock and key—you know, password protected. But guess who's coming to town?"

"A Bee Gees tribute band?"

"Santa Claus. And West Coast Distributors sends poinsettias to all its stores. They did that the first week of December, and my job was to reconcile the invoices."

I studied the sheet in my hand. Twenty-five names a page and six pages. A hundred and fifty wine stores. All in the Sunshine State.

"You think he—Bannon—launders money through some of those stores?" Cole said. We were standing in his front room. A record played on his turntable, but it was a jazz piece I didn't know.

"That's the assumption," I said.

"I've had some time to break it down," he said. "Over here." Cole motioned and the three of us moved over to a round table with swivel chairs.

I took a seat next to him, and Charlotte settled in on his other side. He laid the list in front of us. It was color-coded in yellow, black, blue and red.

Cole said, "We're not looking for chain stores or grocery stores, so I've marked those off in black. The probability is low that he launders money through a store that has been family owned for an extended period. Those"—he picked up a pencil and traced it over a blue line—"are in blue. We can take a pass at them later, but that's not where we start.

"I highlighted the stores in yellow that don't fit either of those two categories. Finally, I tagged in red the yellow stores that opened within the past few years: non-chain, non-family, and newer stores."

"You've done some work," I said appreciatively.

"They can't launder through grocery stores. They would set someone up in a business, and that person would be loyal to them. What's our plan?"

Cole seemed energized to be going after the cartel's money.

"You tell me," I said. "You've put thought into this."

"Our object?" he said as if teaching a class.

"We're looking for businesses that deposit cash every week that is far greater than the inventory they are moving out the door."

"The problem?"

"We can't see the cash," I said. "Therefore we need to gauge the size of their deliveries versus what is walking out the front door."

"Precisely," he said. "Strip centers offer the cheapest leases and usually have loading docks in the back. We start with those. We're looking for ones that are getting a truckload of wine a week, but only have a few customers wandering out the front door. You find that, and you've got your laundromat—assuming a simple walkthrough doesn't reveal a spike in inventory."

"Then what?" Charlotte said. "Say you find a store that unloads fifty cases a week, but doesn't seem to have the business to absorb that inventory. How do you prove there's money in some of those boxes? That is what you're looking for, isn't it?"

"We believe so," I said. "Wine boxes stuffed with cash."

Cole said, "A dozen or so stores taking in less than $10,000 twice a week can filter millions into the system. Do that for a few years, leverage yourself modestly at two to one, and soon you've got a legitimate business, employees with benefits, and chair museum fund-raisers. When you see money, you have no idea whether it's clean or dirty."

"Or brackish," I added.

"Brack-what?" Charlotte crinkled her nose.

"Brackish," Cole said. "It describes water in estuaries and lakes that has more salinity than fresh water, but not as much as the seawater that surrounds us."

"It has elements of both," I said.

"Brackish money," Cole said, as if testing a new concept. "The world is full of it. Sergio Flores likely has many Richard Bannons. He wouldn't risk funneling all his money through one channel, nor can one channel handle all his cash."

Charlotte swiped a strand of hair away from her face and leaned in on the table. She returned to her earlier question. "But even if we find a store with cases of wine going in and little going out, how do you prove there's money in the boxes?"

"Want to take that one?" Cole said to me.

"I'm working on it."

"What stores do you even start with?" she said to me.

"Working on that, too."

"Suggestion?" Charlotte said as she pulled the paper across the table. She flipped through the pages, considered each one, made several marks with a pen, and handed it back to Cole.

"The ones I just marked, with an 'x' by them? They get a white poinsettia and a four-day stay at the Ritz Carlton in Miami—Key Biscayne, I think." She'd been staring at the list and now she glanced at Cole. "Plus, they fit the other criteria you mentioned. They are independent and all opened within the past two years."

"How do you know this?" I asked.

"Lindsay, the woman who hired me? She said Bannon

wanted to give them a little something extra. White instead of red, and four days in paradise."

She turned the list around so that it was easier for me to see. "They were on a separate list of hotel reservations. I couldn't get a copy of it, but I noticed the names and made an acronym."

I looked at the names, but couldn't see how she remembered them.

"Watch," Charlotte said as she observed my perplexity. She underlined the leading letter of each of the stores' locations.

Cole took a stab. "Venice feels . . . no. Very few monsters kill . . ."

"Silly," Charlotte said. "Very Few Men Keep Many Damn Talented Women Around. When I saw the Ritz list, that's what I came up with."

I looked at the marks she'd made on the pages: Venice. Fort Myers. Key Largo. Miami Dade—as there were multiple Miami locations—Tallahassee West and Apokoa.

"The owners of those stores all get the Ritz for four days?" I said to clarify.

"They do."

"Vive la France."

Charlotte blushed. "But that's not that many stores, is it?"

"We only need one," I said.

"Tomorrow, I can try—"

"You're done," Cole said. "Call them. Explain that the museum unexpectedly increased your hours. Offer your deepest apologies. "

"But I told—"

"You're done," I repeated Cole's word. "And the Third Reich never had a prayer."

28

The pungent odor of fresh tar permeated the truck as we pulled into the strip parking lot that housed Fort Myers Fine Wines. We picked Fort Myers as it was a newer location and we thought that might give us an advantage at bluffing the owner. Bluffing was the only ammunition we carried.

We might have missed a weekly delivery by an hour, or the next one could be just around the corner. We couldn't afford to stalk the place for weeks trying to gauge how much merchandise went out the front door versus what entered through the back. We'd have to force the action. I'd known that would be the case while discussing the situation with Cole and Charlotte, but I hadn't wanted to air it in front of them. Better they not know.

We bought a few bottles and exited without more than a "thank you" at the counter. It was a nondescript wine and liquor store, not worth the effort. The top shelf flirted with the $40 mark. A tall glass cooler dominated the rear of the store. A sign over it read, "Champagne, the only drink you can hear!"

They closed at 9:30, so we had time to kill. We headed to the River District and had dinner at Ford's Garage. We formulated our scam, but purposely avoided the details. "If we script it," Garrett said, "we'll never elicit fear, and fear is all we've got."

At 9:25, I pulled between two newly painted white lines in the deserted parking lot. The UPS store next to Fine Wines was closed, as was Annie's Flower Shoppe on the other side.

The same personality-depraved man who had been there previously slouched behind the cash register. He glanced up at us. Garrett parked himself inside the door and crossed his arms in front of him.

I approached the counter. The man's eyes darted between Garrett and me.

"Hands up," I said.

"Hey, I don't want—"

"Let me see your hands. Now."

He floated his hands up.

"Johnny, right?"

Charlotte's list had noted a name beside each address. Fort Myers Fine Wines had a Johnny.

"Yeah, that's right. But it's really Nicholas."

"That's not even close."

"My mom changed her mind after I was born. Due to JFK being shot. What's it to you?"

His tongue darted in and out of his mouth when he talked, and his hair was greased back on the sides of his head. He wore a white, crew cut T-shirt under his yellow shirt, and it was bunched in the front under his chin like it was too large. Sloppy. He should have gone with a V-neck.

"It's everything to us," I said. "We're into details, and one detail we're confused about is the amount we ship to you and the amount that ends up in the bank."

"I don't—"

"Mr. Bannon knows what the deposit is supposed to be, and it's not adding up."

Johnny glanced over at Garrett. At six-three, he filled the

doorframe. Garrett's role was to stand immobile and not to talk. Our bet was that Johnny would imagine far worse scenarios for the evening than we had in mind. For all we knew, the four-day at the Ritz was because he met certain sales quotas for West Coast Distributors.

Johnny's eyes danced back to me.

"Talk to Albert," he said. "He knows I'm straight."

Albert must have been his regular contact. Bannon had to have someone oversee the stores. An extra set of eyes to keep everyone clean.

"We thought we'd talk to you first," I said. "Mr. Bannon knows one of you is skimming."

"I'll show you my numbers. They match perfectly. Albert audits it once a month. I tell you, we're not a penny off."

"Penny?" I snorted. "Your store's off by two grand over the last two months."

"No way . . . I mean if so, it's not me."

"Are you accusing Albert?"

"It's not me," he repeated. "That's all I'm saying."

Garrett let out a low rumble, urging me to wrap it up. I took a step toward Johnny.

"I'll give you the benefit," I said. "When's your next delivery?"

"You know."

"Tell me."

"Got one tomorrow."

"What time?"

"The usual—between ten and noon."

I pretended to think about that and said. "Is Albert going to be here?"

"You tell me," he said with a bit of attitude.

"That was your last hall pass, Johnny."

"Hey, now. I didn't mean any disrespect. I just thought you might know. He never announces when he comes. But I doubt it. He's got a lot of territory to cover, and he was here just last week."

"Mr. Bannon thinks you're clean. But we might have a problem with Albert. Can you keep our little visit quiet?"

"I suppose."

"How about a little team spirit?"

"I won't mention it to anyone. You got my word."

"We'll be by tomorrow. You'll give me the deposit. Mr. Bannon knows how much it is. We'll hand deliver it to Mr. Bannon, but when Albert comes by, tell him you had to make the deposit early—doctor's appointment, whatever. Show him a fake deposit slip minus a grand. Mr. Bannon's going to call Albert in, show him the cash, tell him his stores have been coming up short, and see how he squirms."

"I don't see how—"

"Do as you're told."

"Sure, but he might think I'm in on it."

"Like we don't know that? We're running a little play on the other stores as well. We're not just picking on you. Mr. Bannon's betting that Albert won't keep straight which deposits he actually handled. He'll break."

"I'm supposed to give you the money?" Johnny asked.

"And make the deposit slip for a grand less."

"But—"

"Got a problem with that?"

His face twisted with uncertainty. "I don't really know you g—"

"Nice poinsettias." I tilted my head toward a magnificent white poinsettia plant on a display table in the middle of the store. It was surrounded by bottles of Crown Royal with glittery holiday ribbons tied on them. "Mr. Bannon sent it?"

"He did. He treats me right."

"Also a four-day stay at the Ritz in Key Biscayne, right?"

Johnny nodded as he eyed me with more trust. His hands relaxed, just a little.

"You've been there?" he said, hope rising in his voice.

"Big place. Right on the Atlantic. You'll like it. We look forward to seeing you there. Remember, not a word."

"They'll know I didn't make the deposit. They—you know—have access to the accounts."

"You don't need to worry about that. I'll be sitting in Mr. Bannon's office handing over the money. At the Ritz, Mr. Bannon will likely be thanking you, and a few others who are helping us. And don't call him. He got in a tiff with Emma—his wife. Geez, does she have expensive taste in decorating. He's in no mood for business right now."

I walked over to the display table and picked up a bottle of Crown Royal. "This any good?"

"Some guys swear by it. Take one if you want."

I placed it back on the shelf, nudging it so that it lined up perfectly with the other bottles. "See you tomorrow."

WE CHECKED INTO A MOTEL ON FT. MYERS BEACH. It was a bit of a drive, but I gravitate to water wherever I am. I ran on the beach before the sun rose, and when it did make an appearance, it laid lengthy shadows upon the sand from the condos until a menacing cloud snuffed it out. I sprinted on that last sliver of damp sand that separated Earth from sea. Waves, like rolls of gray carpet, unfolded upon the shore. Willets, also known as sandpipers, animated the beach as they darted nervously away from me, scurrying forward, never figuring out that a step to one side or the other would put them out of harm's way. Birdbrains.

I did push-ups and sit-ups until the pain needled my muscles. I took a seat on a concrete bench—in memory of somebody—and stared into the gulf as a drizzle dampened the air. It occurred to me, halfway through the run, that Johnny might have made a phone call after we left. Agitating a drug cartel probably wasn't such a hot idea. But like the sandpipers on the beach, I couldn't see the quick and easy sidestep out of harm's way.

I bet you anything that a Higher Being was gazing down upon me, shaking Her head—you know that's what causes rain—and mumbling, "Birdbrain."

We picked up the cash on the way out of town.

29

"Jake Travis to see Mr. Bannon."

Lindsay glanced up from her computer screen. "You again? Is he expecting you?"

"That depends, Lindsay. Is he sequestered behind his desk and shriveled up like a dry olive?"

"No." She puckered her face.

"Has he soiled his pants?"

"Nooo."

"Then I doubt he's expecting me."

She huffed out her breath. "Just a minute, please." She rose and headed for the office door behind her. She turned back around and shut the lid to her laptop, landing a nasty look as she did. A moment later she came back out of the office.

"He's busy."

"I'll be at Mangroves at 12:30 for lunch if he'd care to join me."

"You might have a long wait." She opened her laptop.

I took two steps toward the door and pivoted.

"By the way," I said.

She looked up. "Yes?"

"Inform Mr. Bannon that Nicholas, aka Johnny, at Fort Myers Fine Wines has reason to believe that Albert is skimming off the top."
"The who is what?"
"12:30. And Lindsay?"
"Yes?"
"I don't wait."

AT 12:29, RICHARD BANNON SCRAPED A CHAIR ACROSS from me outside Mangroves restaurant in downtown St. Petersburg. Two bland cutouts with stern faces and sunglasses took a table beside us. He brought friends. How thoughtful. Bannon leaned back in his chair. He crossed his legs and drummed his fingers.
"What is you want, Mr. Travis?"
"Why? You're not the waiter."
"I don't have time for this."
"Leave."
He uncrossed his legs and leaned in on the table. "What's your angle?"
"I want Tina Welch."
His eyes crinkled, but he recovered quickly. "She's no longer with me."
"I would have thought you would have asked why I was searching for her."
"Pretend I did."
"She's your ticket to stay alive."
He clenched his jaw. "You are a presumptive man. You have no idea what you're getting into."
"Perhaps we do have something in common. Where is she?"
"I don't know."
We were under an umbrella, and I positioned my chair just a tad to keep the sun off my head. On Beach Drive, a

policewoman in a scooter checked parking meters. A bright blue light rotated atop her scooter. A trolley crawled by and a woman inside stared out a window, her impenetrable face as blank as the Gulf of Mexico on a gray day.

After we ordered, Bannon said, "Perhaps you should tell me exactly what you think I do and why you are here. Start with how you know Albert."

"I don't," I said. An easterly breeze blew over Straub Park, carrying the smell of Tampa Bay to our table.

"Pardon?"

"I don't know Albert. But his name brought you to the table. I seek information on where I can find Ms. Welch."

"Where did you hear of Albert?"

"Johnny, down in Fort Myers. But don't be upset with him. He's an honest dirty businessman."

"How do you know—"

"Tina Welch. Where is she?"

"Clean your ears. I've answered that. She was a part-time assistant, and now she's full-time gone. Why do you want her?"

"I think she participated in the murder of two people last week. I also suspect she was part of a hit and run that resulted in a death north of here."

Bannon took a moment. "What a . . . violent imagination you have. If I see her again, I'll make sure to call the police."

"Did Flores send her to you?"

He tented his hands in front of him. "Who?"

"Sergio Flores. The man you launder money for."

He flipped his hand in the air. "I'm terribly sorry that I can't help you. In fact, I really haven't a clue what or who you are referring to."

"Does Emma know?"

"Beg your pardon?"

"Does Emma know how you make your money?"

Bannon sat back in his chair. His face was like a wedge, wide at his ears and narrow at his mouth and nose.

"I'd advise you to proceed very cautiously. My associates"—he tilted his head to the bland boys a table over—"may have to intercede during our conversation."

I leaned across the table. "Ricky, you blew a layup. You should have said that importing wine is an honorable and ageless profession. And that, yes, Emma knows how I make my millions."

"I'm afraid you think you're amusing while you're merely annoying."

"There's no need to hurt my feelings."

Our lunches came, and Bannon chomped into his grilled fish sandwich. A busker who had been setting up shop a block away started playing a clarinet. A delivery truck drowned out his opening bars, but when it passed, there was music in the air.

I swallowed a chunk of my cheeseburger. "I have a deal for you. You give me Welch, and Flores will never know you and I met this day."

"I told you, I—"

"If you choose not to deal, then this goes to Flores." I pulled a manila folder out of a scuffed leather satchel that had belonged to my father. I placed it on the table, careful not to get it too close to the coaster under his sweating iced tea.

"Save the theatrics," he said. "I don't know the man."

"Then this will be meaningless to him." I reached over and dragged the folder back to my side of the table.

Bannon's eyes swept the patio, buying time, as if looking for someone or something to latch onto. They settled back on me. He flicked his index finger toward him a few times. I slid the folder back across the table, but only half way. I wanted him to reach for it. He did. He opened it, started to look at it, and reached into his shirt pocket and took out a pair of reading glasses. He placed them on and studied the papers in the folder. This first one was a list of all the distributors that earned a trip to the Ritz Carlton. We assumed those were the ones he laundered money through. He went to the second page. It was a photo of Ft. Myers Fine Wines.

"And this?" He held up a bulging envelope that had been in the folder.

"That is the cash deposit from Fine Wines. It didn't hit your account through normal channels, as I'm sure you already know, or will easily verify. Through the kindness and generosity of my heart, I'm presenting it to you in person."

He dropped the envelope on the table and bobbed his head a few times.

"You think you have outflanked me, but you only baffle me. What is it you wish to accomplish by showing me that you can rip off a wine store that I—and numerous others, I remind you—conduct business with?"

"I'll overnight this to Flores. In it will be a note that Albert, your on-the-road bean counter, and you are ripping him off." I dipped my head at the folder. "Those stores will be investigated. We'll be thorough, trace the money, and focus on what's admissible in court. Here's the best part: None of that will matter to you."

"And why is that?"

"Sergio Flores will call you in. Listen to your side of the story. Assure you that everything is copacetic. Ask about Emma. Tell you what a great job you're doing. Do you need me to go on?"

"You're government, aren't you?" he said with disgust. "You think you can use me to smoke out Sergio Flores? Think he's in the white pages?"

"I have my channels."

"Cut the shit. You're DEA. And what? Looking for a slice yourself? You guys are no better than—"

"Than who? It's your call."

"How much to make you go away?"

"Tina Welch."

"I told—"

"Tina Welch," I repeated, although I was starting to believe the guy.

"I cannot *pos*sibly make it simpler for you," he said with irritation rising in his voice. "I do *not* know where she is. I have no way of contacting her. She's one of Flores's lieutenants. I was told she was in town and to accommodate her for a few days."

"Call. Inquire where she is."

"Why would I do that?"

"Make up a reason."

"Right. Like—"

I reached across the table and grabbed his wrist. One of his two men stood. "You've got twenty-four hours. Or my package goes to Flores. What's your life expectancy after he receives my present?"

I placed the envelope stuffed with cash inside the folder. Welch was my best road to the missing children. If Bannon was telling the truth, then I had nothing.

Bannon put his hand on mine. "Wait," he said.

"Yes?"

"Are you DEA?" he asked.

"No."

"But government?"

"Yes."

"I need ears that I can negotiate with," he said, his hand still on mine. "Strike a deal."

"Go on."

"What if I want out? Can you arrange that?"

Was *he* bluffing?

"No," I admitted. "But I can bring those people to the table."

"Do that." He withdrew his hand. "Then we talk. You get Welch. And Flores."

A Beautiful Voice

"What happened to wax in my ears? You said you didn't know where——"

"At the museum, you mentioned something about missing children."

"What about them?"

"I might be able to help you there, but you take care of me first." Bannon stood. I rose to meet him. He stepped into me. "And if you send your pathetic little blackmail packet to Sergio Flores, we'll never talk again. My immunity gives you Flores, Welch and the children."

"You're bluffing. You don't . . ."

He took the folder with the cash and swaggered away, leaving me to wonder how he'd managed to so quickly turn the tables on me. He left me no choice other than to play along.

When I was in junior high, my buds and I had a saying: You think you're hot shit on a tin roof, but you're nothing but cold puke on a paper plate. We thought that was pretty good middle-class smack, although, admittedly, it made no sense. But deep thinking wasn't on the agenda. I hadn't thought of it in years, but it came back to me and it made perfectly good sense.

30

The rising sun bathed palm fronds in celestial glory. As it rose, its astral light sank down the trunks, illuminating the world from the top to the bottom, until it sparkled the azure surface of the swimming pool, still wrinkled with the effects of my swim.

I'd sprinted barefoot on the beach and then had done thirty minutes of laps in the hotel pool, which I use as a country club. Now, slumped in the hot tub, I owned the resort. Not a soul had yet to wander out of the Pink Palace that was constructed during the roaring twenties. Music flipped on and lingered thinly through the crisp air. I sank a little deeper into the tub, feeling sorry for the other seven billion people in the world. On the far side of the southern pool, Jaffe and Fahron tucked towels into lounge chairs. A man dropped to his hands and knees and took a brush around the edge of the pool. Sometimes I wished I had a job cleaning the pool, or tucking towels into chairs. Something that, when I was finished, I could stand back and admire. Something simple, basic, and good.

My phone rang. Janssen. I'd informed him that Bannon was looking for a deal, although I'd honored my commitment to keep the identity of the children to myself. He'd said he'd get back to me. I dried my hands off with a towel on the paver bricks.

"You haven't made a move on Flores yet have you?" I said.

It had occurred to me that if Janssen had another snitch who could put the screws into Flores, he may have acted by now. If so, Bannon would be seriously devalued.

"We're still ironing out the details. It's not what we have that counts. It's what will hold up in court."

"I'm sure that's how the cartels run their operations."

He grunted in rare approval. "We're still interested in Bannon. I'm sending someone down. She'll fill you in. She's intimate with the situation."

"When?"

"Today."

"When today?"

"I told her she'd find you at that hotel bar. Late afternoon."

"Can she negotiate a deal for Bannon?"

"She'll fill you in," Janssen said.

"You said that."

"Then why don't you listen?"

The line went dead.

I climbed out of the hot tub and changed in the locker room. I picked up a coffee, two newspapers, and fired-up my eight cylinder chariot to cover the half-mile to Seabreeze.

The papers weren't worth the meager effort, as I increasingly struggled with the daily news. My interest in current affairs had been deteriorating—like when you try to read late at night and your mind can no longer hold the page. It took a concentrated effort to get past the headlines. The world was becoming an old movie that I'd seen numerous times. A tired script I knew word for word. Only the actors changed, and they seemed oblivious to the superficiality of their roles.

Carol yakked about her kids' classes at school. She didn't

need a paper or a phone app to tell her about her world. I sopped up peppered egg yolk with the corner of a piece of buttered toast and wondered if Bannon was yanking my chain about the children. I decided he was. I pondered Sean Wright's death. Had he suspected his life was in danger? I should talk to people who knew him. Maybe they could shed some light on Tina Welch. Maybe Wright had been threatened before and didn't listen. Maybe he shared that threat with someone. I don't like the word *maybe*—it is a sheepish word and reeks of indecision. Yet it had become the nucleus of my universe.

"Wudja whistling?" Carol said, giving me a refill.

"Nothing."

Sandra, squeezing behind her, said, "Sounds like—oh—what it is? That 'Theme from *Love Story*,' that's it."

"The movie?" Carol asked.

"Mm-hm."

"I never saw it," Carol said. And then to me, "Was that what you were whistling?"

"No."

"Pretty sure it was," Sandra said. "Hard to forget them cryin' violins. Wasn't there some words to it—that guy in those awful Christmas sweaters sang?"

"I don't—"

"Andy Williams. 'Member him? That was some syrupy shit. But that's life."

"Dead or alive?" Carol said.

"Got me," Sandra said and hustled off to a table.

My two hours at the thrift store were quiet, as we hadn't gotten much in during the previous days. Afterwards, I gave *Impulse* a light wax. Garrett dropped by and asked me where we stood. I told him I'd likely gotten into a double bluff and was working my way out of it. He said it looked as if I was working on my boat. He picked up the equipment he kept at Morgan's and went kitesurfing. After I finished, I pedaled my bike over to the *Lauren Rowe*. She floated like a forlorn house waiting for a family to notice her. I piddled around and left, but not before it struck me that Kathleen's enthrallment with the boat and fervent leap into cruising the open waters was likely born of disenchantment. What she was searching for, I wasn't sure. I doubted she was, either.

The hotel purred in low gear when I returned in the late afternoon. Half the lounge chairs surrounding the two pools were deserted. A dozen or so beach umbrellas staked the sand, tilted west to be more effective against the sun that hung low in the southern sky like a sullen lead balloon. If you wanted to be shaded by an umbrella, your chair might be ten feet behind it.

Eddie presented me with a beer, but it didn't taste good. I asked him for an iced tea. My eyes scanned the resort. Nothing. Maybe my contact thought I'd be in the lobby bar. I fidgeted with my phone.

"This seat open?" a woman said from behind me. I recognized her voice and turned around to face her.

Tina Welch must have had serious heels on, for she towered over me like a stately sunflower bemused by the ruffled dandelion below.

31

Welch dragged back a high barstool and positioned it next to me. I sat up straighter. She wasn't a total shock. The night on Bannon's boat, she had recited a list of intelligence courses I'd taken. That wasn't easy information to obtain. I thought it suspicious at the time, but chalked it up to commendable research. Now I chalked it up to being in the same business—or close enough.

But if that were the case, questions multiplied faster than the answers.

She wore dark chocolate leather pants that nuzzled her like a wet suit. The sleeves of her white shirt were partially rolled up. Her hair was again banded behind with the same black hair clip she had on at the museum—the one with a silver spider etched on it. She cut a striking, but unapproachable figure. The honeysuckle perfume she'd worn at the museum wasn't there. Nothing was.

"Hey, bugs, good to see you," I said, trying to sound nonchalant and tanking miserably. "Janssen sent you?"

"Never heard of him. I was just told to show up today. Can I get something to drink?" she said to Eddie as he whisked by her.

"Be right with you," Eddie said. He finished cashing out a bill, circled back, and took her order.

"You DEA?" I said while scrambling past events to make them compliant with the new order.

"Close enough."

"You killed Sean Wright," I said. Might as well let the hammer drop.

She bit on her lower lip and then pursed her lips together. "My, my, my. Aren't you an active child? I might have underestimated you. For the record, it was an accident. Now what, deputy-dawg, you going to cuff my wrist?"

"Drop the attitude."

"Look who's talking."

Her rum Manhattan arrived. She brought it to her lips, closed her eyes, and took a sip. "Sean Wright"—she opened her eyes—"was a piece of shit crooked cop. We think he was involved in multiple murders as well as plugging an innocent kid."

"Did the world a favor, right?"

"Bet your ass."

I pictured Mrs. Wright, watering her white gardenias.

"The innocent kid—that was the pizza store?" I said.

"You know?"

"Only that."

"The pizza store was moving drugs," Welch said. "We recruited a scrappy young guy named Tony Colaprico. Low risk job passing on a little information. Help the kid get a little self-esteem. That sort of thing. Never meant to put him in harm's way. Never would have dreamed of doing it if we knew some psych case like Wright was around the corner."

"Wright killed him?"

"Blasted his face off."

"Was Wright told to?"

"Nope. Just didn't like his attitude."

"Not even suspicious that Colaprico was informing?" I asked.

"Not that we know, and if so, certainly not to that degree. Tony had an edge. Wright was a cesspool with a badge. They collided."

She took a hard swallow of her drink. Her eyes were blank and her face expressionless. I took a chance, for I'd seen that face before—in a mirror.

"You recruited the kid," I said.

She pointed her finger at me like a gun.

"Wright was on the cartel's payroll," she said. "They took out eight people in Ohio without an arrest. We think Wright was part of that. They sent me in to quarterback a scam to get Wright, but there was a leak. We think it was the law firm that represented the cops. Bottom line? I put the kid up to it, and that's on me."

"That justifies murder."

"Want to open your book, Slim? See what tumbles out?"

"You showed your cards. Don't you risk the cartel discovering that you were behind it?"

"Sean Wright left their radar miles ago."

"You recruited Kenny Strawser to tailgate Wright. Put a death on the man's conscience for the rest of his life."

She let out a raspy sigh, which under a different set of circumstances might have come across as seductive, but now sounded more like a mythical Amazon warrior gearing up for battle.

"You talked to big man Kenny?" she said.

"We chatted."

"You're a pesky little number. Here's my statement: I haven't a clue about the specific incident to which you are referring. I do know that the cartel has a trademark on the method that killed Wright. Pulled it off numerous times. It's a textbook play on how to kill without murder. You didn't stir up any cop interest in compiling your theory, did you?"

"What if I did?"

"You don't know what you're getting into."

"I get that line a lot."

"Ever wonder why? Who else did you squeeze?"

"No one," I said.

"I don't believe you."

"You shouldn't."

She took another drink and stole a glance around the bar, her eyes settling on the gulf. No way would I spill about Lee Ann and how the sheriff, her father, had shielded her from the mess. Tina Welch was not someone to confide in. Besides, I'd given Sheriff Sam Bashinsky my word. Nor was I going to weep over Sean Wright. He got what he deserved. I wasn't so sure that was the case with Kenny Strawser. But when you're the low rung on the ladder, everyone steps on you.

I reached for the beer, but changed my hand in midflight and hit the iced tea instead. "Tell me about you and Bannon," I said, getting around to the business that brought us together.

"He thinks I work for Flores," Welch said. "I *do* work for Flores. Been undercover for over a year. He dispatched me to help Bannon."

"You've met Flores?"

"Are you dreaming? Only Flores's friends get close to him, and his friends are dying. Rome is burning. A man named Davido sent me. Davido is Flores's top moneyman. My job with Bannon was to make sure his numbers were right."

"How tight is Bannon with Flores?"

"No one is tight with Flores. Flores lets Davido run the ranch. He's got a lot of cowhands like Bannon. Bannon's dispensable. He's likely made contingency plans."

"Any plan in particular?"

She took another sip of her Manhattan and crossed her legs. A silver ankle bracelet draped over the upper portion of her sandal.

"Not that I know, but you can bet he's been preparing for

this day. Bannon set up several shell corporations and has assets squirreled away. His only concern is whether he can disengage from Flores without retribution."

"Can he?"

She raised her stenciled eyebrow. "After he testifies for us? I could care less."

"His take on it?"

"He knows the risks."

"I confronted him the other day."

"Who?"

"Richard the Lion Hearted," I said.

"Why don't you do us all a favor and go sit in a corner?"

"And what? Watch you screw up the gig by killing people so there's no one else left to talk to?"

"I know what I'm doing," she said in a defensive tone that belied her cockiness.

"It's not what you're doing," I said. "It's who you are."

"Oh, please. I can hardly wait."

"A vindictive Lone Ranger in high heels."

She rolled her tongue over her upper lip and nodded her head in silent approval of my assessment of her. She gave me the same mirthless smile she'd given me at the museum—the one I'd be terrified to wake up in bed next to. I had no proof that Tina Welch was a DEA agent. For all I knew, she was there to milk my mind and then put a bullet in my heart. That might be on the game board even if she was who she claimed.

I told her that.

"If that was my agenda, it would be over by now," she said. "What did you and Richard the Lion Hearted talk about yesterday?"

"I asked him where I could find you."

"How did that go?"

"He said he had no idea where you scuttled off to. How did you get the intel that he has contingency plans? He wouldn't spill that to a Flores operative. Pillow talk?" "Him?" She clenched her teeth. "I had my ways."

"Does Emma know about any of this?"

"Emma knows nothing of his work for Flores. Bannon fears that once she finds out, she'll file."

"That would be a stroke of luck. She could be valuable in collecting information."

"Keep her out of it," Welch said authoritatively. "She doesn't know much, and she'd be an easy target to eliminate."

"Tough luck. She's wed to the—"

"We're not involving her."

"Why? More guilt than the Lone Ranger can handle? What did you do? Engage in pillow talk with Bannon and in the process drive the stake a little deeper into the marriage? You're brewing into quite a storm. They're going to have to name you."

"I never said I screwed him—that's just a Neanderthal male assumption. What else did you and Bannon talk about?"

She had geared the conversation away from Emma and back to Bannon. I took a drink of iced tea and let a smooth piece of ice slide in my mouth. I placed the plastic cup back on the mosaic countertop. Some of the tiles were missing and it rested unevenly, but was in no danger of tipping.

"Not yet," I said. "Convince me that you work for the good guys and haven't crossed over."

"You think I got a union card?"

"Babe, you better have something."

"Don't call me babe. I just gave you Sean Wright. Check it out. The kid. The crooked law firm. And yes, I was told to report here today. I never heard of your Janssen friend, but he must have made contact with my handler. You want more? You have to beat it out of me."

"Wouldn't be the first time."

"You'd win," she said. "But not before I ripped your ear off."

"Just the girl to take home to mom."

"You want the girl next door? Go the hell next door. Your turn."

I pushed my stool back from the counter. She had been positioned a little behind me, and I didn't like that. "I got the list of wine shops where Bannon launders money. We hit one of them and I presented Bannon with the night deposit. Told him I'd express it to Flores with a note that he, Bannon, was double-dipping. He flipped on me and said he wanted to strike a deal."

"Nice. How'd you fence the list of his operations?"

"Tweety Bird gave it to me."

"We can use that," she said with a single bounce of her head.

"We?"

"Oh." She put on a pouting face. "Is someone still having commitment issues?"

"I'll pass it along through my channels."

"I'd expect nothing less."

"Alejandro Vizcarro," I said.

"What about him?"

"Tell me about him."

"Why do you care?" she asked.

"He's my pizza kid."

Her eyes searched mine with a hint of sympathy. She inhaled deeply, her breasts ballooning against her shirt. "I see—you were his handler. I wondered what brought you into the play."

I took another drink of iced tea, but nothing was there. A couple mounted a pair of stools to my left, scraping them on the paver bricks. The woman ordered a rumrunner. She politely asked that it be heavily garnished with fruit. The man ordered a beer. He had a ring on his finger the size of a doughnut, and then I thought of the doughnuts. I switched my gaze to the TV high in the corner, searching for something to erase the doughnuts from my mind. Smiling millennials swooned over cars with red bows on them. End of the year sale. Put a Toyota under your tree.

"You had no chance," Welch said in a kind voice that I didn't fall for. "We—Flores—knew his location. They had a tracking device on them the whole way."

"You were there," I said as a statement, not a question.

"Where?"

"Vizcarro's cottage." I welded my eyes to hers. "You were part of the hit team."

Welch skipped a beat, and revealed herself by her hesitation. "Sorry, Charlie. I don't know what—"

"I got an eyewitness that puts you in Wildwood when Sean Wright bought the farm. I got another that puts you in the passenger seat of a car cruising in front of the Vizcarros' house the night they were killed. Three dead bodies and three missing kids."

She nodded slowly as if simultaneously taking in what I'd just said while also plotting her next move, which, for all I knew, was slicing off my ear to teach me a lesson.

"Okay, hotshot. I'll dive deep with you. I was sent over here to do more than audit books, although I did *not* know that at the time. You ever hear of a hit man, goes by the moniker of the Conductor?"

"Pretend I haven't."

"Frenchman by the name of Rafael Cherez. High-class button man. Flores's favorite go-to man. He does some of the contract work himself, but has invented new methods of murder—he was the first to use a semi truck to ram another car. Nickname's the Conductor because he orchestrates death. Flores dialed him up for Vizcarro."

"Word on the street is that no one's ever seen him."

"Yeah?" she said. "Well, you can delete that footnote."

"How did he track them?"

"I don't know."

"Was it a device sewn into a monkey?"

"I said—"

"Why would Flores want you, an auditor, to tag along on a hit job?"

"Got me," she said. "Rafael could certainly handle two people on his own. I thought maybe my cover was blown and I was on the ticket as well. I was glad to get out of there."

I thought I knew why she was summoned to tag along, but decided to see what she knew first, or was willing to divulge.

"I can't find any connection between Vizcarro and Flores," I lied to her. "I was led to believe he ran numbers for Flores, but I can't substantiate that. I've since been told that he was a red herring."

"Alejandro Vizcarro? Can I have another one please?" She pushed her plastic cup across the counter. Eddie scooped it up, tossed it in a trashcan, and stomped off to make a fresh drink. "I picked up intel that he ran numbers. That's all I know."

"From Flores?"

"Davido."

"Right. And he was the one who told you to ride along that night?"

"He did."

"Which one did you dust?" I asked.

"Piss off. I wasn't there to pull a trigger."

"Did you?"

"No," she said emphatically. I believed her. Despite her admission about Wright, there was something vulnerable and honest about her, although she hid it well. Or maybe I just wanted her to be vulnerable and honest.

"Why *were* you there?" I said.

"I don't know. My orders were to tag along in case he needed help. We did a dry run the night before to scope the area."

That would have been the night Charlotte woke up at 3:17 and went to Cole's front porch.

A Beautiful Voice

"Rafael hit them both?" I said.

"Pop. Pop. And it was over. Rafael searched the house and yard. For what, I had no clue. We split."

"And the children?"

"Children?" Her brow grooved with puzzlement.

"Alejandro's children were there as well. Two girls and a boy."

"I see," she said, nodding her head. "Your quip at the museum. I think we would have noticed three kids." Her hand stroked her drink, and I sensed that she was replaying that evening in her mind.

"Did you help in the search?" I asked.

"Don't try to trap me. I just told you I had no idea what he was looking for. It never occurred to me that he was looking for some *one*. You saw them? You know they exist?"

"I brought them ashore. Took them food."

I also took them flowers, coloring books, doughnuts, and fresh fruit, but what would have been the point of tacking that on?

"Rafael was sent to assassinate the parents and abduct the children," I continued. "That's why you were along, and that's why they wanted a woman. Auditing the books was a cover. You were to be the babysitter. Flores's team manipulated you from the beginning."

She repositioned herself on the stool. "Why would Sergio Flores care about some kids?"

"Just conjecture."

"You're holding back."

"I wish I were."

"I doubled down for you."

"I'm wrung out here."

I'd decided not to tell her that Little Joe was Sergio Flores's son. I had no reason other than I felt more comfortable withholding the information than I did sharing it.

She shook her head in disbelief. "Did Alejandro ever run numbers for the cartel?"

"Not as far as I can tell. He was a bookkeeper. An antiquarian."

"What a shit show. Flores baited me—the government, so that we would—what, smuggle some family into the States? None of it makes sense."

"Cue the clowns."

"One of the kids his?"

"Don't know," I rushed out, maybe a little too fast. "Can you broker a deal with Bannon?" I wanted to adjust the spotlight away from Vizcarro and onto the purpose of our meeting.

"I'll think about it."

"Isn't it your responsibility?"

"I told you I'd think about it."

She took a drink and leaned in on the counter with her elbows. "Assuming this cockeyed theory is correct—that Flores wanted the children, and my role was to be Maria von Trapp, do you know where I was supposed to stash the kids?"

"No."

She gave me a puzzled look. "You didn't know you would have three kids, did you?" She didn't wait for an answer. "Man-oh-man, three little amigos. Where'd they float off to—a competitor snatched them? Blackmail? Tough territory, but it comes with the job. You're going to have to let go of that."

"Just like you did with Tony Colaprico?"

"Screw you, okay?" Welch looked away, but not before I saw a twinkling of moisture in her eyes. I decided I was right about her.

I had no firm reason to believe that, but if I had to justify all my beliefs, precious few would survive.

32

RAFAEL

The masseuse pulled the soft sheet off Rafael's shoulders and folded it neatly across his lower back. The bed radiated heat under his chest, and the pleasant, plucking chords of spa music reminded him of a Japanese garden. He buried his head in the pillowed headrest as she stroked her oiled hands down his side and deep into his lower back, pulling out at the last moment.

The woman.

He'd been instructed to watch her carefully. She was to have taken the children for a few days until Flores decided what to do with two of the three—Rafael had balked at killing them. One must have standards. Then he would eliminate her. But there were no children. He'd decided not to pull the trigger on her that night, as perhaps he might be instructed to work with the woman again if the children were found. And they would be. Meanwhile, the woman was out there. She'd seen him. Smelled him. She could identify him, and that was not acceptable.

Something else bothered him. She was too assured. Too calm for someone who was supposedly a bean counter. A stand-in nanny. Almost as if she faked being afraid in an attempt to hide her professionalism. Was she in the same business as he? Was she that good?

"Maybe she is," he said.

"I'm sorry?" the masseuse said.

"Nothing," he muttered into the headrest. "Press harder. *Feel* me."

The masseuse dug her hands into the muscles of his upper back, the oil allowing her fingers to knead between ligaments, bones and muscle. She ran both of her hands down the long sides of his torso. He felt the tension leave like an evil spirit being banished from his body.

Rafael opened his eyes and stared at the tile floor beneath him. The masseuse was barefoot. He closed them. He'd gone to the house. Did his job. They told him to "hang around" because that is how they talked.

Hang around.

"Roll over, please."

Rafael rolled over, and she placed a warm damp cloth over his eyes. She maneuvered behind him, buried her hands between the sheet and his shoulders, and then pulled them up to his neck and into the base of his skull. She repeated the motion, and Rafael felt his mind ease a bit more. His thoughts emptied, except for one. The one that drove the others, that had seized his mind since he burst into the cottage. The *chalet.*

Where were the *enfants?*

His instructions had been clear. Deliver the boy and then—

"Relax," she said.

"Pardon?"

"You just tensed up. Relax. This is not the place to think about your job."

Rafael let his breath escape him. *Non. What a perfect place to contemplate my job.*

His phone rang.

He bolted upright and stood. The sheet dropped from his

naked body. He snatched his phone from the pocket of the terry cloth robe he'd worn into the room.

"*Oui?*"

"Sir," the masseuse stood back, startled by his nakedness. "We don't encourage guests to bring—"

"Of course," Rafael said into his phone. "Yes. I understand. Immediately."

"Sir, you need to—"

He took a step toward the woman. "I'm sorry, but I need to go."

He put his robe on and walked out the door, leaving it open behind him.

33

On Christmas day, Kathleen, Garrett, Morgan and I were at the refugee house at six a.m. By nine, the sunlit grounds were packed with old cars and young children. The children ran wild, infusing nature with their unbridled glee. I think Mac, the man I'd befriended and who had bequeathed this property, would approve of our efforts—of the little feet who left the doors open, tracked sand inside, and who knew nothing of the man and his land.

Kathleen handed out a sleigh load of presents she'd bought from a list Morgan had provided. She had paid for them herself, refusing to dip into the foundation or accept anything from me. She immersed herself in the children. Garrett and I slaved in the kitchen. I cooked. Garrett scrubbed. We had no time to think. It was a good day. A simple and basic day.

When everyone had finally cleared out, when the last of the old cars had disappeared into the night and the day had exhausted us, I built a fire by the pond. A Puerto Rican family, devastated by the hurricane that had ravaged their island, joined us in a circle of chairs surrounding the fire. Hector and Valeria Casiano, and their four children, were staying in the house a few days until other arrangements could be made. The children sat on the ground with their palms out to the flames and their stockings on the ground in front of them. The night crept in, cooling our backs as the fire warmed our fronts.

The conversation withered. The bottles were no longer passed, but stood crooked on the ground. I whistled "La Virgen lava panales" to the accompaniment of crackling logs. The haunting Spanish Christmas carol had been my father's favorite. I could never discern what the song meant to me, other than it made Christmas a lovely and moving tragedy as if innocence dies with a glorious eternal note. When I finished, one of the children turned to me, the glow of fire soft on her unspoiled face.

"That was pretty," she said.

I glanced over at Garrett. He poured some of his water onto the ground. I did the same with my wine. We nodded our heads at each other and I felt empty and riddled, and the feeling fit me. It fit me just fine.

BEFORE I WALKED THE GANGPLANK WITH WELCH, I wanted more information on her. From someone I trusted. A pair of fresh eyes.

I contacted Natalie Binelli, an FBI agent I'd worked with in the past. I unloaded the story on her, but kept out what I didn't want others to hear—neither of us trusted phones. She called back two days later and said she'd be passing through. We planned to meet at the Caribbean Grille, a restaurant on the island across from mine.

I went by boat, and the bay was middle-of-the-week quiet. The crisp air made the sky higher and made you believe that space really was blue. A flock of roseate spoonbills beat their wings toward the gulf, the sun flaming their pink feathers like match heads.

I idled up to a dock, cut the engines, and drifted in. The forward momentum of the boat yielded to the water and I looped a line around the aft cleat. I trudged up to the restaurant and informed the hostess what shaded table I wanted and that I'd also like an iced tea and a beer. She said that my waitress would be right over. I told her to make sure she arrived with an iced tea and a beer. Although my comment was meant to be lighthearted, it came out with unintentional harshness.

In the adjoining marina, motionless boats rested in lifts and larger ones floated on stagnant water. Each one biding its time until the owners managed to free a few hours of one life to live another. We work today and dream of tomorrow. Tomorrow, we will do the same.

Binelli spotted me and made her way around the indoor-outdoor bar to my table. Her arms swung at her sides and her stride was longer than I remembered it. I stood as she approached. We'd not seen each other in two years.

"Jake," she said, stopping a few feet from me. She rarely used my first name.

"Natalie," I responded. That was also new for me. I usually addressed her by her last name.

She stuck out her hand the same moment I did and our hands clamped together. The first time I'd met her, we'd ended up kissing, although it was part of a desperate attempt to wrestle a gun away from her. I wondered if she remembered the moment like I remembered the moment, and if that didn't sum up all one needed to know about boys and girls, or girls and girls, or boy and boys, or whatever. Life is a temporary, emotional tug that creates a permanent feeling.

She wore a charcoal skirt with a matching jacket and a white blouse. A thin gold chain draped across the front of her neck. Her hair was short. I wanted to ask her if she'd just gotten it cut, but that question was stillborn.

"You look nice," I said, snapping out of my thoughts. Her skin was the color of a suntan that never faded.

A Beautiful Voice

"Thank you. You look . . . you." Our hands disengaged and mine felt clammy. "Meaning?"

"Content," she said.

"It's hard work living an easy life."

"Someone needs to show the way. It's warmer here than I thought." She took off her jacket and draped it over the back of the chair.

"Better lose the shoes as well. They don't serve anyone here in high heels."

"*Really?*"

"Pretty sure there's a sign at the door."

She curled up the corner of her lip, sat down, and kicked off her shoes. I'd given her the view facing the boats. She leaned back as her eyes glazed over the marina.

"What do you got?" I said after a waitress with weight-room arms took our order.

"What did you leave out when we talked?" she shot back.

I told her everything from my original orders—and what I'd been led to believe—to what I now knew, or highly suspected: That Alejandro Vizcarro was a simple bookkeeper. His oldest daughter had a relationship with Sergio Flores that produced a son, and I was uncertain whether Flores or the government had arranged for the Vizcarros to be handed off to Morgan and me in the middle of the night. I told her about Welch, but left Sean Wright and Lee Ann out. I didn't see a way to involve Wright without bringing in Lee Ann and reneging on my commitment to Sheriff Sam.

"What can you add about Flores?" I said.

She swiped away a strand of hair that an unexpected breeze had stirred to life. Her skin was a little tighter and her face paler, as if she were becoming a stranger to fresh air.

"He knows we're hot on his trail." Her contralto voice was kryptonite to my soul. "He's been trying to buy people, but that gig doesn't work like it used to. Oddly, his kingdom is vanishing whether he's incarcerated or not."

"Opioids?"

She nodded. "Are you familiar with Fentanyl?"

"Tell me."

"It's Satan on Earth. Fifty times more powerful than heroin. It's also the great equalizer. It's made a democracy of the drug trade because it's synthetically produced. You don't need a poppy field in Mexico to produce it. It can be mixed with cocaine, heroin, and even marijuana. A good joint can now destroy a life."

"And Oxycodone?"

"Pushed by crooked doctors and greedy pharmacies. Best yet? Medicaid subsidizes it."

"Flores can't beat government bureaucracy," I said.

"No one does. Cost of entry is too low and there's no moat." She leaned in, and the smooth underside of her forearms dented on the table. "Listen, the cartels will do whatever is necessary to protect and expand their business. But this has them panicked. You can buy Fentanyl on the dark web or you can make it yourself. Score a little pot, mix it, and you've got a business with blow-your-ass-off margins and addicted customers. And Oxycodone? Every two-bit hoodlum wants a piece of it. They're multiplying like ants."

"Ants?"

"Rabbits. Whatever."

"No one's corralling the bad docs and pharmacies?" I said.

"State medical boards. But they're woefully unprepared for war."

"And the guys at the top?"

"We try to get them on money laundering. Tax evasion. It is still the easiest way to shut them down."

"You're not working this, are you?"

She shook her head. "A friend briefed me after you called. He's an assistant special agent in charge of northern Florida."

"What can you tell me about Bannon?"

She leaned back. "Richard Bannon is a small time laundry man for the Flores operation. We were already circling him, but apparently you've moved in as well."

"I was—"

"And gathered more information than we had. The poinsettia list you mailed me?"

I had sent her an encrypted email with the list of wine stores that I believed Bannon was using to launder money through.

"What about it?"

"Bannon—in the process of cutting a deal with us—had provided his own list."

"He's cutting a deal with you?" I said, wanting to make sure I heard her right. "He told me he wanted me to bring him someone he could work with. That's how I ran into Welch."

"We'll get to that. Your poinsettia list?"

"Lemme guess," I said. "My list is bigger than the list he gave you."

She curled up the right corner of her lip. "When he got caught with his pants down, he became cuddly-friendly."

"Who led you to him?"

"You know who."

"Welch?"

She nodded.

"How long ago?"

"Couple weeks?"

I punched out my breath. "That leggy little liar. I just met with her—she told me she'd think about it. If Bannon was already working a deal, why try to cut a deal with me?"

"Bannon's smart. He's shopping for the best package."

"They do that?"

"You got to get out more often."

I was going to protest that Bannon had insisted he was clueless as to how to contact Welch, but realized he had to play it that way in order to try and bring other dealmakers to the table—that's why he had asked me if I was DEA. It didn't work, though, as Welch had gotten the call. Both Bannon and Welch had lied to me concerning their dealings with each other. I hadn't realized I was so gullible.

"Why didn't Welch come clean with me?" I aired my thoughts, although I doubted Binelli would have an answer.

"Who knows? People like her are different. While it's a prerequisite for the job, she—water cooler talk—has always been a loose cannon."

I mulled over whether Janssen was privy to this. Probably not. This wasn't his home turf. He likely passed on my request to meet someone who could bargain with Bannon, and didn't give it a second thought.

"So Bannon's working everyone he meets," I said. "Has he given us enough to put Flores away?"

"Maybe too much."

"How so?"

"Last night, Mr. Richard Bannon took a bullet to the head."

"Play that again?" I said.

She raised her eyebrows. "If you heard that Richard Bannon has left the building, your hearing's fine."

"Did he do a Richard Cory or did he have help?"

"He had help."

"Terrific." I leaned back in my chair and the sun caught the back of my head. "His wife? Emma?"

"Not home at the time." Binelli gazed out over the motionless boats. "Is this marina always so dead?"

"No tears for Bannon? You just lost a key witness."

Her eyes darted back to me. "Not my case. Besides, these guys are gangsters even if they dress like you and me. Their closing act is always the same. They want to plea bargain and dry clean their name. Play golf without fingers pointing at them on the tee box and hushed tones trailing them down the fairway. Have their kid's friends not afraid to get within six feet of them. Have people attend their funeral who are not fearful of being photographed. We're the ticket out, but all we do is integrate slime back into society, verifying to a new generation of shitholes that there's always an escape clause."

"D.C. must be a tough place."

She flipped open her hands. "If you believe in turning the other cheek, you don't belong in law enforcement."

I asked her a few questions about the homicide. Due to the similarity of the execution style murders, they believed that it was the same hit man who had taken out the Vizcarros. She was familiar with Rafael Cherez, but had nothing to add concerning his involvement.

"Someone dark lurks in paradise," Binelli said.

"Perhaps not for long," I said. "There's no one left to eliminate. Why would Flores kill one of his money men?"

"Because he sensed he was about to flip on him."

"Or a competitor got a drop on him."

"That's another theory," she said. "My source doesn't think Flores knew that Bannon was turning state's witness. This doesn't smell like that, but Bannon is—was—too small for a competitor to dick around with. Bottom line? We're clueless. Now." She crossed her legs. "Where does that leave us?"

I wasn't sure in what context the question was framed, and hurried out, "Why would Flores want his child out of Mexico?"

"To hide him from the other cartels. They kill family members. In Mexico—what was his name again?"

"Little Joe."

"LJ would have had a life expectancy of a fruit fly. Not to mention the promising scenario of a videoed painful death to serve as a lesson. In the States? His biggest concern might be getting busted someday for underage drinking in Madison."

"Maybe it didn't go wrong," I said, as yet another view surfaced. "We brought them ashore. Flores had someone grab the children, and then killed Alejandro and his oldest daughter. Bannon—"

"Why would Flores kill Martina?"

"We could guess all day. Bannon, through my poking around, gets wind of them. He mentions the missing children to Flores, and Flores kills Bannon because he doesn't want him to know about his son."

She hitched up her shirt toward her neck, although it had not slid down. "Poking around?"

"I mentioned the children to Bannon."

"When was this?"

"I dropped a comment at a museum when I first met him. I had no basis for my remark, but he didn't know that. He passes it up the chain and Flores doesn't take a chance. Bannon is eliminated."

"So you got loose lips." She shrugged. "Fine with me. I made it clear what I think of criminals." She rolled her tongue inside her cheek. "You're over-thinking. It's something much simpler. It always is."

"There's another actor," I said.

"Who?"

I gave her the background on Cole.

"Seems to me he's a person of interest," she said.

"Beyond what his girlfriend saw, he claims to have no knowledge," I said. But as the words came out, I saw an open road I'd yet to explore.

"We might never know," she said. "But I do know one thing."

She stopped, obligating me to come in. "What?"

"I could get used to lunching in bare feet." She took a sip of water.

"Move south. Let your hair down."

"It is down."

"Put it up."

She hesitated and then charged back into business. That had always been the case with us.

"Did Welch say that Rafael popped them?" she asked.

"She did."

"Think she lied?"

"Don't know."

"Listen, Jake, I would disregard everything Welch told you. If I were she, I would have said whatever I needed to keep myself in the clear. Her mantra is to survive the day." She checked her watch. "I gotta go. Listen, double-check your blind side."

We both stood. I took a step around to her side of the table.

"You're out of leads, aren't you?" she said. "That's a side effect of when the bodies start piling up."

"Appears that way."

"You'll figure it out. How's Kathleen?"

That was only the second time Binelli had mentioned Kathleen by name. Previously, she had always been "your woman."

"We're engaged."

Her face blanked with a flash of shock. "You?"

"Jake the Great."

"Congratulations," she said with a grin that initially seemed to take some effort, but then blossomed with sincerity. "When's the tragic day?"

"Not set yet."

"Going to do kids? Get a dog? Buy a van?"

"Cat's enough."

She paused and then said, "I'm happy for you."

"I'm scared for me."

"No, you're not." A silent and lonely moment ticked by. "Well, I'll be seeing you."

"Take care," I said.

Is that all you got?

"You too."

That was hardly a winner, either.

She spun, took two steps, and turned back around.

"It would be good to have some shoes," she said with a sheepish grin.

She bent over to put her shoes on. As she did, a gap opened between two buttons on her blouse, revealing the shadowed skin of her stomach. She stumbled getting the last shoe on, and took an unexpected lurch forward. When she popped up, our bodies were less than a foot apart.

"Married, huh?" Her tongue nervously worked the lower right side of her lip.

I didn't know what to say and she didn't wait. She walked away. Women are much stronger than men in that regard.

As she started to round the corner to the parking lot, where the building would block my view, she turned, paused, and looked at me looking at her. Then she was gone. She might have smiled before her final turn, but all I could think was that I'd never told her I liked her voice. Should we say those things? Or are they best left buried for fear that if uncovered, they would lead to something else—her curves, her edges, her face starting to show the strain of life and her skin hiding behind a gap in two buttons.

I reclaimed my seat and stared at the beer. I hadn't touched it. I picked it up and poured it on the ground where the sand, pockmarked with tufts of grass, eagerly took it in. In the army, we always poured a drink on the ground—a drink for the dead. That is what Garrett and I had done around the Christmas fire.

On the way out, I apologized to the hostess for my unintended rudeness when I'd arrived. Maybe the hostess felt better, but there are some things we never know, aren't there?

34

"There's no answer, sir."

I turned away from the dark-suited man with a crooked tie and a receding hairline sitting behind the concierge desk in the chilly lobby of Emma Bannon's condo building. Her husband hadn't been dead that long. For all I knew, she had gone off to be with her family who still resided in the area.

I took an outside table at an Italian restaurant a block off the entrance to her condo. It was close to dinnertime and the tables were starting to fill. Maybe I'd get lucky and catch her on a trip home. I'm a big believer in luck, as long as you bathe it in opportunity and realize in doing so that luck is not the random element many believe it to be.

Cars crowded bumper-to-bumper, waiting for people to cross the street and for parking spaces to become available. Unlike much of the retirement-dominated west coast of Florida, St. Petersburg boasts a youthful culture to balance the moneyed retirees. Beach Drive teemed with eye-magnet girls in high heels and pierced belly buttons peeking out of short shirts. The cannon fire of their unblemished sexuality intoxicated the air as they strutted, innocently ignorant of the fleeting magic of their carnal beauty. They ruled the sidewalks, dominating the lesser species: guys in tennis shoes, smokers, tattoos, families, couples, foursomes, convention attendees who neglected to shed nametags, and a healthy population of dogs always eager to sniff a new ass.

I called Kathleen and invited her down to the dance.

"Swell of you to think of me," she said. "But I'm booked."

"Booked?"

"I'm having dinner with a different man every night. Don't take it to heart, but I need to be absolutely certain that I can't do better."

"You know I trip over the mere thought of you," I said.

"Wowzee, that's your line?"

"Beats some blind date saying you're a camera because every time he looks at you he smiles."

"Oh, great God," she said. "That's horrible. Is that what's it's like out there?"

"How would I know?"

"How *do* you know?"

"Your chardonnay is waiting."

"It's the man I'm interested in."

"Hurry. We start dying the moment we're born."

She hung up. Another woman would have thought my parting comment to be depressing. Kathleen is not another woman.

Ten minutes later—when she wanted to, Kathleen was a pro at whipping herself together—she rounded the corner dressed down in tight jeans and a white button-down shirt. A shale-colored shawl draped over her shoulders, although you know my color selection was criminally wrong.

"I'm here," she said as a gust of wind whipped her hair, and she knew damn well what those two words meant.

I'm here.

I leapt off my chair and intercepted her three feet from the table. I wrapped my arms around her and stuck my tongue down her throat in a primitive and desperate kiss that tasted like mint toothpaste at the entrance, but was real and unwashed the deeper I went. A car honked. We'd been honked at before.

She broke off our passionate kiss. "You can do better," she rasped out.

I hovered my lips over hers. She parted her lips, and I gently blew into her open mouth as she inhaled. Someone's heart was beating in my chest, and I didn't know whether it was hers or mine or if we had fused a new one.

What if she ever tired of my fatiguing desires, my torrential emotions?

"I don't smell your whiskey," she said.

"I haven't had any."

"I miss it."

"It'll be back."

We settled into our chairs, our hands not breaking until the last moment. She dipped her head toward my whiskey on the rocks, which had become whiskey and water.

"You really haven't touched it, have you?"

"Not in the mood."

"Not in the mood this past week, I'd say."

I shrugged.

"When this is over?" she said.

Another shrug.

"I see."

I asked her how her day was. She had spent most of it with Morgan at the refugee house teaching English.

"There's something terrifyingly meaningful about it," she said.

"Terrifyingly?"

"After all the education, the dissertation, the teaching, the scholarly journals and articles—to master those, or at least to reach the outer abilities of your competence, gives you a false sense of . . . attainment. Accomplishment.

"Terrifyingly?"

"I'm serious. Teaching basic language is tremendously rewarding."

"You're not thinking of giving up the paycheck are you? 'Cause I was thinking that once we walked that aisle, I'd let Trigger out to pasture. Sit around and chew."

"Silly, you're a man of water, not dirt."

"You're right. Then me and the *Lauren Rowe* will sail—"

"I told a man how to say *bread* today," she interrupted me. "Morgan had made several loafs. The man pointed to a cloud. He managed to convey that he thought the warm bread tasted like a summer cloud. There's a lot of situations where you may need to start over in a life; after a hurricane, the pink slip, someone dear dies. Picking up a different language is also starting over. It's a new way of seeing the world. Expressing it. Touching it. I'm finding the experience more rewarding than grading papers in which students hypothesize on whether the oppressed sexuality of a writer was due to beatings administered by his father, although I suppose part of the attraction is that it is different."

"Speaking of sex, how's my friend Danielle doing?"

She rolled her eyes. "Out of my class, with an A. She is a gifted student."

"Still volunteering her services?"

"Not the ones you're dreaming of. She's helping out at an elementary school."

"Finding it as terrifyingly rewarding as you are?"

"I'll let that pass," she said. "It's so . . . wholesome. That's such a corny word, but it's the right one. I don't know."

Kathleen is not an I-don't-know type of woman. I thought she was going to say more, but she clammed up.

"Everything okay?" I asked.

"I'm fine," she said, evoking the most popular two-word lie in the English language.

First, "never mind"—when I'd caught her enchanted

with the mother and daughter ice-skating—and now "I'm fine," with an "I don't know," to boot, snuck in between. My mind flashed to Kathleen's illogical embracement of the *Lauren Rowe*. To her beguilement with teaching English as a second language. The tide was going out. To where, I did not know.

"How was your day?" she said.

I felt a smidgen of relief. She knew we were circling, and she wasn't ready to land yet. At least that's what I told myself.

I unloaded on her, thankful for the familiarity of my problems versus the undefined cauldron of hers. I yapped through the waiter taking our order and the posses of young women with rich curves who passed our table in skirts so tight they required baby steps. Two couples strode by and one of the women's eyes met mine, and I'd swear she was drowning in boredom.

After we split a dish of spaghetti, we corked the rest of the chardonnay and headed down Beach Drive. As we walked, Kathleen kept digging her fingernails into the palm of my hand as if trying to etch our lives into the moment. To mark our time with pain, for it seems to have more staying power than joy. We stopped at the ice cream store, where I ordered a hot-fudge sundae with whipped cream. I politely requested two cherries instead of one. We took a seat on a bench, and she returned to what I had explained earlier, as to why I was downtown waiting for her.

"What is you expect to learn from Emma?" she said. She took a small bite of ice cream and handed the Styrofoam cup back to me. "I'm done," she added.

"What her late husband shared with her," I said. "I think he knew something about the missing children."

"Why do you think that?"

I handed her the cup and she took another bite.

"Because I want to. Because that gossamer thread is all I have left."

"Remember," she said handing me the cup again. "She just lost her husband."

"I can be sensitive when I want."

"You may be a little delusional in that regard."

"Another bite?" I held the spoon up to her lips.

"No more," she said as I slid it in her mouth. "You going to"—she swallowed—"try her again in the morning?" She licked her lips.

"I am. If she doesn't answer, I might camp out at the same table and see if I can catch her coming or going." I handed her the cup and she took it instinctively. She shoveled a bite into her mouth. "Stop doing that. And if you don't run into her?"

"It's a question of when, not if."

I twirled the plastic spoon around the corners of the cup and extracted the last bit of ice cream. I licked the spoon clean and stared at the empty Styrofoam container.

"Holy-schmoly, girl. Get your own next time."

She hit me in the arm. It stung.

I ENDURED A FIVE MILE LOOP THROUGH DOWNTOWN THE next morning while the more intelligent citizens of the city slept. Events of the previous week pounded me with every step, but they were packed with questions and woefully short of answers. I was convinced that Flores had fabricated a story about Alejandro Vizcarro being on his payroll to get the government to smuggle his only child, Little Joe, into the country. But why would Alejandro, when approached about being smuggled into the States, acquiesce? If he suspected that Flores was behind it, wouldn't he and his daughter Martina have refused? Maybe not. After all, they had to roll the dice sometime.

Perhaps Martina was the one the feds wanted. She'd slept

with Flores. *She* was the valuable tool the government might use to construct a case against him.

"Got a cigarette?"

"Excuse me?" I said as my trance was broken by a homeless man with a department store rack of tattered clothing on him. I had stopped running and was cooling down along the waterfront.

"Cigarette?"

"Sorry, man."

"Money?"

"Just out running."

His hollow eyes got lost beyond me and he shuffled off, pushing a small grocery cart piled with blankets. The smell of his body trailed him like a reluctant and groggy shadow.

I strolled back to Kathleen's condo as the forehead of the sun appeared, sharing the sky with the moon. I rode the elevator to the ninth floor. Her neighbor, Ginny Brandenburg, stepped out of her unit as I unlocked Kathleen's door. We exchanged pleasantries and shy grins. Inside, I showered in the guest bath so as not to wake Kathleen. She'd be up within the hour, but coveted that final hour in bed. Out of the twenty-four we get each day, her favorite was the buffer-hour between deep sleep and swinging her legs over the side of the bed. That hour was sleep-heaven.

Fifteen minutes later, imparadised by my morning run, I sat outside in jeans and a short-sleeve shirt sipping a cup of coffee. The air was a few degrees above cold and my body no longer generated heat from my run. I should have brought a sweatshirt.

Emma Bannon bounced out the front door of her condo building at 8:20. She went into a corner café and emerged a few minutes later with a paper bag. She made a beeline back to her condo. I scurried after her.

"Mrs. Bannon?"

She spun around theatrically, as if I'd startled her far more than I would have thought.

"Yes?" Her forehead was creased, trying to place me.

I gave her my name and added, "We met at the museum."

She nodded "Right. The redhead quip."

"I'm sorry about your husband. I'd like to offer my condolences."

"Thank you."

She was in white capris and a floppy gray sweatshirt. A white headband held back her short black hair. She wore leather sandals, and her toenails alternated red and green. Cute. I wasn't sure what a grieving widow was supposed to look like, but Emma Bannon didn't fit any preconceived notions that I had.

"I wondered if I could buy you a coffee," I said.

"Oh, I appreciate that. But I don't have time right now."

"I'd like to ask you a few questions about your late husband."

"What about?"

"I'm not sure, Emma, that's why we need to talk."

I thought of throwing out another plea, but opted to stay silent. I'd been pushy enough.

"There's no need for you to buy. I've got some brewing upstairs."

"I'm not imposing?"

"Of course you are, Mr. Jake Travis. That's your style."

She flashed me her heart-stopping smile, spun, and trotted off toward her building. I trooped after her, wondering if Kathleen would be so receptive a few days after I took a bullet, and wishing I had a little more background material on Mrs. Emma Stratford Bannon.

35

"Can I get you something to eat?" Emma said as she breezed through her front door.

"I'm fine, thank you."

"You sure? I saw you running this morning."

"Actually, I'm starved to de—forgive my rudeness."

I recalled Kathleen's prophetic remark about being delusional regarding my sensitivity.

"Life goes on, doesn't it?" Emma said.

She had planted herself in front of me. Her question impressed me as being more than rhetorical.

"A banana would be good," I said.

"We can do so much better—can't we, you and I?"

That didn't sound rhetorical.

"I'm pretty good with eggs," I said, opting for a safe road.

"And you're talking to the queen of toast. Make yourself at home. I detest guests I need to wait upon."

I got out brown eggs and rummaged through a drawer for a skillet. I helped myself to a yellow onion and a ripe tomato sitting in a ceramic bowl. The bowl had a maroon dragon with a gold tongue wrapped around its sides. True to her word, she made toast as I constructed two omelets. She took a break to turn on music. "Never My Love" by the Association filled the house. I didn't know what audition Emma was performing for me, but it certainly wasn't the role of the distraught widow.

The condo, fifteen floors above Tampa Bay, had commanding views of the bay and Beach Drive. Inside, though, it was a bad poem. Everything rhymed and metered, but it was void of meaning and warmth. The decorations—a brass elephant lamp, hardback travel books angled on top of each other, a world atlas that appeared as if it had never been opened, a series of three candles, none of which had ever known fire—appeared to all have been professionally selected and placed. A picture of a lioness hunching in tall grass hung over a white sofa. Its shining eyes stalked me.

What made you think love will end
When you know that my whole life depends
On you
Never my love

We had breakfast on her balcony while above us the sun warmed the air and below us the city crept to life. After chitchat about the museum, I said, "I am truly sorry about your husband."

"Thank you."

"You seem to be . . . pulling it together rather well."

"Do you want that last bit of fruit?" She dipped her head toward a small bowl of fruit.

"All yours."

She snatched a few blueberries and a sliced piece of strawberry.

"Are you married, Mr. Travis?"

"Jake."

"That's not an answer. That's a name."

"*That is not a name. That is a syllable,*" Martina had said to me.

"No. I am not married," I admitted.

"Neither were Richard and I. At first, yes, but that was once upon a time. He was betrothed to his job, and more accurately, the money it produced. He also had certain habits that I did not appreciate. I was looking for a way out."

"He told me, at the museum, that he came to Florida and fell in love with a young woman. He stayed. He married her. Now's he's been murdered. Shot in the head while at his desk. The killer is unknown and at large."

"Yes. A tragedy," she said.

"Your husband's business activities were somewhat shady."

"So I've heard."

"Perhaps your life, as well, is in danger."

"I doubt it."

"You are remarkably composed."

"Are you judging me?" Her eyes narrowed.

"Observing."

"Why were you waiting for me this morning?" she asked. "That is what you were doing, isn't it?"

"Guilty."

"And?"

"I'm looking for three missing children. Did your late husband mention them to you?"

"No."

"You're positive?"

"Why? You going to take a belt across my back like Richard did if you don't like my answer?"

"You were married to him. Certainly you two talked."

"Did you *hear* what I said?"

I sensed I'd stepped into a minefield, and feared that any further comments would be the wrong thing to say. If Emma had her own agenda, we might as well get on with it.

She leaned back in her chair and considered me, as if she were not sure I was worth the effort. She stood, lifted her sweatshirt over her head, and dropped it on her chair.

Oh boy.

She wore a black bra. She turned her back to me. Her back was crisscrossed with welts. "It didn't start like this," she said, her back still toward me, careening her head over her shoulder. "It started as games. Bondage, shit like that. But he took it a step further each time." She turned back around and slipped off the right cup of her bra. Her breast fell out. It had a nasty bite mark to the right of her nipple. "This was a few nights ago. It doesn't look as bad now. Do you agree?"

"Pardon?"

"That it doesn't look as bad now?"

She slid her breast back into her bra and put her sweatshirt back on, like it was just another day at the office. She dipped her hand in a water glass and rubbed it on her neck. Makeup smeared off. Her skin was yellow and blue underneath. She arched her face up toward the ceiling, exposing the long, sensual nape of her neck.

"The morning after, you could make out his fingerprints. You ever wonder what happens up here in the sky while others dine and drink below? He'd open the doors so he could hear the night. After the belt and the bites, while I begged him to stop, he entered me. He put his hand around my throat and then—you tell me, what would you call what he did?"

"Why didn't you walk out? Call the police?"

She shook her head in disbelief and collapsed in her chair. "Men," she spit out. "Like it's my fault he—"

"I never insinuated that—"

"It's *my* house," she shouted, and I thought she was going to leap across the small table. "*My* money. *My* dreams. And he *fucks* me like it's all his."

She slumped back in her chair.

I glanced down at the street below. A red car waited patiently as an older couple crossed a street, their arms interlocked, their bodes huddled together. The man limped. The woman was patient and kind with him.

A Beautiful Voice

Emma lowered her head and then abruptly brought her eyes up to mine. She sniffled and her eyes welled up with tears.

"I'm sorry," she said.

"There's no need to be."

"It *is* my house. My family has money. I bought it with my money. Richard had nothing when we married. What was I to do? Run from my house? Have the cops pick me over and take a picture of my right tit? Go to court and show my back to a jury? Have my daddy and his golfing buddies follow it in the papers?"

"What *did* you do, Mrs. Bannon?"

She gave me a coy look that shivered my spine.

"I took it, night after night. I pretended to like it and hated myself more each day. The beating my body took was nothing compared to the lashings I gave myself. And when someone stronger than me tired of his bullying, and shot him at his desk? You'll just have to forgive me if it seems to me that the sun is shining just a bit brighter today."

"Why did you invite me to breakfast?"

"He was worried about you."

"Bannon?"

She nodded.

"What did he say?"

"That you were snooping around and asking questions that didn't make sense."

"Concerning?"

"What you said earlier—looking for children."

"You said he—"

"He hadn't a clue what you were referring to."

"You're positive?"

"He couldn't lie. Beat me? Yes. Lie? No."

"Did he tell Sergio Flores that someone was asking about missing children?" I asked.

"I don't know who you're talking about."

"I think you do."

"What you think is—"

"Do you know how your husband made a living?"

"He imported wine."

"He laundered drug money. *Mrs.* Bannon. Despite your act about testifying about abuse, you didn't go to the police because you knew what your husband did, and that scrutiny could have ruined both of you. Drained your holy bank account. Daddy and his golf buddies be damned. I'm not blaming you, but don't peddle self-serving half-stories to me."

"Smart little boy, aren't you?"

"Who killed your husband?"

"I don't know."

"Why did you really bring me up here?"

"To have a smart little boy like you fix me breakfast."

She was a sassy little sax.

I stood up with disgust and picked up my plate and hers. I stomped into the kitchen, rinsed the dishes and placed them in the dishwasher. On the way back to the patio I realized the dishtowel was draped over my right shoulder, which is home position for me when in the kitchen. I returned to the kitchen and folded it into a ring at the end of the counter. Under the counter were open shelves with decorative items: a coffee mug from Venice, a porcelain donkey, a small book: *Olive Oils of the World*. A metal black hairclip with a spider etched into it.

I reached for the large handle of a knife in a butcher block.

"Take it easy, big fellow. Leave the knife and everything will be just fine."

I didn't need to turn and see if Tina Welch had a gun on me, but I did and I was right.

36

"You've got your Eiffels on," I said to Welch.

She was nearly eye level with me. She'd come up behind me at the hotel as well. I was miffed at myself for letting her get the drop on me. I'd lost a step somewhere. Age? Contentment?

Or was she that good?

"Move away from the knives," she said.

I cast my eyes over to Emma, who'd come in from the patio. "Your buddy's the one who saw me," I said to Emma, ticked that I'd fallen for her act. "She sent you down to fetch me." I shifted my attention to Welch. "What's a nice, neighborly DEA agent doing in the house of the not-so-bereaved widow of a recently assassinated cartel moneyman?"

Emma Bannon strutted over to Welch, lifted on her tippytoes, and planted a warm kiss on her cheek. She placed her arm around the small of her back and stared defiantly at me.

Well, bust my heart.

"Peachy," I said.

I strolled over the living room rug—it was a green sea turtle swimming in azure water—and sank into the white leather couch. The picture of the lioness with the shining eyes was over my shoulder. I felt strangely outnumbered.

"Tell me," I said to Welch. "Did plugging Bannon help the government's case against Flores, or do you not care anymore?"

"I don't know what you're talking about."

"You lied to me at the hotel. You didn't admit that you were already brokering a deal with Bannon."

"That's being disingenuous, not lying."

"And I know why: Bannon's death was premeditated."

"The truth shall set you free," she said.

"That's all you got?"

"Let someone else tilt at windmills."

I nodded at her gun. "You can put the timpani away. You already scored your dramatic points for the day."

She placed her gun on a table next to the world atlas.

"I'll let you two chat," Emma said. "I need to shower."

Her fingers slid off of Welch. She padded across the wood floor and slipped into the bedroom, closing the door softly behind her. Welch took a seat across from me in a white chair that was wide enough for two people. She crossed her long legs.

"Why am I here?" I said.

"To let you know there's a possibility that Richard Bannon's death had nothing to do with his business."

"And?"

"To let it go."

"Let it go?"

"Don't look into it," she said.

I opened my hands. "I'm not the police. I have no legal interest in the late Mr. Bannon."

"I can trust you?" she asked.

"As much as I can trust you."

Welch gave that a moment. It was the best she and I would ever do, and we both knew it.

"How long have you and Emma been . . ."
"Lovers?"
"Sure."
"We clicked pretty quick."
"She's had a rough time."
"Wow. Men *are* sensitive. Y'all get such a bad rap."
"She's emotionally vulnerable. You come in and—"
"Don't go Freud on me," she said. "We know what we're doing."
"Don't we all."
She crossed her hands on her lap. "Emma couldn't go another day. It's not a slippery slope to hell; it's one small step after another. And with every step you chant that you can't believe it's happening to you. There are no signs that the end of the road is approaching. You just hit it."
"Enter Tina Welch, caped crusader—no—vindictive Lone Ranger in heels."
She shook her head. "You understand nothing."
"And what? You've got a PHD in twisted lives?"
Her face scrunched, as if racked by an old and particularly nasty memory. "I was an orphan. Great recruiting grounds for my line of work, by the way. Get the orphans, they have nothing to lose. I looked twenty when I was twelve and your twisted imagination can take it from there. So yeah, I'm qualified. The world told me from the beginning that there was no place for me. I was born with that. Emma had it beaten into her. When I tried to get attention?—I was tossed into another juvie center. All Emma could do was silently scream."
"I'm sorry."
"That's meaningless."
"That's good to know. I'll retire it."
"My one and only marriage was a disaster," she said. "Twelve months of hell, and I own most of it."
I hadn't asked her about her marriage, but decided to let her run. She rose and poured herself a cup of coffee. She was

less severe than when we first met. At peace. I could only guess.

"Emma and I never thought we'd get another chance. We thought life was something that was handed to you. A package with your name on it. You can't trade it in. No returns. Suck it up. See if the world gives a damn." She took a sip of coffee and her eyes escaped out the window before coming back to me. "Turns out that we were engineered to survive. But enough of that sugary shit. I brought you up here to ask a favor."

I considered looping back to my recent question for her motive for murder, but who was I to judge?

"Yes?"

"What I said: Let it go. Let *us* go."

"It's not much of a career move."

She coughed out a laugh. "Actually? It's the best. Before I got into this, I talked to some guys—there aren't many female role models in the DEA—who had done it. Got out. Survived. Had a life where they, as much as possible, didn't have to look over their shoulder. They told me I would know when the time came. When it got too hot. When I was sitting in the car with Rafael? That was molten lava, baby."

"Don't call me baby."

Welch tried not to grin, but finally gave in.

I said, "Your coworkers—"

"Are none of your business. I need your word."

"I have no issue with you."

"Or Emma?"

"Or Emma."

"Pinky swear?" she said with a playful tone that was out of character for her.

"Pinky swear. Did you get any information from Bannon before his untimely demise?"

"Again, I had—"

"Answer the question."

"No."

"Shame. It would have been an ideal time to—so to speak—kill two birds with one stone."

That earned a sardonic smile. "You're not seeing what this is about."

"I've got a good idea. You think it's that easy? Running away?"

"I never said it was easy."

"I asked Emma earlier if she knew what her husband did for a living."

"She didn't know. Does now."

"Your turn," I said.

"Meaning?"

"Does she know what you do?"

"Every last detail," she said.

"Rafael?"

She blew her breath out. "I'm not sure what was supposed to happen at the cottage that night. Perhaps I was sent to babysit and when my job was done, it was my turn. Bannon's death certainly will draw suspicion from Flores, and—"

"You think?"

She ignored my jab. "I have a safe house. I just need to get us there by unconventional means."

I didn't think unconventional would be a problem for her. After all, shooting your employer, who you are spying on, and running off with his wife is pretty unconventional.

"Then what?" I said. "Step out of the wheelhouse and start over?"

"Absolutely. Emma's got some business she needs to attend to around here. But in a few days, we're gone."

"A bullet takes a second."

"I know how it works," she said with a false sense of bravado. Then, she rushed out, "He was at the museum."

"Rafael?"

"The night you went. He was there. I didn't know him

then, nor him me. But I'm sure he remembered me. We could see it in each other's eyes when we met—the night we went to the cottage."

"Describe him to me."

She did.

I, too, had seen the man. He had delicately held a glass of Champagne while contemplating *Woman Sitting at a Table*. I thought of something she had said at the hotel beach bar.

"You said—concerning your operation in Ohio—that there was a crooked law firm that helped Sean Wright."

"Not so much the law firm as we suspected one of the lawyers was on the take. We could never prove it, though. The firm represented the police union. We let them know we were in town. That was probably a mistake."

"Any lawyer in particular?"

"It was more a feeling or innuendo. There was this one attorney that was too interested in the case. You know, like you act when you're *not* trying to act like it matters."

"His name?" I didn't want to lead her unless I had to.

"I'm not sure."

"Stephen Cole?"

"No. Some grease ball. Type of guy who could fall into a sewer and climb out wearing a new suit. No one ever called him his name—used some nickname. Handle? I don't know."

"Handel like the Messiah?"

"I was using it as a word association. That wasn't his name. Like I said, we never had proof. Why do you ask?"

"Just fishing."

"For what?"

"I questioned a guy across from the Vizcarros. Odd bird. Told me he used to practice law up north. His firm represented Sean Wright."

She scooted forward in her chair, her dark eyes bright. "My, what a tiny little world. Is that this Cole fellow?" She didn't wait for my response, but continued. "And he ends up across from your mark?"

"Coincidental. He's been there well over a year. He was suspicious of Wright's murder. Called it a drug hit."

I'd made an unforced error. I never should have brought Cole up. Welch certainly didn't want anyone snooping around the death of Sean Wright.

"Why would he even know of it?" she asked, her interest piquing.

"Not sure. He called Wright 'Pepperoni.'"

"What else does he know?"

"Nothing," I said. "He's a burned out round-table knight who thinks Florida is the Holy Grail."

"You know this or is it just your poor judgment?"

"The same poor judgment I'm using regarding you."

"Touché. Is he a threat to me?" she asked.

"He's a fisherman."

"Is he a threat to me?"

"Back off, Welch. He's curious, nothing else." I settled my eyes on her. I didn't want to bring any harm to Cole and felt an urge to protect him, although I wasn't sure why. "I'll circle back to him, but he's fine."

"Is there more that you're not—"

"Emma and Cole are safe, understand?"

"You vouch for him?"

"I do."

She nodded in closure and settled back into the chair. "Why did you say Rafael's mission here is not done? What are you holding back?"

"I didn't say that."

"You said a bullet takes a second. Same thing."

"He'd not fond of people who have seen him."

"There's more, though, isn't there?"

"Do you know that Sergio Flores has a son?"

"I might have overheard," she said.

"Did you overhear that he was trying to bring him to the U.S.?"

"No," she said.

"We don't have all day."

"Over a year ago—that's how long I've been on the case—I picked up that he had a son. I did *not* suspect that he was trying to bring him in. Is that what this is all about? Was one of the missing children his son?"

"Yes."

"My," she said, swaying her head side to side. "What petty little liars we are—you and me. You didn't just find that out this morning."

"And you told me you didn't know why you were told to tag along with Rafael."

"What I know and what I suspect are two different things. Could Flores have used me, through Davido, to plant information compelling us to grant safe passage of his son to the States? And then used me to help kidnap three children? Then have Rafael eliminate two of the three and finish with me—meaning my cover was blown? That's where we're headed, right?"

I arched my eyebrows.

She swiped the side of her forehead as if to displace a strand of hair that wasn't there. "Entirely possible." She massaged her forehead with her fingers. "Shit . . . Shit. Shit. I can see that, but who knows? The riddles come faster than the answers. Nobby."

"Nobby?"

"That was the lawyer's nickname," she said. "Nobby, like a doorknob."

"Or a handle."

"Right. Real name Norbert something."

"Last name?"

She swayed her head side to side. "I don't have it."

"And you think he would have been the one who told Wright to get your pizza kid, Tony Colaprico?" I said.

"Perhaps not directly, but at the least through a channel. But it all may be a product of my hallucinations."

"Not much to go on."

"No. But I'm sure you can do better."

Why do people tell me that?

"Any particular requests?" I asked.

"Avenge Tony's death."

"You already did that," I pointed out in the disturbing possibility that she had forgotten that she had orchestrated Wright's death.

"I just took out a small cog in the wheel. Rafael ran Wright. I want to cut the head off, but this town might get a little hot for me."

"You want me to go after Rafael," I said, "while you hide from the local homicide detectives? I'm not into suicide runs. Besides, despite our budding friendship, I don't owe you."

"What makes you think we have a budding friendship?" she said in a schoolmarm tone.

"Lay off the act. I know you told Emma you're mad about her just to make me jealous."

She rolled her eyes. "You are a piece. Do us both a favor and look into Nobby. I'd do it myself—it's on my list—but I'm best out of circulation right now."

I didn't want to know about her list.

"How'd you select Tony in the first place?"

She paused, as if considering whether to answer my question. Her eyes flashed down at the floor before coming back to me.

"Tony needed the job. He had one more year of payments to pay off his used car. Some beat-up piece of rust you heard four blocks away. That was all he cared about—having his car paid off."

I thought of Lee Ann working to pay off her car. The

early admission to UF. The travel abroad programs. Two kids who were dealt different hands.

"I gave him the opportunity. It cost him his life." She rolled her lower lip between her teeth and her face collapsed. Her eyes went blank, like when you can no longer think because everything inside of you is molasses and mud. "You want to know how I found him?"

Welch didn't strike me as someone who frequented a confessional booth, but she seemed to be in one now.

"You don't have—"

"I thought I could be a positive influence in someone's life. That's what we're supposed to do, right? Help others we can relate to? Someone who maybe had a rough start like you? Is that bad? Is it wrong?"

The questions were for her and not me. I let the film roll.

"I scouted around for juvie offenders who were also orphans. I told you they make the best recruits."

37

Tina Welch was responsible for the deaths of Sean Wright, Richard Bannon, and in her mind, Tony Colaprico, who was the only weight she carried. Those were just the names in the circle of her life that intersected with mine. It was good that she was hanging up her badge. I didn't think she lied about who plugged Alejandro and Martina Vizcarro, but I wouldn't put money on it. Not mine, at least.

Welch and I had exchanged cell numbers before we parted. I would be surprised if our paths didn't cross again. She didn't strike me as a woman who walked away from unfinished business—safe house or not. She had mentioned a crooked lawyer—Nobby someone—in connection to her pizza-boy case. A lawyer who worked at the same firm that Cole had and who had been snooping around the Wright case. It wasn't hard from there.

I couldn't see how any of that came back to the missing children. But you can drive a thousand miles at night without ever seeing more than twenty feet in front of you. You just have to trust the headlights.

And they kept shining on Cole.

I slammed my truck door, and the bells from the Pass-a-

Grille church sliced the thin winter air. The goofy bells and I must be on the same schedule. Cole wasn't home. I found him at the end of the short pier by the jetty where the channel dumps into the gulf. The seaweed clumped together so thick you would think you could walk on it. White egrets perched on the rocks that formed the break wall, and an ugly gull stood with them as if it yearned to be part of the flock and was unaware that it was a different bird.

Cole sat on a chair facing the flat endless water. A wide-brimmed hat shielded his eyes. One white egret had ventured from the flock and kept him company, but both man and bird looked bored. It was late morning, in the middle of a sun-drenched tide—not an ideal time to be fishing. But fishing is as much about meditation as it is about food. Except for the bird.

Cole's pole was slumped against the pitted and rusted railing. His feet were propped up on the lowest rail.

I tugged on his line.

In one motion he popped up, lost his hat, grabbed his pole, and glared at me. The bird backed off a few paces, but did an admirable job of maintaining its position considering its incalculable weight disadvantage.

"Don't you ever knock?" He reached for his hat on the ground.

"Door was open."

"There is no door."

"Then how could I knock?"

He shook his head at the meaninglessness of our words. "What is it this time?" He slouched back down in his chair and pulled his hat over his eyes.

"Norbert—Nobby—Larrison," I said.

Cole nudged his hat off his forehead and sat up straight. "Say it again."

I did.

"What about him?" he said with an aggressive edge. He squinted his left eye.

"He worked at your former law firm, correct?"

Instead of answering, Cole rose and reeled in his line. He cast it far out to the south, toward the edge of the channel where the fish lay. He brought it in, a slender piece of sea grass riding up his line, and again tossed his bait toward the channel.

The third time, I grabbed his pole.

"Cut the act," I said.

"I don't—"

"Tell me what you know about Nobby Larrison."

"Why do—"

"We're done with whys. I got a drug hit across the street from you, and another, Sean 'Pepperoni' Wright two hours north of here. He plugged a kid, and your firm represented him. I have reason to believe they are related, or at least, the same parties were involved. Someone in your firm was tainted. That may or may not have anything to do with my problems. But I'll be the judge of that. Maybe you're the crooked nail."

"You know better than that."

"Don't be so sure, pal."

"I'm not your pal."

"The way it's starting to look, you better hope I am."

He propped the pole up against the railing. The bird stepped back.

"Nobby and I shared a secretary," he said. "Other than that, I didn't know him that well. Forty-five lawyers are more than you can keep up with. I hear he split the firm not long after I did."

"You never did say why you left."

"Too cloudy for half the year and law . . . wasn't in my blood."

"What is in your blood?"

"Trying to fish without you interrupting me."

"You weren't fishing," I said. "Was Nobby crooked?"

"Was Nobby crooked?" Cole repeated, as if it had never

occurred to him that those three words could be arranged in that order.

"Your firm represented the police union," I said. "I was informed that Nobby Larrison might have abetted Sean Wright in identifying a plant in the pizza store. Did Larrison tell Wright about the kid?"

"What's this got do to with the search for missing children?"

"You tell me."

"Who told you this?" he said.

"I ran into someone who had knowledge of the massacre across from you and they also had knowledge of Sean Wright. This person thinks Wright might have been tipped by someone at your old firm."

"Let me talk to your source," he said.

"You go on the offense pretty fast."

"I need to talk to him."

I didn't want to slip and tell him that the him was a her. Welch needed all the protection she could afford, although I questioned why I was sheltering her.

"Why the sudden interest in an associate you barely knew, which we both know is a lie seeing as how you shared a secretary?"

"Nothing," Cole said, but he knew he'd fumbled. "I'd just like to know what your source knows."

"He was passing on a rumor."

"No he wasn't. You said he had knowledge. Know what your problem is?'

"My problem?"

"You're always holding back," he said.

"I'm in the presence of the master."

His face went expressionless. He picked up his pole and cast far out into the gulf. He leaned the pole against the railing. He settled in the chair and pulled his hat over his eyes. The white egret inched closer.

I drove back home, my hands squeezing the steering wheel and blood boiling out of my ears.

"A PICNIC ON THE BEACH?" I SAID.

Kathleen planted her hands on her hips. We were in my kitchen and it smelled like bug repellant. I'd gotten a little too aggressive with a can of indoor ant spray.

"Why does that sound so foreign to you?" she said.

"We've never done it before."

"Man-oh-man," she said. "Where does this fuddy-duddiness come from? Indulge your left-bank bohemian inner self."

"We won't see the sunset boats go by."

"Will they make it without us?"

"That's just it. You don't know."

"Be a pioneer," she said.

"They got scalped."

"Father help me."

"Besides, I—"

"Fetch us a bottle," she said and stuffed—with more force than was necessary— some napkins into a picnic basket I didn't know I had. "If that's not asking too much."

It was an hour before sunset and I had trout in the oven. That, along with Morgan's leftover seafood gumbo and fresh bread from a bakery on Gulf Boulevard, was to be dinner. They still were, but now Kathleen had it in her to move the feast to the beach. Blanket and all.

I took the trout out of the oven and kept it in the glass cooking bowl. It fit snug into a yellow, insulated cloth tray with burn marks from the time I'd left it in the oven for too long. Kathleen put the gumbo into a travel coffee cup, and the rice into another. She had already scrounged through the house and collected the blanket, utensils, and paper plates. It seemed like a lot of work to me, considering our cushy chairs overlooking the bay were five feet away. Even Hadley III meowed in protest at the inefficiency of our dinner as we ditched her. I did grab a camping table and two chairs—mainly to avoid being guilty of contributing nothing in the event it turned out to be a good idea.

I also snatched two Krewe of Carrolton plastic cups. Alcohol is illegal on St. Pete Beach unless it is in a plastic Mardi Gras cup. The police may not be aware of that particular law, but as they will tell you, ignorance of the law is no excuse.

Kathleen spread the blanket on the cooling sand and flipped the corners out. She patted the center like she was a cat. I poured red wine into the cups so that we could pour it into our bodies. A woman on a paddle board stroked her way south, caressing the glass water and trailing a miniature wake that rolled in the failing sunlight. Terns sat like statues staring out at the gulf. People freckled the beach, sitting in chairs and standing—couples, families, friends, and solo acts, all waiting for the greatest show on Earth. We settled in our chairs and placed the food on the camping table between us. Kathleen gave me credit for thinking of the chairs and table. It's great when a hedge pays off.

I took a sip of wine, kicked off my shoes, and said, "I'm glad I finally convinced you to do this."

"*Are* you now?"

"Been after your fuddy-duddy highness for years."

"I do recall."

"I knew you'd like it."

"I feel so foolish for my childish whining," she said with mock sincerity. "Can you ever forgive me?"

"Happens to the best of us."

She reached over the table and punched me. Same spot as before.

"Loosen up, hear me?"

"Yes ma'am."

"How was your day?" she asked.

"How was *your* day?"

"First day of classes," she said.

"I know."

Actually, I'd forgotten that. But I covered well.

"I stood in front of eighteen twenty-year-olds and, for the first time, had to take a deep breath before talking."

"Meaning?"

"I don't know," she said. "It was like pulling a cord to start a lawn mower and it doesn't start, so you pull again."

"What do you know about lawn mowers?"

"I just told you."

"But then they start."

"But then they start," she repeated and took a promising sip of wine from the plastic cup. "Your day?"

"The same."

"What's with your mower?"

I downloaded on her. Recapped my run-in with Emma and Tina Welch as well as my brief encounter with Cole. As I talked, the sun slid farther down the horizon, inching its way into the giant bathtub. It hid behind a cloud that it transformed into pink tissue paper, and then dropped out on the underside as if the paper couldn't hold it. The cloud blazed into flames as the sun singed it from underneath. The terns and the willets were gone, and I wondered where they went.

After dinner, we ditched the chairs and nested on the blanket. Kathleen pulled on the sweatshirt I'd brought for her. It spread far beyond her and she looked like a blonde mushroom.

"Will Tina and Emma be safe?" she asked. I'd just told her that I feared for them, as Rafael was not fond of people who could identify him.

"I think so."

"That's hardly a ringing endorsement. Look, there they are." Kathleen pointed south toward the channel. Two of the charter boats that sail past my house drifted at the mouth of the channel. They had front-row seats. "See, you didn't miss them. We still haven't done it."

"We will," I said.

"I know."

Kathleen had always wanted to be on one of the sunset sailboats that cruise past my dock. I'm not sure why, for we often take *Impulse* out to catch the sunset. I think it's because she wants to view my house from the boat. To see what other people see when they look at us. Don't we all want to do that?

"Welch knows the risk," I said. "Although I doubt she shared the full extent of it with Emma."

"Your high-heeled friend is quite the little murderer, isn't she?"

I didn't say anything, and I sensed that Kathleen regretted her comment. My record had a few asterisks on it.

"What now?" she said, distancing herself from the previous strain of conversation.

"Might track down Nobby Larrison."

"Why?"

"To make sure that the events at Cole's old firm aren't tied to my problems."

"You think they are?"

"Might be."

"What's the end game here?"

"I want the man who killed Alejandro and his daughter, and who likely killed two

of the three children."

"Is that wise?"

"Is what wise?"

"Chasing a professional hit man," she said.

"The alternative?"

"I want Garrett with you 24/7."

"Done."

"There's more, isn't there?"

I thought of Martina calling me an amateur, a clown.

Janssen's you're-as-low-as-we-go smirk. If I walked away, I'd limp with that for the rest of my life.

"Let's go," I said. "Temperature's dropping. You'll be getting cold."

She hesitated—I could never fool her—but then started cleaning up. We gathered our belongings while high above us, streaks of red stained the sky like the smeared blood of a fallen Greek god.

38

Norbert Larrison, Esq., lived in Lakewood Ranch, an invasive ground-cover housing development east of Sarasota. I had called Cole's old firm, gotten hold of his ex-secretary, and said I was an old friend.

The secretary—it sounded as if she were smacking gum while we talked—had informed me that Nobby "retired somewhere around Sarasota." She declined to give me an address, but that wasn't necessary. She asked if I would tell Nobby to give her a call someday, and then inquired if I also knew Stephen Cole.

"Don't think so," I said. It was misleading yet sincere. "Who is he?"

"He used to work here."

"Why do you ask?"

Silence.

"It's nothing."

"LEFT," GARRETT BARKED FROM THE PASSENGER seat of my truck. I took a hard turn and cut my speed. Lakewood Ranch was stuffed with Mediterranean-style, single-story homes that lined manicured, curved streets like a video game. A late-afternoon winter shower had glistened the grass, darkened the pavement, and turned the stucco homes two shades darker. While we had Larrison's address, it would be easy to zip by his house as they came upon us one after another, until they lost all sense of individuality.

"Just passed it," Garrett said.

"Wonder how?"

I did a U-turn in a driveway with a manatee mailbox and pulled over to the rounded curve.

"We'll go by foot," I said as I stepped out of the truck.

Larrison's garage door rolled up, and a black, two-door Mercedes backed out. Garrett and I scampered back to the truck and followed the man we presumed was Norbert Larrison. The Mercedes pulled into the Mall at University Town Center in front of a trio of restaurants. A man got out and marched into a steak house. We followed.

He was perched at the bar when we entered, chatting with the bartender. Desk lamps with low-glowing red shades and white lace, apparently lifted from the reading room of a bordello, were planted every few feet on the bar. The far side of the bar opened to the outdoors and liquor bottles were stacked in the middle. The outdoor light reflected through the liquid, creating amber waves of distilled grain.

Expensively attired older people were scattered around the curved bar. Sarasota: Top-income. Midwest retirees. A genealogy tree with deep European roots. No St. Petersburg, Beach Drive, tattooed, short-skirt, high-heeled, low-cut, eye-magnet crowd here.

I took the high bar stool on Nobby's immediate right, although there was no need to sit next to him as the bar wasn't crowded. Garrett camped out at a table behind us.

"I was hoping to keep that available for a blonde," Nobby said to me. He gave me a come-on-good-buddy smile.

"I'm a blonde," I said with a be-careful-what-you-wish-for smile.

"Sorry, pal. Not my type."

"Are you Norbert Larrison?"

"Do we know each other?"

"What can you tell me about Sean Wright and the pizza kid he blew away?"

His eyes narrowed and the deep feathered lines around them folded together. But he recovered quickly. "I never heard of this Nor . . . whoever you're looking for."

The bartender placed a cocktail glass in front of him. "What's your pleasure Nobby?" she asked. "Menu or wait a few minutes?"

Larrison rubbed his forehead with his hand. He glanced up at the bartender. "I'll wait a few minutes."

"Anything I can get you?" She directed her question to me. I ordered a Jameson on the rocks.

She turned away and I said to Larrison, "You were saying?"

"Who are you?"

His tone was two parts accusatory and one part fear. It was the fear element that I wanted to cultivate.

"Told you. I'm your blonde tonight."

He shrugged and took a drink. "Yeah? Well, don't get too excited about launching your rocket. I can't talk about any of it. Attorney privilege. Even if I could, why would I spill to you?"

His voice cracked as he talked, and carried a natural element of condescension and haste.

"Look behind you," I said.

"Why?"

"Do it."

He turned around. Garrett tipped his head.

"What about it?"

"What about *him*, Norbert?"

"Get to the point."

"You and I are going to join my friend and have a civilized conversation. You can enter willingly and leave willingly. If you do not cooperate, your willingness will not be a concern the next time we meet."

"Are you threatening me?"

"Definitely."

The bartender deposited my drink. It had a large circular ice cube in it. I picked it up, stepped off the stool, and joined Garrett at the table. A few minutes later, Larrison, drink in hand, ambled over.

He was dressed in creaseless beige pants and a black shirt that pushed at the buttons. His complexion was sallow and his eyes were like oysters—wet, slimy, and gray. His short neck and cheeks were rusted with tiny broken veins. It was as if he was inflicted with the curse of Dorian Gray, and his soul had mutated into his skin.

"Fine. You got my attention," he said, sitting down. His glossy eyes slipped between Garrett and me.

"Sean Wright," I said.

"What about him?"

"Did you tip him off that Tony Colaprico was working with the feds to gather information on a drug cartel?"

He skipped a fraction of a beat.

"Jesus, what are you guys drinking?"

"Water," Garrett said and leaned in. "Answer the man's question."

"No. We done here?" He leaned back. He could lie all night.

So could we.

"We hear the next hit's on you," Garrett said.

"Pardon?" His eyes narrowed. The top button of his shirt was chipped, perhaps damaged at the cleaners.

"You might be my next paycheck," Garrett said, his voice thick with disinterest.

Larrison stroked his glass with his hand. Our bluff held dire consequences for him.

"I don't know what you're referring to," he rasped out.

"You know Wright got wasted, right?" I said. "Truck rear-ended him. He talked. Got a little religion. People are worried that you're next. Maybe you can convince us, maybe you can't." I leaned in toward him. "If I were you, I'd sure as hell want to try."

He placed his palms out toward us as if to ward us off. "Hey, I had a simple deal. I fed you guys information and you did the rest. Why would I squeal? All I would accomplish is to indict myself. You know how it works."

"Tell us, so we can report that you understand the agreement."

"I'm not telling you shit."

"That's your prerogative, Nobby," I said. "And it's reassuring that you understand your rights. But there's a version floating around that doesn't bode well for you. You don't tell us shit? We go with that version."

"The hell you talking about?"

"We're done talking," Garrett said. "It's decision time for you: Talk to us or go back to the bar. Can't honestly say we care one way or the other—bank account's getting a little low."

Larrison swung his head side to side a few times, trying to shake his life away.

"I'm clean, man. Did everything they asked of me. Wright was taking money on the street, protecting the dealers. Stupid prick—he'd bite his own dick for a buck. The pizza joint was raking street cash. The feds put some kid—Tony what's-his-face—in there. Yeah, I passed it along. Wright was told to make the problem disappear. We got Wright off the hook. Hey, everybody's entitled to a defense attorney, right?"

Garrett said, "You told him Tony Colaprico was wired by the feds?"

Larrison nodded.

"How did you know?"

"You know."

"Pretend I don't."

"Some federal agent came to us and wanted to know about Wright. We represented the police union. I stonewalled them, just like I'd said I would. She told us they were going to put the kid in the store. Like I said, I passed it up the chain. That's proof right there that I did my job."

"The agent," I said. "Was she tall?"

"Yeah. A real female praying mantis."

"Tony Colaprico's dead," Garrett said. "How's your conscience, counselor?"

"Hey, I had no clue Wright would do that. You think I'd go along with that? No way, man. I thought he'd just bust his lip."

"How'd you get Wright off the hook?" I asked.

"We planted another kid in the store." Nobby's voice had taken on an air of accomplishment as he recalled his days of corporate glory. "Found out what type of knives they used. Had the kid plant one by the take-out window. Our line was that Wright encountered a kid high on drugs who pulled a knife on him. He had no choice but to protect himself. Jurors hate to convict a policeman. I mean, if Colaprico was black, it would have been different, you know? But he was lily white—so there you go. Not that any of that mattered." He spread his hands. "We got lucky, you know."

"How so?" I said.

"You know damn well how so," he said irritably.

"Keep pretending. It's important that you haven't changed your story."

"What's the deal? You get your rocks off gloating over this shit?"

I waggled my finger at him. "I'll clue you in if I want editorial comments."

Nobby reached for his chin but just as quickly withdrew his hand. He hunched over the table and folded his arms in front of him.

"There was a guy in our firm, Stephen Cole. He looked like a goddamn cherub on a Christmas card. We were going to put him on as lead defense. Let the jury dwell on his rosy cheeks. Cole and I shared the same secretary. I saw some papers she had left out. Cole was crossing the aisle. Going to the prosecution. I passed it along. While he was bound not to talk about the case, we all knew that was a pile of crap." He lowered his voice even more. "I never told anyone about the accident. Is that what they think? Why you're here? That I'm gonna' put two and two together? Talk? Look around, man. It's Sarasota for God's sake. Place is stuffed with eighty-year-old Tommy Bahamas. I'm down here sailing into the sunset, got it?"

I wanted to ask him about the accident, but we'd already been lucky in bluffing him this far. Garrett must have felt the same way, for he said, "Keep going."

He reclined back into his chair. "The rest was in the papers. Wright got off on self-defense. The department ushered him out the door. I paid off my gambling debts, which is how they found me in the first place. I'm clean. Haven't been to a track in over a year. They know I'm mum for life, right? You tell 'em that."

"Wright's death makes everyone a little uneasy," I said.

"Yeah, well the tailgating truck act is getting a little old." He eyes flooded with fear, and I knew what he was thinking. "I'm not being critical. Trying to help, you know?"

Garrett leaned in and nailed his eyes to Larrison's. "We think the DEA agent who put the kid in the pizza store did the number on Wright. She's gone rogue. She's gunning for you."

His eyes narrowed as if he were doing internal calculations. "Who the hell are you guys?"

"We're the men who are going to save your life," Garrett said.

"I thought you were with . . ."

"Who?" Garrett said.

"Nothin'."

"Talk to us about your contact." I said. "In return, we won't repeat your story to anyone."

"Contact?"

"Who put you up to it—who you passed info to."

"You've been bullshittin' me?"

Garrett said, "You give us who recruited you, and we won't press charges."

"Fuck me." Nobby leaned back in his chair and slapped his hand on the table. "You're government, aren't you? Making me believe you're on the other side. Assholes are as crooked as the thugs you chase."

"Talk or walk," I said.

"Can you give me immunity?"

"No," Garrett said. "But—"

"Then why—

"—we can give you tomorrow."

He talked. He talked about his gambling debts, trying to elicit sympathy from us. About his divorce. How he lost half his money in the Great Recession of '08 and then half of what was left when his wife booked five years later. About a tall man "with a hawkish nose" and a French accent who found him and wanted only a little bit of information for thirty pieces of silver. How he knew it was wrong, but what's right about your wife, who never worked a day in her life, skirting with half of your retirement plan? What's right about overleveraged bankers taking the whole fucking country to its knees? Fuckers didn't even go to law school, and you wanna guess what they pull down every year? You want to talk to me about what's right?

"You know what's left when you lose fifty percent twice?"

he implored us. "Jack Shit. I lost seventy-five percent of my net worth."

"Should have taken your wedding vows more seriously," I said.

"Hey, what do—"

Garrett cut him off. "Seems like a lot of attention paid to a single cop on the take."

Larrison took a few seconds. "There were others," he said. "The eight killings south of Columbus? Wright was involved with that. They wanted to protect him. He'd done good work for them. In the end, though, it was Cole deciding to cross the line that saved Wright's ass. I tell you what, man, what they did to Cole? Unbelievable. Go after Cole and it reeks of interference. Draws attention. Go after his. . . "

His voice trailed off, and he gazed toward the bar and the empty stool he had sat in. His hand slipped off his drink then tightened around it.

"I had nothing to do with that," he said, his lips quivering. I thought the man might cry. "Nothing. No way would I have cooperated if I knew that. I liked the guy, you know?"

"What did they to do Cole?" I asked.

He combed his hand through his hair. He glanced again at the empty bar stool. He started to look away, but, perhaps finding nothing else to settle his troubled soul, rested his eyes back upon the empty bar stool. He was shutting down. Curling up into the mental corner of his bed where the blanket of illusions kept him safe and warm.

"You want to be back in that chair, don't you?" I said. "Look at me." He didn't. "You think some woman's going to drop out of the sky and crave to be the center of your universe? That's your salvation? And what? She'll want your body. Your mind. Your face. Your wit. Your dick. Here. Now. Tonight. All from that chair. That's not going to happen. Look at me. *What did they do to Cole?*"

Larrison pivoted his head to me. I'd seen the dead eyes of

living men on the battlefield before, eyes that see the other side, ghosts that no one else sees. But seeing them in a restaurant in Sarasota spooked me. Chilled me to my core.

"You know," his voice wavered, "made him quit. They knew that would destroy the man. I never would have told them Cole was moving across the table if I had a notion that. . ."

He sucked in his cheeks as his face collapsed into an ugly frown. His oyster eyes glistened.

"You goddamned people are all the same," he said. "*Fuck*ing animals. All of you."

He bolted out of his chair and stalked out of the restaurant.

39

RAFAEL

A cool air swayed the towering palms, and the scent of freshly brewed coffee flitted from an open door. A sailboat threaded its way out of the marina, its main sail taut and full of the morning wind.

Rafael sat at the outdoor table on the expansive front porch of the Vinoy hotel in downtown St. Petersburg. He'd had no clue that there was a city in Florida named after a city in Russia. He thought the Spanish killed the natives in the new world and seized the land before the English colonists decided it was *their* right to kill the natives and seize the land. Apparently Ivan had found his way here as well. And what about Pass-a-Grille, where the job had been? We were here as well? *Oui!* This country, he thought. They want to keep immigrants out, but everyone here is from somewhere else.

A man took the chair next to him. He was a compact creature with no neck, for the ripped muscles of his back and shoulders had morphed into his head. Tattoos crawled out from under his tight black shirt. He wore jeans and running shoes. His dark sunglasses shielded his eyes, but Rafael knew they, too, were dark and masked. Rafael and the man had done several jobs together, each calling the other when an accomplice became desirable.

Such as now.

Rafael knew he'd shown his hand. If nothing else, the *grande femme*, who had accompanied him and who he had planned to kill, had disappeared. No trace. She had seen him. Could point him out.

That may not have been enough to summon his loyal comrade. But then Sergio Flores, not Davido, had called and spurted out that Richard Bannon had taken an execution shot to the head. *What the hell is going on over there? What the hell am I paying you for? You better finish the job. Get my boy, goddammit. I'm paying you a lot of money—Oui, we will get—don't fucking "we" me like some squiggly little pig, get my boy—yes, of course—eliminate all survivors—naturally.* Click.

Flores had asked if Rafael had any clue who plugged Bannon, even suggesting that Rafael himself might have had a hand in the execution. Rafael knew that Flores had called himself because he wanted to hear Rafael's voice, to judge for himself if it contained elements of deceit. Of betrayal. Perhaps one of Flores's competitors had gotten to Rafael and made an offer he couldn't refuse. Being in possession of Sergio Flores's only son could create strategic business advantages. Give one a leg up—so to speak—on the competition.

"You have good news?" Rafael said to the man across from him.

"Yes."

"You know where they are?"

"I do."

"Tell me."

He did.

"How?"

"I trailed her one day. She went to the grocery store. She bought more than she would need for herself. I followed her. They are there."

"She took them?" Rafael asked.
"How could I know that? I only know what I saw."
"Do not be smart with me, Fredrick."
"I meant—"
"They are there now?"
"Yes."
"Then why do you sit here?"
"You called me to—"
"Go. Now. Watch them."

Fredrick slid off his stool. Rafael reached inside his silk jacket for his phone. The corner of his lip curled up as he dialed. *She bought more than she would need for herself.* Rafael knew that large events often pivoted on the most miniature and inconsequential act. For the world spun and wobbled on it axis, like a warped record on a turntable, playing the same mournful sound over and over to a naïve and impressionable audience.

While the phone rang, his eyes made love to his watch—a Patek Phillippe Nautilus. A little large for his frame, but such an exquisite design. Time seemed more majestic when measured with such an eloquent instrument. Each passing second a finely tuned note from a flawless orchestra.

From Rafael's phone: "What?"
"We found him," he said.

40

Florida in the rain is a picture of lost dreams and busted fantasies. Canceled beach days and ruined outdoor weddings. It might be sunny for nineteen straight days, but the day you get hitched? A day that's been on the calendar for over a year? Boom. Buckets of it. Monsoon mania. Nature is a shifty little rascal and plays no favorites. And in a state that packages and sells sunshine, that outlawed both state and municipal income taxes because it egregiously taxes those visiting souls who rent its sunshine, rain is financial depression.

When you live on an island and it rains, water is everywhere. It is a river running up to the sky.

I stood outside Cole's house and banged on his door. A flash of lightning veined through a threatening cloud and a rumble of thunder reverberated in from the gulf. My hair was damp from the short hop from my truck to his front porch. I peered inside. Everything was the same, but nothing was the same. It was my third trip that day, all three the same experience. Rain. Distant thunder. No Cole. Or car.

The day before had been sunny, but no Cole.

I wanted to tell him I'd run into Norbert Larrison. That he'd spilled the beans and then sit back and hear what Cole had to say. I gave one more frustrated, angry pound on the door and turned away. A garbage truck grumbled down the street. It was wet. Grungy. Its pungent odor mixed with the rain and soiled the air. On its side, a sign read, "Our business stinks, but it's picking up."

On the way back to my house, I swung by to check on the *Lauren Rowe*. The sky and the water were the same dismal metal gray. What had we been thinking?

No.

What had *she* been thinking?

SEA FOG ROLLED IN OVER THE NEXT FOUR DAYS. It chased the rain away, but it was like trading a head cold for the flu.

The fog sat low and threatening off the shore for half a day, like a fallen cloud, and then moved in with no sound or fanfare—a Tolkien army on a silent beat. Guests at the hotel were cast into the dark ages. It blocked the sun in Biblical proportion and made navigating the water dangerous. The birds were gone. The red channel marker in front of my house came on during the day, and then it too got swallowed by the milky gray silk. The only sound was the dolphins serenading in the mist. At night, the fog lifted enough to shroud the moon with swirling wisps of vapor, creating a witch's brew of Black Death.

We scuttled our plans to take the *Lauren Rowe* out. We were all revved up, but had no place to go. The short winter days dragged by. Garrett thought of flying back to Cleveland, but decided to hang for a while. I suspected that Kathleen had a few words with him. He stayed with Morgan. They both worshipped kite surfing and kept hoping the fog would lift. They ran north and south trying to outflank the fog, but it was not to be. We were in the doldrums.

Cole was AWOL. I found excuses to head downtown or

destinations east, as the fog lifted once I got a mile or so inland. The days there were bright, sunny and blue. You drove in and out of the fog, like driving in and out of a cave.

I did a stint at the thrift store and then spent two days at the refugee house, but I don't possess the talent and patience to teach. Instead, I cooked, did landscaping, and performed odd jobs that Morgan had taped to the refrigerator. It felt good to cross them out, one by one. After my chores, I sat on the dock that reached into the pond at the back of the property. The world was wet and small and pressed in all around me. I believe that fog is made up of the pureed dead who no longer have anyone alive who remembers them. I dreamed that once and it's never left me. Someday I'll come back as fog, blot out the light, and crush someone else's day.

I went back inside and told Morgan I was headed downtown for good. By the time I hit I-275, the fog had lifted and a hundred million angels broke forth in song.

I spent the night with Kathleen. I would not go home until the fog was gone.

"KIDS' ART," I COMPLAINED TO KATHLEEN, WHO, I suspected, was tired of my attitude.

"Can you suck it up?"

Told you.

"We'll be in and out," she assured me. "Danielle— remember I said she was volunteering at a school? Her class was selected. I want to support her."

"I thought you didn't like sex-kitten."

"Not purring around you, I don't. But she's doing good work. You're sure Morgan can't join us?"

"Just me."

"Guess you'll have to do," she said putting a sweater on.

The museum was displaying children's artwork from local schools. Maybe Charlotte would be there. If so, I planned to corner her and choke out of her where Cole had bustled off to and why.

I paid admission for Kathleen and myself. After I received my change, I inquired of the man behind the counter if Charlotte was working that evening.

"She no longer works here," he said. He was dressed in jeans and a striped shirt. A light saber hung from his belt.

"Where did she go?"

"I don't know."

"When did she leave?"

"I'm not sure," he said.

"Who can I talk to who might know?"

"Why do you ask?"

"I think she's pregnant with my child."

"Jake," Kathleen said from behind me.

"I'm concerned for her safety," I said to the Jedi knight.

"Charlotte quit—I don't know—week or so ago. Sorry. That's all I know."

"Is that thing real?" I nodded at his light saber.

"Dude, you know it is."

The museum was packed with ebullient parents who had turned out in blabbering legions to support their gifted children. Two of the galleries had been converted to display the children's art, which ran the gamut from stick figures to impressive seascapes and haunting self-portraits. I circulated with Kathleen until we got separated when she broke off with friends.

I swung by *Woman Sitting at a Table* to let her know I was there that evening—she still wouldn't look at me—and then stalked off in search of Danielle's class. It was sequestered in the Cannova Gallery, a cul-de-sac gallery reached by walking through four other galleries. She had arranged her class pictures by age. I started with the upper classes, as they held the most promise to be something other than crayon drawings of Santa Claus.

One prominently displayed easel held a painting of a man scrummaging through a garbage can on a beach while in the background children played in the sand. The man wore heavy clothing and the children were in swimsuits. He reminded me of the homeless man who had approached me after my run. The picture was done with colored pencils, but the man and his surroundings were in black and white, creating a stark contrast to the rainbow beach scene behind him. Like *The Wizard of Oz*, it was part color and part black and white.

"That's Colleen's," Danielle said. She'd snuck up beside me, the stealthy little lynx. I must have been more engrossed in the picture than I thought.

"I like it," I said.

"Colleen's parents are here illegally—although no one discusses such things. She lives in fear every day of being deported. She sees everything as two worlds. Coexisting. See the couple strolling the beach, where there's color?" She pointed at the picture. "They're looking straight ahead. They don't notice the children or the homeless man. And here," she pointed to a bird facing the man, "the bird represents nature. It is aware of the man's plight."

I said, "The man over the garbage can is a drug addict, and there's nothing the system can do for him. Give him a buck and he'll shoot it up his arm. The bird's hanging around for food."

"Hmm. We see what we want to see. Excuse me, Jake." She touched me lightly on the shoulder. "I need to spend some time with the parents."

She took a few steps to her right and started talking to a man who stood proudly before a picture of a sea turtle. Danielle had deftly reduced me to sand. The picture we'd viewed and discussed was a modern day *Gathering at the Church Entrance*, the painting I admired of a young Parisian peasant woman holding her child while the rich stood haughtily by. What else was I failing to see?

I lollygagged around the galley. Pictures ranged from sunsets to cars to manatees and dolphins with Broadway smiles. Some were surreal, like a watercolor of Poseidon riding a wave down a city street, and another of a marching band made up of creatures of the sea. But none stopped me dead in my tracks like the crudely drawn and sloppily painted picture of a troll with warts on its face chasing a giraffe with the head of a lion.

When the fog finally lifts, everything is so clear.

41

Danielle was talking to a man twice her age. His tongue drooled out his mouth.

"Beat it, buddy," I said as I inserted myself between them. "You're old enough to be her father."

"We were just—"

"I a*m* her father."

The man blushed and backed away before realizing he was in reverse. He turned and scuttered off.

"Who did this?" I demanded, holding up the picture.

"Daddy?" Danielle said with a twinkle in her eye.

"Who did this?" I repeated.

"A young girl in—"

"What's her name?"

"Sally. It says there." She pointed to the lower left hand corner of the picture.

"Describe her to me."

"Why do you want to know?"

Good question, Danielle.

"I was hired to find a missing girl," I lied. "And this," I held up the picture, "looks like something she might draw."

Then I tacked on, fending off a question she might ask, "I've seen some of her other drawings and this looks similar."

It beat telling Danielle that I had squatted on my knees in front of Gabriela as she told me I looked like a giraffe with a lion's head on it, after I'd told her that Walt Disney World had trolls with warts on their faces.

"Why were you hired to find her?"

"Listen," I said, my breath escaping as I attempted to regain my composure. "I'm not even sure it's the same young girl. I'm just curious, that's all."

She eyed me suspiciously. "She's a nice girl—a real talker, I can tell you that."

"Age?"

"We have mixed ages in our classes. Ten? Nine? Somewhere in there, I'd guess."

"Nationality?"

"I'm not sure," she said defensively.

"Nordic blonde?"

"You know better."

"How long has she been in the school you volunteer at?"

"She was there when I started, but I just signed on after the semester."

I didn't want to tip my hand or scare Gabriela away. Furthermore, if it was her, she had to be staying somewhere. I couldn't go barging in, my six-shooter leading the way. For all I knew, Flores was in possession of the children.

I didn't think that was the case.

"She may or may not be the child I'm looking for," I said. "How can I come by your class tomorrow and take a peek?"

"I don't know. What if she is? Is she a runaway? I don't understand why you're looking for her."

"*Might* be looking for her. I'll drop by. If she's not the one, there's no need to get worked up about it."

Danielle pursed her lips. "You didn't answer my question. Why are you looking for her?"

"I'm not going to answer that question until I know if she is the one."

She gave that some thought and then gave a perky, "Okay."

We agreed that it would be best if I casually observed from a side street during recess.

"But don't creep people out," she said.

"I understand."

"I mean, you just can't loiter around—"

"I got it."

"Because sometimes you come across—"

"We're cool. Ten-thirty, right?"

"That's when recess starts. But you know if it rains, we stay inside."

KATHLEEN SIPPED DECAF COFFEE, WHICH WAS NEW for her. She never had coffee at night. Straws, and now decaf coffee—which is coffee without the coffee part. That was all pretty radical for me. I'm not big on change. I took a sip of twenty-year port.

"You think Danielle has Gabriela in a class she volunteers at?" Kathleen said as we sat on her balcony. A car honked below. But up in the air, everything down there seemed a different world.

"I do."

"Then what? Assuming it is her?"

"See who picks her up." I leaned back in my chair and turned on the ceiling fan.

"Pretend time—who do you think will pick her up from school?"

"Don't know."

"I said pretend."

"Couple thugs for Flores. Thug one and thug two."

"Probability?" she asked.

"Low. Flores wouldn't enroll them in a local school. I didn't even look at all the pictures. Maybe giraffes and lions were a theme. Maybe a dozen pictures looked like that."

"Any long shots?"

"Tina Welch."

"That would be interesting," she said. "What would be her angle?"

"Got me. She's a long shot, remember?"

"You can do better than that."

Geez, was I tired of that line.

"Let's leave it at this," she said. "Your Ms. Welch is a horse of many colors. Any other contenders?"

Silence.

"Hey, super-sonic. I'm talking to you."

Shrug.

"You're not going to answer my question, are you?"

"No."

"You think you know, don't you?"

"Not really."

"I don't blame you. You thought they were dead and nothing crushes us more than broken hope."

She drew her legs into her and wrapped her arms around them. I turned the fan off.

IT RAINED DURING MY RUN IN THE MORNING. THEN, IN an apologetic manner, the gray clouds ushered themselves away and surrendered the day to puffy bunny tails that floated under a robin-egg sky. A soft breeze petted my damp skin just enough to make me think I should turn and see who had touched me.

At ten-thirty, I sat in my truck across the street from an elementary school north of downtown St. Petersburg. I sipped warm coffee and tried to recall when I had last changed the oil.

The door flung open for recess, and children exploded into freedom like dry leaves in front of a blower. I bolted up in my seat. There were too many of them. Dozens and dozens. All ages. Sexes. Nationalities. Place looked like a Coca-Cola commercial from the 1970s.

And then . . . I recognized one.

And then another.

SAME PLACE. SAME DAY. TWO-THIRTY. A CARAVAN OF cars block my view as they queue up to collect the little people. I leave the truck. I walk briskly across the street as the first of the cars start to pull out. Children dart about playing with each other. Screaming. Laughing. Some parents are out of their cars and talking. Others wait patiently for the cars ahead of them to inch forward. I slow my pace. I pull my baseball cap low over my face.

Don't creep people out.

She stands like a great blue heron, tall, erect, motionless. Scanning the crowd for the children, *her* children. All the noise and confusion does not matter, for her world is on mute. She peers between the bodies and heads as she searches for them. Ana Maria finds her. Of course. She is older. More mature. She knows not to keep the woman waiting. Gabriela sees the woman and runs to her. She is wild, that little one. Stuffed with life so hard it springs out of her. I position myself behind their surrogate mother. It is easy. I could drop an H-bomb behind her and she would not flinch. She is drowning with the girls. She is rejoicing in life. How was your day? Was the lunch I packed okay? Did you see the happy note I put in? Uncertainty hides in her voice. She's not used to packing lunches or writing happy notes. It's new and exciting for her. Gabriela holds up a paper she wants to show off. Ana Maria stands politely behind her little sister. Ana Maria's eyes shift. They meet mine. Her expression changes. Not fear. Shock?

Gabriela's blathering. Something needs to be done by tomorrow and can we start it when we get home? Right away? Of, course dear. But then the woman sees that Ana Maria's eyes are catatonic, staring at something beyond her.

Gabriela spots me. "Hey, it's lion head. I thought you said we wouldn't see him again."

I feel for her—in that briefest moment. *Turn your head. Quick. It is only me. And you know I bring you no harm, my apple girl.*

She turns her head.

"Hello, Charlotte. You don't mind if I follow you home, do you?"

42

RAFAEL

"*Oui*," Rafael said into his phone. "By tomorrow this time, they will be no more."

He disconnected and his gaze, unleashed from the chewed thoughts of his mind, floated out toward Straub Park and the marina. Children played like squirrels in the massive trunk of the ancient banyan tree. A boy on a skateboard swerved around them, the sinuous sway of his hips curving up the sidewalk.

Rafael took a sip of his coffee. He said to Fredrick, "They are safe?"

"Yes."

"Still, you must get back."

"Soon. Are we staying afterwards?"

"Not this time. We must take the cargo and leave."

Fredrick took a bite of a croissant. "Our usual method?"

"No. Fire."

"Fire?"

"It is the best way to hit all targets and cover our tracks," Rafael said.

They discussed their plan.

"What time?" Fredrick asked.

"Tomorrow. The part of clock that is neither night nor day."

"Are you sure we must wait?" Fredrick said. "That is not what we do."

"Our escape is not finalized. This job requires a quick exit. It would be hard to hide him, and I have no patience for that."

Fredrick spread his hands. "This man? He will be there at the appointed hour? If not, we are . . . "

"He will be there," Rafael reassured his accomplice who, although quick of body, was ponderous with his thoughts.

Fredrick leaned back. "I should very much enjoy being on a boat."

Rafael tried to think of the boat, but his mind stuck on Tina Welch. Had he recognized himself in her? What if he had? Even if I were to chase her, he thought, where would I start? *I'm over-reacting. I can potentially expose myself more by pursuing her than simply returning to France. But then what? Glance over my shoulder every—*

"What are you thinking?" Fredrick said.

"Pardon?"

"Your lips were moving, but no words came out."

"There is something else I may need to do."

"What is that?"

Rafael told him.

Fredrick said, "For all we know, she may be sunbathing in the Virgin Islands."

"The Virgin Islands," Rafael murmured. Of all the places in the world, they had the most lascivious name. "I don't think so."

"Why not?"

Rafael had to dig inside for the answer, for his doubt stemmed more from an unexamined feeling than from a coherent memory. This did not mean that he denied his emotions. He considered emotions to be an untamed river to be viaducted into his mind, where they could be sorted and arranged. Calculated like a math equation.

The museum. Tina Welch. Emma Bannon. How they looked at each other. How Welch had stepped in to defend Emma when the man who had arrived with the elegant woman had approached her. Welch, pulling herself up to her considerable height, a bird spreading its feathers. Touching Emma on her shoulder when she turned to leave.

"I don't think she's in the Virgin Islands," Rafael said, although Fredrick could barely hear him. "I think she's . . ."

Emma Bannon sprang out of the front door of her high-rise and rounded the corner. Rafael tracked her.

"Is it her?" Fredrick asked, following Rafael's gaze. "I thought you said she was tall."

"It is her lover," Rafael said, for he prided himself with a sixth sense in such matters.

"Ah. You are certain?"

"I am."

"You were always gifted at such things."

"The boy," Rafael said.

Fredrick stood. "Yes. I will go."

Rafael glanced at his 1934 Rolex Oyster stainless steel watch. The most desirable of all watches, his had never been refinished. It was in pristine condition. At the bottom of the face, there was a watch within a watch—a wheel within a wheel—where the seconds mechanically ticked by. He considered his body to be a timepiece, and wondered how long it would tick—the last tick only recognized as such by the absence of a following tick. *The watch will outlive me,* he thought. *It will grace someone else's wrist.*

For the first time in a long time, Rafael Cherez felt truly sad.

43

Twin dormer windows with peaked tops interrupted the flat roofline of Charlotte's home. Cole wasn't there when we entered the house. But Little Joe was. So was a nanny—Nanny Suzy. Unbelievable. Charlotte asked Nanny Suzy to take the children to the backyard.

"Where's Cole? Attending a school board meeting?" I said to Charlotte, who was doing a sterling job of avoiding eye contact.

"He's working. He's practicing law three days a week."

"Better be his last will and testament unless he's got a good story for me. Or do you want to take a whack at it?"

"I need to help the children with their homework."

"You just sent them out back."

"We have fun time when they first get home, then we do homework."

"Did you text him?"

"No," she said.

"Going to?"

"Yes."

"Mind if I wait outside?"

"It's a free world."

"Look at me."
She didn't.
"Look at me."
She did.
"Why did you keep me in the dark?"
"I think Stephen should—"
"I thought they were—look at me. What the *heck* were you thinking?"

Charlotte's lips trembled. She planted her eyes on mine. "Don't take them from us. They are all he has. They are the world to him, and us to them. Their father, mother, older sister—we are all they have."

"Do they know?"

"No." Her chest heaved and she struggled to control her breathing. "We didn't know how to tell them, or where this all ends up. We told them their sister and father had to leave for a few weeks."

"You let me believe . . ."

I stopped talking as Charlotte covered her mouth with her hand. She flew out of the room, her heavy sobs echoing down the hall.

What? Am I the bad guy here?

I stole two beers from the refrigerator and stalked out to the covered front porch. I grabbed a chair and took a long draw from the bottle, lecturing myself to count to ten before bashing Cole's head in. I stood. I paced. I drank. I killed a fly. I looked for another one.

Although agitated, I was relieved that the children were fine. It wasn't a total shock that Cole and Charlotte had them. Cole had been the name I kept from Kathleen when she had asked me who I thought had the children. It had first hit me when Binelli asked if Cole was a person of interest. Her question had sparked a new road to consider—a road that had nothing to do with Cole. Instead, it gave me a backstage pass inside Alejandro's head. His POV. What would he do if he felt his family was in imminent danger? What did Sheriff Sam do? What would I do if I ever had children?

Protect them. Move the children to safety.

Cole pulled in fast and vaulted the front steps in two strides.

"Where are they?"

"Let me see," I said idly. "First they have fun time. Then homework. You know the routine."

He started to go inside. I grabbed his arm.

"Not so fast," I said.

"I want to see my—the children."

"I don't even know where to start with that."

"It's not—"

"Tell me why I've been suffocating in hell the past few weeks thinking they were dead while you and your bunk mate were enrolling them in school and playing Ward and June Cleaver."

His breath escaped him. I imagined it had been a tense drive in from wherever he had come from. I freed his arm and gave him the second beer. "Have a seat, counselor. Consider yourself lucky that you don't have broken teeth."

He plopped down like a Raggedy Ann doll.

"Alejandro brought them to you, didn't he?" I said.

Gabriela bounded around the corner of the house. "I knew you were home," she said and flung herself onto Cole's lap. He wrapped his arms around her and planted a kiss on her cheek.

"Tell you what," he said to her. "Mr. Jake and I need to talk, so we're going out for a while." He glanced at me. He didn't want to discuss anything when the children might bomb his lap at any moment. "Let's go tell Ms. Charlotte."

She bounced off his lap and said, "I'm on it like Blue Bonnet." She dashed inside.

Cole followed her in. A moment later he came back out.

"Let's ride," he said.

. . .

WE GRABBED TWO STOOLS at the Riptides bar that was open to the beach. The Gulf of Mexico was a flat, massive sheet of tarnished silver. Exhausted from cold fronts ripping it from the northwest, and a tumultuous year of typhoon winds attacking its unprotected flank from the south, it lay quiet and spent, finally left to its own immobile solitude. And left alone, the Gulf of Mexico has no quarrels with anyone; it spawns no storms to torment some distant shore.

Cole and I did the silent act on the short trip over. I wanted to explode on him, but that would serve no useful purpose other than to make me feel better. But what's wrong with making me feel better?

After we ordered drinks, the bartender asked if we wanted to round up our bill to the next dollar to donate to the hurricane relief effort. I told her to round it to the next ten. Too many businesses had lost inventory, operating income, and suffered structural damage from the hurricane.

"Speak," I said. "And just so you know where we stand: You have exhausted every untruth, lie, falsehood and innuendo that I ever granted, or—for some unfathomable cosmic reason—you assumed you were entitled to."

"Okay," he said.

"You lied and were deceitful."

"Guilty."

"I want to break every bone in your body and bury them at sea."

"I understand," he said, refusing to put on the gloves.

"Hold a ceremonial fire first."

"Of course."

"Sell tickets. Roast weenies over your ashes. Roast *your* weenie in the ashes. You can forget malice toward none and charity for all."

"I don't blame you," he said in an irritatingly calm voice.

"Good. 'Cause I blame you."

I glanced out toward the water to calm myself and fought a crushing urge to chuck it all. The sun dropped out from underneath a dark cloud that looked like a galactic spaceship. The world brightened, like sunrise at sunset. Jet vapors stenciled the sky. I'd give half my record collection to be in one. Six miles high, sipping a whiskey, winging 600 hundred miles an hour away from it all.

"We meant to tell you," Cole said to the back of my head. "We *were* going to tell you, but we were afraid you would force us to give up the children."

I faced him. "From the top."

Cole took a second and then started in. "He—Alejandro—asked me to keep the children. He—"

"When?"

"The first time he came over."

"When he came for the plunger?"

"Uh, the plunger was actually the second time he came over."

"I told the man not to leave and what? He goes door-to-door soliciting bleeding hearts?"

"He spoke to no one but me."

"You know this?"

"I do," he said.

"But you lie."

"No more."

"I'll judge that. Go on."

"He knew he was in danger. Said the men after his daughter and Little Joe never failed. That they—"

"You're telling me you *knew* that someone was after Little Joe."

"That's correct. Sergio Flores. He is Little Joe's father."

"Kiss my grits, Stevie. Is there anything you haven't previously lied to me about?"

He seemed to give that serious thought. "Not much," he said in a dismissive tone. "I do fish."

"Charlotte's not married or getting a divorce, is she?"

He bounced his head. "I might have been blowing smoke there, too. Trying to keep her out of it."

I leaned back in my stool. I found myself admiring Cole and I didn't know why, and then I did. He was keeping to his agenda. He had made a promise to Alejandro to protect the children. Unlike my promise to Martina, he had honored his.

"Keep it rolling," I said.

"Like a drummer," Stephen Cole said.

"Pardon?"

His eyes clouded over. "Nothing." But he had momentarily zoned out. He recovered quickly. "Alejandro told me that Flores would win. That—"

"He told you that?"

"It would be a more efficient conversation if you didn't interrupt."

I spread my hands. "By all means, Great One."

He took a swig from his bottle of beer. "He told me everything. How he married young and had Martina and then he and his wife waited years before having more children. How his wife, Nicole, died of cancer. How his oldest daughter, Martina, got a job as a maid at the Flores compound. Sergio Flores is a hero in his hometown. He showers charities with money, bankrolls the school, and funds the hospital. It's blood money, but tell that to the mother whose kid is getting a vaccine shot, an education, a backpack and a free laptop in a country where the average worker earns $843 a month. Dirty money doing good deeds. Brackish money.

"Martina and Flores had an affair that produced a child. He wanted to marry her. She refused. She understood where the money came from. Worse yet, she felt compelled to do something about it. She stole away one night with Little Joe."

That would explain why Flores wanted to kill Martina.

Binelli had questioned me on his possible motive when we had met.

"Alejandro asked me to take the children, at least until the feds"—he glanced at me—"your people arrived to relocate him. He didn't have confidence that would happen. He didn't entirely trust you, which is why I may have been more evasive than I should have. It wasn't anything you said, it's the system. I was caught between helping you and honoring my pledge to him."

He chose correctly, and had performed commendably, but I didn't feel like telling him that.

"Why not ship Martina to you as well?" I said.

"She refused to leave him. I think she *wanted* to be separated from her son. To increase his chance of survival. I sensed that both Alejandro and Martina had greater confidence in Flores than . . . in their new situation."

I let that slide.

"What was his reason for coming here?" I said.

"He saw it as an opportunity to move his family to America and be free of Flores. He misled our government to believe that he had information on Flores. Anything he knew, he garnered from Martina, but he wanted her out of it. Although it happened with such ease, he suspected Flores might have been behind the whole show. You know, have the feds bring Little Joe in and then snatch him from underneath their eyes.

I again thought of Alejandro and Sheriff Sam and the lengths they went to protect their children. I could fault neither man.

"Did Alejandro give you anything concrete?" I said.

"No. He said Flores was a master marionette—pulling strings all the time. He didn't really add to that."

"And you said what? Give, me your tired, your poor? Your huddled children yearning to breathe the free American air?"

"Absolutely not," Cole spit out. "No way did I want three

kids and one of them with a bull's eye on his back. But Charlotte saw it another way. The right way."

"What's the right way, 'cause I'm all twisted around here?"

"Seize life," he said with earnest, ignoring my attitude. "Charlotte lost her parents at an early age."

"My apple picker from Wisconsin?"

"What?"

"Nothing. What's her story?"

"Her parents were killed in a car accident. Some white-trash in a pickup with a pair of balls hanging from his trailer hitch. Guy was so boozed-out he had no memory of it. Third offense. She was six and raised by an aunt who prayed to Jesus in the morning, drank JD and Coke at night, and who thought her sister got what she deserved because she'd had an abortion when she was fifteen. Charlotte was dragged through six schools in twelve years. She never thought she'd get a clean swing at anything."

"When did—"

"She can't have children," Cole said.

"Charlotte?"

"Due to inflammation when she was young. Her aunt refused to seek medical treatment for her. God's way and all of that."

I was going to say I was sorry, but recalled Emma lecturing me that that was meaningless.

"When did Alejandro bring over the children?" I said, sounding insensitive—and then wishing I'd thrown an apologetic remark out.

"He came over the evening he and Martina were murdered. He had a premonition that his time was getting thin. Something about you can hide in a hole for only so long. He made me—made us—promise that we would raise them. Love them." Cole shook his head. "I told him that he was overreacting, that everything would be fine, but Charlotte—she wanted to take them."

"What was he going to tell me when I showed up the next morning and his children were gone?"

"They stayed with Charlotte that night. The plan was to move them back in the morning."

A thought flirted with my mind but I couldn't hold it, nor would it ever find its way back to me. Cole continued.

"We planned to keep them at nights until you came and moved them. No big deal, right? He left. Brought them back ten minutes later. We told them, a few days later, that their father and older sister had gone back to Mexico for a while."

"When did you know that Alejandro and Martina were murdered?"

"When he didn't come to collect them. I saw you break in the house and I knew."

"When are you going to tell them?"

"We don't know. Charlotte worries about Ana Maria. She's old enough to smell the truth but too young to challenge a lie. That's not how to start a relationship, but we hesitate to tell them until we feel safe. Little Joe will never remember his true mother, and Gabriela?" He swung his head and squinted his left eye. "That engine never stops."

"When we met at Hurricanes, you had them then, at Charlotte's house."

"We did."

"Straight out lied to me," I said.

"We did."

"I'm not getting even a whiff of remorse."

"The children are safe."

I scored him a point there. He'd done a better job at guarding the hole than I had.

"Did you hear anything that night?"

"No."

"If you—"

"I heard nothing. I've played the night over in my head a hundred times."

I planted my elbows on the counter. A thin, orange wafer of sun remained on the horizon, and then slipped into Poseidon's arms. Straggling sunset worshippers turned their backs to the horizon. They slogged toward higher ground, their heads down, shoulders bent. I reached for my whiskey, but just fondled it as the playlist went from reggae to country.

"They're not seashells you collect on the beach," I said. "You just can't pretend they're yours."

"We're not pretending. They are ours."

"How do you plan to legally—"

"That's my problem, not yours."

"We'll let that slide for now. How do you and Charlotte feel about the real problem in your life?"

"Which is?"

"You are in possession of Sergio Flores's only known son."

"She is aware," Cole said.

"You told her?"

"Yes."

"You're lying."

"I am not," he said.

"It's all you do."

"It's all I did."

He tented his hands in front of him. He was different from when we first met. His mind was quicker. His voice was confident. His eyes bright. He had shed a few worthless pounds. A moment of silence passed between us. A monk parakeet screeched from somewhere.

"He'll grab his son," I said. "Kill you all."

"Not again."

"Pardon?"

He hesitated, as if he'd been processing something internal.

"Did you hear what I said?"

"Why do you think we went along with you?" he said. "That's why Charlotte got the list of distributors for you. We can't rest until Flores is put away." He rested his eyes on mine. "We were hoping you could help us."

For a moment, I thought the man was going to break down. *What was his story?*

"After your deceit?" I said. "Why would I?"

"To make things right. That's what people like you do." His eyes were hard on mine. "You can't believe how effortlessly we formed a family. Charlotte is so good with them. We knew it was stupid—putting them in school. But you're either up, or you're getting up. You are never down," he said more to himself, like a mantra he'd repeated a thousand times.

"That's all great until a bullet weighs in."

"I have a contract on a house in Jacksonville."

"You won't make Jacksonville. You, Charlotte, Ana Maria and Gabriela will be dead before your loan clears."

Cole rubbed his forehead with his hands.

I stood up. "Let's go."

"Where?" Cole asked.

"Charlotte's house. Fast."

AS WE STEPPED ONTO THE FRONT PORCH, GABRIELA shrieked from inside. She burst through the front door, and much like she had the first morning in the cottage, nearly ran into me. She held Bongo, the stuffed monkey in her right hand.

"Beep, beep. I'm a jeep," she said.

"Scram Sam, but leave Bongo with me," I said.

"My name's not Sam."

"Is now."

"Why do you want Bongo?" she asked.

"So I can whisper in his ear that the trolls are after him."

She twisted her fingers as she'd done before. "The one with warts?"

"And pointy ears." I took Bongo from her.

"Go on," Cole said. "Help Ms. Charlotte with dinner."

"Are you staying for dinner?" she said to me.

That wasn't my call.

"He's invited," Cole said.

She ran back in the house, yelling to whomever that I was staying.

I took out my pocketknife and slit Bongo's throat, where the loose thread was. Inside was a chip. I pulled it out and held it up for Cole to see.

"If it's still operational, they know we're here," I said. "That's how they found Alejandro."

"We need to move," he said.

"No."

"No?"

"Bongo needs to move. And I won't be staying for dinner."

44

I saw God that night.

I never expected to see Her—She appeared in the masculine form—as I do not acknowledge Her existence, although that is not to say I deny Her. I write this down so that as I age into that dark bar of senility, I will have set my God in stone. Put forth my sacred script for someone to unearth in a dark and dusty cave. Or was I delusional and under the spell of a stealth senility that had unknowingly taken up presence in a decaying mind? You decide. I've lived with that night long enough and can't say I care one way or the other.

Garrett and I decided to keep Bongo on the boat. Rafael would follow the tracking device to the *Lauren Rowe*—assuming it was still active—where we would host a surprise party. Morgan would keep an eye on Charlotte's house.

Our vaudeville-worthy plan was a ninety-pound weakling that hadn't eaten in three days, but it was all we had. If the tracking device was still operational, why hadn't Rafael made his move? If it wasn't, it wouldn't lead him to the *Lauren Rowe*. We could only assume that the Goddess of Luck had shone down upon us and in some manner altered Rafael's plan.

What if Rafael wasn't interested in the Brady Bunch? He

could snatch Little Joe when Charlotte was out strolling with the kids and be on a private jet within an hour. We weren't banking on that. Leaving the group alive was to invite trouble later. But on the other hand, a mass murder would invite an all-fronts investigation. Unless it was an accident.

Rafael might have previously scouted out the location and knew the children were in the house. Why he hadn't acted was another "what if" followed by "maybe." If that were the case, then we had tipped our hand by moving Bongo to the boat. We thought of running the tracking device down to MacDill. At least we could learn if it was still operational or not. Unfortunately, if it wasn't operational, we wouldn't know when it had died. We decided not to waste the time. We had no choice but to juggle a galaxy of maybes, contemplate a universe of what-ifs, and flounder in a sea of unknowns.

AT TWO A.M., I CLIMBED INTO MY TRUCK AND WENT TO check on Morgan. Charlotte's street slept, except for Morgan, who was coughing and rubbing his throat. The man had been working himself to exhaustion. Rising earlier each day to work on his book without sacrificing time at the refugee house, frequently forgoing his morning mediation at the end of his dock. Perhaps he, too, felt the clock crawling up his spine.

I insisted that he go home. Between Garrett and me, we could keep a watchful eye on the house. He hacked out a protest, but I told him to get lost—and to sleep in.

I slumped exhausted in my truck. My legs hurt. In the darkest hours of the night, when my body battled fatigue and the siren bosom of sleep whispered my name, the things I hadn't done in my life paraded in front of me. A tormenting procession of destinations and accomplishments that would not be checked off by a certain age. The lost opportunities pulled equal to my aspirations. Worse yet, they had the inside rail. Would they pass at one point? Switch positions? Is age a lengthening pageant of what could have been, of what will never be? Perhaps mortality is a gift. A final resolution to the cathedral of empty questions that bother us so.

I slapped my face.

I slapped it, hard, twice again.

AT 4:15, GARRETT SAID, "I SMELL SMOKE."

I'd driven over from Charlotte's house and we were standing in front of the *Lauren Rowe*. We'd been discussing our next move if the succeeding nights were as quiet as that night. The Cole house had been unguarded for no more than ten minutes. Or had it been twenty? We'd foolishly gotten too engaged in our conversation and hadn't paid attention to the clock.

My phone rang. Welch. In the middle of the night? I started to punch it, but Garrett stepped into me. He pushed my phone down and away.

"From the direction of Charlotte's house," he said.

When Garrett communicates in non-verbal methods, it is wise to pay attention. The phone kept ringing while I took in a deep breath through my nostrils. A light north-northwest breeze carried a whiff of charred wood.

"Maybe he's trying to draw us out," I said.

A tendril of flame flickered above the treetops, as if a distant palm frond had gone ablaze.

"We can't ignore it," he said. "We have to split. You want the boat or the house?"

"I'll take the house," I said, and that is how I came to see You-Know-Who.

45

I gunned the truck down the street, the engine nearly leaping off the block. Flames now erupted above the trees like an oil well blowout. It could be any one of the streets close to Charlotte's. But I knew. Just like you know something bad will happen to you and you're almost relieved when it does. *At least now I don't need to worry about it anymore.*

I careened around the corner. Charlotte's house was an inferno.

Fire lashed out of the upstairs dormer windows. The intense heat invaded the truck. A siren wailed in the distance. A neighbor to the right watered his house with a hose. He kept trying to get closer, but was driven back by the heat. His stream of water looked like he was pissing on an angry sun. I couldn't imagine a drop getting close before it boiled.

I vaulted out of the truck and raced toward the house.

I am super-sonic. Watch me fly.

Impossible. The heat was the tormented soul of the devil. It formed a ring of gaseous lava around the house. To even approach it beyond the barrier would be certain death. Maybe Cole got his family out.

Then where are they?

I bounced on my feet. Garden hose.

I bolted to the north side of the house, opposite from where the neighbor was, and where the flames, due to the light breeze, were not as fierce as the other side. I uncoiled the neighbor's hose and raced around to the front. I dosed myself and shot a stream into the cauldron. Worthless. I pressed forward. My eyebrows were singeing, my face starting to blister. The heat drove me back. To move in would be suicide.

Stephen Cole walked out the front door.

Later, when recounting the tale to Garrett, he interrupted me and said, "You mean he *ran* out the front door."

"No, he *walked* out the front door."

Garrett, never one to grant the metaphysical a possibility, or the surreal a seat at the table, had remained silent. Morgan, on the other hand, upon hearing my declaration that Cole had walked out of the house, merely said, "My father says that even at our best, we are faintly what we can be."

What do you do with that?

Charlotte was his backpack. Her arms clasped his neck and her legs hiked around his hips. Ana Maria rode one hip and Gabriela the other. The flames roared at him in frustration. He, nor the angels he carried, showed any effect. They displayed no panic. Gave no sound.

A dream, right? *Then wake up, man.* I tried to run to his side, but the flames that held such reverence for Cole found a mere mortal victim in me. My legs were immobile. They would not be a willing party to suicide. There would not carry me into the Valley of Death. I turned the hose on Cole. Worthless. All I could do was witness the fire peel skin off their faces. They became a crumbling ball of fire as Cole collapsed to his knees. Ashes to ashes.

But that didn't happen. My mind was playing tricks on me. It took what it saw, processed it based on past experience and knowledge, and envisioned the inevitable conclusion.

This is what happened:
Cole walked.

He kept his madly measured and steady pace, the water hitting him as it shot from my hose. The flames pushed me back. I could not maintain my position against a superior force. I adjusted the nozzle so that it was more a spray and less a hard stream. Cole walked forward. I retreated. Forward. Backward. Finally, safe from the heat—*had it ever threatened him?* —he bent down and Charlotte hopped off his back. He lowered each of the girls to the ground.

"They got Little Joe," he said.

Gabriela wore a nightgown two sizes too large. She had just come through the flames and—

"Did you hear what I said?" Cole demanded.

"Are you okay?" I stammered out.

"I said they got Little Joe."

"You're not burnt?"

"There were two of them. They took him and torched the house. Who are you calling?"

"911. You need—"

"We're fine."

"How did you—"

Cole stepped into me. "Snap out of it. You're ten minutes behind them."

My phone rang. Welch again.

"What?" I said, relieved for the intrusion, thankful for something real.

"I'm on him," Welch said.

"Rafael?"

"Who else, bucko?"

"How—"

"You listen, I talk," she said. "He was staking Emma and me out, but missed that I was watching him watch us. He broke into our condo last night, but we were gone—I left him a note on the pillow. I called in a favor from some friends and we kept a tail on him."

"He burned down—"

"You're listening, remember?" she said in a hushed voice. "I followed him to a house. But when I got there it was in flames. There was nothing I could do. Rafael and another man were running out of the house. Rafael had a small boy in his arms."

"That's Sergio Flores's son."

"I know—the others—I'm sorry. I made the decision to follow. There was nothing—"

"They're fine."

"How? The house was—"

"Later. Rafael?"

"Headed toward Fort De Soto," she said. "I don't know the area. Is there a different road off?"

"No. One road in and out. He must be planning to leave by boat. Where exactly are you?"

"The entrance. It's a long road. I came to a T and—"

"See what direction he goes and then pull up. Anything beyond that and he'll make you. I'll pick you up."

The line was quiet. Welch was on a lonely patch of road. She couldn't follow Rafael without revealing herself. I was about to supplicate my case to her again, when she said, "Okay."

The line went dead.

"You know where he is?" Cole said, his eyes piecing mine.

"I do. He's—"

"Go."

"You sure you're—"

"Go."

I picked up Garrett. We chased the truck's headlights to my house, where we snatched the red spinnaker bag—the Steiner eOptics night goggles were in it—as well as the Remington sniper rifle. I called Morgan, stirring him from a deep sleep, and told him what we needed him to do. I felt bad recruiting him, but he did not hesitate.

As we pulled away from my house, I touched my face. Skin peeled off. Yet Cole had . . .

There'd be time for that later.

46

I didn't bank on the paranormal bailing me out twice, although that is what happened. The second time, however, can be largely attributed to Welch's vociferous outcry.

Fort De Soto State Park is comprised of five separate islands, or keys, and boasts over seven miles of waterfront. Three of those seven miles are sandy beaches. The remainder is a web of interlocked and inhospitable mangroves—not conducive to a rendezvous with a boat. The main island is shaped like a crooked V. A single road leads onto it but then splits at the conjuncture of the V. One leg goes to North Beach and the other to South Beach. Off to the side at that intersection was a black car. Welch.

Or not.

I pulled up behind it. Garrett swung open the passenger door and crouched behind it, using it as a shield. His drew his gun. I called out to her. She stepped out of the car and swung her head behind her toward North Beach.

"He headed down the road," she said.

Garrett told her to get in the truck as I reminded myself

that I didn't wholly trust her. She was in black jeans and a dark T-shirt. No heels tonight.

I swung to the right and killed the lights. The straight road serviced a series of expansive parking lots abutting the beaches. I stopped at the first one. We got out of the truck. We listened.

Nothing.

We did the same at the next parking lot. Double nothing. At each one, Garrett and I took turns with the Steiners, scanning 360° for anything that moved.

The road took a sharp right at the old fort. It had been built to keep the Spanish out of Tampa Bay, and the Spanish, getting sight of her entrenched guns, never bothered to make an appearance. Alejandro had been right: *A fox will not approach the hole if he knows a lion is guarding it.* We repeated our futile exercise at the fort's parking lot as well as each successive parking lot. The possibility grew alongside my mounting anxiety that Rafael was either wading out to a boat, or he had rendezvoused at a break in the mangroves. Such a rendezvous, though, would be difficult for someone intimate with the area and nearly impossible for anyone else.

The road ended in a wooded cul-de-sac. Before we reached it, I swung the truck into the shadows by the trees and killed the engine. Either they had found that elusive spot, or they were in front of us, trapped at the end of the island. Assuming they weren't skimming over the gulf popping Champagne. I didn't think that was the case, as Morgan would have notified me. My instructions to Morgan had been to take *Impulse* and idle off Bunce Pass. If Rafael had a boat, I didn't want to be standing dry-foot watching him wave adios to me.

Kathleen in my head, for she is always there: *That would be bon voyage, darling, not adios, remember?*

We spilled out of the truck. Garrett took the Steiners and scanned the area. I explained to Welch that Morgan had my boat and would text me if he saw anything. We were shrouded on one side by pine trees and mangroves. The three of us crouched in the dark shadows of the trees, straining to both hear and see. I rubbed my forehead. More skin peeled off on my hand. Yet Cole had appeared un—

My phone vibrated with a text message just as Garrett, with the Steiners welded to his face, whispered, "Two o'clock."

The text was from Morgan.

boat inside sandbar

There was a sandbar that ran a couple hundred feet off North Beach. Between it and the shore, the water ran deep, even at low tide. Someone knew what he was doing. I texted *ok* back to let Morgan to let him know I received his message. I told Garrett and Welch.

"What do you see?" Welch said to Garrett.

"Two men. One is carrying something—or someone. Their vehicle is parked behind them in the curve of the road." He gave me the Steiners. "Our plan?"

Welch jumped in. "We move to their left, there," she jutted her chin toward the other side of the road. "Along those bushes. We cut underneath them—"

"Those are mangroves," I said. "Their above-ground roots are a steel web." I turned to Garrett. "We'll hug this side of the mangroves. When we reach positions, we wait until they're in the water."

"You'll need to get across the road," Garrett said. "See the taller of the pines? I'll be on the east side of those. On the count of fifteen. One—" Garrett sprinted low to the ground hugging the mangroves.

Welch said, "I don't—"

"He'll go straight in. We'll come in ninety degrees to his left. Never stay together. Always split. Con—"

"I think I can—"

"—fusion is their enemy and our friend. You sign on or stay back."

"I can—"

"Sign on or stay back."

"Fine. But how are we going to cross the road? We'll be exposed."

I said, "Thirteen, fourteen, fifteen."

To our right, where Garrett had vanished, came the sound of breaking sticks. Not loud enough to be suspected as a trap, but not soft enough to ignore.

I grabbed Welch's arm. "Now."

We darted across the exposed pavement just as the moon broke free of a cloud.

I'm a fast runner, but Welch had no problem keeping pace. We crossed the road and hustled to the shielded side of an oak tree. The sand was cool and littered with twigs and shells. I opened my mouth so as to breathe easier and with less noise. Welch did the same. In front of us were stumps from Australian pines that had been cut down. I made a note to avoid them when we moved out.

"Hear anything?" I said to Welch. My hearing sucks. I put the Steiners up to my face.

"Only the sound of an old man wheezing," she said in a stage whisper.

"I thought I was going to have to carry you back there."

"You mean when I slowed down so I didn't run into you? When do we advance?"

"When they first hit the beach, I get a text."

"That's so cute. What are you doing, arranging a golf outing?"

"Might," I said keeping the binoculars in front or my eyes. "Why don't you slip into something more comfortable and meet us at the nineteenth hole."

"And leave you out here with only your wits? The birds

would eat you alive. We need to move now. We have the advantage of surprise."

I put down the Steiners. "Fine, super-agent. You want to draw your gun and charge ahead with the moon on your back?"

"What if your guy in the boat is compromised?"

"He won't be."

"Is he ex ops like you?"

"More like an enterprising hippie," I said.

"You're screwing with me, right?"

"I'm spoken for. But I do dig tall women."

"I'm with Emma, you ignorant dildo."

"Still trying to make me jealous."

"Just so we're clear, I get Rafael."

"We don't—"

"He's mine. He controlled Wright."

I was getting a glimpse at why Tina Welch fled the burning house. It wasn't a pretty sight.

"Listen, toots," I said. "We can't count how many ways there are to die out here. We focus on staying alive. If a jellyfish sends Rafael to his maker, that is victory. No style points. You got that?"

"He—"

"You got that?"

"Sure, *toots*."

I put the Steiners back to my face. The shadows were moving. I hadn't been paying attention. A whistle pierced the night. Garrett.

"What was *that*?" Welch whispered, a little too loud for my taste.

"Garrett. We move in five, four—"

"The hell? You guys do this every—"

"Watch out for the stumps." I vaulted out of my crouched position and ran toward the beach, sprinting hard to keep up with Tina Welch.

47

Welch and I ran stride for stride, breath on breath, arms pumping together, as if we were one, but separated into two halves. I could have run forever like that, clean off the planet and into the great beyond.

Shadowed figures formed in the darkness, but they were upright instead of laid upon the ground. We couldn't blindly open fire when they had Little Joe in their arms. The what if's came crashing down: What if we hit the little fellow? What if they spin and shoot? What if they get to the boat before we get to them? What if a man in the boat has a machine gun and methodically rakes the area behind his approaching men?

We had a winner. A man in the boat introduced himself with the staccato burst of a machine gun.

I hit the ground and yanked Welch down with me. Bullets combed the beach, thudding into the sand. As we fell, I twisted my body so she would land on me and not on the jagged stump of an Australian pine. She plopped on top of me with an umph, blowing her hot breath on my face. A root impaled the left side of my rib cage, and I involuntarily winced in pain.

"You okay?" Welch said. She had to cock her head back so

our faces wouldn't touch. Her hair was down, and I realized I'd never seen her like that. It was thin and made her face more delicate.

"Ouch. I think you broke my heart."

"They got a machine gun."

"I didn't notice."

"That's not fair," she said, her face hovering over mine. Her breath was moist on my face. Strands of her hair were plastered on my cheeks.

"It sucks when they don't read the rules," I said.

"Why'd you yank me?"

"So you wouldn't hit a stump."

"You know I don't like you, right?"

"Roll to your right. It's clear there."

She rolled off, and I brought the Steiners up to my face. A narrow-beamed boat with a row of engines across her stern anchored close to the beach. A man stood in the bow hoisting a machine gun. Another man was at the wheel. With the two on shore, that meant four. A damn regiment.

I gave the layout to Welch.

"We're screwed," she pointed out, in the event my brain had drained out the hole in my ribcage. "How good is your buddy with the sniper gizmo?"

"The best."

"What do we do?"

"Stay low. Stay alive."

"He raped me."

"Who?" I asked.

"Rafael. The night we went to the cottage."

"No he didn't. You're just saying that so I give you get the kill shot, assuming we survive the machine gun."

"Worth a try."

"Pathetic."

A fusillade of bullets kicked up dirt, and I instinctively

rolled my body on top of Welch's. Branches above us splintered. I pressed down hard on her.

"You're suffocating me," she said, her mouth on my ear.

"Shh."

"Don't 'shh' me. I—"

I placed my hand over her mouth as a solitary pop pierced the air. The Remington. There was an eruption of small arms fire, but no machine gun. Garrett had found his mark.

I raised my head. Two men were running low to the boat. One held Little Joe— or a sack of wood, it was hard to see— in his arm. The kid had not screamed. I assumed they had his mouth taped.

I rolled off Welch. The narrow-beamed boat was faster than *Impulse*. Our only hope would be to stop it with a hail of bullets, which came with a low probability of survival for either side. Nor would it help our cause if we clipped Junior in the process. The runner with Little Joe stumbled and fell on a log that had washed up on the beach. If I thought about it, I'd rationalize myself out of it.

I dashed to the beach. There was no need to sneak up on them. Time was far more precious than surprise. Time *is* surprise. The lead man had his back to me, and the man with Little Joe was scooping the kid up off the sand. The captain of the boat shouted out to his companions. The Remington popped again, but a ping ricocheted from an aluminum rail.

I tackled the man who had fumbled Little Joe. He jumped to his feet. I rolled and took his legs out from under him. He went down. We both sprang up. I took two giant steps back, as if I wanted nothing to do with him. The Remington again. He went down for the third and final time.

There is an incalculable advantage of two people who think as one.

I picked up Little Joe. He had a large patch of duct tape over his mouth. Shots rang from the boat and someone yelled. I crouched to my knees.

Silence.

Idiot.

I'd put myself between the boat and Garrett. *Good move, Jake the Mistake.* Garrett couldn't protect me without shooting into me. I had to move north or south up the exposed beach, and the two men with hot firearms knew that.

Morgan coughed.

He had positioned *Impulse* between the sandbar and the beach, north of the other boat. Once I broke free of the direct line between Garrett and the men, Garrett would be free to fire at will. Still, *Impulse* wasn't my objective. I planned to give Garrett room, and then angle in back toward the safety of the mangroves and underbrush.

"Jesus, you're stupid," Welch said as she slid into me. *Where did she come from?* "He can't cover you here."

"I know that."

"We got a problem," she said. "There's another boat."

"That's ours, dimwit."

Bullets traced well over our heads. Holding Little Joe was keeping us alive and responsible for the tepid fire. But they might decide the hell with him. Kill them all. Live to fight another day.

"How good's your buddy?" Welch said.

"Once we give him a few feet, he'll protect us. We'll cut back toward land. Remember to leave him a clean line of fire."

"Like you just did?"

"On three. One, Two."

I tucked Little Joe under my right arm, using my body as a shield, and made for the woods. Guns popped from my left. Garrett let loose with the Remington. I figured it was the captain of the boat and Rafael who were still alive and shooting at us. The man I grappled with certainly didn't match the description of Rafael Cherez. I assumed the machine gunner Garrett took out had been a hired hand.

Welch screamed and went down, clutching her right thigh.

"Oh sweet Jesus," she said, wincing in pain.

I stopped and nearly dropped Little Joe. The boy's eyes were wide with fear, and his arms and legs flayed against me.

"I don't think I can walk," Welch said. Her face contorted in pain as if it was breaking apart at the seams.

"Any last words for Emma?"

"Screw you."

"I knew I'd win you over." I hovered over her to protect her from the line of fire.

"Get the kid out of here," she said. "They want him, not me."

I couldn't carry Welch and Little Joe. I had only one option. *Impulse* was less than half the distance than our Omaha Beach sprint.

"We're going to my boat," I said as the Remington continued its nonstop assault on the other boat.

Garrett's going to run out of ammo soon.

"I can't—"

I lifted her up and she wrapped her arm around my neck. With Little Joe tucked under my right arm, and Welch draped on my left side, I did my best potato sack race toward Morgan and *Impulse*. Morgan idled the boat closer to the beach as Welch dragged her worthless right leg in the sand. Morgan jumped over the bow of the boat and grabbed Little Joe from me. He stowed him in the cuddy. Welch threw her good leg over the gunwale and then flopped on the deck. She did not cry out, and I had great admiration for her.

I jumped in after her as Morgan threw the twin 300s into hard reverse. Nothing.

The tide was going out.

I'd witnessed numerous boats maroon themselves on the sandbar in front of my house. In an outgoing tide, throwing the engines in reverse was a futile effort. What worked was another boat towing the grounded vessel, or enjoying a cool one while listening to Buffett and waiting for the tide to reverse itself. Sadly, neither option was on our menu.

"Let me have her," I said to Morgan and brushed him aside with unnecessary force.

Morgan went to the stern to keep the bow as light as possible. I grabbed the twin throttles and slammed them in reverse. The engines roared. Water and sand churned. I backed away from the throttles to add a little more weight to the aft. *Impulse* seemed to be thinking about it. She rocked. She hesitated.

Welch screamed. To this day, her tempest echoes in the cosmos.

"*Move, you fucking bitch!*"

And then the second miracle occurred.

Impulse, as if recognizing the voice of authority, jerked backward. She was now 600 hundred horsepower in reverse with no one at the helm. Morgan jumped behind the wheel, did a boat version of a U-turn, and then shoved the throttles down, barreling *Impulse* around the corner and through Bunce Pass.

Behind us, the chase boat did a similar movement. As the boat turned, moonlight silhouetted it. I'd been right in my assessment. Sleek. Narrow beamed. Four engines. Three engines—we might have had a chance. Four—not so much.

"We're cooked," I said to Morgan.

"How so?"

"He's a racer. Four engines."

"Low tide," Morgan said a disturbingly serene voice. "When you know the water better than the other guy, the low tide is your friend."

I've yet to have that serious conversation I promised myself with my next-door neighbor regarding his uncommon calmness under trying circumstances while on dark water. He didn't get that out of a book.

"Two minutes on the outside," I said, stating the obvious.

Morgan coughed and kept darting his eyes at the black shoreline in order to keep his bearings.

The water through the pass ran over twenty feet deep. But on the northern edge, it shot to a foot with no warning. Once we cleared the bridge that carried the road into the park, the shallow shelf was on both sides. Whether or not we'd get there before the chase boat caught up to us was difficult to calculate.

I opened the cuddy and checked on Little Joe. He was curled up on top of a pile of life jackets. Eyes bulging. I thought I should remove the duct tape, but none of us needed the distraction. *What if he has difficulties breathing through his nose?* I worked the tape off, trying to make it as painless as possible. He whimpered, but he was a tough little nut. I gave him a bear hug and murmured some nonsense about everything being all right. I buckled him into a lifejacket, although I had none that was small enough for him. I strung the vinyl straps around him twice. A Mickey Mouse bobber, courtesy of a former girlfriend, was on the floor. I gave it to him and told him to hold it tight and that it was a gift from a deranged woman. I wrapped him in a large beach towel, picked up a clean, smaller towel, and closed the door. I withdrew a fishing knife from a leather sheath attached to a seat and bent down over Welch.

"You're messing up my boat." I sliced open her jeans with a fishing knife, careful to not slice her as well.

"I heard you say the other guy has a bigger boat."

"Faster boat."

"Same thing." Her faced pinched in pain. "Sorry about the blood on the floor."

"It's a deck, not a floor." I wrapped the towel around her leg. "It's no different than fish blood—it'll wash right off."

"Comforting."

I unfastened her belt.

"What are you doing?"

"Getting in your pants."

"God, you're boorish."

"No big words on the boat."

I took her belt and wound it tightly around the towel. Her wound didn't look bad, but there was no way of knowing. Arterial bleeding can be fatal.

"I think you're fine for now," I said. "If we don't lose these guys, none of us this will matter."

I gave a final tug on the belt and she bit her lower lip.

"I get Rafael," she said.

"I forgot. Everyone picks their part."

"You don't understand."

"I know, doll. And that's why we're going to get out of this alive."

"Don't call me doll."

"I thought it was babe."

"Christ, I hate you."

"That's not my name. Besides, you don't want hate to be your last feeling on Earth, do you?"

Instead of an answer, her breath shuddered out of her. Her eyes pinched with fear and sorrow, and tears splotched her face. She shut her eyes tight. I wished to hell I hadn't joked with her, but it was too late.

48

The chase boat strayed from the channel and thrashed into sand. For a moment, I thought that was it. Cue the ticker-tape parade. Morgan the Magnificent and Jake The Great save the day. Tina the Terrible arrives safely at the hospital. All three will be autographing Playbills after the show.

But the other captain freed his vessel. Apparently the fickle Goddess of Luck equally bestows her favors upon the bad guys. Then again, a boat the width of seaweed, with the starting gate of the Kentucky Derby packed across her stern, requires more than the edge of a sandbar to ground her.

He came at us with a vengeance, straight down the middle of the channel. Jerk wasn't taking any more chances. I gave us a minute, at best the opening seconds of another, before the whole thing turned into a shootout on the high seas.

I said to Morgan, "The cut?"

"It's our only chance, assuming he doesn't ground himself."

"He'll follow us," I said. "He needs less draft than we do. Figures if we make it, he'll make it."

"But he'll have no margin of error and be glued to his GPS."

"Which will fail him."

"Which will fail him," Morgan concurred, and coughed.

The channel back to my house—not that we needed to go there, but it afforded us the best opportunity to lose the chase boat—runs straight toward I-275 and then takes a ninety degree hard left. It follows the highway for a mile and then takes another sharp left. One can cut out that unnecessary box by slicing through the shallow water off Tierra Verde. It is a naturally shallow area, and even at high tide, I avoid it. You could beach a bathtub toy in some parts. Running it on a flats boat is one thing, running it in a thirty-foot Grady at night was another. But a narrow and shallow channel that ran through it. Morgan knew where it was. Whether it remained after the hurricane was unknown, as was whether he could keep to it at night. The tide was still running out, but it had three hours before the moon tugged it in the opposite direction.

The chase boat would have no choice but to follow. If he stuck to the marked channel, he could never make up the time, assuming he even found us.

"Give me a gun," Welch said from the floor.

"You still with us?"

She gave an angry grunt and struggled to stand. Her face was pallid. I put my arm around her and eased her back on the deck. She didn't fight me.

"Listen, Tina. We—you—are going to come out of this. Don't be a hero. Think of Emma." I took a bottle of water from the cup holder and unscrewed the cap. I gave it to her, contemplating how long it had been in the boat and hoping I wasn't poisoning her. "Drink this."

She took a long drink. "I lost my gun on the beach. Gimme a gun."

"No."

"Gimme a gun."

A Beautiful Voice

"You going to shoot me?"

"Only if you don't gimme a gun."

I got a Smith and Wesson out of the radio box and handed it to her. She couldn't help us without one.

"Ready to cut," Morgan announced.

"What are we doing?" Welch asked me.

"Going where we have no business going."

Morgan took a hard port turn and then brought the throttle back. The chase boat, by my calculations, was less than thirty seconds behind us. He followed Morgan's path, dead center in our wake.

"He figures that if you make it, he'll make it," I said. "We get a little reprieve at Little Bird Key, right?"

"We do."

I told Morgan what to do. He muffled a cough and nodded in silent approval. Only then I realized he was wearing his pajamas—a bleached pair of swim trunks and a T-shirt with the name of his family's charter service on it. No shoes. I went back and gave Welch the plan. I drew my gun and sat next to her while we waited for Morgan to commence the movement. Her body expanded and contracted against mine as if breathing had become a conscious effort. Dampness leaked into my jeans. Blood.

"Hang in there," I said to Welch. Her eyes were closed.

"Welch. You hear me?"

She didn't answer.

"Tina, look at me."

Nothing. I started to reach for her just as Morgan cut the engines, spun the wheel, and thrust the throttle down. We were now gunning straight at the chase boat, like a medieval jousting match.

Except Morgan slammed the twin engines into neutral then screamed them into reverse, bringing *Impulse* to a dead stop. We scraped ground but stayed buoyant. He brought the throttles back to neutral. It was quiet. I peered over the side.

The chase boat skimmed the water, approaching us on our port side. He wouldn't have time to stop. He slowed down, likely confused by our maneuver and glancing nervously at his GPS. At about fifty yards, with the chase boat still closing fast, I raised out of my crouched position. I started to rest my forearms on the gunwale, but the boat was still bobbing in its own wake. The chase boat was less than twenty yards out and slowing. My window of surprise was closing.

I sprang up, spread my legs, clasped the gun with both hands, and fired into the center of the boat where two men huddled. I emptied my chamber. They were likely too far away when the first bullet left the barrel, but I couldn't wait for them to zip past me.

The boat veered off course, first away from us, and then sharply toward us, as if the captain had overcompensated, although he had not been one to make such errors. Morgan reversed the throttles to clear *Impulse* out of the way. The chase boat crossed our bow. I put another clip in the gun, raised it, and got off three more rounds. There was no return fire.

"He's in shallow water," Morgan said. "He'll never make it."

"Get us as close as you can."

The chase boat roared into the sandy bottom with a deafening crunch. Her four engines stalled, whipping up sand. Morgan idled in its direction. I kneeled in the bow of the boat. One man was slumped over the bench behind the wheel and another fidgeted with the controls as if he were uncertain exactly what to do. Rafael. The captain must have been the man I hit. That would explain the boat getting grounded.

I stood, aimed high, and fired two rounds. The man hit the deck. He could raise his hand over the side of the boat, fire indiscriminately, and a lucky bullet could mean victory for either side. I grabbed the Mossberg Maverick double barrel shotgun from inside the cuddy.

"Hang in there, little buddy," I said to Little Joe. He clasped the Mickey Mouse bobber in both hands.

I pumped and shot into the bow of the boat. The boom from the recoil put the pop of the handguns to shame. Fiberglass splintered on the chase boat. I pumped again and waited for him to stand, which he would never do. The equipment on the battlefield had changed. It was a new war.

The bay was silent except for Welch's breath. It was wet. Raspy.

"Lights," I said.

Morgan flicked on the spotlight. Its beam was a white tunnel in the dark. It hit the water and he adjusted it to bathe the boat. Four black Mercury Verado 300 horsepower engines crowded the stern. A man lay still on the driver's seat, his body wedged between the opening between the seat and the back support. The seat glistened red in the light. A fish jumped.

A hand fluttered above the aft port side, facing us.

"Stand up slowly," I said.

"You shoot?" A voice came from the boat. Welch moaned from behind me.

"Hands high above your head. If not, I'll shoot until there is nothing but splinters left of your boat."

"You give me little choice."

He stood slowly. Halfway up, he put his hands over his eyes to shield himself from the blinding spotlight. He was a thin man, dressed in tight black clothing.

"Hands up."

"I cannot see."

Morgan lowered the light so the beam hit the water yet still illuminated the boat.

"Up," I repeated.

He raised his arms. "It is you," he exclaimed. "*Voila.* What an interesting turn."

He was the man I'd seen at the museum holding a glass of Champagne and looking at *Woman Sitting at a Table.* Rafael.

As if he had pirated my thoughts, Rafael said, "We admired the same painting, that night, at the museum. We are in the same business, no? You are the man who took Alejandro and his family to that minuscule chateau, that... cottage. Am I right?"

Rafael had been watching me watching Alejandro? Well, that wasn't something I was going to admit on our first date.

"Climb out of the boat," I said. "Hands over your head at all times. Move five feet from the boat and stand in the water."

"You are lucky. I wasted days arranging my transportation. I knew where the boy was all along, but he was less trouble to me where he was until I could leave. But luck is what we make, is it not?"

"How so?"

"I am Rafael Cherez, but you know this, no? I have valuable information that your government will want. We can talk."

"In the water," I said.

He lifted a leg over the side of the boat, and then swung his other leg around. He reached for the boat to steady himself.

"Hands in the air."

"But I will fall if I don't support myself."

"You will die if you do."

Rafael seemed to consider his options. Keeping his hand over his head, he plopped over the side of the boat. He landed in no more than a foot and a half of water.

"Who knew," he said, "that such a large body of water could be so shallow."

"Your captain."

"You got lucky."

"So you insist. Move away from the boat. Five paces."

He waded a few feet away, and then faced me with annoying confidence.

"I am worth far more to you alive than dead. This, we both know."

"All I know is you killed Alejandro and Martina."

"Oh, I have killed far more than them. And you are no stranger to killing either. Hashing each other's past will get us nowhere. You can deal with me. I can give you direct information on Sergio Flores as well as Josef Santiago."

"Who?"

"Santiago. He is the new breed of Mexican drug lords. He is why men like Sergio Flores are retiring. Why you and I meet at this time and place."

"How's that retirement working out?"

"It is a difficult business to withdraw from. Flores only seeks to take his son and set up shop—as you like to say. How is the little boy?"

"Missing his mother."

That shut the shit-bag up. But he regrouped.

"Perhaps," he said, "I can take the boy off your hands, and then I will tell you all my secrets."

"Not even close to happening. How did you trail them? The monkey?"

"I was told they were carrying a tracking device. How it got there, I cannot say. Unfortunately, it ceased operating soon after they came ashore, otherwise I would not be ruining my shoes. You are more fortunate than you realize. Is there a better place to conduct this conversation?"

"Not if I kill you here."

"You would have done so already."

"How were Vizcarro and his family set up?"

Behind me, the water splashed. Morgan had tossed out an anchor.

"You want to test me?" Rafael said. "See if I can be honest? I understand. I will tell you what I know, but remember, like you, I am a hired gun. He does not indulge me with—"

"Get on with it."

"*Bien sûr*. Of course. Flores suspected that the DEA had infiltrated his circle. He talked loudly that Alejandro was running numbers for him. It was ridiculous, of course. But Flores wanted his son in the States, and what better way of getting him here than having your government arrange transportation? He fabricated that Alejandro was working with Bannon, because Richard Bannon is the most expendable of the Flores moneymen. He had to act. The boy had no future in Mexico. He was easy bait."

"Alejandro went along?"

Rafael shrugged. "I am a contractor. In such a capacity, I am not privy to all the workings. I believe that Alejandro felt his family was no longer safe in Mexico. The extent he played along? I can only guess. He likely thought it was the safest manner in which to relocate his family. Me? I think your government wished to get hold of the boy's mother. Flores was adamant that I . . ."

"Kill her in cold blood?"

"Must we stand out here all night?"

"The DEA agent," I said. "Did Flores ever find out who it was?"

"One of his auditors accompanied me on the job. She was to take care of the little boy. I believe now that she was a DEA agent. She picked up Flores's talk—from his lieutenant, Davido—about Alejandro running numbers without realizing she was being used. I told this to Flores. He sees it clearly now."

"How—"

"I am done. If you want more . . . *significatif* information, I need a pair of dry slacks. I can help you battle the drugs that ravage your country. That is what you were hired to do, is it not?"

Natalie Binelli's words concerning plea-bargaining came back to me: *Just a way to integrate slime back into society.*

A Beautiful Voice

Rafael continued to lobby his case. "Your government will be keenly interested in many past cases as well. I suggest—"

"Jake," Morgan said as Rafael abruptly halted his plea.

I partially turned my head. Tina Welch—*DEA agent*—was out of the boat and sloshing toward Rafael, lugging her right leg behind her like an anchor. Her outstretched hands held the gun that I'd given her. Her hair was tangled and matted with blood. Clumps of it shrouded her face. The moon cast her rippled shadow on the water.

"Tina," I said.

No response. Rafael shifted his weight. Welch kept her zombie pace.

"Tina," I said again, but she wasn't listening.

She steadied her gun and reached out as if she wanted the end of the barrel to touch Rafael's heart. She looked like Paul Jennewein's sculpture, *The First Step*, in the museum courtyard, in which a mother helped her child take his first steps, his legs unsteady, his arm stretched out to the world that awaited him. But this hand held a gun and yearned for death, not life.

"Tina." I wondered what made me think her name would work magic the third time when it whiffed the first two times.

"It is her," Rafael stammered out. "She is mad. *Demented*. You need to talk to her. I can't help you if I'm dead." His head darted back and forth between Welch and mine. "You want to stop drugs from entering your country? I can help you."

He undoubtedly had valuable information about the drug trade and the men who employed him. I recalled Janssen spewing statistics about the number of deaths each year from drugs, as well as the financial strain on both health care and law enforcement. Maybe with Rafael's information I could put a dent in that, or at least make as much difference as one person was capable of.

Welch muttered something. She started to stumble, but then steadied herself. Her hand slipped down a few degrees.

She brought it up, but overcompensated. She leveled it at Rafael's chest.

"This is for Tommy," she said in a remarkably clear voice. She fired. But her energy had been wasted on words. Her shot went high. She collapsed in the water.

"That was a . . . gallant effort," Rafael said. He glanced at his watch, as if it represented his world and he was relieved that it had survived. He was a cocky bastard. He looked down at Welch's body, half submerged in the shallow water, and then up to me. "People like us know not to let guilt seep into the soul. I will come aboard. I will tell you—"

I blew a hole in his chest and vaulted over the side of the boat. My feet hit sand. Two feet deep. Too high to run in. I threw myself into a shallow dive, stood, and repeated. Morgan and I got to Welch at the same time. We hauled her back to the boat. I frantically tore open the first-aid kit, thinking what a fool I'd been to leave her bleeding on the deck.

PART III
STEPHEN COLE

49

Palm fronds thudded against the side of the house as a southwest wind gusted off the gulf. Kathleen came around the bay side, entered the screened porch, and collapsed on a chair. She'd toiled all day grading papers. A black racer—a handy snake to have around, as it eats roof rats—slithered across the side of the outdoor concrete patio. I was glad its schedule had not coincided with Kathleen's, although Hadley III was on the windowsill staring intently at the ground. Cats miss nothing.

"Tough day on the loading docks?" I said.

I took an epic swallow of whiskey. The smoky, tangy liquid tingled down my throat and fired my insides. It was phenomenal. Hadley III tepidly approached Kathleen, leapt on her lap, and gently sniffed her face. Convinced Kathleen was who she thought she was, the cat curled up into a tight furry ball. She wrapped her tail around herself until it reached her mouth, like a muffler on a winter's night.

"How can I sit all day," Kathleen said, "and be so physically exhausted?"

"Lack of alcohol will do that."

"I'm serious."

"As am I."

"I'd asked my class to write a paragraph describing a desert without using the words, hot, sand, sun, flat, or sky. Kurt Sadell—who is a marine biology major, yet clutches a book of James Wright poems like the Baptists tote a Bible—wrote, 'Never describe a desert.'"

"And?"

She shook her head. "I think he's right."

I refilled my tumbler and poured a glass of wine. I handed Kathleen the glass.

"Sweatshirt," she said as a single-word command. I went to my—our—room and got her favorite sweatshirt of mine. I draped it over her.

"Hot chocolate?" I said.

"The sweatshirt will do. I dropped by Tina and Emma's place today."

Welch had a close call in the hospital, and Kathleen had gotten to know Emma as they kept a vigil. The three of them had gotten tight, which left me pondering what, or whom, they were talking about.

"How is she?" I said.

"Back in form. It's hard to believe she lost all that blood."

"I had to turn the bilge on."

"You did no such thing. They're flying in two days. Tina's house on St. John sounds enchanting, although she hasn't seen it since the whirly blew through."

"Whirly?"

"You know what I mean.

"She finally confess and tell you she's madly in love with me?"

"She said you are arrogant, conceited and self-centered."

"That's a compliment, right?"

"For some bizarre reason, she thinks I'm the luckiest woman in the world."

"Emma's not far behind in the rankings."

"No, I don't think so. You're seeing her again before they leave?"

"I am."

"How are Cole's efforts coming along?"

"He's filing papers like Gutenberg on Adderall to get legal custody of the children."

"What are their odds?" Kathleen asked. Hadley III perked her head up. She tracked a gecko that, sensing danger, sought refuge high on the screen.

"Even Stephen. Cole's tenacious as hell. He's got a hearing to grant temporary custody."

"Can Janssen help?"

"Not his arena."

"But he knows people."

I took another sip. Might have to start using a larger glass.

"The real bookkeeper, the man who laundered most of Sergio Flores's money, took a deal. Flores is staring at bars for the rest of his life. Janssen has no further interest."

"Good news for Stephen and Charlotte, right? No one's after Little Joe."

"Not that we know of. More wine?"

"When is sunset?"

"Fifteen minutes."

"Make it to go. I *do* sit too much."

Five minutes later, we strolled on the beach. It was low tide, and the sand was hard and smooth and flat. The south wind gummed the air with salt. The crystal green sea was the color of her eyes and . . .

Never describe a desert.

EMMA WAS ON HER way out, and we met at the door. She gave me a lovely hug and a tender thank you. I told her I would always remember her fantastic toast. She said she would always remember our time at the museum and gave me a wink that reminded me that women, ultimately, destroy men. And that when we die, what also passes is the haunting remnants of every smile, every glance, and every lingering scent that the heart ever held in sanctuary.

"I got you something," Welch said when I stepped into the living room. She handed me a box wrapped in red paper.

"How do I know it's not a bomb?"

"A bomb would say 'open later.' And the package would be from Acme. Mind if I ask you something?"

"Beep-beep."

That earned a kind smile, a facial expression I didn't know Tina Welch was capable of. I placed a little silver star next to my name.

"Do you think we become like them?" Welch asked me. "That in the end, there really isn't much of a line?"

"That's a little deep for a coyote."

"Do you?" she said.

"Become like who?"

"You know."

"What do you think?"

"I'm asking you," she said.

"Not even close."

"Because what I've—"

"Not even close," I repeated. "Do you need a lecture?"

"Not from you."

"One for you," I said to change the subject. "The night of the fire. Cole walked out carrying Charlotte and the two girls. The flames never touched him."

"That's what you said."

"Believe me?"

"It's what you saw."

"But my skin peeled."

"You're thin skinned, in case you don't know."

"Right. I'm sure that was it."

"Open it," she said.

I unwrapped the box. It was a new shirt.

"What's this for?"

"I ruined your shirt that night."

I'd worn the new/old shirt that I had bought at the thrift store. The one Kathleen had said she liked.

"This one is far nicer," I said.

"Yeah, well you could use a little dressing up."

I had brought up Cole to give her the opportunity to describe the fire when she'd gotten there—and she'd passed. I thought of asking point-blank how bad the flames were at Charlotte's house when Welch decided to high-tail it after Rafael instead of trying to rescue the people in the house. To question if she had traded the opportunity to save four souls for the opportunity to avenge the death of one—Tony Colaprico. But if she told the truth, I wasn't sure I wanted to hear it, and if she lied, I didn't want her to hear herself.

50

Cole and I met at the hotel on a day I ran in the morning, but stopped halfway through and sat in the sand in front of the sea oats. It had rained during the night and the sand was damp and pitted. It was the first time I had ever stopped during a run, and I worried that I would like it and never run the same again.

The hotel is a pink Moorish structure built in the 1920s by an Irishman from Virginia, named after a character in a play by a French dramatist that was turned into an English opera, and is located in a city named for its Russian counterpart.

Like the country it is located in, it is the parts that make the whole.

Every stool at the poolside bar had a body on it. A man stood with his shirt unbuttoned, eager to share his tangled nest of dark chest hair with the world. Someone's T-shirt read "Send Help." A kid screamed. A voluble man parked on a corner stool was like the moon blotting out nearby stars—no one close to him could get a word in. A woman in a thong, with grapefruit cheeks, paraded past in high heels. Another woman, wearing a white crochet see-through cover up and a wide-brimmed brown sun hat that shadowed her face, breezed past with a drink in one hand and her cell phone in another. She lifted her head. Our eyes met. Blenders ripped, music played, and oiled bodies reflected the sun. The air was drunk and thick with the smell of *eau de* sunscreen, skin, perfume and salt air. Everyone was happy. Everybody was young. I said let's split. Cole said sure. We tramped down the beach.

We settled on the bench where a few years before a homeless man had died. The police had covered his body with a blanket, but his feet stuck out. Beach-walkers started to point, and even the birds developed an interest until the police decided it wasn't a crime scene and moved the body. It's the first bench south of the hotel. The death bench.

Without the buzz of the bar, it was the silent bench. We sat in that silence.

Speak that I may see thee.

A welcoming breeze carried over the cool waters of the gulf like a fan blowing over a block of ice. Cole seemed comfortable in a short-sleeve shirt. I asked him how the hearing went. He was engaged in the long and tedious process of legally adopting the three children.

"Good."

"That's your best essay?"

He humped his left shoulder. He favored that side.

"The system has a unique structure and pace," he explained. "Undocumented immigrants fall into their own category. The children are minors. Nothing can be legal until they live with us for two years, and then we file a visa petition. I'll petition the courts for legal custody. I don't think that will be a problem. They can also be deported on a whim. While that used to be unlikely, that is no longer the case."

"Any problem with how they entered the country?" I asked.

"Big time. They came in without inspection."

"Meaning?"

"Illegally. Fortunately, the courts are lenient in cases of minor children."

"What are your odds?"

"Actually, quite good. Charlotte and I aren't going to sit around and worry about what can go wrong. A family is not a legal document. We won't love them any more, or treat them any differently the day they become citizens."

"You've told them the truth?"

"Their father and sister?"

I nodded.

"Yes."

"And?"

Cole looked out over the water and then at me. "It was hard. Hard for everyone."

I thought of prying for more details, but let it go.

"I've got two sisters up north we're going to visit," he said. "After that, we're moving to Jacksonville. I've accepted a job there. We need to get them out of this area."

"Going to drop by your brother's as well?"

"I don't have a brother."

"I didn't think so."

"Then why ask?" He eyed me suspiciously.

"The pictures in your house."

Cole bobbed his head a few times, like he knew we were at the end of the road we'd inched toward since the day we met. I slipped off my sandals, using the heel of each foot to free the other foot, and scrunched my toes into the sand.

I said, "You told me—when you were explaining why you and Charlotte decided to indulge Alejandro and take the children—that you knew how quickly it could all go. This has always been about that, hasn't it? Getting back something you lost. Not trusting me. Your carefully crafted lies, your gentle persuasions. They've all served a purpose."

"You never get it back."

"But we move on."

Cole squinted and focused beyond the horizon. "I didn't know that—that we move on. It wasn't even a conscious choice. But we do. We put one foot in front of the other. Like robots."

I said, "For whatever you are going to say, I am deeply sorry."

He studied me a moment and gave a slight nod of his head. We were two warriors who had finally reached a truce.

"I was married," he said. "We had two children. Another on the way. Worked at a law firm. It was a beautiful day."

"Take it easy, man."

"Only Charlotte has heard this."

"I don't need to," I said, fervently hoping he didn't take me up on my offer.

"You deserve to. And I need to be able to say it." His chest rose and fell. "My wife's name was Julie. I couldn't say her name for a year. I was once in love, and will always be in love with Julie. Charlotte understands that apparent contradiction. Accepts it. Julie and I had two wonderful girls. April and Corrie. Julie was pregnant, although we hadn't told the girls. How much of this do you want?"

"How much am I entitled to?"

"I imagine the whole thing."

"Totally up to you."

He gazed out to the water. A flock of five pelicans flew along the shoreline, their giant wings riding the air, flaunting their majestic gift of flight.

"It was such a pretty day," he said, as if he were talking to the air. "I can never get over that—how nice it was. I drove out of my neighborhood that morning with the windows down, riding high, on top of the world. Before I left the house, I'd checked on the girls. They were both asleep, but a beam of sun was on April's face. I couldn't understand . . ."

His head fell. He jerked it back up, talking again to the sea.

"Julie and the girls were coming downtown to have lunch with me. I was changing jobs that afternoon; leaving my firm and moving to the prosecutor's office. I was nervous. Excited. I was glad they were coming to take my mind off it for at least an hour. Crystal, my secretary, told me that two men were in the lobby waiting for me. She didn't know them. I went out to see who they were. My girls were due within a few minutes."

His eyes met mine. "Looking back at those few seconds, when I was walking out to the lobby? You can't imagine.

"I opened the door. A policeman and a guy in a suit—I remember thinking it wasn't expensive, the shoes gave him away—just stood there. Hands folded in front of them. They shifted their weight. The cop looked down. We represented the police union, and at the time the Sean Wright case was in the news. I assumed it was about him."

"How far in advance of Wright's trial was this?" I asked.

"Month. He would have walked. He *did* walk, but for different reasons."

"The men?"

"Asked me to sit down. I did. They did. The man in the worn shoes said he was a minister, and then the police officer introduced himself as a captain and said he was sorry, that there had been an accident on 315 that involved my wife and two daughters, and he was sorry but there were no survivors. And then they sat there like I was supposed to say something, but what would I say? I was numb thinking it wasn't true but knowing it was, and the captain said he would like me to accompany him to the hospital, and I was trying to wake myself up, and the minister touched me. I stared at the coffee table where someone had left a magazine and had ripped off the address label and I didn't know why people did that—tear the label off. Who cares about your address, it's in the damn phone book."

Cole was quiet. And in the quiet, my problems dissipated like a sea fog burnt by the sun. My advancing age halted, and like the tide, receded. The doldrums and slumber had been squatters. They were transitory, not permanent. They held no permit.

"Before I left my office, I stuck three pieces of candy in my pocket in case they came and I didn't have time to go back. One for each girl and—I don't know, maybe the third for our unborn child. That night, when I undressed—I was at my sister's house and pretty heavily medicated—I felt something in my pocket. I reached in and took out the three pieces of candy." He glanced over at me. "After that? I don't remember much of the next month of my life."

"How old were your girls?"

"April was five. Corrie seven. Corrie was more like her mom. April probably more like me. I didn't give that much thought, when they were alive, but I do now. They're close to two years older now. But I don't see that. I know now that I will never see that. I used to think of their future. What will they look like? Who will they bring home? So much of our lives were ahead of us. The future was a constant companion. We were going to Hilton Head in a week. The girls would vault out of the car, hold hands, and skip into the surf before we even went to the condo."

He paused. I racked my mind for a comment, but Cole said, "They are frozen like that forever. They grow no older."

He interlocked his hands and rubbed his thumbs. His face sagged into a frown, and I thought he might break. He unlocked his hands, straightened his back, and squared his shoulders. His jaw tightened and he fought the empty sea with his eyes. I thought of putting my arm around him but did not, and I wonder to this day if I should have.

I held immense respect for Cole. I oftentimes run across people who are better than I. Not better as in faster, smarter, nicer, or doer of good deeds, but better in the sense of the humanity they encapsulate. A wholeness to the soul that makes me wonder if it is an element they are born with, or, at the least, they have cultivated. Or perhaps, as in Cole's case, it is thrust upon them. They see the world in a different realm than the rest of us who stumble day-to-day, swatting anxiety, bemoaning the trivial, and reading the weekly country music awards in the same breath as we inhale the death of a child. They are Wilder's saints and poets, the silent flag bearers of the human race.

"I lost them," he said, booting up the conversation. "I know now that when a person dies, more than a life vanishes. Everything yet to come is also gone. Aborted. It nearly killed me. My mind had to stop projecting. I had to *learn* to do that. I didn't think there would ever be room for anything—anyone else."

"But there is," I said.

"We are not born to be down. We are either up, or we are getting up. But to think of it without treason, without guilt . . . that took—that *takes* an effort. But they would want me to be happy, to carry them with me. Death does not alter love."

I recalled he had made the same comment about getting up at Riptides when he confessed to having the children. Had those been his marching orders from repeated therapy sessions?

"That's it." He perked up and looked at me. "I moved down here a little over a year ago. I told people I went by my last name, Cole. I don't know whether I left part of me up north, or part of me died there, or whether there's even a difference. I met Charlotte. She's been wonderful."

"You have remarkable will to—"

"Do you want to know how they died?"

I was pretty sure I knew how they died.

"It's up to you."

I expected him to hesitate, but Cole charged ahead. I stopped wiggling my toes in the sand. I had been unaware that I was moving them.

"Julie was in the left lane. A truck was following them too

close. A car swerved in front and Julie slammed on her brakes. The truck hit our car. It bounced off the concrete barrier that divided the highway and burst into flames. Witnesses said they saw Julie climb over to the back seat and frantically try to unbuckle the girls. They think she got one of the girls undone, but the flames totally enveloped the car. No one got out."

I knew where we were headed, but kept quiet.

"They said they saw her—"

"I don't need this part," I said, but to no avail for Stephen Cole plowed ahead.

"People stopped, but all they could do was watch. Watched as she fought in the back seat. Small arms flailing. Reaching out. Watched as her frantic movements slowed. Watched until she was still. Until she died and the flames had won. The heat drove the bystanders back. There was nothing anyone could do."

We were silent, and in the silence, I tried to think of some odd job that needed doing around my house. Anything to flush the image out of my mind.

"I was going to the prosecutor's office that afternoon. I never made it. I quit law. Wright got off. What do you think of that?"

"I—"

"It was the same type of accident that killed Wright."

Janssen had mentioned a similarly staged accident in North Carolina that had taken out a potential witness. I would not share that with Cole. Instead, I lied and said, "I don't think that had anything—"

"Of course it did. Don't you see? Someone told them I was crossing the aisle. Killing me would have been too obvious. They knew that if they got my family, I wouldn't prosecute."

"The police report?"

"Failure to maintain a safe distance. Vehicular homicide. Whatever. They made a sincere effort to find the car that cut

Jules off, but were never able to locate it. I got no quarrel with the police. They looked hard for that car. Blue four-door sedan. Ohio plates. But no one got any reliable digits from the plates."

"How would they even know she was coming to see you?" I knew the answer. I had to see if Cole did, as well.

"Larrison," he said. "We shared a calendar, although any one could probably have gotten access. But he wasn't what he appeared. That's just a gut call. You said, when you snuck up on me when I was fishing, that you had a source who thought he might have been a leak. Did you ever talk to him?"

"No," I lied. Again.

"He's in the Sarasota area."

I was surprised that Cole hadn't challenged my lie, and I considered how much of the harsh truth he wanted.

"Should I?" I said.

We both knew what I was asking.

He gazed down at his feet. "No. If he did it, he had no idea what they were capable of. He's a victim himself."

Cole was so much more than I.

"The night of the fire," I said. "When you brought Charlotte and the girls out of her house."

"What about it?"

"I couldn't get within twenty, thirty, feet of the house. But you didn't burn, you or the girls."

An immortal silence hung between us, and then Cole said, "Do you believe in God?"

"Not—"

"That makes two of us. But you don't have to believe in God for God to believe in you."

"That's cute, man. But their clothing didn't even—"

"Julie—I mean Charlotte—wanted to walk out on her own, but that wasn't what I'd practiced."

"Practiced?"

"After the accident, the fire burned every night. Months of

it. I couldn't close my eyes without seeing the car in flames. Julie fighting to free the girls. The screaming. The panic. The heat. I'm their father and I'm not there, and I'll never get over that no matter how long I live."

He punched his breath out.

"I took those nightmares and made them my own. You know what a lucid dream is, right? When you're aware that you're dreaming, starting to leave one world and enter another, but you still have a grasp on the dream. You can shape your words and your actions. I coveted those fleeting seconds; I nurtured and mastered that surreal mist. Night after night, the fire came. They're struggling to get out of the car. I awake. I'm sweating. I walk back into the dream. I walk into the flames. I take them in my arms."

Stephen Cole gave a final shrug.

"I am imperishable."

51

Blaise Pascal said, "We know the truth, not only by the reason, but also by the heart."

Did Stephen Cole walk through fire? Did my measly effort with the hose make a difference? I don't know, and that's the best I can do. Feel free to put your own spin on it. I long ago tossed logic out the window and this remains: with age comes questions, for answers belong to the young.

Welch said that as far as she knew, no agency seriously investigated the truck driver who rammed Julie's car. She agreed that it sounded like Rafael's doing, but at the time, they weren't looking for that. She pointed out that someone would have had to know that Cole was crossing the aisle, and what time his wife and daughters would be driving downtown to meet him. Do you know who that might be, she asked? No, I lied, because lying is what Tina Welch and I did to each other.

I honored Cole's unspoken policy of no retribution against Nobby Larrison. Living with himself was more painful than dying. Garrett disagreed.

Cole and I were flipping through his records when he popped did I know who "arranged" his family's death, and whether that person masterminded Wright's and Tony

Colaprico's deaths. I had wondered when he would parade the question out. I said yes, smudging the truth a bit regarding Wright. He asked me if I'd handled it in "the manner in which you handle such things." Yes. He paused, and then showed me a Pink Martini album he'd bought when they came to the Mahaffey. As we listened to the excerpt from Tchaikovsky's Piano Concerto No. 1 in *Splendor in the Grass*, I was damn glad I'd laid Rafael Cherez in the chilly waters not far from the end of my dock where I sit at night with Kathleen and listen to the dolphins blow.

Cole might have been better than I, but I'm not.

COLE AND CHARLOTTE DECIDED TO PUT THEIR move off until after the school year. They started hauling their horde to the local church on Sundays. I gave Cole and Charlotte credit. I didn't see much divine intervention in either of their lives.

Cole joined the choir. Kathleen insisted we attend on a day that he had a solo. It was a gorgeous day to take the *Lauren Rowe* out, but it would have to wait. First the museum, then the picnic on the beach, and now church. I complained. Acted a fraction of my age. Exasperated with me, she said she and Morgan would go. Only then did I man up.

Before we entered the sanctuary, we lingered in the vestibule where local photographers had set up an exhibit.

"This one looks like you," Kathleen said. She pointed at a silhouetted runner on the beach. Behind him, the gulf shimmered in light from a moon that was missing its top third due to the recent lunar eclipse.

"Close," I said, admiring my form. "Look at this one."

I pointed to a photograph of an osprey tearing apart a fish, but my eyes stayed on myself. I was so small and everything else so vast. Yet, I was centered in the picture.

We sat in the second row with Charlotte, Ana Maria and

Gabriela. Charlotte had both girls dressed for an Easter parade. Little Joe was in nursery care. The sheer Wisconsinness of Charlotte's face illuminated the church like sun dazzling a stained-glass window. Gabriela talked. Charlotte said, "Hush." They repeated that worthless exchange numerous times.

I didn't last. I moved to the back of the church where I could quickly exit in the event of being discovered as a fraud. God is a curious creature to me. I am equally baffled by Her presence and Her absence.

My mind, through no fault of the minister, toggled in and out during the sermon. I rearranged who I would look up when I first crossed the river—a favorite game of mine. Martina now held honors. After all, my ineptitude had denied her a life with her son. What cancerous seed had that failure planted in me? She bumped off Victor, a man I had killed nearly five years ago. The Cardinal as well—he'd not visited my dreams in over a year.

Gabriela had as much control over her body as she did her mouth. She climbed on top of Kathleen. Kathleen wrapped her arms around her. The minister called for the children to come forward to receive their message. Ana Maria went willingly but Gabriela hesitated. Kathleen whispered in her ear. Gabriela jumped off and skipped off to join the other children who had made a quarter moon circle around the minister. Kathleen followed her at a distance—that must have been part of the pact—and knelt a few feet behind Gabriela. When the message was over, they both returned to the pew. Gabriela climbed again on Kathleen's lap. Kathleen wrapped her arms around her, as if she'd joyously found something she never wanted to let go.

Kathleen turned her head. Our eyes locked. She snuggled her face against Gabriela's and gave me a canonical smile. Great God.

Great Holy God.

A Beautiful Voice

I knew then what lay behind her, "never mind." Her dismissive, "I'm fine." It was never about the promise of a boat, or teaching English as a second language. Her dissatisfaction with the status quo and desire to experience life on a different plane stemmed from a yearning rooted in deep evolutionary crevices. I trembled with the joyous and terrifying clarity of our lives together.

The small choir performed and Cole sang. St. Augustine decreed, "He who sings prays twice." I liked to think Cole sang for both families that he loved so much, both of whom he could equally touch.

A little sappy? Too syrupy for your judicious palate? Preach it to the dead. The unborn. On my toe of tropical sand—where the undiminishable wonder of a woman's smile scythes your heart, where fire holds no court over man, where mornings are an open window to heaven, and the sun and the moon are the twin symphonies of life—that's how it rolls.

That is how it rolls.

I got antsy. Hadn't had a Bloody Mary since God knows when. I slipped out and hustled down the street toward Hurricanes with unstinted enthusiasm.

Behind me, high on the roof of Howard's house, church bells tolled.

———

Acknowledgements

The writing muse appears at different places. While I may not be at those locations for an extended time, their magic travels within. *A Beautiful Voice* owes a nod to my northern home of green, where deer munch on my landscaping and I pound the path of deciduous woods, and my Florida home of blue, where dolphins jump and I hike the beach, scuffing my feet in the shallow water. If you are blessed with a life of deer and dolphins, you are blessed. To the Sunflower Café in Sonoma, California, the Naples Grande Beach Resort and the Vanderbilt Beach Resort, both in the Sunshine State. And, always, to the Pink Palace on the impassioned beaches of the Sunset Capital of Florida.

It is there, as always, that I lose all excuses.

Special thanks to my editor, Jessica Nelson and proofreader, Ellie Oberth, both with Indie Books Gone Wild.

For those astute readers who realize I took liberty with the timing of the partial lunar eclipse, please forgive me. It is, for the most part, fiction.

Robert Lane
    Pass-a-Grille, Florida
    June 2018

ABOUT THE AUTHOR

Robert Lane is the author of the Jake Travis stand-alone novels. *Florida Weekly* calls Jake Travis a "richly textured creation; one of the best leading men to take the thriller fiction stage in years." Lane's debut novel, *The Second Letter*, won the Gold Medal in the Independent Book Publishers Association's (IBPA's) 2015 Benjamin Franklin Awards for Best New Voice: Fiction. Lane resides on the west coast of Florida. Learn more at Robertlanebooks.com.

Receive a free copy of the Jake Travis series prequel, *Midnight on the Water*.

As much mystery as love story, *Midnight on the Water* is the saga of how Jake and Kathleen met, tumbled into love, and the drastic measures Jake, Morgan, and Garrett took to save Kathleen's life—and grant her a new identity. *Midnight on the Water* is available only to those on Robert Lane's mailing list. The newsletter contains book reviews across a wide range of genres, both fiction and nonfiction. It also includes updates and excerpts from the next Jake Travis novel.

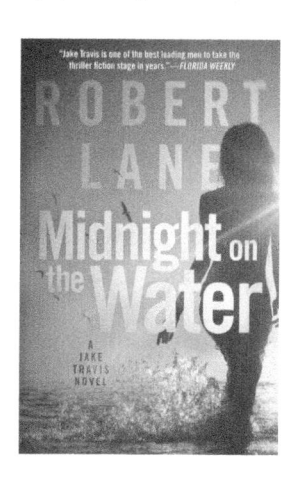

Enjoy *Midnight on the Water*.

Also be sure to read these previous stand-alone Jake Travis novels:

The Second Letter

Cooler Than Blood

The Cardinal's Sin

The Gail Force

Naked We Came

The Elizabeth Walker Affair

A Different Way to Die

The Easy Way Out

Visit Robert Lane's author page on Amazon.com: https://www.amazon.com/Robert-Lane/e/B00HZ2254A/

Follow Robert Lane on:

Facebook: https://www.facebook.com/RobertLaneBooks

Goodreads: https://www.goodreads.com/author/show/7790754.Robert_Lane

BookBub: https://www.bookbub.com/profile/robert-lane?list=about

Learn more and receive your free copy of *Midnight on the Water* at http://robertlanebooks.com

Made in United States
Cleveland, OH
01 May 2025